The Mystic Chronicles
Book 2

When darkness rises across worlds, destiny calls the light within.

The Mystic Chronicles

Between Realms

By Erhrole Navarro

BETWEEN REALMS.
Book Two of the Mystic Chronicles Series

Copyright © 2024 by Erhrole Navarro.
Cover art by Luisa Galstyan.

This book is a work of fiction. Names, characters, places, and incidents either are the product of the author's imagination or are used fictitiously. Any resemblance to actual persons, living or dead, events, or locales is entirely coincidental.

First Edition.
Self Published in the United States.
San Diego, California. Visit us online at erhrole.com or www.mysticchronicles.com

Library of Congress Control Number: 2024924154
Hardcover ISBN: 979-8-9905744-4-1
Paperback ISBN: 979-8-9905744-5-8
Ebook ISBN: 979-8-9905744-3-4

1 John 4:19
"We love because He first loved us."

Because of and for Ethan Matthew Navarro
November 20, 2002 to October 27, 2023

PROLOGUE

The old stories say that some souls are too important to fade, that they return again and again when destiny calls—for Maya and Myst Durant, nineteen years seemed a short time to prepare for the weight of two lifetimes.

In ancient Italy, they had died once before, defending sacred relics from those who would use them for darkness. When they were reborn in 2005 to Elan and Kaira Durant, the memories stayed buried deep—until Dante Malvagio forced them to remember.

Last summer, Dante's quest for vengeance nearly destroyed everything. Allied with Verendana, he manipulated St. Valentine's sacred dagger, twisted its power of love into a weapon of hate, and unleashed chaos on an unsuspecting world. But the Durant-Mazza family, alongside the reborn Knights of St. Michael, stood against him. Maya and Myst reclaimed their past-life memories, embraced their heritage as guardians of ancient power, and with their family's help and the sacred relics they had gathered - from Jupiter's Bolt to Neptune's Tears - they defeated Dante. Though Verendana escaped into the shadows, her ultimate fate is unknown.

Yet victory came with a price.

In the battle's aftermath, their mentor Nykronus—a powerful sage and longtime friend of their family—vanished without warning. The only clue he left behind was a cryptic message about a realm between heaven and hell and a darkness rising that would test them all.

As summer fades into autumn, new threats gather like storm clouds on the horizon. The Malefic Assembly, under Verendana's hidden guidance, grows bolder, their shadow magic corrupting sacred ground. The Order of St. Michael works tirelessly to maintain the balance, but ancient gateways sealed for centuries begin to crack.

Maya dreams of battles yet to come, the visions growing stronger each night. Her connection to the mystical grows deeper while Myst's strategic mind works to unravel the cryptic clues left in ancient texts. Their parents sense the change, too; Elan's blessed sword *Winterstar* hums with restless energy, and Kaira's magical artifacts pulse with unprecedented power.

But this time, they aren't just fighting for survival. This time, they're fighting for answers. What secrets did Nykronus discover? What realms lie beyond the boundaries of their world? Most importantly, are they ready for the price those answers might demand?

The Durant-Mazza family has always been more than blood. They are guardians, warriors, and protectors of an ancient legacy. And as darkness gathers and barriers between worlds grow thin, they will need every ounce of strength, every fragment of wisdom, and every bond of love they possess.

The old stories are true—some souls return when destiny calls.

Destiny is calling now.

ACT ONE

"The only limit to our realization of tomorrow is our doubts of today."
— *Franklin D. Roosevelt*

CHAPTER
ONE

Deep within Prairie Creek Redwoods State Park, Orick, California

Maya Durant jerked awake, her heart pounding against her ribs. The same dream again—ancient battles, forgotten temples, and a bow that sang with moonlight. Throwing off her covers, she padded to her bedroom window, where pre-dawn light cast long shadows across the grounds of her family's estate in Prairie Creek Redwoods State Park.

Below, a figure moved through the morning mist. Her twin brother, Myst, was already up and training. Maya watched as he executed a perfect flip over one of the obstacle course walls, his movements fluid as water. Show-off.

She pressed her hand against the cool glass, and her reflection stared back—olive skin, dark hair wild from sleep, and eyes that held too many memories for a nineteen-year-old. Or was she really nineteen? The dreams of her past life in ancient Italy felt as real as yesterday.

A sharp rap at her door made her jump. "Maya." Her father's voice, firm but warm. "Time for training."

"Coming, Dad!" She quickly pulled on her workout clothes, mind still dwelling on the dream. The memories—or whatever they were—

had been getting stronger lately. She and Myst dying in Italy, being reborn in 2005, finding each other again. Sometimes it felt like her head would split trying to reconcile two different lives.

Maya jogged down to the training grounds, where her father, Elan Durant, waited. His muscled frame and military bearing spoke of his years as a Marine, but the slight shimmer in the air around him betrayed his supernatural heritage. Behind him, ancient statues of Catholic saints watched with stone eyes, including an imposing figure of St. Michael himself.

"You're late," Elan said, but his eyes crinkled with affection. "Bad dreams again?"

Maya nodded, dropping into stretches beside Myst, who bumped her shoulder in greeting. "The same one. Something's coming, Dad. I can feel it."

Elan's expression darkened. "We've been hearing whispers. The Malefic Assembly is on the move again."

Maya's hands stilled mid-stretch. The Malefic Assembly—a cult that had hunted her family for generations, seeking the sacred relics they protected.

Before Maya could respond, the air crackled with energy. Her mother, Kaira, materialized beside them, her dark hair dancing with static electricity. "Sorry I'm late. Had to secure the vault." She held up a hand, cutting off Maya's question. "Training first. Then we talk."

The next hour was brutal. Maya and Myst ran the obstacle course until their muscles screamed, then moved to sparring.

Elan and Kaira, stood to the side, their eyes sharp and evaluating their every move. Maya took her place beside Myst, her heart pounding with anticipation. She knew the drill and had been through this routine countless times before, but each session brought new challenges and opportunities to push herself further.

At Elan's command, they took off running, their feet pounding against the packed earth. Maya focused on her breathing, finding a rhythm that matched the cadence of her steps. She could feel Myst's presence beside her, his energy catalyzing her own.

As they reached the first obstacle, a towering wall loomed before them. Without hesitation, Maya leaped up, and her fingers found purchase in the nooks of the uneven surface. Hand over hand, she hauled herself up as her muscles burned with every effort. Beside her, Myst matched her pace, and his movements were fluid and graceful.

They paused momentarily at the top of the wall as their chests heaved with exertion. Their parents watched them below, and their expressions were unreadable. Maya exchanged a look with Myst, and silent communication passed between them. Their connection, forged by blood and bolstered by a common goal, propelled them forward.

They dropped down the other side of the wall, landing lightly on their feet. The rest of the obstacle course stretched, a gauntlet of dilemmas designed to test their mind, body, and soul. Maya tackled each one with menacing determination, pushing herself to the limits of her abilities.

By the time they reached the end of the course, Maya's muscles were trembling with fatigue, and her skin was drenched in sweat. She bent over with her hands on her knees, gasping for air. Myst cheered her on, his chest heaving with exertion.

Their parents approached, their faces gleaming with pride and satisfaction. "That's what I'm talking about," Elan said, his voice gruff with feeling. "You both continue to impress us every day."

Kaira smiled in agreement, her eyes shining with love. "Remember, your physical strength is just one aspect of your training. Your mental and emotional resilience is just as important."

Maya straightened up, her heart swelling with a sense of achievement. She had only a moment to catch her breath before Elan motioned toward the sparring ring, where the next phase of training awaited. The ancient statues of St. Michael and other Catholic saints watched from above, their weathered faces a reminder of the legacy she carried. Maya rolled her shoulders, centering herself as Reagan stepped forward, her first opponent of the morning.

Reagan grinned at her, her stance relaxed but ready. They circled each other, eyes locked in a silent battle of wills. Maya feinted to the left, then lunged forward, her fist connecting with Reagan's jaw. She staggered back, shaking her head to clear the stars from her vision.

They grappled, their bodies locked in a fierce embrace. Maya twisted Reagan's weight against her to flip her onto her back. As Reagan tapped out, Maya helped her to her feet, both breathing heavily.

Next up was Austin, a new face in the training area as he recently retired from the United States Marines. He was tall and broad-shouldered, with a friendly smile that belied his fierce determination. Maya sized him up, noting how he moved with a fluid grace that spoke of years of training.

They engaged in a flurry of blows, their fists and feet a blur of motion. Austin was quick, and his movements were precise and calculated. Maya matched him strike for strike, moving with fluid, adaptable grace. They danced around each other, each seeking an opening.

Finally, Maya saw her chance. She ducked under Austin's guard, sweeping his legs out from under him. He hit the ground with a grunt but rolled quickly to his feet, grinning at her with newfound respect.

Austin, Reagan's fiance, conceded, "You did well, Maya!"

"Thanks, Uncle Austin! My dad showed me some of those same moves. Not bad for an old man!" Maya grinned, shaking out her arms to keep the muscles warm. The morning's matches had been intense, but she wasn't finished yet.

A familiar presence entered the ring. Myst stood before her, and though his stance was relaxed, Maya recognized the calculating look in his eyes—the same one she'd seen countless times across the Stratego board. Their sparring matches were always different, neither twin quite able to predict how the other's style had evolved since their last bout.

Myst struck first, his fist whistling past Maya's ear as she dodged to the side. She retaliated with a swift kick to his midsection, forcing him back. They traded blows, their movements a blur of speed and power.

Finally, it was Elan's turn. Maya squared off against her father, a mix of trepidation and excitement coursing through her veins. His skills, honed by forty years of training and experience in the military across two different timelines and with the Order of St. Michael, made him her most formidable opponent yet.

They circled each other, eyes locked in a silent battle of wills. Maya could feel the energy crackling between them, a palpable force that set her nerves on edge. She knew that her father would not hold back and that he would push her to her limits and beyond.

Elan struck first, his fist a blur of motion. Maya dodged to the side, her hands coming up in a defensive posture. They traded blows, each seeking an opening in the other's defense. Maya could feel the sweat trickling down her back, her muscles burning with exertion.

Finally, she saw her chance. As Elan lunged forward, Maya dropped low, sweeping his legs out from under him. He hit the ground with a grunt but rolled quickly to his feet, a proud smile on his face.

"Well done, Maya," he said, his voice steely with emotion. "You've come a long way in your training."

Maya grinned, her heart swelling with pride. She knew that she still had much to learn, but moments like these made all the hard work worthwhile.

Maya followed her mother, Kaira, to a secluded corner of the estate, where intricate runes were etched into the ground, forming a protective circle. The air crackled with energy as they stepped inside, the runes glowing faintly in response to their presence.

Kaira turned to face her daughter, her eyes glinting with pride and determination. "Today, we'll be focusing on elemental magic," she said, her voice calm and steady. "The key is to feel the energy flowing through you, to connect with the elements on a deep, intuitive level."

Maya nodded her mind deep in concentration. She closed her eyes, reaching out with her senses attuned to the world around her. She could feel the earth beneath her feet, solid and unyielding, and the air swirling around her, alive with potential.

"Good," Kaira said, watching her closely. "Now, focus on the element you feel most strongly. Let it fill you up and become a part of you."

Maya took a deep breath, feeling the earth's energy rising through her body. She could feel it gathering in her hands, tingling and pulsing with power.

"I feel it," she whispered, her eyes still closed. "The earth, it's... it's like it's a part of me."

Kaira smiled, a glimmer of satisfaction in her eyes. "Now, channel that energy outward. Shape it, mold it to your will."

Maya raised her hands, feeling the power flowing through her. She focused on the image of a stone, solid and unyielding, and felt the energy in her hands shifting, taking on a new form.

When she opened her eyes, a small, perfectly formed stone hovered above her palm, its surface smooth and polished, Maya stared at it in wonder, hardly daring to believe what she had done.

Kaira placed a hand on her shoulder, her touch warm and reassuring. "You have a natural affinity for earth magic," she said, her voice filled with pride. "But don't neglect the other elements. They all have their strengths and weaknesses, their unique properties."

Maya nodded, setting the stone down gently on the ground. "What about air magic?" she asked, curiosity sparking in her eyes.

"Air is the element of freedom, of movement and change," Kaira explained. "It can be unpredictable but also incredibly powerful when channeled correctly."

She raised her hands, and a gust of wind swirled around them, tugging at their hair and clothes. Maya watched in fascination as her mother shaped the wind, forming it into a miniature cyclone that danced and spun above her palm.

Maya leaned in closer and whispered to her mother, "Mom, how did you pick this up so quickly? Is Nykronus a really good teacher, or are you naturally skilled?"

"The key is to find balance," Kaira said, her voice barely audible over the rushing wind. "Earth and air, fire and water - each have their purpose in the grand scheme. It's in our blood. And he wasn't my only mentor; I also learned the basics in Benevento."

Maya grinned, her mind racing with the possibilities of elemental magic. The morning's lessons had revealed just glimpses of her potential, but she knew there was far more to master—countless ways to blend the physical and mystical aspects of her training.

"That's enough for now," Kaira said, dispersing the swirling winds with a gesture.

The walk to the armory gave Maya time to ground herself, transitioning from pure magical energy to the more focused power of enchanted weapons. She found her father in the familiar room, his fingers trailing reverently over the artifacts that held centuries of history—sword hilts and gun stocks gleaming in the soft light.

"These were the weapons of our predecessors in the Order of St. Michael," he said, his voice low and solemn. "Each one has a story, a history of battles fought and won."

He lifted a sword from its stand, the blade singing as it sliced through the air. Maya watched in awe as her father moved through a series of complex forms, the sword an extension of his body.

"*Winterstar*," Elan said, his eyes fixed on the blade. "It requires skill, discipline, and honor to wield her effectively."

He handed St. Michael's sword to Maya, adjusting her grip and stance. She could feel the weapon's weight in her hand, the balance perfect, and the razor-sharp blade.

"Feel the connection between you and the sword," Elan instructed, his voice calm and steady. "It's an extension of your will, a tool to be used with precision and intent. Focus on the energy and power she can conjure."

Maya nodded, focusing on the sensation of the sword in her hand. She moved through the forms her father had shown her, the blade slicing through the air with a satisfying hiss.

Next, Elan led her to a display of bows, each one crafted from the rarest materials and strung with care. He lifted one from its stand, running his fingers along the smooth wood.

"As I know you're aware, the bow is a weapon of patience and focus," he said, his eyes distant as if lost in memory. "Our ancestors used it to hunt and protect their families and lands."

He handed the bow to Maya, showing her how to nock an arrow and draw the string. She could feel the tension in the bow, the potential energy waiting to be released.

"Breathe," Elan instructed, his voice soft and steady. "Focus on your target, and let the arrow fly true."

Maya drew in a deep breath, her eyes fixed on the target at the end of the range. She released the string, and the arrow flew straight and true, thudding into the center of the target.

He grinned at her, his eyes glowing with pride. "Excellent work," he congratulated, patting her shoulder.

"Thanks, Dad." Maya couldn't wipe the joy off her face if she wanted to.

"You've done well, Maya," Elan praised, his eyes shining with pride. "Your hard work and dedication over the past year have paid off."

Maya accepted the bow from Elan, her fingers curling around the grip with a mixture of hesitation and reverence. "Dad, this bow... it's extraordinary. What's its story?"

Elan's expression grew solemn as he revealed the weapon's legendary origins. "This bow is called *Moonbow,* and it possesses a divine power that resonates with its wielder."

Maya's eyes widened in astonishment. "*Moonbow*? I can feel its energy, like a whisper in my mind."

Excitement surged through her veins, and she grinned. "I can't wait to tell Myst about this!"

Elan laughed, recognizing his daughter's enthusiasm. "Your brother will be thrilled, no doubt. But remember, Maya, this bow is a sacred responsibility. It's said to embody the strength and accuracy of Artemis herself, the goddess of the hunt."

Curiosity piqued, Maya asked, "What kind of abilities does *Moonbow* possess?"

"According to the ancient tomes your mother and Reagan have studied," Elan explained, "the bow's powers manifest differently depending on the individual wielding it. It's a mystery that unfolds uniquely for each archer."

With solemnity, he placed the bow in Maya's hands. "She's yours now, Maya. Cherish it, protect it, and let it guide you on your path."

Maya's heart swelled with gratitude as she pledged, "I will, Dad. I promise to honor this responsibility and become the warrior I'm meant to be."

Elan embraced his daughter, his voice filled with conviction. "I have no doubt you will, Maya. You have the potential to become a formidable force for good in this world."

~

Maya followed Kaira to a quiet corner of the estate, away from the bustle of training. The sun-dappled leaves cast intricate shadows on the ground, and a gentle breeze carried the scent of blooming flowers. Kaira sat on a weathered stone bench, patting the space beside her for Maya to join.

As Maya settled beside her mother, Kaira's eyes held warmth and solemnity. "Maya, my darling," she began, her voice soft yet filled with purpose, "there is much to discuss about the power we wield and the responsibilities that come with it."

Maya listened, her gaze fixed on her mother's face, eager to absorb the wisdom she was about to impart.

"Our magic is a gift, but it's also a burden," Kaira continued, her words measured and thoughtful. "We should always strive for balance, never allowing ourselves to be consumed by the seduction of power. We have to use our abilities for the greater good, to protect those who can't protect themselves."

Maya frowned as she considered her mother's words. "I know, Mom," she said, her voice filled with strong-mindedness. "I want to use my magic to help others, just like you and Dad do. After all, we've been through. I know."

Kaira smiled, pride shining in her eyes. "I know you do, Maya. But remember, with great power comes great responsibility. It's not just a comic book quote. We *have* to always consider the consequences of our actions, both in combat and life."

Maya nodded, her mind racing with the implications of her mother's words. "Mom," she said, her voice hesitant, "Myst and I have always done everything together, both in our past life in ancient Italy and since we were born again in 2005. Why are we not training together now?"

Kaira reached out, gently taking Maya's hand in her own. "Baby girl," she said, her voice filled with understanding, "you and Myst share an unbreakable bond, but each of you must also walk your own path. By growing stronger individually, you'll be better equipped to protect each other and yourselves when the time comes."

Maya's eyes widened as she absorbed her mother's words, a newfound sense of purpose filling her heart. She knew the journey ahead would be challenging, but with her family's guidance and determination, she was ready to embrace her destiny.

Maya and Myst sat cross-legged on the plush carpet of their family room, a well-worn Milton Bradley's Strategy board game, Stratego, between them. The room was filled with personal touches—family photos, handmade crafts, and souvenirs from their adventures.

Myst leaned forward, his forehead wrinkled in concentration as he studied the board. "I'm not letting you win this time, sis," he said, a playful grin tugging at the corners of his mouth.

Maya laughed, her eyes sparkling with mischief. "You say that every time, little brother," she teased, emphasizing the 'little' despite their status as twins.

Myst rolled his eyes, but his smile never wavered. He moved his piece, capturing one of Maya's in the process. "Ha! How's that for strategy?"

Maya puckered her lips, assessing the new arrangement on the board. She tucked a strand of her dark hair behind her ear, a habit she'd developed when deep in thought. After a moment, she moved, skillfully outmaneuvering Myst's piece.

"Not bad," Myst conceded, his competitive nature shining through. "But you're going to have to do better than that to beat me."

The siblings continued their game, their banter flowing easily as they each sought to gain the upper hand. Myst's determination and adaptability evenly matched Maya's quick wit and strategic mind.

As the game progressed, their strengths became more apparent. Maya's moves were calculated and precise, while Myst's were more intuitive and spontaneous. Despite their different approaches, they were evenly matched, and the game remained close.

Ultimately, Maya emerged victorious, her final move securing her win. Myst groaned in sarcastic frustration, but his eyes shone with pride for his sister's accomplishment.

"Good game, Maya," he said, reaching out to shake her hand. "You may have won this round, but I'll get you next time."

Maya grinned, pulling her brother into a hug instead. "I wouldn't have it any other way," she said, her voice filled with affection.

As they packed away the game, their laughter and good-natured ribbing filled the room, a testament to their unbreakable bond. No matter the challenges they faced or the paths they walked, Maya and Myst knew they would always have each other's backs.

Maya sat in the estate's library, surrounded by her family and the weight of their collective history. Ancient texts and relics adorned the shelves, each a testament to the legacy she was born into. Newly written texts, tracing the echoes of their past lives, could also be found scattered throughout the room. The air was thick with the scent of old books and the anticipation of the coming discussion.

Elan, filled with pride, began to speak of his family's military history. "I served in the U.S. Marines," he said, his voice steady and robust. "My uncle, a Master Chief in the U.S. Navy, brought my grandmother, father, and other uncles from the Philippines to the States, giving us a better life than our ancestors had known. My grandfather served in the Philippine Army, and their bravery and dedication run through my veins."

Maya listened intently, her heart swelling with admiration for her father's family and their sacrifices. She knew their strength and resilience were a part of her, shaping the person she had become.

Her eyes shining with the wisdom of generations, Kaira took her turn to speak. "The Mazza women have always been protectors," she said, her voice soft but powerful. "Every woman in our family has played a crucial role in safeguarding ancient relics and working with secret organizations like the Order of St. Michael. Our lineage dates back to before the days of Jesus Christ, and our ability to harness magic and intellect has been passed down through the generations."

Maya felt the weight of her mother's words settle upon her shoulders. She knew she was a part of something greater, a legacy stretching back through the centuries. The responsibility of carrying on that legacy was both daunting and exhilarating.

As the discussion wound down, Maya felt the weight of generations settling on her shoulders. Each story shared around the library's ancient table added another thread to the tapestry of her heritage—Elan's military lineage, the Mazza women's ancient magic, all of it flowing together in her veins. The responsibility was overwhelming, and she needed time to process it all.

The afternoon sun streaming through the library windows beckoned, and Maya found herself drawn to her private sanctuary. The secluded garden had always been her refuge, a place where the burden of legacy felt more like an embrace than a weight. Wind chimes tinkled softly among the blooming flowers, their melody mixing with the whispers of long-ago memories as she ran her fingers along a weathered statue —a relic from a past life that seemed both distant and achingly familiar.

As she settled onto a worn wooden bench, Maya's mind drifted to the day's events. The training sessions with her family had been intense, pushing her to the limits of her physical and magical abilities. She knew they were preparing her for the challenges ahead, but part of her longed for a simpler life where she could choose her path.

Maya sighed, her eyes fixed on the horizon. She felt confined, trapped by the weight of her family's legacy and the expectations placed upon her. While she loved her family deeply and understood the importance of their mission, she couldn't help but feel a sense of restlessness, a yearning for something more.

She closed her eyes, allowing her mind to wander. In her dreams, she saw herself as a warrior, a protector of the innocent, and a champion of justice. She imagined herself wielding *Moonbow* with skill and precision, her magic flowing through her veins like a raging river. But even in her dreams, she felt uncertain, a nagging doubt that this was the path she was meant to walk.

Maya opened her eyes, her gaze falling upon a delicate flower that had pushed through a crack in the stone pathway. Despite the odds, it had found a way to thrive, to carve out its existence in a world that seemed determined to hold it back. She smiled, a sense of kinship washing over her.

Like the flower, Maya knew she had the strength and resilience to forge her path. Although she was born into a legacy of power and responsibility, she also had the power to define her purpose. With renewed determination, Maya rose from the bench, her feet carrying her deeper into the grounds than she'd ever ventured before.

The path twisted through ancient trees until she found herself in a secluded corner of the estate she'd never explored. The air grew heavy with a sense of ancient mystery and the world's sounds seemed to fade away. She stood before an old stone well, its weathered bricks covered in intricate carvings that whispered of forgotten tales.

Curiosity piqued, Maya approached the well, her fingers tracing the worn engravings. As her skin made contact with the cool stone, a sudden surge of energy coursed through her body, causing her to gasp in surprise. The carvings began to glow with an ethereal light, pulsing in rhythm with her heartbeat.

Maya's vision blurred, and the world around her fell away. In its place, a series of vivid images flashed before her eyes. She saw herself, tired and battle-hardened, wielding *Moonbow* with deadly precision. The scenes shifted, revealing ancient ruins, hidden temples, and other-worldly creatures that terrified and mesmerized her.

Maya felt a deep sense of purpose settle over her as the visions continued. She saw herself standing alongside Myst, their powers combined in a dazzling display of magic and might. Together, they faced unspeakable dangers, their bond unbreakable in the face of adversity.

Just as suddenly as they had begun, the visions faded, leaving Maya breathless and disoriented. She stumbled back from the well, her heart racing and her mind reeling from the experience. She steadied herself and noticed a small object lying at her feet.

Bending down, Maya picked up the item, revealing it as a small, intricately carved stone. It was warm to the touch, and as she held it, she felt a gentle thrum of power emanating from within. Somehow, she knew this artifact was connected to her destiny, a tangible reminder of the path before her.

With trepidation and excitement, Maya placed the stone in her pocket and turned away from the well. The sun was setting as she returned to the main house, and the aroma of Kaira's cooking drew her toward the dining room where her family was gathering for dinner. Despite the weight of her discovery, the familiar scents and sounds of home wrapped around her like a comforting embrace.

The Durant-Mazza family settled around the warm, inviting dining room, the table laden with a feast fit for kings. The aroma of Kaira's home-made pizza filled the air, making stomachs growl in anticipation. Reagan and Austin joined them, their presence adding to the joyous atmosphere.

As they settled into their seats, the room buzzed with lively chatter. Elan regaled them with tales of his time in the Marines, his eyes sparkling with pride as he recounted the camaraderie and adventures he had experienced. Reagan and Austin shared their own stories, their laughter mingling with the clinking of cutlery against plates.

The conversation flowed seamlessly, from lighthearted anecdotes to more serious discussions about the future. Maya and Myst listened intently, absorbing the wisdom and experiences of their elders. They chimed in with their thoughts and dreams, their voices filled with the enthusiasm and optimism of youth.

As the meal progressed, the family debated various topics, their opinions diverse yet respectful. They discussed the challenges facing the world and the role they each played in making a difference. Kaira spoke passionately about her work with ancient relics and the importance of preserving history. At the same time, Reagan shared her experiences as a police officer and the need for justice and equality.

Throughout the evening, the sense of belonging and normalcy enveloped them all. At that moment, they were not warriors or guardians but simply a family enjoying each other's company. The laughter, the teasing, and the heartfelt conversations reminded them of the unbreakable bonds they shared.

As the plates were cleared and the dessert was served, the family lingered at the table, reluctant to let the moment end. They savored each other's presence, knowing these precious times were a respite from the challenges ahead.

In the warmth of the dining room, surrounded by the love and support of their family, Maya and Myst's eyes sparkled with happiness and hope as they looked around the table at their family. The flickering candlelight cast shadows on their faces, highlighting their expressions of determination and strength. They knew that no matter the future, they would always have this foundation and unwavering support system to guide them through the darkest times.

As the laughter and chatter from dinner began to subside, the conversation took a more somber turn. Elan leaned forward, his eyes flickering with concern and determination. "We've been hearing whispers," he said, his voice low and severe, "of a growing threat to the relics we protect."

Kaira nodded, her brow furrowed. "The Order of St. Michael has been monitoring the situation closely. They suspect that the Malefic Assembly may be on the move again, seeking to harness the power of the ancient artifacts for their clandestine motives."

Maya listened intently, her heart quickening at the mention of the relics and the potential danger they faced. She had grown up hearing stories of the Order's mission, fought them herself, and understood the importance of safeguarding these powerful objects from those who would misuse them.

Reagan chimed in. "We've been seeing an uptick in unusual activity around the city," she said, her voice tinged with worry. "Thefts of ancient texts and artifacts, whispers of dark rituals being performed secretly. It's like something is stirring in the shadows."

As evident in his posture, Austin's military background added, "The Order has been increasing their patrols and surveillance. They're trying to stay one step ahead of the cult, but it isn't proving easy. These guys are slippery and well-connected."

Maya's mind raced with possibilities as the adults continued to discuss the growing threat. She felt excitement and purpose, knowing her training and abilities could be used in the fight against the Malefic Assembly. She longed to be out there, actively protecting the relics and circumventing the cult's plans.

Sensing his sister's restlessness, Myst squeezed her hand under the table. He, too, felt the call to action, the desire to make a difference in the face of this looming danger.

As the conversation continued, Maya's determination grew more vigorous. She knew her time to step up and take her place in the more significant conflict was drawing near. With each passing moment, the urgency of their mission became more apparent, and Maya found herself eagerly anticipating the challenges ahead.

Maya sat on the edge of her bed, her eyes wandering around her bedroom. The space reflected her journey, with artifacts and symbols of her past lives and future aspirations adorning the walls and shelves. A mosaic depicting the Order of St. Michael's crest hung above her desk, a constant reminder of her family's legacy and the responsibility that rested upon her shoulders.

As she reflected on the conversations from dinner, Maya felt a mix of hope and tenacity coursing through her veins. The revelation of the growing threat posed by the Malefic Assembly and the whispers of their wicked activities had ignited a fire within her. She knew her time to step up and take her place in the fight against the cult was drawing near.

Maya's fingers absently traced the intricate carvings on the mysterious stone she had found by the well. The artifact seemed to hum with faint energy as if calling out to her, urging her to embrace her destiny. She couldn't shake the feeling that this stone was somehow connected to the challenges ahead.

As she lost herself in thought, Maya's mind drifted to the visions she had experienced at the well. The images of herself, battle-hardened and wielding *Moonbow* with deadly precision, filled her with purpose and determination. She knew her training and abilities would be tested in the coming days, and she was ready to face whatever obstacles stood her way.

Maya's gaze fell upon a photograph of her family. Their smiling faces reminded her of the love and support that surrounded her. She drew strength from their unwavering belief in her and the knowledge that they would always guide and support her, no matter her challenges.

Maya's fingers absently traced the intricate carvings on the mysterious stone she had found by the well, its faint hum of energy resonating with the power of Moonbow still lingering in her muscles from training. The two artifacts seemed to call to each other, whispering of destinies yet to unfold.

As she lost herself in thought, the visions from the well flickered through her mind—herself wielding Moonbow with deadly precision, standing alongside Myst against unknowable threats. But unlike the dreams that had haunted her sleep, these images felt less like memories and more like promises of what was to come.

Maya's gaze drifted to the photograph on her nightstand, the one taken last summer at the beach. In it, her family beamed at the camera, sun-kissed and laughing, caught in a moment of pure joy. Myst had Maya in a playful headlock while their parents looked on with matching expressions of amused affection. Reagan and Austin were there too, part of the tapestry of love and strength that made up her world.

She traced their faces with a gentle finger, drawing strength from their unwavering belief in her. The Malefic Assembly might be rising, but they didn't understand what they were truly facing—not just a single warrior, but the combined legacy of generations of protectors, bound together by something far more powerful than ancient relics or mystical forces.

Family.

CHAPTER

TWO

San Francisco, California

The vibrant cityscape of San Francisco stretched out before Maya as she gazed through the window of the sleek, black car that ferried her into the heart of the city. The towering redwoods that had enveloped her during the journey gave way to the urban landscape, a tapestry of historical buildings and modern structures woven together in a captivating display of architectural diversity.

As the car navigated the winding streets, Maya's eyes were drawn to the iconic Golden Gate Bridge, its striking orange hue a beacon against the azure sky. The bridge stood as a testament to the city's resilience and ingenuity, symbolizing the indomitable spirit that had shaped San Francisco over the centuries.

The car turned onto a quieter street, away from the bustling main thoroughfares. Maya's gaze settled on a sleek, modern building that seemed to emerge from the surrounding historical sites like a hidden gem. Its façade was a masterful blend of contemporary design and classical elements, a nod to the city's rich heritage.

As the car approached the building, Maya noticed the emblem of St. Michael discreetly adorning the entrance. The symbol, representing the archangel's unwavering strength and protection, was a subtle yet unmistakable marker of the Order's presence. The building exuded an air of secrecy and purpose, its very existence a closely guarded secret known only to a select few.

The car came to a smooth stop at the entrance, and Maya stepped out, her senses heightened by the anticipation of what lay ahead. She stood before the building, taking in its imposing presence and the weight of the responsibility that awaited her within its walls. With a deep breath, Maya approached the entrance, ready to embrace her destiny.

As Maya entered the building, she was greeted by the sight of her mother and aunt engaged in a lively discussion. Kaira exuded an air of quiet confidence and determination. Her attire was a seamless blend of modern practicality and traditional elements, a testament to her deep respect for the Order's rich history and effortless ability to navigate the contemporary world. She held a tablet in her hands, her eyes intently focused on the digital reports on the screen. Deep in concentration, she analyzed the information before her, a strategic thinker always seeking to unravel the complexities of their challenges.

Reagan stood beside Kaira, her presence commanding attention. She was a visionary leader known for her keen eye for innovation and ability to inspire those around her. Her sharp attire was complemented by an array of high-tech accessories, reflecting her dynamic approach to leadership and her embrace of cutting-edge technology. As Maya approached, Reagan turned to greet her, her enthusiasm infectious. She engaged with the other Order members present, her words sparking motivation and igniting a sense of purpose in their hearts.

"Maya, welcome," Reagan said warmly, her eyes twinkling with excitement. "We've been eagerly awaiting your arrival. Kaira and I have been discussing the latest developments, and we believe your unique skills and perspective will be invaluable in our upcoming mission."

Kaira looked up from her tablet, a smile gracing her features as she acknowledged Maya's presence. "Indeed, Maya. Your training and dedication have not gone unnoticed. We have a critical task, and your involvement will be crucial to its success."

As Maya followed Kaira and Reagan through the headquarters, she marveled at the seamless fusion of ancient artifacts and cutting-edge technology surrounding them. The walls were adorned with intricate tapestries depicting legendary battles and mythical creatures, their vibrant colors illuminated by the soft glow of holoprojectors displaying digital archives. Ancient tomes, their spines cracked and weathered with age, shared shelf space with sleek tablets that members used to access limitless knowledge repositories.

Kaira and Reagan walked side by side, their voices low as they discussed the latest updates and strategies. Kaira's tablet flickered with real-time data, its screen casting a soft blue light across her face as she analyzed the information. Reagan, her eyes sharp and focused, listened intently, occasionally interjecting with insights and suggestions.

As they navigated the corridors, they encountered other members of the Order, each engaged in their tasks. A young man, his fingers dancing across a holographic interface, manipulated a complex magical sigil, his brow furrowed in concentration. Nearby, an older woman, her silver hair tied back in a neat bun, carefully examined an ancient artifact, her hands glowing with a faint magical aura as she probed its secrets.

Kaira paused beside a large, ornate door, its surface adorned with intricate carvings depicting the archangel Michael. She placed her hand against a small, unassuming panel, and the door silently swung open, revealing a spacious chamber beyond. The room was bathed in a soft, ethereal light, and at its center stood a large, circular table, its surface a mosaic of ancient symbols and modern digital displays.

Reagan gestured for Maya to sit at the table, her eyes alight with anticipation. "This is where we gather to plan our most critical missions," she explained, her voice filled with reverence. "The fusion of magic and technology in this room is a testament to the Order's commitment to adapting and evolving to face the challenges of our time."

As Maya settled into her seat at the table, Kaira stood at the head, commanding the attention of all those gathered. She tapped the table's surface, and a holographic display sprang to life, bathing the room in a soft, blue glow. Ancient texts and manuscripts flickered across the screen, their pages worn and weathered with age.

"Our knowledge is our greatest asset," Kaira began, her voice clear and confident. "For centuries, the Order has safeguarded these ancient texts, preserving the wisdom and secrets of our ancestors. But as we move forward, we must adapt to the changing times."

She swiped her hand across the display, and the images transformed, revealing a sleek, modern interface. "After our last encounter with Dante Malvagio, and after the dreams from my previous life stopped for me, I realized there is so much knowledge we still don't understand. So, I propose a new initiative," Kaira continued, her eyes sparkling with excitement. "We'll digitize our entire collection, creating a secure online archive that members can access worldwide. No longer will our knowledge be confined to the walls of this chamber or spending an entire lifetime or two to learn about our past. It will be at the fingertips of every member, no matter where they may be."

"This is madness," Elder Chen interrupted, his weathered hands clutching an ancient tome. "These texts have survived centuries because we protected them properly."

Kaira met his gaze steadily. "And they'll survive centuries more, Master Chen. But they'll do more than survive - they'll live, breathe, and teach in ways our ancestors could only dream of."

"I understand your reservations," she said, her tone gentle yet firm. "Change can be intimidating, and the thought of our sacred texts existing in a digital realm may seem like a departure from tradition. But I assure you, preserving our knowledge is my utmost priority."

She tapped the table again, and the display shifted to reveal a complex network of security protocols and encryption algorithms. "We'll implement the most advanced security measures to protect our archive from unauthorized access. The younger generation, those who have grown up in a world of technology, will be able to engage with our teachings in a way that resonates with them."

Kaira paused, her gaze sweeping across the room, meeting the eyes of each member. "I value your input and expertise. Your years of dedication to the Order have been invaluable, and I believe that together, we can navigate this new path while honoring our traditions. I welcome your thoughts and suggestions as we embark on this journey."

Reagan Mazza stepped forward, her eyes alight with excitement as she prepared to unveil her latest project. The room fell silent, all eyes fixed on her as she began to speak.

"I've been working on something special," she announced, her voice filled with enthusiasm. "A training program that will revolutionize how we prepare our members for the challenges ahead."

Reagan flicked her wrist to activate a holographic display in the center of the room. The image shimmered and took form, revealing a virtual reality simulation of a historical battle. The scene was so lifelike that Maya could almost feel the flames' heat and hear swords clashing.

Reagan's voice softened as she manipulated the holographic display. "Two years ago, we lost three young members in their first field mission. If they'd had this training..." She let the sentence hang, but Maya saw Kaira reach for her sister's hand, a gesture of shared pain.

Maya's throat tightened at Reagan's mention of the lost members. Her own training had been rigorous, but the thought of facing real combat without proper preparation sent a chill down her spine. She'd heard whispers about that tragic mission - three promising initiates, not much older than herself, caught off guard by an unexpected enemy. Looking at Reagan's pained expression now, Maya understood why her aunt had thrown herself into developing this new training system with such dedication.

"This is more than just a simulation," Reagan explained, her words filled with passion. "It's a fully immersive experience that combines the wisdom of our past with the cutting-edge technology of the present."

She gestured towards the holographic figures engaged in combat, their movements fluid and precise. "Through these virtual reality simulations, our members will be able to train in the most challenging scenarios, facing the same obstacles and adversaries that our ancestors did centuries ago."

Reagan's excitement became infectious as she continued, "But it's not just about reliving the past. These simulations are designed to adapt and evolve, presenting new challenges and scenarios based on the individual's strengths and weaknesses. It's a dynamic training program that will push our members to their limits, helping them enhance their physical and magical abilities in ways we never thought possible."

Maya watched in awe as the holographic figures moved and interacted with their environment, their actions seamlessly blending with the virtual landscape. She could see the potential in Reagan's vision and how it could prepare the Order for the unknown threats ahead.

"By combining the wisdom of our past with the possibilities of the future," Reagan declared, her voice filled with conviction, "we'll be better equipped than ever to face whatever challenges come our way. This training program is just the beginning of what we can achieve when we embrace the power of technology and innovation."

As the meeting progressed, an urgent alert flashed across the holographic displays, casting a spooky, flashing red glow. Kaira's eyes widened as she read the incoming message, and her voice grave as she addressed the assembled members. "We have a situation," she announced, commanding attention. "One of our sacred sites, the Catacomb of the Everlasting Storm, is under attack."

Maya's breath caught in her throat. The Catacomb - she'd read about it countless times in her studies. Hidden beneath the city's ancient streets, it housed the Storm Crystal, an artifact said to harness the very essence of lightning itself. In the wrong hands, its power could devastate entire cities.

"The forces of darkness have launched a coordinated assault," Kaira continued, her voice grave, "and they're using a combination of ancient magic and advanced technology to breach the temple's defenses."

Reagan stepped forward with urgency. "We need to act fast," she declared, her mind racing with possible strategies. "This is no ordinary threat. They've clearly done their homework and are exploiting the site's weaknesses."

Kaira nodded, her gaze sweeping across the room. "We'll need a team to handle this attack's magical and technological aspects. Reagan, I want you to assemble our best operatives with expertise in both fields. We can't afford to underestimate our enemy."

Reagan's fingers danced across the holographic interface, pulling up profiles of potential team members. "I have just the people in mind," she said, her voice confident. "We'll need a mix of seasoned veterans and fresh talent who can think on their feet and adapt to the ever-changing battlefield."

As Reagan rattled off names and skill sets, Kaira listened intently, her mind already formulating a plan of action. "We'll need to secure the perimeter first," she mused, studying the temple's schematics. "If we can cut off their access to the temple's power source, we can weaken their assault and buy ourselves some time."

Reagan grinned, her eyes sparkling with excitement. "I have just the thing," she exclaimed, pulling up a holographic image of a sleek, high-tech device. "This is the Arcane Disruptor, a little something I've been working on in my spare time. It can temporarily nullify magical energy within a localized area, giving us a tactical advantage."

Kaira raised an eyebrow, impressed by Reagan's ingenuity. "Brilliant," she praised, her mind already incorporating the device into their strategy. "We'll need to deploy it at key points around the temple, creating a barrier preventing the enemy from drawing upon its power."

As the plan took shape, the assembled members watched in awe, marveling at Kaira and Reagan's seamless collaboration. Their contrasting yet complementary styles merged into a cohesive strategy, each bringing their unique strengths.

Maya watched with admiration and determination, her resolve strengthening with each passing moment. Though part of her yearned to join the mission, she understood that her time would come. For now, she could learn from watching the Mazza sisters in action. With them at the helm, she did not doubt that the Order would emerge victorious.

As the team prepared to depart, Kaira placed a hand on Reagan's shoulder, a gesture of trust and respect. "Together, we'll show them what happens when they dare to threaten our sacred grounds," she declared, her voice filled with unwavering conviction.

Reagan nodded, her eyes alight with the thrill of the impending battle. "Let's give them a fight they'll never forget, sis," she grinned, her words a rallying cry that echoed through the hearts of all those present.

With a final nod of determination, Kaira and Reagan led the team out of the command room, ready to fight. The Catacomb of the Everlasting Storm awaited their defense, and they would not rest until its sanctity was preserved.

The next few hours passed in a blur of activity. Teams were dispatched, equipment was gathered, and strategies were refined. Maya watched as her mother and aunt coordinated the response with precision and grace, their years of leadership experience evident in every decision. When the immediate crisis was contained - the attackers driven back from the Catacomb's outer defenses - the Order's headquarters slowly settled into an uneasy calm as they awaited updates from the field teams.

As the sun slowly descended over the San Francisco skyline, Kaira and Reagan found themselves in a rare moment of tranquility on the rooftop garden of the Order's headquarters. The bustling city below seemed a world away, its distant sounds muffled by the gentle rustling of leaves and the soft chirping of birds.

Kaira leaned against the railing, her gaze fixed on the horizon, where the golden hues of the setting sun painted the sky in a breathtaking array of colors. "It's moments like these that remind me why we do what we do," she whispered, her voice filled with fierce contemplation.

Reagan nodded, her own eyes tracing the outline of the city's iconic buildings. "The weight of our responsibilities can be overwhelming at times," she admitted, her fingers absently tracing the intricate patterns on the railing. "But the hope for a better future keeps us going, right?"

Kaira turned to face her sister, a soft smile on her lips. "Absolutely," she agreed, her voice filled with conviction. "We're not just fighting for the present, but for future generations. The decisions we make today will shape the world they inherit."

Reagan's eyes sparkled as she met Kaira's gaze. "And that's why it's so important that we lead by example," she declared, her words filled with passion. "We have to show them that change is possible, that we can adapt and evolve without losing sight of who we are and what we stand for."

Kaira reached out and took Reagan's hand, gently squeezing it. "Together, we'll inspire them to embrace the future while honoring the past," she said, her voice filled with unwavering faith in their shared mission. "We'll show them that the Order is more than just a collection of ancient traditions, but a living, breathing entity that can grow and change with the times."

As the last rays of the sun dipped below the horizon, casting the rooftop garden in a soft, ethereal glow, Kaira and Reagan stood side by side, their silhouettes etched against the darkening sky. At that moment, they knew they had the strength, the wisdom, and the unwavering commitment to face them head-on.

CHAPTER
THREE

The fluorescent lights of East Los Angeles buzzed beyond the bookstore's grimy windows, but inside, time moved differently. Dust motes danced in the few slanting beams that penetrated the towering shelves, each packed with leather-bound secrets and forgotten lore. The scent of aging paper and binding glue wrapped around Elan like an old friend's embrace.

His fingertips ghosted over the map's surface, feeling each ridge and valley where ancient hands had pressed their knowledge into parchment. New marks layered over old, telling stories within stories - if you knew how to read them. And after twenty years of chasing history's shadows, Elan knew.

"What do you see?" Myst's whisper barely disturbed the bookstore's respectful silence. His son leaned in closer, his eyes sharp with intelligence inherited from his mother.

"Cartography wasn't just science back then," Elan murmured, tilting the parchment to catch the light differently. "It was art. Magic. Prayer. Every line carries meaning - you just have to know which language it's speaking."

"There's something here," he murmured, leaning closer to the parchment. "Like ripples in still water - a pattern just beneath the surface."

Beside him, Myst leaned in closer, his forehead wrinkled in concentration as he examined the cryptic notes scattered across the table. His eyes, alight with keen intelligence, darted from one inscription to another, seeking the threads that would unravel the mystery before them.

"The compass Nykronus gave you," Myst whispered, his fingers hovering over a faded illustration. "It's the key to unlocking this puzzle."

Elan nodded, his gaze never leaving the map. "The Malefic Assembly is moving in the shadows," he said, his voice tinged with urgency. "We have to decipher these clues before they can unleash their dark designs upon the world."

Myst's lips curved into a wry smile. "Then it's a good thing we're the best at what we do," he quipped, his confidence evident in his tone.

Elan chuckled softly, the sound a welcome respite from the heavy tension in the air. "Yup," he agreed, his eyes sparkling with determination and anticipation.

As they worked, the bookstore seemed to fade away, the outside world receding until only the map and the notes remained. Elan's keen eye for detail, honed through years of navigating treacherous territories and, lately, deciphering ancient texts, proved invaluable as he pieced together the disparate elements of the puzzle.

Myst's intuitive grasp of magic, guiding his every move, worked perfectly with Elan. His insights illuminated the hidden meanings behind the cryptic inscriptions. Together, they formed a formidable team—father and son, with their combined skills and knowledge, a force to be reckoned with.

Myst's fingers skillfully manipulated the intricate mechanisms of the green and gold compass, his brow furrowed in concentration. Elan watched, his breath held in anticipation, as his son worked to unravel the secrets hidden within the ancient device.

Suddenly, a soft click echoed through the bookstore, and a light beam erupted from the compass's face. It projected a shimmering constellation upon the map, the stars aligning perfectly with the cryptic symbols on the parchment.

"I've got it!" Myst exclaimed, his voice filled with triumph. "The constellation, it's a map!"

Elan leaned in closer, his eyes widening as he traced the path revealed by the celestial projection. "It's pointing us to a location," he whispered, his mind racing with the implications. "Somewhere in the heart of Mexico."

Myst nodded, his gaze locked on the map. "Mexico City," he closed his eyes, his voice tinged with reverence. "It was the birthplace of empires and the cradle of secrets."

Elan's hand clasped his son's shoulder, a gesture of pride and camaraderie. "We have our destination," he said, his tone resolute. "Honestly, I don't know what we're looking for."

Myst met his father's gaze, his eyes alight with determination. "We'll find out together," he declared, his voice unwavering. "Road trip!"

Cuicuilco Archaeological Zone, Mexico City, Mexico

Elan and Myst followed Ana Garcia, their enigmatic guide, through the overgrown ruins of Cuicuilco. The ancient temple, nestled on the southern tip of Mexico City, was a labyrinth of crumbling stone and twisted vines, its secrets hidden beneath layers of history and magic.

Crickets serenaded the night while distant creatures called from the shadows. Elan's fingers traced the familiar grip of his knife, every nerve crackling with the ancient energy that seemed to pulse through the temple grounds.

"The stones whisper of forgotten truths," Ana said, her voice barely above a whisper. "Listen closely, and they will guide your path."

Elan glanced at Myst, his brow furrowed in concentration. They had come to Cuicuilco seeking answers, following the trail of clues that had led them to this ancient site. They could feel the weight of the temple's secrets pressing upon them as they navigated the twisting pathways and crumbling stairs.

The compass shuddered in Myst's palm like a living thing, its needle jerking sharply left. He froze mid-step, and Elan's hand immediately went to *Winterstar*'s hilt - years of partnership had taught them to read each other's signals.

"There." Myst's voice barely carried over the chorus of night insects. His free hand reached out toward what looked like just another temple wall, but ancient stone spoke beneath his touch as his fingers brushed aside centuries of creeping moss.

Elan moved closer, the moonlight catching the silver in his hair. "The map's markings," he breathed, recognition lighting his features. His weathered hand joined Myst's on the wall, tracing channels worn into the rock. "But these aren't just copies, son. They're deeper. Older."

"The originals," Myst finished. The compass hummed against his skin, responding to something their human senses couldn't detect. "The map wasn't showing us where to go - it was showing us what to look for when we got here."

Ana nodded, her dark eyes glinting in the moonlight. "The key to unlocking the temple's heart, this is as far as I go," she said, her words cryptic and meaningful.

Elan's gaze fell upon a small slot, perfectly sized to fit the compass. With a nod from Myst, he placed the ancient device into the opening, holding his breath as he waited for the magic to take hold.

For a moment, nothing happened. Then, with a grinding sound that echoed through the night, the stone wall began to shift, revealing a hidden chamber that had lain untouched for centuries. Elan and Myst exchanged a look of triumph, their hearts racing with anticipation, as they stepped forward. An ethereal glow emerged from the walls, casting an otherworldy light upon the ancient stone. The air was heavy with the scent of incense and the whispers of forgotten secrets, a living energy that seemed to pulse with every breath they took.

Their footsteps echoed as they descended deeper into the temple, the passage leading them further underground. The walls were adorned with intricate carvings and symbols, a language lost to time but imbued with power and meaning.

A dark shape merged from the temple shadows, wrapped in robes that seemed to drink in what little light remained. Elan's hand flew to his blade, but Myst caught his wrist. His son's eyes had that distant look they got when he sensed magical energies, and he gave a slight shake of his head - no threat, not yet.

The figure emerged from the darkness like a piece of shadow taking form. Their movements were too fluid, too precise - not quite human. The air grew heavy with the scent of ozone and ancient incense.

"The stars remember you." The voice seemed to come from everywhere and nowhere, neither male nor female, young nor old. It brushed against their minds like silk over steel. "They have carried your echo forward through time, waiting for this convergence."

Elan shifted his weight, positioning himself slightly before Myst - an instinct born from years of facing the unknown. But Myst laid a hand on his father's shoulder, a gentle restraint. The magic in the chamber responded to the figure's presence like ripples spreading across still water, but there was no threat in the disturbance.

"The compass led us here," Myst replied, his voice steady despite the power thrumming through the ancient stones.

The figure's hood tilted slightly. "The compass?" A sound like distant chimes colored their words with something almost like amusement. "No, young one. You led the compass here. It has waited centuries for the right hands to hold it, the right eyes to read its truth."

Elan and Myst exchanged a glance, their eyes widening in surprise. The figure stepped forward, extending a hand that held a small, intricately carved object. It was a fragment of an ancient relic, its edges jagged as if it had been torn from a larger whole.

"This is but a piece of the puzzle," the figure explained, their words cryptic and meaningful. "A fragment of a greater whole, a key to unlocking the secrets that lie ahead."

Myst reached out, his fingers closing around the relic. As he held it up to the light, he noticed that it seemed to complement the compass, the two objects fitting together like long-lost companions.

"The path ahead..." The figure's voice dropped to a whisper that seemed to echo from the stones themselves. "The Malefic Assembly hunts you even now. They cannot allow you to succeed, to fulfill what was written in the stars. But succeed you must - or watch our world fall into shadow."

Elan's jaw clenched his resolve hardening with every word. He knew the risks, the weight of the responsibility that rested upon their shoulders. But he also knew they could not turn back, not when so much was at stake.

"We won't fail," he declared, his voice steady and confident. "We *will* see this through, no matter what."

The figure nodded, a hint of a smile playing at the corners of their lips as they faded into the darkness. "Then go forth, bearer of the compass," they said, their voice a whisper that seemed to echo through the ages. "Embrace your destiny and let the ancient wisdom guide your path."

As they stepped out of the temple, Elan and Myst found themselves in a secluded area, the night sky stretching endlessly above them. The weight of their journey seemed to press down upon their shoulders, the enormity of the task ahead suddenly overwhelming.

Elan sank to the ground, his back against a crumbling stone wall. He ran a hand over his face, his eyes filled with a weariness beyond physical exhaustion. "What if we're on the wrong path?" he whispered, his voice barely audible above the chirping of the crickets. "What if this is just a wild goose chase, and we're risking everything for nothing? Nykronus had this compass for who knows how long, and he obviously never got to this point."

Myst knelt beside his father, his hand resting on Elan's shoulder. "Dad," he said, his voice gentle but firm. "We can't let doubt consume us. We've come this far because we believe in what we're doing and our mission's importance. Plus, he gave it to us for a reason. Grandma always says, 'Things happen for a reason.' You know that."

Elan looked up, his gaze meeting his son's. "But the stakes are so high," he said, his words heavy with the weight of responsibility. "If we fail, if the Malefic Assembly succeeds..."

"We won't fail," Myst interjected, his eyes blazing with determination and squeezing Elan's shoulder tightly. "We stopped them before. We'll stop them again. And again. For as long as we're alive. We have each other, and we have the compass and the relic. We have the strength and the knowledge to see this through. You, out of all people, have shown me this. Believe Dad. Just believe!"

Elan smiled, his son's unwavering resolve a beacon of light in the darkness of his doubts. "You're right," he said, his voice growing stronger. "We've faced challenges before and always found a way. This time won't be different."

Myst helped his father to his feet, their hands clasped in a gesture of unity and support. "Together," he said, his voice filled with conviction. "We'll unravel the secrets of the past and protect the future, no matter what it takes."

Elan nodded, at ease by his son's words.

The campfire cast dancing shadows across the temple stones, its warmth barely reaching Elan and Myst as they hunched over their discoveries. The compass caught the firelight, its brass face gleaming like a cat's eye in the dark, while the relic seemed to drink in the shadows. Their makeshift camp - little more than a tarp strung between weathered pillars - kept the worst of the night wind at bay, but neither man noticed the cold. Their focus belonged entirely to the puzzle before them.

Myst cradled the relic in his palms, its surface cool despite hours by the fire. Moonlight caught the edges of symbols that seemed to shift when viewed directly, like trying to remember a dream. The familiar tingle of magic danced across his skin, but this was older, wilder than anything he'd encountered.

"Dad," he said softly, "look at this pattern. It's almost like…" He tilted the artifact, watching shadows pool in its ancient grooves. "It's like it's waiting for something. The way a lock waits for a key."

Elan's hands stilled over the compass. Twenty years of hunting artifacts had taught him to trust his son's instincts about magic. He held the compass closer to the relic, and suddenly, the air between them seemed to thicken with possibility.

"The compass's markings," Elan breathed. "They're not decorative. They're half of a whole." His fingers traced the intricate patterns that wrapped around the compass's edge. "All this time we thought it was meant to point the way…"

"When it was meant to complete something," Myst finished. Excitement threaded through his voice as he shifted closer, holding the relic to the firelight. 'These aren't two separate artifacts, are they? They're fragments of something bigger. Something that was broken apart…"

"Or hidden deliberately," Elan added, his eyes narrowing with the familiar gleam of puzzle-solving. "Nykronus gave us the compass knowing we'd find our way here. To this moment."

Elan leaned in closer, his eyes narrowing as he studied the cryptic markings. "There has to be a connection," he said, his mind racing with possibilities. "The compass led us to the relic for a reason."

Hours passed as they pored over the artifacts, their minds straining to unravel the hidden secrets. They tried every combination and every angle, their frustration mounting with each failed attempt.

Myst ran a hand through his hair, his eyes tired from the strain. "Maybe we're coming at this all wrong," he said, his voice tinged with exhaustion. "What if the answer isn't in the symbols but in the spaces between them?"

Elan's eyes widened, a spark of understanding igniting within him. "Of course," he breathed, his fingers tracing the empty spaces on the relic's surface. "The negative space forms a pattern."

Together, they worked to align the compass with the relic, the two objects fitting together like long-lost pieces of a puzzle. As they turned the dial, the symbols on the relic began to shift, revealing a hidden message that had lain dormant for centuries.

Myst's adrenaline spiked as he read the words, his voice trembling excitedly. "The path to the lost city lies within the heart of the dragon," he recited, his eyes wide with wonder. "Only those who bear the mark of the ancient ones may enter."

Elan's mind raced with the implications of the message, the weight of their discovery settling upon his shoulders. They had come so far and faced so many challenges, and now, they stood on the precipice of a revelation that could change everything.

As the campfire crackled and the night wore on, Elan and Myst huddled closer, their minds racing with the implications of their discovery. The hidden message within the relic had opened up a new path, a tantalizing clue that pointed towards their next destination.

Myst's fingers traced the words etched upon the ancient artifact, his voice barely above a whisper as he read them aloud once more. "The path to the lost city lies within the heart of the dragon. Only those who bear the mark of the ancient ones may enter."

Elan's brow furrowed, his mind grappling with the cryptic message. "The heart of the dragon," he uttered softly, his gaze drifting towards the compass beside the relic. "What could it mean?"

Elan's hand froze mid-motion, his breath catching. The firelight caught the compass's intricate etchings, and suddenly, the patterns shifted in his mind like pieces of a kaleidoscope clicking into place. His fingers trembled as they traced the ancient mechanisms.

"The dragon," he breathed, excitement bleeding through his measured tone. "We've been thinking too literally. Look at these markings - they're not depicting a beast; they're mapping force lines. The dragon is Earth itself, its heart beating in magnetic pulses beneath the ice and stone."

Myst leaned in closer, his mind racing to keep pace with his father's revelation. "And the heart of the dragon," he said, his words tumbling out in a rush, "must refer to a place where the magnetic field behaves differently, where it uniquely interacts with the compass."

Elan nodded, his fingers already moving to adjust the compass's settings. As he turned the dial, the needle spun erratically as if pulled by an invisible force. Slowly, it settled upon a single point, a direction far from their current location.

"The South Pole," Elan whispered, his voice filled with awe and trepidation. "Antarctica. That's where we need to go next."

Myst's eyes widened, their discovery settling upon him like a physical weight. They had come so far and faced so many challenges, and now, they stood on the brink of a journey that would take them to the ends of the earth itself.

But even as excitement surged through their veins, they knew the path ahead would be dangerous. The lost city, the heart of the dragon, lay waiting, its secrets guarded by forces they could only begin to imagine.

As the first rays of dawn crept over the horizon, Elan and Myst set about packing up their makeshift camp.

Myst carefully wrapped the ancient relic in a soft cloth, his fingers lingering on the intricate carvings on its surface. He then gently placed it into his backpack, nestling it securely between layers of clothing and supplies.

Elan, meanwhile, focused on gathering their notes and maps, his mind still racing with the implications of the hidden message they had uncovered. He meticulously folded each piece of paper, his movements precise and deliberate, as if organizing their findings could clarify their next steps.

As they worked, a silence settled over the camp, broken only by the rustling of fabric and the occasional clink of metal. But beneath the quiet was a thrumming undercurrent of determination, a shared resolve that bound father and son together in their quest.

Finally, Elan reached for the compass, his fingers closing around the cool metal with reverence. He looked up, nodding to Myst's gaze.

"We have a long journey ahead of us," he said, his voice steady and filled with conviction.

Myst returned the nod, his eyes blazing with the same fierce determination. "We won't stop until we find the lost city," he declared, a vow that seemed to hang between them. "No matter what or how far we have to go."

Elan clasped his son's shoulder in a gesture of solidarity and support. "We've come this far," he said, his voice filled with quiet strength. We won't turn back now. I'll call your mom and tell her we're not coming home for dinner."

With their gear packed and resolve unshakable, Elan and Myst set out from the temple ruins, their footsteps carrying them toward the next leg of their journey.

Mexico City fell away behind them as their jeep wound through pre-dawn streets toward the outskirts. The rising sun painted the sky in watercolor strokes of pink and gold when they finally turned onto a narrow access road, revealing a private airfield nestled between hills.

A sleek aircraft waited on the tarmac, its polished surface reflecting the dawn like liquid metal. The Order's insignia marked its tail - subtle enough to miss unless you knew where to look. Elan caught Myst studying the symbol, his son's expression unreadable in the early light.

"Is this really your first time flying Order transport?" Elan asked, shouldering his pack.

Myst nodded, eyes still on the aircraft. "First time knowing what it really means."

They moved towards the aircraft, courtesy of the Order, their foot-steps echoing in the early morning stillness. His palm pressed against *Winterstar's* hilt, the archaic artifact's heft and the compass an ever-present symbol of the odyssey that awaited them.

Myst paused as they approached the plane; his gaze drifted toward the horizon. The enormity of their mission seemed to settle upon his shoulders, a physical weight that threatened to overwhelm him.

Elan turned to face Myst. "We've come this far," he said, his voice steady. "There's no turning back now."

Myst grinned. "I know," he replied, his words a whisper that hung in the air between them. "It's just... the South Pole, the lost city... it all seems surreal."

Elan smiled, a flicker of understanding in his eyes. "I feel it too," he admitted, his gaze drifting towards the plane that awaited them. "Admit it, this is exciting."

With a final nod, they boarded the plane, their movements precise and purposeful. As they settled into their seats, Elan pulled out the compass, its needle pointing resolutely toward their destination.

The engines roared to life, the vibrations thrumming through the cabin as the plane began to taxi down the runway. Myst's fingers tightened around the armrests, his heart pounding as the aircraft gathered speed.

And then, with a sudden surge of power, the plane lifted off, its wheels leaving the ground behind as it soared towards the sky. Elan and Myst exchanged glances, their eyes locked in silent communication.

They were airborne, the next phase of their adventure unfolding before them. They would see this through, no matter what.

~

Antarctic Plateau, South Pole

The endless white of Antarctica stretched below them like a blank page in Earth's story. Elan pressed his forehead against the cold window, watching his breath fog the glass. Beside him, Myst sat unnaturally still, his fingers absently tracing the relic's edges through his jacket pocket.

"It's like nothing else exists," Myst murmured, breaking their hours-long silence. "Just ice and sky."

Elan glanced at the compass resting in his palm. Its needle swung with unwavering purpose, pointing them deeper into the heart of this frozen continent. The sensation building in his chest since Mexico grew stronger - that peculiar mix of anticipation and dread that always preceded their most significant discoveries.

"Something exists down there," he replied, watching the shadow of their plane race across the pristine surface. "Something old. Something waiting."

Elan's fingers tightened around the compass, its needle pointing resolutely toward their destination. He glanced at Myst, a flicker of pride in his eyes as he took in his son's determined expression.

For his part, Myst couldn't tear his gaze away from the view below. The sheer scale of the landscape was humbling, a reminder of how small they were in the grand scheme of things. And yet, he knew that their mission was anything but insignificant.

As the plane continued its journey, the two men sat silently, each lost in their thoughts. The weight of their responsibility hung heavy in the air, a palpable presence that seemed to fill the cabin.

But beneath the solemnity was a flicker of excitement and anticipation for what lay ahead. They were on the brink of something extraordinary, a journey that would test their limits and push them to their breaking points.

And yet, as they looked out at the frozen landscape below, Elan and Myst knew they were ready for whatever challenges lay ahead. They had the compass and the relic to guide them.

The plane flew on, carrying them toward their destiny. The lost city, the heart of the dragon, lay waiting, its secrets hidden beneath the ice and snow. But Elan and Myst were determined to uncover the truth, to see their mission through to the end.

CHAPTER
FOUR

Benevento, Italy

Sunset painted Benevento's Roman arches in blood-red hues as Order members hurried through the ancient streets. Above, the medieval castle's towers pierced the darkening sky like accusatory fingers, casting long shadows over the compound below. The Order of St. Michael's headquarters had stood here for two millennia, its high walls blending seamlessly with the city's historic architecture while concealing decidedly modern secrets.

Inside, the compound hummed with nervous energy. Ancient incense mingled with the sharp ozone smell of electronics as members moved purposefully through corridors where security cameras shared space with centuries-old wards. Tonight, like every night for over two thousand years, the Order stood guard over the thin line between mundane reality and forces that would shatter that reality's foundations.

Within these walls, the members of the Order gathered to study the arcane arts and to plan their next moves in the eternal struggle against the forces of darkness. They were a diverse group, hailing from all corners of the world, but united in their purpose and their faith.

The compound was more than just a building; it was a living, breathing entity pulsing with the energy of the Order's collective will. It was a place of power, a nexus of mystical energy that hummed with the promise of secrets yet to be uncovered.

In a secluded wing of the Order's headquarters, Stanley Wyatt's domain was a testament to the fusion of ancient wisdom and modern technology. The room hummed with the constant whir of machines, the glow of screens casting an ethereal light across the space. Ancient runes danced alongside lines of code, their secrets waiting to be unraveled.

Stanley stood at the center, his muscular frame contrasting the delicate artifacts surrounding him. He moved with a fluid grace, his hands gliding over the keyboards and touchscreens as if they were extensions of his own body. Now streaked with silver, his red hair was tamed beneath his ever-present cowboy hat, a reminder of his roots.

Stanley's domain reflected the Order's evolution. Holographic displays projected ancient texts into three-dimensional space, allowing him to manipulate prophecies with gesture controls. "The old masters would have killed for this setup," he said, expanding a section of text with a flick of his wrist. "We've merged their wisdom with quantum computing. Each scroll, every prophecy, digitized and cross-referenced against centuries of Order knowledge."

He pulled up another display showing the compound's defense grid. "But it's more than just fancy lights and databases. Every stone in this place is fitted with sensors that can detect both technological and magical threats. The old ways and the new, working in harmony."

"Check this out," Stanley called out, his voice filled with excitement. He gestured towards a sleek, black device on a nearby workbench. "This beauty can decipher any ancient text, no matter how obscure. It's like having a thousand linguists and cryptographers at your fingertips."

He picked up the device, his fingers tracing the intricate patterns etched into its surface. "But that's not all. It can also detect hidden magical properties, things that have been lost to time." His eyes sparkled with the thrill of discovery. "Imagine what we could learn, the secrets we could uncover."

Stanley effortlessly lifted a heavy piece of equipment as he spoke, his muscles straining beneath his shirt. He moved it aside, making room for the device on the workbench. "I've been working on this for months, tweaking the algorithms, refining the sensors. It's not perfect yet, but it's a start."

He set the device down, his hands moving with practiced precision as he connected it to the network of computers that surrounded him. "With this, we can bridge the gap between the old ways and the new. We can harness the power of technology to unlock the mysteries of the past."

As the sun dipped below the horizon, painting the sky in hues of amber and violet, Zoe found solace in her sanctuary within the compound. The verdant garden was a testament to the harmonious blend of nature and magic, where the lines between the two blurred into a seamless tapestry.

The air was filled with Zoe's electric lute's gentle strumming, the melodic notes dancing on the breeze like ethereal whispers. The garden responded to her music, the plants swaying in rhythm, their leaves rustling in a symphony of life.

Zoe sat amidst the greenery, her beach blonde hair cascading over her shoulders, her piercing green eyes focused on the injured bird cradled in her hands. She hummed softly, her voice weaving with the lute's melody, creating a soothing balm that seemed to envelop the undersized creature.

"The key to bardic magic," Zoe explained to the bird, her voice as gentle as a lullaby, "is to find the resonance between the melody and the essence of life itself. Every living thing has its unique frequency, a song that echoes through the fabric of existence."

As she spoke, the bird's wounded wing began to mend, the torn feathers knitting back together as if guided by an invisible hand. Zoe smiled, her fingers never faltering on the lute's strings. "When we attune ourselves to that frequency and allow our music to harmonize with the natural world, we can tap into a power that transcends the physical realm. We become conduits for the very essence of life, channeling its energy to heal and restore."

The bird, now fully healed, fluttered from Zoe's hands, its wings beating perfectly with the rhythm of her lute. It soared above the garden, a living testament to the power of Zoe's magic.

Zoe's gaze drifted to the other inhabitants of her sanctuary, the plants and animals that thrived under her care. Each was a thread in the tapestry of life, a part of the more incredible symphony she had learned to orchestrate.

"This is the true power of bardic magic," she said, her voice filled with reverence. "It's not about control or domination. It's about understanding, finding the harmony between all living things and nurturing it, allowing it to flourish."

Olivia stood at the head of the large table, her pixie-cut black hair framing her face with an air of determination. The dimly lit library was a sanctuary of knowledge, its walls lined with ancient tomes and dusty scrolls. The flickering candlelight cast an ethereal glow over the maps and texts spread out before her, their secrets waiting to be unraveled.

The Order members gathered around the table, their faces etched with anticipation and reverence. They looked to Olivia for guidance, their trust in her unwavering. She was a beacon of faith and wisdom, a strategist whose plans were as precise as they were inspired.

Olivia's eyes scanned the maps, her mind weaving together the threads of ancient prophecies and current intelligence. She spoke with a quiet intensity, her words carrying the weight of centuries.

"The prophecies speak of a time when the forces of darkness will rise, threatening to engulf the world in chaos," she said, her voice cutting through the silence like a blade. "But they also speak of hope, a path that will lead us to victory."

She traced her finger along a faded parchment, its edges worn by time. "Here, in the heart of the ancient city, lies the key to our success. A relic, long hidden, that holds the power to turn the tide of battle."

The Order members leaned in closer, their eyes fixed on the map. Olivia's faith was a tangible presence in the room, a force radiating from her very being.

"But we must act quickly," she warned, her gaze sweeping over the assembled team. "Our enemies are cunning and relentless. They will stop at nothing to prevent us from claiming the relic."

She tapped a series of markings on the map, her mind already three steps ahead. "We will divide our forces, striking from multiple angles. Each team will have a specific role to play, a part to contribute to the greater whole."

Olivia's words were met with nods of agreement, and the Order members were ready to follow her lead. They knew that her strategies were not just born of intellect but of a deep and abiding faith that guided her every move.

"Remember," she said, her voice filled with conviction, "we are not just fighting for ourselves but for the very soul of humanity. Our faith is our shield and our weapon, a light that will guide us through the darkest of times."

Zoe's lute strings hummed in response, finding the resonance in Olivia's words. Without thinking, she began to pluck out an ancient melody—one of the Order's oldest ballads:

"Stand Fast, Brothers and Sisters
By blade and faith, we take our stand,
Guardians of this sacred land.
Not for glory do we fight,
But for all souls caught in night.
Our shield is forged of burning faith,
Our weapon is the ancient grace.
Through shadows deep and trials dire,
We'll light the way with sacred fire.
For in this hour when darkness falls,
We'll answer humanity's desperate calls.
Together bound by holy light,

We'll guide all souls through endless night."

As the meeting drew to a close, the Order members rose from their seats, their spirits livened by Olivia's words and Zoe's song.

The common room was a testament to the unique blend of personalities that comprised the Order's leadership. It was a space where ancient relics sat alongside cutting-edge technology, where mystical tomes shared shelves with scientific journals. The room hummed with a quiet energy, reflecting the diverse talents and perspectives that had come together in this moment.

Stanley, Zoe, and Olivia sat at the heart of the room, their faces illuminated by the soft glow of the screens before them. They were joined by a handful of trusted advisors, each chosen for their expertise and loyalty to the Order's cause.

Olivia leaned forward, her eyes scanning the data scrolling across her screen. "The signs are clear," Olivia said, spreading the ancient texts across the table. "A new power is emerging—"

"Like the Shanghai incident?" Stanley's fingers stilled on his keyboard. "Because we all remember how that turned out."

"This is different." Olivia touched the scar on her neck—a reminder of Shanghai. "The energy signatures match the Durant prophecies perfectly. I've triple-checked."

"So had Master Chen before Shanghai." Stanley's voice softened. "Look, I trust you, Liv. I just can't watch another team get decimated because we rushed in."

Zoe's lute strings thrummed discordantly. "Neither of you is helping. The Council expects our assessment by morning, and we still haven't agreed on the approach to Maya's training.

Zoe closed her eyes, her fingers absently plucking at the strings of her lute. "I can feel it too," she breathed, her voice almost lost in the gentle melody. "A new song is being sung, a melody that speaks of great potential and even greater challenges."

The room fell silent momentarily, and each group member was lost in their thoughts. Stanley finally spoke, his voice cutting through the stillness like a blade.

"Maya," Stanley said, pulling up her combat footage on the main screen. The image froze on her hands wreathed in silver fire—Durant fire. "Look at the energy signature. It's exactly what the Codex predicted: a warrior carrying both bloodlines."

Olivia leaned forward, her crucifix glinting. "The emergence of Durant and Mazza lines. The gateway opening. It hasn't happened in—"

"A thousand years," Zoe finished. "Not since Valencia Durant sealed the Crimson Gate." She gestured to the ancient mural depicting the event. "And now the gate's weakening again."

"And Maya's the only one who can reinforce it," Stanley added grimly. "If we can't prepare her in time, everything Valencia sacrificed will have been for nothing."

Olivia paced the strategy room, holographic prophecies shifting beneath her feet. "A Mazza," she said, waving her hand through the ancient text. The words rearranged themselves, revealing new patterns. "The warrior rising from shadow—"

The lights flickered. On the detection grid, a dozen red dots appeared.

"Speaking of shadows," Stanley muttered, fingers flying across his keyboard. "Perimeter breach in sectors seven through twelve. They're testing our defenses again."

Olivia squared her shoulders. "They know about Maya. Get Zoe—we'll need her wards." She pulled her blade from its sheath, blue light crackling along its edge. "The prophecies can wait. Right now, we prove why the Order has survived over two thousand years of nights like this."

Zoe's fingers stilled on her lute, her green eyes sparkling with interest. "And what better warrior than one who has been trained by the best? I know Myst is equal in many aspects," she asked, a smile tugging at the corners of her mouth. "Maya has the skills, but more than that, she has the heart. She understands the true nature of our struggle, the balance between light and dark."

The advisors murmured their agreement, their voices blending in support. Stanley leaned forward, his hands clasped together on the table before him.

"So, it's decided then," he said, his voice filled with great determination. "We extend an invitation to Maya, bring her into the fold. We guide her, test her, and help her reach her full potential."

Olivia nodded, her face set in a mask of resolve. "But we must be cautious," she warned, her eyes scanning the faces around the table. "The path ahead will not be easy, and Maya must be ready for the challenges that await her."

"Twelve hours," Stanley muttered, watching the calibration numbers flash red again. The device sparked, filling his lab with the acrid smell of burnt circuits. Third failure tonight.

His phone buzzed: another text from the Council. "Status update required."

Stanley glanced at the ancient scroll propped beside his keyboard—the one warning of the Crimson Moon's approach in three days. If the attunement device wasn't ready before Maya arrived, she'd have no defense against what was coming. He'd seen the projections: a psychic backlash strong enough to shatter an untrained mind.

"Not on my watch," he growled, reaching for his tools. The burns on his hands could wait. Maya's safety couldn't.

He paused momentarily, his eyes scanning the lines of code that scrolled across the screen. Maya's potential was immense, and he knew that the Order would need every tool to help her harness that power. With a final keystroke, he completed the calibration, a sense of satisfaction washing over him.

Stanley's message echoed through Zoe's phone: "Device failed again. Need your harmonics expertise."

"On my way," she replied, but her hands kept weaving the protective wards in her sanctuary. The welcoming ritual had to be perfect—she'd seen how the Order's energies had overwhelmed their last candidate. The poor girl still hadn't woken up.

This time would be different. She'd sync her wards with Stanley's device, creating a buffer for Maya's transition. They couldn't risk another failure. Not with the Crimson Moon so close.

She knew Maya's journey would have significant challenges and greater rewards. The welcoming ritual was just the first step, a way to help Maya find her place within the tapestry of the Order's magic. Zoe's heart swelled with pride as she thought of the role she would play in guiding Maya along her journey. For the first time, she would be alone, forging her own path toward her destiny.

In the library, Olivia pored over ancient texts and modern strategies, weaving together a series of exercises designed to test Maya's resolve and insight. She knew that Maya's potential was not just a matter of raw power but of the strength of her character and the depth of her understanding.

The exercises she had planned were not just physical challenges but mental and emotional ones as well. They would push Maya to her limits, forcing her to confront her doubts and fears. But Olivia had faith in Maya's resilience, in her ability to rise to the occasion and emerge more robust than ever.

As the three leaders worked, each in their own domain, they shared a common sense of purpose. Maya's arrival marked a turning point for the Order, a moment when fate could shift in their favor.

As the sun set, painting the sky in hues of deep purple and inky blue, the leaders of the Order gathered in Zoe's garden. The air was filled with the gentle rustling of leaves and the soft chirping of nocturnal creatures, a soothing symphony that underscored the moment's significance.

Zoe sat cross-legged on the grass, her lute cradled in her lap. Her fingers absently plucked at the strings, the notes blending seamlessly with the natural sounds of the garden. Stanley leaned against a nearby tree, his arms folded across his chest, his eyes fixed on the stars above.

Olivia stood at the center of the garden, her hands clasped behind her back, her gaze distant and thoughtful.

For a long moment, no one spoke. The weight of their shared responsibility hung in the air, a palpable presence that seemed to bind them together. They knew that the path ahead would be fraught with challenges, that the fate of the Order and the world rested on their shoulders.

But as they stood there, surrounded by the beauty and tranquility of the garden, a sense of resolve began to take hold. They were not alone in this fight, not anymore. With Maya by their side, they had a chance to turn the tide, to bring balance to a world that had been teetering on the brink of chaos for far too long.

Zoe's fingers stilled on her lute, and she looked up at her companions. "We have a long road ahead of us," she said, her voice soft but filled with determination. "But I believe in Maya. I believe in us. Together, we can face whatever challenges come our way."

Stanley nodded, his eyes still fixed on the stars. "She's got the skills, the heart, and the legacy. With our guidance, she'll become the warrior we need her to be."

Olivia's gaze shifted to her friends, a small smile tugging at the corners of her mouth. "The prophecies have spoken, and now it's up to us to see them through. We must be ready for the trials ahead, to support Maya and each other every step of the way."

The garden seemed to come alive as they stood there, united in their resolve. The wind whispered through the leaves, carrying with it the promise of change, a future yet to be written. And though the path ahead was uncertain, one thing was clear: with Maya's arrival, the Order stood on the precipice of a new era, one that would be defined by the strength of their unity and the power of their purpose.

CHAPTER
FIVE

The Durant Estate within Prairie Creek Redwoods State Park, Orick, California

The morning sun cast a warm glow across the Durant-Mazza family dining room, illuminating the faces of those gathered around the table. Maya sat beside her Great Grandma Gianna Mazza, her eyes sparkling excitedly as she discussed their upcoming trip to Benvenuto. Lola Rose, her aunt Kristinn, and Uncle Jhan listened intently, their smiles reflecting the Durant family's shared joy.

The peaceful mood in the room was abruptly broken by an unexpected rapping at the entrance. Jhan stood up, his tone laced with unease as he declared, "Maya, you expecting someone at this hour? I'll see who's there." After a brief absence, he reentered the room, followed closely by one of his most reliable counselors, whose countenance was marked by a somber and serious look.

"I bring troubling news," the advisor announced, his voice heavy with worry. "Nykronus has disappeared, and rumors have surfaced of a mysterious realm that has come to light."

The family exchanged looks of shock and disbelief, their once cheerful conversation replaced by a tense silence. The advisor reached into his coat and produced a sealed letter, holding it out to Maya.

"This letter is believed to be from Nykronus himself," the advisor explained, his hand trembling slightly. "It's addressed to you, Maya."

Maya accepted the letter, her fingers brushing over the ornate seal as her eyes grew large with astonishment. "It's for me, not mom or dad?" Bewilderment rapidly transformed into a profound, disturbing inquisitiveness within her. Glancing at her relatives, she noticed their expressions reflected the same perplexity and unease she felt.

Lola Rose reached out and placed a comforting hand on Maya's shoulder. "Whatever it says, we're here for you," she reassured, her voice steady despite the uncertainty.

Apprehension gripped Maya as she stared at the mysterious letter, the family's unease palpable in the stillness. Months had passed without any word from Nykronus, and even Maya couldn't escape the feelings of concern that now entwined her thoughts. With a subtle nod of acknowledgment to her grandmother's reassurance, Maya refocused on the unopened envelope, an unspoken understanding that its contents would irrevocably alter her path and potentially reshape the very destiny of the Order.

Maya's fingers trembled slightly as she broke the seal on the letter, her heart pounding. The family gathered closer, their eyes fixed on the unfolding parchment. As Maya read the cryptic message aloud, her voice wavered with confusion and unease.

"Nykronus speaks of a hidden realm," Maya said, her brow furrowed in concentration. "A place where the very fabric of reality is woven differently."

Grandma Gianna leaned forward, her eyes sharp with concern. "And he's disappeared? Without any warning or explanation?"

Maya nodded, her gaze still locked on the letter. "He mentions a mirror, one that can guide passengers to this mysterious realm."

The family exchanged glances, a silent understanding passing between them. They rose to the private study, a room steeped in history and secrets. The walls were lined with ancient tomes and artifacts, each holding a piece of the family's legacy.

In the center of the room stood a large, worn map, its surface marked with mystical sites and ley lines crisscrossing the globe. Maya and her family gathered around the map, their eyes tracing the intricate patterns.

"These are the last known locations associated with Nykronus," Jhan said, pointing to a cluster of marked points. "And here, this area is where the rumors of the mysterious realm originate. Mom, you know where this is, right?"

Rose sighed. She stood up and looked out the window. "Your dad's province, Palawan."

Maya's fingers brushed over the map, her mind racing with questions. She had always known that her family was different and connected to something greater than themselves. But now, with Nykronus's disappearance and the revelation of this hidden realm, she couldn't shake the feeling that her destiny was somehow intertwined with these events.

As the family discussed the implications of Nykronus's message, Maya found herself lost in thought. She had always felt a stirring within her, a sense of untapped potential and unexplored abilities. Could this be the key to unlocking the mysteries that had always seemed out of reach?

Maya sat in her room, the late afternoon sun casting elongated shadows across the space she had grown up in. Mementos of her childhood and training surrounded her, each holding a memory of the path that had led her to this moment. Her gaze lingered on Vulcan's shield momentarily as the memory of the day her mother bestowed it upon Myst and herself resurfaced in her mind. She held the letter from Nykronus in her hands, the weight of its contents seeming to grow heavier with each passing minute.

Maya touched the broken seal with a deep breath, her fingers trembling slightly as she unfolded the parchment. The cryptic message within seemed to dance before her eyes, the words speaking directly to her soul. It was as if Nykronus had known the very depths of her being, the untapped potential that lay dormant within her.

As she reread the message, a sense of awe washed over Maya. The words hinted at a destiny far more significant than she had ever imagined, a path inexplicably intertwined with the mysteries of the hidden realm. The responsibility to uncover the truth behind Nykronus's disappearance settled upon her shoulders, a weight that she knew she must bear.

Maya rose from her seat, a newfound determination coursing through her veins. She moved to her window, gazing out at the world beyond. The sun was setting, painting the sky in hues of orange and pink, but Maya's focus was elsewhere. Her mind raced with the possibilities ahead, the challenges she would face in her quest for answers.

She knew that the journey would not be easy, that there would be obstacles and dangers at every turn. But Maya also knew that she could not turn away from this calling. It was a part of her, woven into the very fabric of her being.

With a resolute nod, Maya returned to the letter, her eyes scanning the words again. She would not rest until she had uncovered the truth, found Nykronus, and discovered the secrets of the hidden realm. It was her destiny, and she would embrace it with every fiber of her being.

Maya walked through the dimly lit corridors of the estate, her footsteps echoing off the ancient stone walls. The moon's soft glow filtered through the stained glass windows, casting a kaleidoscope of colors across the floor. She approached the family's library entrance, a room steeped in history and secrets.

As she pushed open the heavy wooden doors, Maya was greeted by the sight of her grandparents, Gianna Mazza, and Rose Durant, seated at a large oak table. The room was illuminated by the flickering light of candles, their warm glow dancing across the shelves lined with ancient tomes and artifacts.

Grandma Gianna looked up from the book she was studying, her eyes softening as she saw Maya approach. "Come, sit with us," she said, gesturing to an empty chair beside her.

Maya sat, her gaze drifting to the open book on the table. The pages were filled with intricate illustrations and ancient scripts, the ink faded with time.

"We've been expecting you," Lola Rose said, her voice gentle but firm. "The path you're about to venture is not an easy one, but it's a path that our family has walked before."

Grandma Gianna nodded, her fingers tracing the edges of the book. "Nykronus has been a part of our family's history for generations," she explained. "The Mazza family has encountered other realms, and our connection to Nykronus runs deep."

Maya leaned forward, her eyes wide with curiosity. "And what about the Durant family?" she asked, her gaze shifting to Lola Rose.

Rose sighed, a distant look in her eyes. "It's no coincidence that Nykronus's last known location is in Palawan, your grandfather's province in the Philippines," she said. "The Durant family has its own ties to Nykronus, though they have been buried beneath the sands of time."

The elders exchanged a knowing glance, a silent understanding passing between them. They turned back to Maya, their expressions grave.

"The path you must walk is filled with danger," Grandma Gianna warned. "Trust your instincts, Maya, but do not let your bravery turn to recklessness."

Lola Rose reached out and touched Maya's shoulder, her touch comforting and reassuring. "Prepare yourself, both in mind and body," she advised. "The challenges you'll face will test you in ways you can't yet imagine."

Maya nodded, her determination growing with each passing moment. She knew the journey ahead would be difficult, but she also knew she could not turn away from her destiny.

Maya stood before her family in the grand hall, the room filled with an air of solemnity and anticipation. The ancient tapestries adorning the walls seemed to whisper the tales of their ancestors, their presence a reminder of the legacy that Maya now carried. The family members, both physically present and those joining through the virtual call, focused their attention on the young woman at the center of the room.

Grandma Gianna was the first to speak, her voice filled with concern and pride. "Maya, my dear, the path you wish to embark upon is not an easy one. The quest to find Nykronus and explore this mysterious realm will test you in ways you cannot yet imagine."

Maya nodded, her eyes shining with determination. "I understand, Grandma. But I feel in my heart that this is something I must do. It's as if Nykronus's message was speaking directly to my soul. He has done so much for us in this life and in our previous life. I can't let him down."

Elan, his image projected on the virtual screen, leaned forward, his eyes focused on his daughter. "Maya, as your father, I want nothing more than to protect you from the dangers that lie ahead. But I also know that you have been trained for this moment, and I have faith in your abilities. Remember what we talked about. This is *your* moment."

Kaira, seated beside Reagan, added, "Your father and I have faced our own challenges in the past, and we know the importance of following your instincts. If this is the path you feel called to, then we'll support you every step of the way."

Myst, emanating from the speakers, said, "Sis, you have always been the one to push the boundaries and seek out the truth. I have no doubt that you'll face whatever obstacles come your way with courage and wisdom. I'm proud of you!"

Reagan, commanding even through the virtual connection, spoke with a mix of pragmatism and affection. "Maya, as your aunt and a member of the Order, I understand the weight of the responsibility you are taking on. But I also know that you are not alone in this. We are all here to support you and lend our strengths to your cause—whatever you need, we've got your back."

The family members in the hall nodded in agreement, their faces reflecting a mix of worry and pride. Lola Rose, eyes misty with emotion, stood and approached Maya, placing a gentle hand on her shoulder.

"Maya, you carry the spirit of both the Mazza and Durant families within you. You have the courage of your father, the wisdom of your mother, and the determination of your grandparents. Trust in yourself and in the love and support of your family, and you will find the strength to face whatever lies ahead."

As the council drew to a close, the family members, both near and far, united in their decision to support Maya's quest. They knew that the path ahead would be filled with challenges and uncertainties, but they also recognized that it was an essential step in Maya's journey to discover her true purpose and powers.

Maya stood in the center of the family's armory, her gaze sweeping over the ancient weapons and artifacts that lined the walls. The room swirled with activity as her family members moved about, each focused on a specific task to aid her preparations for the impending quest.

In one corner, Grandma Gianna and Lola Rose huddled over an ancient tome, their fingers tracing the faded ink as they searched for any information that might shed light on the mysterious realm Nykronus may have entered. They whispered to each other, their voices low and urgent, as they jotted down notes and cross-referenced various texts.

Meanwhile, Jhan and Kristinn worked together to gather supplies, carefully selecting items essential for Maya's survival in the dense jungles of Palawan. They packed a sturdy backpack with provisions, medical supplies, and tools that could prove helpful in navigating the treacherous terrain.

Maya was engaged in intense training, her focus unwavering as she honed her physical and magical abilities. She moved through a series of complex combat forms, her body flowing with grace and precision, Vulcan's shield her mother had bestowed upon her and Myst held firmly in her grasp. The air crackled with energy as she channeled her powers, the *Moonbow* responding to her every command.

As the preparations continued, Rose approached Maya with a solemn expression. She held a beautifully crafted weapon in her hands, its surface shimmering with an otherworldly light.

"Maya," Gianna said, her voice filled with reverence, "this is the Axiom of the Celestial Divide. It has been kept by our family for generations, waiting for the right person to wield its power. I believe that person is you."

Maya's eyes widened as she reached out to take the weapon, her fingers closing around the worn metal. She could feel the power emanating from it, a thrumming energy that seemed to resonate with her soul.

"Thank you, Grandma," Maya whispered, her voice thick with emotion. "I'll do everything in my power to live up to the legacy of our family and find Nykronus."

Gianna smiled, her eyes shining with pride. "I have no doubt that you will, my dear. You have the strength and courage of both the Mazza and Durant families flowing through your veins. Trust in yourself and in the love and support of those around you, and you will overcome any obstacle that stands in your way."

As the family continued their preparations, the atmosphere in the armory was one of unity and determination. Each member brought unique skills and knowledge to the table, working together seamlessly to equip Maya for the challenges ahead. They knew that the path she was about to embark upon was fraught with danger, but they also knew she had the strength and resilience to face whatever trials came her way.

A thin mist clung to the Durant-Mazza estate as Maya stood at the edge of the landing field, her shadow stretching long across the wet grass. The waiting helicopter's blades caught the first light of dawn, flashing like signal fires. A chill wind whipped at her jacket—the same wind that had carried her mother to her own adventures years ago.

The Durant-Mazza family formed a half-circle behind her, their presence as familiar as her own heartbeat. Jhan's footsteps in the wet grass made her turn. His usually steady hands trembled slightly as he reached for her shoulder.

"That summer when you were seven," he said, voice rough, "you spent three weeks learning to climb the estate walls. Scraped knees, torn clothes—but you never quit." He pulled her into a fierce embrace. "That's who you are, Maya. That's who you've always been."

Kristinn pressed something cold and metallic into Maya's palm—a small arrowhead, its face weathered by age. "Your grandfather used this to find his way home," she said softly. "Now it's your turn." She joined the embrace, and Maya caught the familiar scent of vanilla and old books that always lingered in her aunt's home.

Maya turned to her grandmothers, who stood like pillars of strength in the growing light. Grandma Gianna's hands were warm against her cheeks, fingers calloused from years of wielding both weapons and cooking spoons. "The Mazza blood runs true," she murmured in Italian, the words carrying the weight of generations. "*Fidati della sua saggezza.* Trust its wisdom."

Lola Rose pressed her forehead to Maya's, a gesture so familiar it made Maya's throat tight. "I love you, apo," she whispered, using the Tagalog word for grandchild.

The helicopter's rotors began their slow arc, stirring the morning mist into ghostly wreaths. Maya felt the weight of Nykronus's letter against her chest, tucked safely in her inner pocket. The path ahead was uncertain, but uncertainty had always been the Durant-Mazza way. She squared her shoulders, feeling the familiar pressure of Vulcan's shield against her back.

Each step toward the helicopter felt both terrifying and inevitable, like walking into a dream she'd had a thousand times. The ground trembled beneath her boots, and the rotor wash battered at her clothes. Maya paused at the helicopter's door, one hand on the frame. The metal thrummed beneath her fingers, alive with possibility.

The helicopter lifted, and Maya's stomach lurched with more than just the sudden altitude. Below, her family drew together, their upturned faces growing indistinct in the swirling mist. Lola Rose's silver hair caught the light like a beacon. Jhan's steady stance, Kristinn's raised hand, Grandma Gianna's proud chin tilt—she memorized each detail, storing them like talismans against the loneliness ahead.

The estate shrank beneath them, the carefully tended gardens and ancient stone walls blurring into a familiar patchwork. Maya's gaze was drawn westward, where the morning sun painted the distant ocean in shades of fire. Somewhere beyond that horizon lay Palawan, where Nykronus and the mysterious realm waited, with answers to questions she'd only just learned to ask. The arrowhead in her pocket seemed to grow warmer as if responding to their direction.

The helicopter banked west over the dense, mist-shrouded forest that marked the border of Durant-Mazza land. Ancient trees stretched toward the clouds, their branches like gnarled fingers grasping at the helicopter's shadow. Maya watched as tendrils of fog pulsed with almost otherworldly energy, and the Axiom of the Celestial Divide hummed softly at her side in response.

The helicopter banked sharply, and Maya's breath caught as she spotted the vessel waiting below—her first stepping stone toward Palawan. The ship's weathered hull stood dark against the gleaming water, somehow both imposing and welcoming. Her grandmother's Italian words echoed in her mind: "*Fidati della sua saggezza.*" Trust its wisdom. Whatever trials lay ahead, the path was set.

The helicopter settled onto the ship's landing pad with a gentle shudder. Maya shouldered her pack and stepped out onto the deck, her boots splashing through puddles of seawater. Salt spray stung her face, and the crash of waves against the hull thrummed through her bones. The ocean stretched endless in every direction, but somewhere ahead lay Palawan—and answers.

Maya scanned the horizon one last time, noting how the rising sun had burned away the last traces of dawn mist. Only open water lay ahead now. She touched the letter in her pocket, felt the reassuring weight of Vulcan's shield on her back, and headed below deck. The Durant-Mazza blood ran true, and it was leading her to Palawan.

CHAPTER
SIX

he Pacific Ocean

The Spirito del Viaggio carved through jewel-toned waters, its brass-fitted bow scattering dolphins like silver coins. Maya's fingers found the familiar grooves in the teak railing, her homeland dissolving into watercolor streaks behind them. Adventure stretched across the horizon in shades of possibility—though her grandmother would call it destiny.

The shore shrank with each swell, excitement and apprehension warring in Maya's chest like opposing tides. The vastness of the sea stretched before her, its endless expanse a reminder of the uncertainty ahead. Yet, the steady progress of the ship, its hull slicing through the waves with unwavering purpose, reassured her that she was on the right path.

As the sky lightened, the first rays of the sun painted the horizon in a breathtaking array of oranges and pinks. The colors danced across the water's surface, casting a warm glow on Maya's face. She closed her eyes for a moment, allowing the warmth to seep into her skin and the gentle rocking of the ship to soothe her nerves.

At that moment, Maya felt a profound connection to the journey ahead. The call of destiny, once a distant whisper, now resonated deep within her, urging her forward. She knew that her chosen path would be fraught with challenges and obstacles, but she also knew that she could not turn back now.

As the ship pressed onward, Maya's resolve only grew stronger. She thought of Nykronus and his countless sacrifices for the mysterious realm that awaited her discovery. The weight of her family's legacy rested upon her shoulders, but rather than feeling burdened, Maya felt empowered.

Maya opened her eyes with a deep breath and gazed at the horizon again. The coastline had all but disappeared, replaced by an endless expanse of blue. The Spirito del Viaggio continued its steady progress, carrying Maya towards her destiny.

Maya's cabin had evolved from sanctuary to command center, where centuries collided. Dog-eared star charts spilled across holographic displays, their ancient constellations dancing through digital grids. At the heart of this organized chaos, Nykronus's letter held court, its cryptic symbols writhing like living things beneath the cabin's spectral glow. Each character seemed to pulse with its rhythm as if trying to whisper secrets beyond her understanding.

With a deep breath, Maya turned her attention to her pack, carefully reviewing its contents. The essentials, meticulously chosen for the journey ahead, were neatly organized. Her hand brushed against the protective amulets her family gave her, each imbued with their love and prayers for her safety. The amulets seemed to pulse with a gentle warmth, a constant reminder of the support and strength she carried with her.

A soft chime echoed through the cabin as she continued her inventory, signaling an incoming holographic call. Maya activated the device, and the shimmering forms of her family appeared before her. Their faces, etched with concern and pride, filled the small space.

"Maya, my brave girl," her grandmother spoke, her voice filled with wisdom and love. "You carry the strength of our ancestors within you. May their spirits guide and protect you on this journey."

Maya felt a lump form in her throat as she looked at the faces of her loved ones. "Thank you, Grandmother. Your words give me courage."

Her parents, Elan and Kaira, stepped forward, their eyes glistening with emotion. "We are so proud of you, Maya," Kaira said, her voice trembling slightly. "Remember, you are never alone, baby girl. We are with you every step of the way."

Elan nodded, his gaze filled with a fierce determination. "Trust in yourself, Maya. You've trained for this moment, and we believe in you."

Maya's twin, Myst, grinned at her through the hologram. "Show them what you're made of, sis. And don't forget to bring back some awesome stories to tell."

Laughter mixed with tears as Maya smiled at her family. Their love and support washed over her, strengthening her resolve. She knew that no matter the challenges, she carried their love and the weight of their legacy with her.

As the holographic call ended, Maya took a moment to absorb the silence of her cabin. She glanced again at the mysterious letter from Nykronus, its secrets waiting to be unraveled. She put away her pack with a deep breath, ready to face the unknown.

The ship's common area thrummed with the whispered dreams of seasoned wanderers. Maya sank into a leather armchair, its arms polished to a butter-soft sheen by generations of restless hands. The brass telescope beside her stood sentinel, its lens catching stray light like a trapped star. Her digital tablet cast blue-white shadows across yellowed manuscripts, technology and tradition merged in her lap.

Away from the comfort and safety of her home and family, the enormity of her mission became all too real. Doubt and fear crept into her thoughts, their icy tendrils wrapping around her heart. What if she wasn't strong enough? What if she failed to find Nykronus and unravel the secrets of the mysterious realm?

Maya's gaze drifted to the letter from Nykronus, its cryptic words etched into her memory. She pored over the message, searching for any clue or sign that she was on the right path. The letter spoke of destiny and the importance of her journey, but it offered little concrete guidance.

As she sat there, surrounded by the laughter and chatter of those around her, Maya felt a deep sense of responsibility settle upon her. The fate of Nykronus, and perhaps even the world, rested on her shoulders. The thought of failure, of letting down those who believed in her, was almost too much to bear.

Yet, even as doubt and fear threatened to overwhelm her, Maya clung to the belief that her destiny was intertwined with finding Nykronus and understanding the secrets of the mysterious realm. She had been chosen for this task and knew she could not turn back now.

Crystal chandeliers swayed with the ship's ancient rhythm, casting kaleidoscope shadows across the dining hall's mahogany panels. Each table cradled its constellation of stories—merchants with ink-stained fingers plotting routes on digital maps, scientists arguing theories in five different languages, weather-worn adventurers whose tales grew taller with each glass of port.

The elderly explorer across from Maya—Captain Lin, he'd introduced himself with a bow that spoke of Asian naval tradition—tapped his teacup with a scarred index finger. His Mandarin accent wrapped around English words like silk around steel. "The sea calls to certain souls," he mused, eyes bright beneath snow-white brows. "I see that call in you, young lady. The same hunger that drove old fools like me to chase horizons."

Maya traced the rim of her water glass, buying time. "I'm on a quest," she admitted, barely stirring the air between them. Her finger found a chip in the crystal, much like the flaw in her confidence. "But sometimes I wonder if I'm equal to it."

The Captain's laugh rumbled like distant thunder. "Equal? Child, the ocean doesn't ask for your credentials. Neither does destiny. They ask only for courage—and you have that in spades, or you wouldn't be here."

Maya listened intently as her fellow diners shared their stories, each tale more captivating than the last. A young couple spoke of their dream to explore uncharted islands, their eyes sparkling with excitement and anticipation. An elderly gentleman recounted his decades at sea, his weathered hands gesturing animatedly as he described the wonders he had witnessed.

Maya was drawn into the tales of adventure and discovery as the conversation flowed. Yet, a nagging sense of doubt tugged at her heart. She hesitated, unsure of how much to reveal about her journey.

"And what brings you to the sea, young lady?" a seasoned explorer asked, keenly examining Maya's face.

Maya hesitated, choosing her words carefully. "I'm on a quest of sorts," she began, her voice barely above a whisper. "But I'm afraid I might not be up to the task. What if I let down those who believe in me?"

The explorer leaned back in his chair, a knowing smile on his lips. "Ah, the weight of expectations," he mused. "It's a burden we all carry at some point in our lives."

He fixed Maya with a steady gaze, his eyes filled with wisdom and understanding. "But let me tell you something, young lady. Great discoveries often start with a leap of faith. It takes courage to embark on a journey into the unknown, to face your fears head-on."

Maya felt a flicker of hope ignite at the explorer's words. She looked around the table, taking in the faces of her fellow passengers. Each of them had their own dreams and aspirations and their own challenges to overcome.

"Thank you," Maya said softly, a small smile tugging at the corners of her mouth. "Your words give me strength."

As twilight deepened, the night wrapped around the Spirito del Viaggio like a velvet cloak studded with ancient secrets. Maya stood at the rail, salt spray kissing her cheeks as constellations wheeled overhead—each pattern a lesson Nykronus had branded into her memory through endless nights of study.

"The stars are more than light," his voice echoed in her mind, rough as sandpaper but warm as summer wine. "They're the original wayfarers, girl. Learn their dance, and you'll never be lost."

The Wayfinder's Crown hung low on the horizon, its five brightest stars pulsing in the sequence Nykronus had taught her to trust: one-two-three-pause-two-one. Like a heartbeat. Like a code. Her fingers unconsciously tapped the rhythm on the rail, cold metal warming beneath her touch.

Far below, phosphorescent creatures traced luminous patterns in the ship's wake, as if the sea itself sought to mirror the celestial dance above. Maya's breath caught—Nykronus had described this exact phenomenon in his letter, calling it the 'Mirror of Ways.' Another piece of the puzzle, clicking softly into place.

Charts and ancient texts had colonized every surface of Maya's cabin, their cryptic patterns merging into a maze of possibility. Her grandfather's compass spun lazy circles beside Nykronus's letter, while three generations of explorers' journals formed a paper pyramid on her bunk. In the corner, her pack waited like a crouching beast, ready for the adventure ahead.

As the night wore on, Maya could not sleep, her mind consumed by the impending quest. She paced the small confines of her cabin, her bare feet treading a well-worn path amidst the sea of parchment. Every step was accompanied by the rustle of paper, the sound of her thoughts giving tangible form.

Maya paused as she picked up a necklace with the emblem of St. Christopher, the patron saint of travelers and voyages. She knelt at the side of her bed, her hands clasped in silent prayer. The cool metal of her family's amulets pressed against her skin, a constant reminder of their love and support.

Rising from her knees, Maya returned to her desk, eyes scanning the meticulously organized notes before her. She had spent countless hours studying the ancient texts, deciphering the cryptic clues left behind by Nykronus. Each scrap of information, no matter how seemingly insignificant, had been carefully cataloged and cross-referenced, a tapestry of knowledge woven together by her hand.

As the first light of dawn began to creep through the porthole, Maya felt a surge of excitement coursing through her veins. The anticipation came in waves, a living thing that seemed to fill the air around her. She knew that the challenges ahead would be significant and that it would not be easy.

Yet, at that moment, Maya felt an undeniable sense of confidence, a deep conviction that she was competent and was exactly where she was meant to be. She had trained for this moment and spent her entire life preparing for the quest ahead. And now, as the ship drew closer to her destination, Maya knew she was ready.

After glancing at her notes, Maya began to pack her belongings, each item carefully chosen for the journey ahead. She knew that the search for Nykronus and the mysterious realm would test her skills, courage, and resolve. But she also knew that she would not face this challenge alone, that the love and support of her family and the guidance of the ancient texts would be with her every step.

Puerto Princesa, in the Province of Palwan, Philippines

Puerto Princesa materialized from the dawn mist like an ancient prophecy fulfilled, its harbor a patchwork of past and present. The Spirito del Viaggio's horn echoed off limestone cliffs, startling a flock of white-bellied sea eagles into flight. Modern research vessels bobbed alongside weather-beaten fishing boats, their crews calling to each other in a symphony of languages that felt older than the tide.

Maya's first step onto the gangway sent vibrations through her bones—the shift from sea legs to land legs was as much metaphor as reality. Each footfall marked a countdown: five steps from passenger to explorer, four steps from student to seeker, and three steps from daughter to destiny's child.

The dock's wooden planks creaked beneath her boots, speaking of countless arrivals and departures. She turned, one hand still on her pack's strap, to face the Spirito del Viaggio. The morning sun caught its brass fittings like fallen stars, and for a moment, Maya saw more than a ship—she saw the bridge between who she had been and who she must become.

"Thank you," she whispered to the ship, the sea, and the stars that had guided her here. Then she squared her shoulders and strode into the bustling port, where the air thrummed with possibility, and the scent of adventure rode every breeze. The true journey, she knew, was beginning—but now she carried not just her family's legacy but the strength of the voyage itself in every step.

CHAPTER

SEVEN

Ushuaia, Argentina

The icy wind whipped across the rugged airstrip in Ushuaia, Argentina, the southernmost city in the world. Elan and Myst, a father-son duo, moved with purpose, their faces determined as they loaded the last of their gear onto the specially outfitted ice-capable plane. The early light of dawn painted the sky in hues of orange and pink, casting long shadows across the tarmac.

Elan hoisted a heavy duffel bag into the cargo hold, his muscles straining under the weight. He had spent months preparing for this moment, pouring over ancient texts that spoke of a lost civilization and deciphering cryptic clues that hinted at a powerful artifact hidden in the heart of the South Pole. Standing on the precipice of his most excellent adventure, he felt excitement and trepidation coursing through his veins.

Myst, his ever-faithful companion, worked alongside him, his movements precise and efficient. He had been by his side through countless trials and tribulations, his unwavering loyalty and sharp intellect repeatedly proving invaluable. As he secured the last of their supplies, he turned to Elan, his eyes glinting with fierce determination, a sight that inspired those around him.

"We're ready," he said, his voice steady and sure, instilling a sense of reassurance in those around him.

Elan nodded, his jaw set. "Let's do this."

Together, they climbed into the plane's cockpit, settling into their seats with practiced ease. Elan's hands moved over the controls, his fingers dancing across the buttons and switches as he prepared for takeoff. The engines roared to life, reverberating like a mighty heartbeat through the cabin.

As the plane lifted off the ground, Elan felt a rush of adrenaline surging through his body. This was the moment he had been waiting for, the beginning of a journey that would test his limits and push him to the brink. He knew that the path ahead would be fraught with danger, that they would face challenges unlike any they had encountered.

But he also knew that he was ready and had spent his entire life preparing for this moment. With Myst by his side and secrets waiting to be uncovered, with the help of his compass, Elan felt a rush that he had never known before.

As the plane soared over the rugged landscape of Patagonia, Elan's mind raced with the possibilities of what lay ahead. He knew that the journey to the South Pole would be perilous, that they would face the harsh and unforgiving elements of one of the most inhospitable places on Earth. But he also knew the rewards would be great—unlocking secrets beyond anything he had ever imagined.

The plane shuddered as it hit another pocket of turbulence, jostling Elan and Myst in their seats. Elan gripped the controls tightly, his knuckles turning white as he fought to keep the aircraft steady. Outside the cockpit windows, the world had turned a blinding white, an endless expanse of ice and snow stretching out in every direction.

Myst leaned forward, his eyes fixed on the navigation instruments. "We're getting close," he said, his voice barely audible over the constant buzz of the engines. "The compass is starting to react."

Elan glanced at the ancient device, watching as the needle twitched and spun increasingly. It was as if the compass was being pulled towards some unseen force, drawn inexorably towards the heart of the frozen continent.

As they flew deeper into the icy wasteland, the weather outside the cockpit windows grew increasingly violent. Howling winds buffeted the plane, throwing it from side to side like a toy in the hands of a petulant child. Snow and ice battered against the fuselage, obscuring their view and making navigating nearly impossible.

Elan gritted his teeth, fighting to keep the plane on course. He had flown in difficult conditions before, but nothing like this. The sheer isolation of their surroundings was unnerving, a stark reminder of the danger they faced.

Myst, too, seemed on edge. His usual calm demeanor gave way to a tense, focused intensity. He scanned the maps and charts before him, searching for clues to guide them toward their destination.

As the plane pushed on through the storm, Elan couldn't shake the feeling that they were being watched. It was as if the very land was aware of their presence, an ancient and powerful force that resented their intrusion. He shook his head, trying to clear his mind of such thoughts. They had a mission to complete, and he would not let fear or superstition stand in their way.

Antarctic Plateau, South Pole

The plane touched down hard on the Antarctic ice, skis screaming against the frozen surface. Elan fought the controls, compensating for a savage crosswind that threatened to flip them. In the co-pilot's seat, Myst braced himself, his eyes fixed on the compass that had guided them here. The ancient device pulsed with an intense blue light that matched *Winterstar*'s glow.

"That landing was more like a controlled crash," Myst said, managing a grin despite his white-knuckled grip on the console. "Is that how they taught you to fly in the Marines?"

"You try landing on a magnetic anomaly, wise guy." Elan nodded toward the compass, which was spinning wildly. "Something down there doesn't want modern instruments working properly."

As they unloaded their gear into the brutal cold, Myst paused, his expression distant. "Maya would love this. Remember how she used to track energy signatures back at the Order?"

"She's where she needs to be," Elan said, but his tone softened. "Your sister's research into the Malefic Assembly's artifacts might be the only reason we found this place. Without her translation of those texts..."

"I know." Myst shouldered his pack. "Still wish she was here to see what her work led us to."

With their gear unloaded and camp established, Elan and Myst turned their attention to the compass, watching as it vibrated with otherworldly energy. The needle pointed unerringly towards the distant mountain range, a silent guide in the frozen wilderness.

As they stood there, the vast silence of Antarctica enveloping them, Elan couldn't shake the feeling that they were on the cusp of something truly extraordinary. The secrets in this icy wasteland called to him, beckoning him forward with a force he couldn't resist.

With a final glance at the compass, Elan shouldered his pack, mounted their snowmobile, and turned to Myst. "Let's get moving," he said, his voice filled with determination. "We have a long way to go and little time to get there."

The icy wind howled across the vast expanse of the Antarctic plateau as Elan and Myst trekked through the frozen landscape. The sun hung low on the horizon, casting long shadows across the snow-covered ground. It felt as if they had been astride the snowmobile for an eternity, following the guidance of the ancient compass, which vibrated with increasing intensity as they drew closer to their destination.

Elan held up a hand as they crested a slight rise, signaling for Myst to stop. Before them lay a field of deep crevasses, their dark, shadowed depths cutting through the ice like gaping wounds. The sight was breathtaking and terrifying, a stark reminder of the raw power and danger that lurked beneath the surface of this frozen world.

Elan pulled out the compass, watching as the needle spun wildly before settling in a direction that led directly into the heart of the crevasse field. He exchanged a glance with Myst, who nodded grimly. They both knew they had to press on despite the risks.

As they carefully made their way across the treacherous terrain, Elan couldn't shake the feeling that they were being watched. The hair on the back of his neck stood on end, and he scanned the horizon for movement. But there was nothing, only the endless white expanse, and the Antarctic wilderness's eerie silence.

Suddenly, Myst let out a sharp gasp. Elan whirled around and stopped the snowmobile, his hand instinctively reaching for Winterstar. But Myst was not in danger. Instead, he dismounted and crouched next to one of the crevasses, his eyes wide with excitement.

"Dad, look at this," he said, his voice barely above a whisper.

Elan moved closer, his heart pounding in his chest. A series of cryptic markings etched into the ice at the edge of the crevasse were ancient symbols that matched those they had studied in the texts back at the Order's headquarters. The sight sent a thrill of excitement through Elan's body. They were on the right path.

But before they could investigate further, the ground beneath their feet began to tremble. It started as a low rumble, barely perceptible at first, but quickly grew in intensity until it felt like the ice was shaking apart. Elan and Myst stumbled, struggling to keep their balance as the world heaved and bucked.

The ground's first tremor was subtle - just a vibration through their boots. But the compass's reaction was immediate, its steady pulse becoming a violent rhythm that matched the shaking earth. Elan and Myst exchanged glances. They'd seen this behavior only once before, in the presence of a major Malefic artifact.

"There!" Myst pointed toward a massive crevasse ahead. Ancient symbols had begun to glow along its edges, pulsing in sync with the compass. But reaching them meant crossing a field of unstable ice, with cracks spreading beneath their feet like spider webs.

Elan drew Winterstar, its electric-blue energy illuminating the growing fissures. "I'll anchor us. Like we practiced."

Myst nodded, pulling a length of rope from his pack. They'd trained for this in the Rockies, but never in conditions like these. As Elan drove Winterstar into the ice, channeling its energy to create a stable point, Myst began weaving a spell of reinforcement through the rope.

The crossing was treacherous. Each step had to be tested, each rope length carefully managed. Twice, the ice cracked beneath them, and only their teamwork prevented disaster. But as they reached the crevasse wall, the glowing symbols intensified, responding to their presence.

"These markings," Myst breathed, brushing snow from the ancient script. "They're like the ones Maya found, but these are the original forms. Everything in the Order's archives must be copies of this. They're connected to the compass somehow," he said, his voice filled with wonder. "It's like they're part of the same puzzle."

Elan nodded, his mind racing with the implications of their discovery. But the fragment of a map carved into the ice wall truly caught his attention. The markings on the map were unmistakable, the same symbols used by the Malefic Assembly. And there, etched into the center of the map, was a depiction of an underground passage leading deeper into the realm.

"The location we're looking for," Elan said, his voice barely above a whisper. "It's beneath the ice itself. A passageway. I think it might be a secret lair for the Malefic Assembly. This may lead us to Verendana."

As Elan and Myst trekked back to their camp, the ethereal glow of the aurora borealis danced across the night sky, painting the icy landscape in shades of green and purple. The silence was broken only by the crunch of their boots on the snow and the occasional gust of wind that whipped across the frozen tundra.

But as they drew closer to their camp, a sense of unease settled over Elan. He held up a hand, signaling for Myst to stop. They dismounted the snowmobile. Something was wrong. The hairs on the back of his neck stood on end, and he could feel the weight of unseen eyes watching them from the shadows. Elan placed his hand on *Winterstar*, prepared for the inevitable danger.

Suddenly, the stillness was shattered by a flurry of movement. Elan and Myst reacted instantly, dropping into defensive stances as the attackers closed in. The attackers emerged from the storm like wraiths, their white tactical gear blending with the swirling snow. But what caught Elan's attention wasn't their camouflage - it was their weapons. Each carried a blade that hummed with a familiar energy, similar to Winterstar but corrupted somehow, their glow a sickly green instead of blue.

"Malefic tech," Myst growled, magic already coursing through his hands. "Modern design, though. Someone's been updating their arsenal."

The first attacker crossed blades with Elan, the clash of energies sending sparks of blue and green across the ice. Their fighting style was familiar - too familiar. The same forms the Order taught, but with a brutal efficiency that spoke of years of practice.

"You don't have to do this," Elan called out, recognizing the implications. "The Order can protect you."

The only response was a flurry of synchronized attacks. Myst's shield spell barely activated in time, deflecting a barrage of energy bolts. He countered with a blast of his own, the magic leaving traces of frost in the air.

"Dad!" Myst's warning came just as one attacker's hood fell back, revealing a face covered in ritualistic scars. Not random patterns - mathematical formulas etched into flesh. Before Elan could process the implications, the attackers retreated as quickly as they'd appeared, leaving behind only a single dropped item: a medallion bearing the same symbols they'd found in the crevasse.

Elan picked it up carefully, noting how the compass reacted to its presence. "Well," he said grimly, "I think we just confirmed Maya's theory about infiltrators in the Order."

Elan drew his sword, the blade glinting in the otherworldly light of the aurora, pulsing with blue lighting-like energy. He lunged forward, his movements a blur as he engaged the nearest assailant. The attacker was skilled, their own blade flashing in a deadly dance as they parried Elan's strikes.

Beside him, Myst unleashed a blast of magical energy, the force of the spell sending another attacker flying backward into a snowdrift. But more kept coming, and their numbers multiplied with each passing moment.

Elan and Myst fought back to back, their movements perfectly synchronized as they fended off the onslaught. Elan's blade found its mark repeatedly while Myst's magic crackled and sizzled through the air, leaving a trail of destruction in its wake.

But the attackers were relentless, their determination fueled by some unknown purpose. Elan gritted his teeth as a blade sliced through his parka, drawing a thin line of blood across his arm. He retaliated with a savage kick, sending his attacker sprawling into the snow.

The attack was over as quickly as it had begun. The remaining assailants melted back into the blizzard, their forms vanishing into the swirling white. Elan and Myst stood panting, their breath clouding in the frigid air as they surveyed the aftermath of the battle.

Questions raced through Elan's mind as he wiped the blood from his blade. Who were these attackers, and what did they want? Who had sent them, and how had they known where to find them in the Antarctic wilderness?

But one thing was clear: their mission was far from over, and their opposition was more formidable than they had ever imagined.

Elan and Myst returned to the camp. As they limped back into the warmth of their airplane, the adrenaline from the fight slowly faded as the pain from their injuries began to set in. The Southern Cross constellation glimmered overhead, a silent witness to their ordeal.

Myst slumped down in the cargo bay of their private plane,

wincing as he peeled back the layers of Elan's parka to examine a deep gash on his arm. "Those guys were no joke," he groaned, rummaging through their supplies for the first aid kit.

Elan nodded grimly, his body aching from the exertion of the battle. He held steady as Myst began to clean and bandage his wound. "They were well-trained, and they knew exactly where to find us. This was no random attack."

As they tended to their injuries, their minds raced with the implications of the day's discoveries. The hidden cavern, the ancient relics, the map fragment—each piece of the puzzle seemed to raise more questions.

Myst looked up at his father, his eyes blazing with determination. "We're getting close, Dad. I can feel it. Whatever secrets that map holds, they're worth fighting for."

Elan met his son's gaze, a fierce pride welling up in his chest. Despite the danger they faced, despite the unknown forces arrayed against them, Myst's resolve never wavered. At that moment, he saw not just his son but also a true partner in this quest.

"You're right," Elan said, his voice rough with emotion. "We can't let this stop us. We'll rest tonight and heal up, and tomorrow, we'll follow that map wherever it leads. Together."

Myst grinned, the pain in his arm forgotten as he clasped his father's hand. "Together. Just like always."

Under the watchful gaze of the Southern Cross, father and son sat in companionable silence, their bond more vigorous than ever. The Antarctic night stretched beyond them, vast and unknowable.

As the unending Antarctic sun illuminated the frozen landscape, Elan and Myst readied themselves for the upcoming stage of their expedition, the hours slipping by unnoticed in the constant daylight. The campsite was a hive of activity, the two men moving with purpose and determination as they refueled their snowmobile, packed their gear, and checked their supplies.

Elan stood at the edge of the camp, his gaze fixed on the horizon as he cradled the ancient compass in his gloved hand. The device vibrated with a steady, insistent pulse, its needle pointing unerringly toward the hidden passage revealed by the ice map. He could feel the weight of the secrets that lay ahead, the anticipation and trepidation that came with delving deeper into the mysteries of this frozen realm.

Beside him, Myst shouldered his pack, his eyes gleaming with a fierce resolve. The attack from the previous night had only strengthened his determination, his desire to uncover the truth behind Verendana and the Malefic Assembly. He knew that the path ahead would be fraught with danger, but he also knew that he and his father were ready to face whatever challenges lay in store.

As Elan and Myst navigated their snowmobile through the treacherous mountain range, the compass in Elan's hand pulsed with an ever-increasing intensity. The ancient device seemed to guide them toward a specific destination, its needle unwavering in its direction. The icy wind whipped around them, but their determination never faltered.

Suddenly, the compass vibrated with a fierce, almost unbearable energy. Elan brought the snowmobile to a halt, his eyes widening as he surveyed the scene before them. They had arrived at a hidden valley nestled deep within the mountains, and at its center stood an ice-covered entrance pulsing with an otherworldly light.

Elan and Myst dismounted the snowmobile, their boots crunching on the frozen ground as they approached the entrance. The air around them seemed to crackle with energy, and they could feel the power emanating from the ice-covered doorway.

Myst placed his hand on the icy surface, his brow furrowed in concentration. He could sense the ancient magic that sealed the entrance, a force that had kept this place hidden for centuries. Elan drew *Winterstar*, the blade humming with anticipation as he channeled his energy into the sword.

Father and son combined their abilities, Myst's magic intertwining with the power of *Winterstar*. The ice began to crack and splinter, shards flying through the air as the entrance slowly yielded to their efforts. With a final surge of energy, the doorway shattered, revealing a stairway that descended into the darkness below.

Elan and Myst exchanged glances, their hearts pounding with excitement and trepidation. They knew whatever came their way would bring them closer to the truth behind Verendana and the Malefic Assembly.

As they descended the stairway, their path illuminated by the soft glow of *Winterstar*, they found themselves in a chamber filled with ancient artifacts and cryptic inscriptions. The relics pulsed with a power that seemed to resonate with the energy of the compass, and the inscriptions hinted at a guardian of immense knowledge and strength.

Elan ran his fingers over the symbols etched into the walls, his mind racing as he tried to decipher their meaning. The name Verendana appeared repeatedly, and he couldn't shake the feeling that she was the key to unlocking the secrets they were meant to find.

As Elan and Myst stood at the threshold of the underground passage, the weight of their discovery and the night's events pressed upon them. The ancient relics, the cryptic map, and the sudden attack all pointed to a larger mystery that seemed to revolve around the enigmatic figure of Verendana.

Elan's mind raced with questions, trying to piece together the fragments of information they had gathered. The Malefic Assembly's involvement, the hidden cavern, and now this secret passage hinted at a complex web of secrets that they had only begun to unravel.

Beside him, Myst's eyes gleamed with determination, his resolve hardened by the attack they had faced. He knew that whatever lay ahead would be dangerous, but he also knew that they had no choice but to press on. The clues they had uncovered were too significant to ignore, and the connection to Verendana was a thread they had to follow.

As they prepared to descend into the unknown, Elan placed a hand on Myst's shoulder, a silent gesture of support and trust. Despite the uncertainties that lay ahead, their bond was unshakable. They had faced countless challenges together, and this would be no different.

Myst met his father's gaze, a small smile tugging at the corners of his mouth. "Ready?" he asked, his voice steady and sure.

Elan nodded, his grip tightening on *Winterstar's* hilt. "Ready."

Together, they stepped into the passage, the darkness swallowing them as they descended. The air grew colder as they moved deeper underground, the walls of the tunnel glistening with ancient ice. But their resolve never wavered, their determination fueled by the knowledge that they were on the right path.

As they navigated the passage's twists and turns, Elan's thoughts turned to Verendana, the mysterious figure who seemed to be at the center of it all. Who was she, and what role did she play in this ancient conflict? The questions burned in his mind, but he knew that the answers lay ahead, waiting to be discovered.

The hidden passage descended at a steep angle, its walls lined with the same mineral veins they'd seen above. But here, the patterns were more intricate, telling a story in symbols that spiraled downward with them. Elan held the compass in one hand, Winterstar in the other, both pulsing in an increasingly rapid rhythm.

"These aren't just decorative," Myst said, studying the patterns as they descended. "Look - they're showing energy flows, like a circuit diagram. This whole place is some kind of machine."

The passage eventually opened into a vast chamber that stole their breath away. Columns of ice rose like frozen waterfalls, each containing suspended objects: artifacts, weapons, and devices that hummed with power even after centuries of imprisonment. At the chamber's center stood a raised platform, and upon it...

"That's impossible," Elan breathed. The compass nearly jumped from his hand as they approached the platform. There, suspended in crystalline ice, was another compass - identical to theirs in every detail.

Myst stepped closer, his expression a mix of awe and concern. "Dad, look at the inscription."

Beneath the frozen compass, ancient letters spelled out a name they knew too well: 'Verendana's Key.'

Elan said softly. "This isn't just a storage facility. It's—"

A sound like cracking glass echoed through the chamber. The ice around the suspended compass began to splinter, and deep within the chamber, something ancient began to wake.

CHAPTER

EIGHT

San Francisco, California

Ancient wards pulsed dimly along the corridors of the Order's San Francisco headquarters, their usual golden glow muted to a sickly pale yellow in the dawn light. Where morning usually brought the buzz of apprentices practicing cantrips and the sharp scent of brewing enhancement potions, now only silence pressed against the spelled windows. The sun's first rays penetrated the building's magical defenses, casting long shadows across the marble floors inscribed with protective runes, but even the strongest illumination spells seemed unable to dispel the supernatural chill that had settled over the building. In the west wing, a protection crystal cracked with an audible ping, its failure a herald of the horror about to be discovered.

In the heart of the compound, a junior member of the Order hurried through the corridors, his footsteps echoing in the eerie quiet. His face was pale, his eyes wide with disbelief and horror. He had stumbled upon a sight that would forever be etched in his memory, a discovery that would shake the very foundations of the Order.

Junior member Jordan approached Professor Xicato's study, his protection amulet growing ice-cold against his chest. The professor's usually impenetrable wards hung in tatters of golden light, their broken strands writhing like wounded serpents. His trembling hand pressed against the oak door, its surface still warm from discharged magical energy. Inside, the professor's body lay slumped over his ancient desk, the rare grimoire he'd been studying still open beneath him. Arcane symbols burned into the ceiling above told a story of a fierce magical battle, while the professor's defensive crystals lay shattered across the floor, their power wholly drained. Most disturbing was the perfect circle of ash surrounding the desk, suggesting a ritual Jordan had only read about in forbidden texts.

With trembling hands, the Jordan reached for his phone, his fingers fumbling as he dialed the emergency number. His voice shook as he relayed the grim news, the words catching in his throat as he struggled to comprehend the magnitude of the loss.

Within minutes, the headquarters was in a state of upheaval. Members of the Order rushed to the scene, their faces etched with a mixture of shock and disbelief. Whispers of confusion and speculation filled the air as they gathered outside the professor's study, each trying to make sense of the tragedy that had befallen them.

Kaira and Reagan pushed through the crowd, their eyes wide with alarm. As they entered the study, the weight of the moment crashed upon them. Kaira's knees buckled, and she gripped the doorframe for support, her heart-shattering at the sight of her mentor's lifeless form. Reagan stood beside her, her hand on her shoulder, her face a mask of sorrow and determination.

The loss of Professor Xicato reverberated through the very core of the Order. He had been a guiding light, a beacon of wisdom and knowledge, and his absence left a void that seemed impossible to fill. As the members of the Order gathered around, their faces etched with grief, they knew that this was a turning point, a moment that would test their resolve and their faith.

Kaira's office was dimly lit, and the weight of the news she had to share was pressing heavily upon her. With a deep breath, she initiated the virtual call, the faces of her fellow Order members appearing on the screen before her. Maya's visage, though small, was etched with concern, her quest momentarily forgotten in the face of this unexpected gathering.

The communication crystal pulsed to life, its faceted surface projecting spectral images of Order members from across the globe. Each face flickered with a colored aura that reflected their emotional state - a security measure Professor Xicato himself had designed. Maya's projection sparked with irregular bursts of indigo, betraying her turbulent emotions despite her composed expression. Stanley's aura burned a fierce crimson, while Olivia's normally steady green light wavered like a candle in wind.

Kaira activated the Truth Circle with a gesture, causing runic symbols to spiral around each participant's image. Reagan stood at her shoulder, fingers moving in a subtle pattern that strengthened their collective magical connection. When Kaira spoke, her words carried the weight of old magic, bound by the ancient protocols of the Order's emergency protocols.

Kaira cleared her throat, her voice heavy with emotion as she began to speak. "I'm afraid I have grave news to share with you all. Our beloved Professor Xicato was found murdered in his study this morning."

A collective gasp rippled through the virtual gathering, the shock palpable even through the digital connection. Zoe's hand flew to her mouth, her eyes wide with disbelief. Stanley's jaw clenched, a flicker of anger flashing across his features. Olivia bowed her head, her lips moving in a silent prayer.

Maya's reaction was perhaps the most profound. From her distant location, her face paled, her eyes darkening with a mixture of grief and determination. The news of the professor's murder struck a chord deep within her, a stark reminder of the dangers they all faced in their pursuit of truth and justice.

Kaira continued, her voice steady despite the tremor in her hands. "In this time of great loss, it is more important than ever that we stand united. We must be cautious, for the threat that took Professor Xicato's life may still be lurking in the shadows."

Reagan stepped forward, her presence a pillar of strength beside

Kaira. "We will not let this tragedy break us. We will honor Professor Xicato's memory by continuing our work, by protecting the innocent and fighting against the forces of darkness."

As the call drew to a close, Maya's mind raced with the implications of the professor's murder. It was a chilling warning, a sign that the dangers they faced were far more significant than she had initially realized. Her thoughts turned to Nykronus, the Grand Magus at the center of her quest, and a sense of urgency gripped her heart. If the professor could be targeted, then Nykronus, too, was in grave danger.

Kaira raised her hand, her enchanted rings casting prismatic light across the threshold of Professor Xicato's study. The magical forensics team had erected a containment sphere, its iridescent surface rippling as it preserved every trace of residual energy. Reagan moved methodically around the perimeter, her Enhanced Sight Charm revealing layers of magical combat: there, a deflected curse had scorched the wallpaper; there, a hasty protection circle had been drawn and broken; there, the professor's final spell had left its signature in the etheric plane.

"Look at the pattern of spell residue," Reagan said, sketching symbols in the air with her athame. The glowing marks hung suspended, creating a three-dimensional reconstruction of the battle. "He was defending something specific, not himself."

Kaira nodded, her own Truthseer's Pendant growing warm as she approached the professor's desk. "The grimoire's gone," she said, running her fingers over the leather blotter. "But he managed to hide something before..." Her voice trailed off as her rings detected a subtle manipulation in the room's magical architecture. With a complex gesture, she revealed a secret compartment beneath the desk's surface, sealed with the professor's personal sigil.

Kaira's eyes scanned the room, her mind racing with questions and possibilities. She had known Professor Xicato for years, in two lifetimes, had studied under his tutelage, and sought his guidance on countless occasions. The thought of someone harming him, of violating the sanctity of his study, filled her with a mixture of grief and anger.

Reagan, ever the pragmatist, was already coordinating with the external experts who had been called in to assist with the investigation. She moved through the room with purpose, her keen eyes taking in every detail, searching for any clue that might lead them to the killer.

As the investigation progressed, a member of the Order approached Kaira, holding a small piece of paper in his gloved hand. "We found this hidden among the professor's research notes," he said, his voice low and urgent. "It seems to be some sort of cryptic message."

Kaira looked at the note with concern as she read the words scrawled upon it. The message was indeed cryptic, a series of symbols and phrases that hinted at a more greater mystery. A chill ran down her spine as she studied the note more closely. The professor had been on the verge of a significant discovery that seemed connected to the very realm Maya was searching for.

Reagan peered over Kaira's shoulder, her eyes widening as she took in the note's contents. "This could be the key to finding Nykronus," she said, her voice tinged with a mixture of hope and trepidation.

Kaira nodded, her mind already racing with the implications of the discovery. Suppose the professor's murder was connected to his research. In that case, they were dealing with a more significant threat than they had initially realized. The Order would need to proceed with caution, but they could not afford to let this lead go cold.

Whispers and rumors swirled through the communal areas of the Order's headquarters, the air heavy with a palpable sense of unease. The murder of Professor Xicato had sent shockwaves through the ranks, sowing seeds of fear and doubt among the members. They gathered in small groups, their faces lined with worry and uncertainty as they struggled to face the grim reality that had befallen them.

Kaira and Reagan stood before the assembled members, their expressions somber yet determined. They knew that the Order's morale hung in the balance, that the future of their mission rested on their ability to inspire and reassure their fellow members.

Kaira stepped forward, her voice clear and steady as she addressed the crowd. "My friends, I know that the loss of Professor Xicato has shaken us all. His murder is a tragic reminder of the dangers we face in our pursuit of truth and justice."

She paused, her eyes scanning the faces before her, taking in the fear and doubt that lurked in their eyes. "But we can't let this tragedy break us. We must remain resilient, united in our cause and our commitment to protecting the innocent."

Reagan nodded, her voice ringing out with conviction. "The professor's legacy lives on through each and every one of us. We will honor his memory by continuing our work, by standing firm in the face of darkness, and by fighting for what is right."

Despite their leaders' impassioned words, a palpable tension remained in the air. Members exchanged uneasy glances, their whispers tinged with a newfound sense of vulnerability. They had always known that their work was dangerous, but the murder of one of their own had brought that reality into sharp focus.

Questions began to circulate, quiet and urgent. Who could have committed such a heinous act? Was the Order still safe? What did this mean for their future and the future of their mission?

Kaira and Reagan could sense the unease rippling through the crowd, the doubts that threatened to diminish the very foundation of the Order. They knew they would need to work tirelessly to maintain morale and keep their members focused on the task at hand even as the specter of danger loomed.

As the gathering dispersed, the moment's weight hung heavy. The path ahead was uncertain, fraught with new challenges and dangers, but Kaira and Reagan remained resolute. They would not let fear and doubt destroy what they had worked so hard to build.

Maya stood alone, her figure silhouetted against the stark, unforgiving landscape that stretched out before her. The barren terrain seemed to mirror the turmoil that raged within her heart, the emptiness a reflection of the void left by Professor Xicato's untimely demise. The wind whipped through her hair, carrying with it the echoes of the virtual call that had shattered her world, the news of the professor's murder still ringing in her ears.

As she gazed out at the desolate expanse, Maya's mind raced with thoughts of Nykronus and the mysterious realm that had consumed her every waking moment. The quest that had once seemed like a distant dream now took on a new sense of urgency, a desperate need to unravel the secrets that had cost the professor his life.

At that moment, standing alone in the wilderness, Maya made a decision. She would not let Professor Xicato's death be in vain. She would intensify her search for Nykronus, delving deeper into the mysteries that surrounded his disappearance and the enigmatic realm that called to her. If there were answers to be found, she would uncover them, no matter the cost.

With renewed purpose, Maya reached for her communication device, her fingers trembling slightly as she initiated a private call to Kaira and Reagan. As their faces appeared on the screen, etched with the same grief and determination that she felt in her own heart, Maya took a deep breath and began to speak.

"Kaira, Reagan," she said, her voice steady despite the emotion that threatened to overwhelm her. "I know we're all reeling from the loss of Professor Xicato, but I can't shake the feeling that his murder is connected to something larger, something that threatens us all."

She paused, her eyes meeting theirs through the digital connection, a silent plea for understanding. "I believe that finding Nykronus and unraveling the secrets of the realm may hold the key to unmasking the professor's killer. We need to dig deeper into his recent work to follow the threads that he left behind."

Kaira and Reagan listened intently, their expressions a mix of concern and resolve. They knew that Maya's instincts were rarely wrong and that her connection to the mystical forces surrounding them gave her a unique perspective on their challenges.

"By the Ancient Protocols," Kaira intoned, her words activating the oath-binding runes carved into her office walls, "I invoke the Right of Vengeance. Professor Xicato's death demands answer." The runes flared blue-white, recording her formal declaration.

Reagan stepped forward, her practical nature asserting itself. "I'll alert our agents in the field. If anyone's detected unusual magical signatures in the past forty-eight hours, we need to know."

"The dimensional barriers are weakening," Maya added, her projection flickering with concern. "Whatever the professor discovered about Nykronus's realm, someone wanted it buried with him. But they failed to account for one thing."

Reagan nodded in agreement, her eyes blazing with a fierce intensity. "The Order stands with you, Maya. We'll leave no stone unturned in our investigation, and we'll support you every step of the way in your quest for Nykronus."

Kaira and Reagan sat in their shared office, the weight of the day's events pressing heavily upon their shoulders. The dim light of the desk lamp cast long shadows across the room, mirroring the dark thoughts that swirled within their minds. They had spent hours poring over the professor's personal effects, searching for any clue that might shed light on his untimely demise.

Reagan held up a small, crumpled note, her eyes narrowing as she read the cryptic words aloud. "'The key lies within the realm, where ancient powers dwell. Seek the truth in Nykronus's name, and the path shall be made clear.' What do you think it means?"

Kaira leaned forward, her brow furrowed in concentration. "It seems the professor was on the verge of a breakthrough, something connected to the realm Maya is searching for. But why would someone want to silence him?"

They sifted through the professor's recent communications, piecing together the fragments of his final days. Emails hinted at clandestine meetings and whispered conversations, a trail of breadcrumbs leading to a truth that had cost him his life.

As the night wore on, Kaira and Reagan found themselves grappling with the enormity of the challenge that lay before them. It was not just a matter of solving the professor's murder but of navigating the crisis that had erupted within the Order itself. They knew that their leadership would be tested as never before, that they would need to draw upon every ounce of wisdom and courage to guide their members through the dark times ahead.

Kaira reached across the desk, her hand resting on Reagan's. "We can't let this break us," she said, her voice steady despite the turmoil within her. "The Order needs us now more than ever. We have to be strong, for them and for ourselves."

Reagan nodded, her jaw set with determination. "We'll find the truth, no matter where it leads us. We owe it to the professor and everyone who has put their faith in us."

At that moment, as the first light of dawn began to creep through the windows, Kaira and Reagan made a silent pact. They would not rest until they had unraveled the mystery of Professor Xicato's death and brought his killer to justice.

The Order's courtyard shimmered with memorial magic, hundreds of spell-lights floating like stars above the gathered members. Protection wards hummed at maximum strength - no one would risk another attack, not today. The professor's portrait hung suspended in a field of pure energy, his kind eyes watching over the assembly as they had in life.

Kaira stood at the podium, her ceremonial robes catching the ethereal light. "Professor Xicato understood power," she said, her voice carrying to every corner of the space through ancient acoustical enchantments. "Not just magical power, but the power of knowledge freely shared, of wisdom passed from teacher to student." She touched her Truthseer's Pendant, and suddenly the air filled with images - the professor teaching, laughing, working alongside his students. Living memories, shared by those present, combining into a tapestry of the man they'd lost.

Reagan stepped forward, raising her athame. A beam of pure white light shot skyward, piercing the evening gloom. One by one, other members raised their magical implements, adding their light to hers until a brilliant column stretched from courtyard to clouds. Within it, written in letters of fire, burned their oath: "By your teaching we grew strong. By your example we grow wise. By your sacrifice we grow determined."

The magic faded slowly, but its effect remained. Where there had been a crowd of grieving individuals, now stood a unified force, their shared loss transformed into shared purpose. As the assembly dispersed, the protection wards recorded an unprecedented surge of magical energy - the combined power of hundreds of renewed commitments to the cause."

As the memorial drew to a close, the last rays of the setting sun cast a somber glow over the headquarters of the Order of St. Michael. The gathered members began to disperse, their hearts heavy with the weight of their shared loss. Kaira and Reagan lingered, their eyes meeting in a silent exchange of determination and resolve.

Maya's face, still visible on the screen of their communication device, bore the same expression of grim purpose. "We can't let Professor Xicato's death be in vain," she said, her voice steady despite the emotion that threatened to overwhelm her. "His murder is connected to the mysteries we've been unraveling, to the quest for Nykronus and the secrets of the realm."

Kaira nodded, her jaw set with a fierce determination. "We'll intensify our investigation, leave no stone unturned. The professor's death has given us a new sense of urgency, a reason to push harder than ever before."

Reagan placed a hand on Kaira's shoulder, a gesture of support and solidarity. "We'll follow every lead, no matter where it takes us. We owe it to Professor Xicato and to everyone who has put their faith in us."

As the three women stood together, united in their resolve, they could feel the path's weight before them. The murder of Professor Xicato had added a new layer of complexity to their already daunting mission, a darkness that threatened to engulf them at every turn.

But they knew that they could not falter, not when the stakes were so high. They would press forward, guided by the legacy of the fallen and the strength of their own convictions. The quest for answers would lead them into uncharted waters, into the heart of the mystery that had claimed the professor's life.

ACT TWO

"Hardships often prepare ordinary people for an extraordinary destiny."
  — *C.S. Lewis*

CHAPTER
NINE

A   Maya stood at the precipice of the unknown, the ancient stone archway looming before her like a sentinel of forgotten times. The dense jungle surrounded her, its lush foliage and thick vines seeming to pulse with an otherworldly energy. As she stepped forward, her boot crunched over shards of broken glass, the sound echoing through the eerie stillness.

Curiosity piqued, Maya glanced down and spotted a tome lying amidst the debris. Her heart quickened as she recognized the distinctive binding style of the Arcane Archives. She bent down, fingers trembling slightly as they brushed against the weathered leather cover, carefully clearing away broken glass fragments. Her name was etched upon its surface in Nykronus's distinctive silver script - the same elegant hand that had penned countless warnings in her father's journals. The letters seemed to pulse with a faint luminescence as if responding to her touch.

As her eyes scanned the pages, Maya's breath caught in her throat. The handwriting was unmistakable—it belonged to Nykronus. Questions swirled in her mind as she tried deciphering the cryptic messages across the parchment. What secrets did this tome hold? Why was her name inscribed upon its cover?

Tucking the tome securely into her satchel, Maya turned her attention back to the archway. The air hummed with an ancient power as if the very fabric of reality was stretched thin at this junction. She could feel the energy thrumming through her veins, calling her forward.

With a deep breath, Maya stepped through the archway. The tome in her satchel grew warm against her hip, its energy resonating with the ancient stones. As she crossed the threshold, reality fractured and reformed around her - the transition feeling eerily similar to the phenomena Nykronus had described in his final message. The world shifted dramatically, the familiar jungle dissolving like watercolors in the rain.

In its place, a new realm materialized before her eyes. Vivid hues painted the sky in shades she had never seen before, and the air crackled with tangible magic. Maya's senses were overwhelmed by the sheer intensity of it all—the scents, the sounds, the sensations that danced along her skin.

A mixture of awe and apprehension washed over her as she took in her surroundings. This was unlike anything she had ever experienced before. The realm seemed to beckon her forward, promising answers to the questions that had haunted her for so long. Yet, a flicker of uncertainty lingered in the back of her mind. What challenges awaited her in this strange new world? And what role did the mysterious tome play in all of this?

～

Another Realm

Maya ventured deeper into the otherworldly realm; her senses were heightened, and her mind was racing with possibilities. As she navigated the unfamiliar terrain, the landscape around her shifted and morphed in ways that defied the laws of nature.

In the distance, mountains rose and fell like the chest of a slumbering giant, their peaks reaching toward the kaleidoscopic sky before crumbling into dust. Forests sprouted from the barren ground, trees shooting upwards at an impossible rate, their branches intertwining to form dense canopies. Yet, as quickly as they had appeared, the trees withered and decayed, their leaves turning ash and scattering in the ethereal breeze.

Maya's training with the Sentinel Guard kicked in as she encountered a rapidly changing riverbed. Professor Xicato's voice echoed in her memory: "The most dangerous terrain is the one that refuses to stay still."

She analyzed the water's pattern, noting how it mimicked the fluid drawings she'd glimpsed in the tome's early pages.

The once-tranquil stream suddenly surged with raging waters, threatening to sweep her away. With nimble movements, she leapt from rock to rock, the shifting currents testing her balance. Just as she reached the other side, the river vanished, leaving a deep chasm with no bottom.

Undeterred, Maya pressed forward, her mind focused on maintaining her direction amidst the chaos. She relied on her instincts and the subtle cues of the environment to guide her path. The time in her satchel seemed to grow heavier with each step, as if it held the weight of the realm's secrets.

As she climbed a steep incline, the ground beneath her feet began to tremble. Cracks appeared in the earth, widening into gaping fissures. Maya's agility was tested as she dodged falling rocks and leaped across the widening gaps. Her heart pounded in her chest, but she refused to let fear overtake her.

When she thought she had found stable footing, a sudden flash flood engulfed the valley. Water rushed towards her from all directions, the roar of the torrents drowning out all other sounds. Maya scrambled to higher ground, her muscles burning with exertion as she clambered up a rapidly eroding hillside.

Perched atop a precarious ledge, Maya caught her breath and surveyed the ever-changing landscape below. The realm seemed to be testing her, pushing her to the limits of her physical and mental endurance. Yet, amidst the chaos, she felt a strange sense of exhilaration. This was the challenge she had been seeking, the opportunity to prove herself and unravel the mysteries that lay ahead.

A peculiar sight caught her eye as Maya pressed on through the ever-shifting landscape. Amidst the chaos and turmoil, a tranquil clearing emerged, seemingly untouched by the realm's unpredictable nature. The clearing was bathed in a soft, eternal twilight, casting a gentle glow upon the lush grass and delicate flowers that swayed in a gentle breeze.

Intrigued, Maya cautiously approached the serene oasis. As she stepped into the clearing, a sense of peace washed over her, as if the very air itself was imbued with a calming essence. The tumultuous sounds of the realm faded away, replaced by a soothing silence that enveloped her like a warm embrace.

In the center of the clearing, Maya noticed a group of ethereal creatures, their forms shimmering and shifting between animal and humanoid shapes. They moved with fluid grace, their luminescent bodies leaving light trails in their wake. The creatures seemed composed of pure energy, their essence radiating a soft, mesmerizing glow.

As Maya drew closer, the creatures turned their attention towards her. If they could be called eyes, their eyes held a depth of wisdom and understanding that transcended mortal comprehension. A silent communication passed between them, a language of thoughts and emotions that Maya couldn't quite grasp yet somehow felt familiar.

The creatures approached her, their movements gentle and non-threatening. They circled around her, their light-infused forms brushing against her skin, leaving behind a tingling sensation that sent shivers down her spine. Maya found herself captivated by their ethereal beauty, her mind struggling to comprehend the sheer wonder of their existence.

At that moment, surrounded by these enigmatic beings, Maya felt a profound connection to the realm. The beauty and peace of the clearing offered her a glimpse into the potential for wonder amidst the danger and chaos. It was a reminder that even in the darkest of times, there could be moments of breathtaking beauty and tranquility.

As the creatures continued their silent dance around her, Maya lost herself in the mesmerizing display of light and energy. Time seemed to stand still, and for a brief moment, all her worries and doubts melted away. She allowed herself to be fully present, to bask in the ethereal glow and the sense of unity that permeated the clearing.

As Maya reluctantly left the ethereal clearing behind, she was engulfed in a dense fog that seemed to materialize out of nowhere. The once-vibrant colors of the realm faded into muted shades of gray, and the air grew heavy with an unsettling chill. The path ahead, which had been so clear moments ago, now lay obscured by the swirling mists.

With each step, Maya felt the weight of unseen eyes upon her. Shadows danced at the edges of her vision, darting in and out of the fog like ghostly apparitions. Disembodied whispers echoed through the haze, their words indistinct yet alluring. They called to her, promising secrets and shortcuts, urging her to stray from her intended course.

Maya's training kicked in, and she steeled herself against the temptation of the whispers. She knew the dangers of letting her guard down in unfamiliar territory. Instead, she relied on her instincts, trusting the subtle cues of the environment to guide her forward. She focused on the ground beneath her feet, searching for signs of hidden traps or treacherous terrain.

Maya caught glimpses of shadowy figures lurking just beyond her sight as she pressed on through the fog. They moved with a predatory grace, their silhouettes blending seamlessly with the swirling mists. Low growls and feral snarls echoed through the haze, sending shivers down her spine. She knew that these creatures were not to be trifled with, their intentions as dark as the fog itself.

Maya's senses were on high alert, her body poised for action. She scanned the surroundings, seeking any sign of an impending attack. The fog seemed to play tricks on her mind, distorting distances and shapes, making it difficult to discern friend from foe. Yet, she refused to let fear overtake her, knowing that any moment of hesitation could prove fatal.

With each step, Maya navigated the treacherous landscape, her intuition guiding her around hidden pitfalls and through narrow passages. She moved with silent grace, her footsteps barely disturbing the eerie stillness that enveloped her. The whispers continued to call out to her, their voices growing more insistent with each passing moment, but she remained steadfast in her resolve.

As Maya ventured deeper into the mysterious realm, she stood at the edge of a labyrinthine garden of thorns. The twisted brambles rose high, their razor-sharp edges glinting menacingly in the ethereal light. The paths before her seemed to loop back on themselves, creating a dizzying maze that threatened to ensnare any who dared to enter.

Maya's brow furrowed as she studied the intricate patterns of the thorns, her mind racing to make sense of the perplexing layout. She closed her eyes briefly, reaching deep within herself to recall the ancient teachings passed down through her family. The symbols etched into the thorns began to take on a new meaning, their hidden secrets unraveling before her mind's eye.

With a newfound understanding, Maya stepped forward, her movements deliberate and precise. She navigated the winding paths, her eyes scanning the thorns for the subtle markings that would guide her way. The teachings of her ancestors echoed in her mind, their wisdom a beacon of light amidst the darkness.

As she delved deeper into the garden, Maya's intuition began to awaken, guiding her steps with a surety that surprised even herself. She could sense the hidden traps and false paths ahead, her instincts warning her of the dangers within the thorns.

With each twist and turn, Maya's confidence grew. She moved with a fluid grace, her body responding to the challenges of the garden as if it were an extension of her own being. The thorns seemed to part before her, revealing secret passages and hidden alcoves that had remained unseen to the untrained eye.

Time seemed to blur as Maya navigated the labyrinthine garden, her focus unwavering. She relied on the knowledge passed down through generations, the ancient symbols serving as her compass in this strange and treacherous realm.

Finally, as she emerged from the garden's heart, Maya stood in a tranquil clearing, the thorns giving way to a serene landscape of soft grass and gentle streams. She took a moment to catch her breath, her mind reeling from the intense focus and concentration that had guided her through the maze.

As Maya stepped into the heart of the thorn garden, she found herself standing at the edge of a serene pond. The water's surface was as clear as glass, reflecting the chaotic sky above in a mesmerizing display of colors and patterns. Despite its tranquil appearance, the pond seemed to hold an unfathomable depth, its secrets hidden beneath the mirror-like surface.

"Well, this is unexpected," Maya muttered to herself. "A peaceful oasis amidst the chaos."

She cautiously approached the pond, eyes scanning the surroundings for any signs of danger. As she drew closer, a shimmering figure materialized above the water's surface. It was a spectral guardian, its form ethereal and translucent, emanating an otherworldly glow.

The guardian's voice echoed through the clearing, its tone ancient and enigmatic - yet somehow familiar, carrying traces of Nykronus's cadence. "Seeker of truth," it intoned, its form shimming with the same ethereal energy that had drawn her mentor into this realm, "To pass this trial, answer me: What is the key that unlocks the door to wisdom?"

Maya's hand instinctively touched the tome, remembering the countless hours spent debating similar riddles with Nykronus in the Archive's lamp-lit halls.

Maya meditated as she pondered the riddle. She closed her eyes, delving deep into her mind and drawing upon the knowledge and insight she had gained throughout her journey. The teachings of her ancestors whispered in her thoughts, guiding her towards the answer.

Opening her eyes, Maya met the guardian's gaze steadily. "The key to wisdom is understanding. It's the ability to see beyond the surface, to grasp the underlying truths that lie hidden from plain sight."

The guardian remained silent momentarily, its ethereal form shimmering in the soft light. Then, a smile graced its spectral features. "Well spoken, seeker. You have demonstrated your growing connection to this realm and its wisdom."

With a gentle wave, the guardian conjured a small talisman that floated through the air toward Maya. She reached out, her fingers closing around the extraordinary, metallic surface. The talisman pulsed with faint energy, its intricate engravings glowing with a soft, comforting light.

"This talisman shall offer you protection and guidance on your journey," the guardian explained, its form flickering like a candle in wind. "It is one of seven sacred anchors Nykronus sought, though he never survived to claim it himself."

The medallion's surface rippled, revealing intricate patterns that matched the mysterious diagrams Maya had noticed in the tome's margins. "Each victory here strengthens its power - and your connection to Aethoria's essence. It symbolizes your first victory in this realm, a testament to your unwavering spirit and keen intellect. Welcome to the Aethoria— a realm few from your world have seen with their own eyes."

Maya smiled, a sense of pride swelling within her chest. She carefully placed the talisman around her neck, feeling its gentle weight resting against her skin.

As Maya stepped beyond the thorn garden, she found herself atop a hill that offered a breathtaking view of the realm's ever-shifting landscape. The kaleidoscopic sky above cast an ethereal glow upon the land, painting it in hues of vibrant colors that seemed to dance and swirl with a life of their own. The distant mountains loomed on the horizon, their peaks shrouded in an enigmatic mist that beckoned her forward.

Maya took a moment to catch her breath, her eyes scanning the panoramic vista before her. The realm of Aethoria was a place of unimaginable beauty and danger, a reflection of the journey she had embarked upon. Each trial she had faced and obstacle she had overcome tested her resolve and pushed her to the limits of her abilities.

As she stood there, the weight of the talisman around her neck reminded her of her growing connection to this mysterious realm. It symbolized her first victory, a testament to her unwavering spirit and keen intellect. The talisman pulsed with a gentle energy, its intricate engravings glowing softly in the ethereal light.

Maya's thoughts turned inward, reflecting on the path that had led her to this moment. The teachings of her ancestors, the rigorous training she had undergone, and the love and support of her family had all prepared her for this journey. Yet, the challenges she had faced in Aethoria had begun to shape her understanding of her power and purpose.

She closed her eyes, feeling the gentle breeze caress her skin and the soft grass beneath her feet. At that moment, Maya felt a profound connection to the realm, as if it were a part of her, guiding her towards a greater destiny. The whispers of the wind seemed to carry the voices of those who had come before her, their wisdom and knowledge echoing through the ages.

With a deep breath, Maya opened her eyes, her gaze fixed upon the distant mountains. She knew that the realm's heart lay beyond those peaks, holding the secrets of Nykronus and the answers she searched for. The path ahead would be fraught with danger and uncertainty, but Maya's resolve was never stronger.

Her hand instinctively reached for the talisman resting on her chest, its smooth metal surface serving as a source of courage. As she touched it, a wave of revitalizing energy seemed to flow through her, readying her for whatever obstacles lay ahead. Maya was prepared to face any challenges head-on, drawing upon the skills and knowledge she had acquired on her journey.

With a final glance at the awe-inspiring landscape before her, Maya set her sights on the mountains, ready to embark on the next leg of her quest. The realm of Aethoria had tested her, but it had also awakened

something within her—a power and purpose that she was only beginning to understand.

~

As Maya descended from the hill, the tome's pages rustled of their
own accord, drawing her attention to a hastily sketched forest map
where light and shadow danced in eternal twilight. She looked up to
find that very forest materializing before her, just as Nykronus had
documented. The ancient trees seemed to whisper with magic, their
twisted forms perfectly matching the illustrations to the luminescent
fungi that marked safe passages through the darkness. But something
about the margins of Nykronus's notes suggested he'd encountered
more than mere plants in these woods.

The trees towered above her, gnarled branches reaching out like
skeletal fingers. The air was heavy with the scent of moss and decay,
and a faint mist clung to the ground, swirling around her ankles with
each step.

Maya ventured deeper into the realm, her senses heightened by the
surreal beauty surrounding her. The forest floor was carpeted with
luminescent fungi, their soft glow casting an otherworldly light upon
the twisted roots and fallen leaves. Strange flowers bloomed in the
shadows, their petals pulsing with an inner light that seemed to
beckon her closer.

Yet, despite the mesmerizing beauty, Maya remained vigilant,
aware that danger lurked in every corner of this unpredictable realm.
The talisman pulsed against her chest, its energy guiding her forward,
warning her of hidden threats and unseen perils. She moved with a
cautious grace, her footsteps barely disturbing the eerie stillness that
permeated the forest.

As she ventured deeper into the heart of the twilight forest, Maya
couldn't shake the growing sense that she was being watched. The
whispers of the ancient trees seemed to carry a hidden message, a
warning of an impending encounter. The shadows danced at the edges
of her vision, hinting at the presence of something powerful and
mysterious.

Maya's hand instinctively reached for the talisman, its smooth metal surface providing a reassuring touch. She knew that whatever lay ahead, whether friend or foe, would be a crucial step in her journey through this enigmatic realm. The talisman's energy pulsed in response as if acknowledging the challenges that awaited her.

CHAPTER
TEN

As Maya ventured deeper into the whispering woods, the eerie sensation of being watched intensified. The bioluminescent flora cast an otherworldly glow, illuminating the path before her with a soft, ethereal light. The ancient trees seemed to lean in closer, their whispers growing more insistent as if trying to impart some secret knowledge.

Suddenly, the shadows around her began to shift and take form. Creatures emerged from the darkness, their bodies as black as the night, with glowing eyes that pierced through the gloom. Maya's heart raced as she instinctively reached for her weapon, but something about these creatures made her hesitate.

As she studied them more closely, Maya realized that these beings resembled the Diwata from the stories Lola Rose had shared during their secret evening lessons—lessons that now felt less like folklore and more like preparation for this moment. The Diwata were powerful spirits, guardians of nature, and protectors of the realm. Their presence here, in this strange and mystical place, filled Maya with a sense of awe and reverence.

The creatures began to communicate with each other in a language Maya couldn't understand, their voices a haunting melody that seemed to blend with the whispers of the trees. Despite the unfamiliarity of their speech, Maya sensed no hostility from them, only a deep curiosity and perhaps even a hint of recognition.

Remembering her grandmother's teachings about the importance of respect and understanding, Maya decided to approach the situation differently. Instead of reacting with fear or aggression, she slowly lowered her weapon and raised her hands in a gesture of peace.

With deliberate movements, Maya began to draw symbols in the dirt at her feet, hoping to convey her intentions through the universal language of art. She sketched images of the talisman, the realm, and the path she had taken to reach this point. The Diwata watched intently, their glowing eyes following every line and curve she traced upon the ground.

As Maya continued to communicate through gestures and symbols, a sense of understanding grew between them. The Diwata's curiosity seemed to deepen, and they responded with their own intricate patterns and shapes in the dirt, as if sharing their own stories and knowledge.

In that moment, Maya realized the true power of understanding and the importance of approaching the unknown with an open mind and heart. She had entered this realm seeking answers and allies, and now, in the heart of the whispering woods, she had found both in the most unexpected of places.

As Maya followed the path through the enchanted forest, she eventually came upon a crystal-clear river blocking her way. The water shimmered with a dreamlike glow, and the air around it seemed to hum with a mystical energy. Maya approached the riverbank, her eyes scrutinizing the surroundings for a way to cross.

Suddenly, a figure emerged from the mist, seemingly material- izing from the water. It was a woman with long, flowing hair and clothing that appeared to be woven from the elements of nature. Her eyes, an impaling green, locked onto Maya's, and a smile played upon her lips.

"I am Maria Makiling, guardian of this river," the woman spoke, her voice melodic and soothing. "If you wish to pass, you must first prove your worth."

Maya straightened her posture, meeting Maria's gaze with determination. "The Diwata? You're real! My grandmother told me stories about you. What must I do?"

Maria gestured to the river, her movements fluid and graceful. "This river has been corrupted by a force that cannot be seen with mortal eyes. To prove your worth, you must cleanse it of this taint."

Maya looked at the river, its waters still appearing pristine and clear. She closed her eyes, reaching out with her senses as her family had taught her. As she focused, faint, sickly energy began to reveal itself, like tendrils of darkness weaving through the water.

"I sense it," Maya said, opening her eyes. "A magical pollution, tainting the very essence of the river."

Maria grinned, a glimmer of approval in her eyes. "Indeed. Now, show me how you will purify it."

Maya stepped forward, kneeling at the riverbank. She reached into her pouch, retrieving a small vial of sacred water and a handful of purifying herbs. With practiced movements, she began to perform a ritual she had learned during her training with Nykronus, chanting softly as she sprinkled the herbs into the river and poured the sacred water in a circular pattern. Maya's fingers moved through the purification ritual just as Nykronus had taught her, though she never imagined she'd be performing it before Maria Makiling herself. Each gesture carried the weight of both his teachings and her grandmother's stories.

As the ritual progressed, the sickly energy dissipated, the tendrils of darkness unraveling and fading away. The river seemed to come alive, its waters shimmering with renewed vitality and power.

Maria watched with a smile of satisfaction on her face. "Well done, Maya. You have proven yourself worthy of passage."

Maya stood, bowing her head in respect to the guardian. "Thank you, Maria Makiling. This experience has taught me the importance of perceiving beyond the physical and the responsibility we have to protect and maintain the balance of nature. Can I just say one thing? You are really, I mean *really*, beautiful."

As Maya crossed the river with Maria Makiling's blessing, she found herself standing at the edge of a vast chasm. The depths below seemed to stretch into an endless void, and the only way forward was a bridge made of pure, dazzling light.

Upon closer inspection, Maya noticed the bridge was divided into three distinct paths. Each path pulsed with a different hue, beckoning her to choose. The path on the left glowed with a golden radiance, promising wealth beyond measure. The central path emanated a deep, powerful red, offering the allure of unrivaled power. The path on the right shone with a soft, mesmerizing blue, inviting her to explore the depths of knowledge and wisdom.

The golden path whispered promises of resources to fund her search for Nykronus, while the red path offered power that might help her protect her family from whatever had taken her grandmother. But as she stood there, Rose's voice echoed in her memory: "Knowledge, apo, is the key that opens all doors."

Maya felt the pull of each path, their temptations tugging at her heart and mind. The promise of wealth and the ability to provide for her loved ones was enticing, as was the prospect of wielding power to protect those she held dear. However, as she contemplated her choices, the lessons of humility and the pursuit of wisdom over material gains, instilled in her by her family and mentors, echoed through her thoughts.

She recalled her mother's words, who had always emphasized the importance of knowledge and understanding above all else. She reminisced about the countless conversations she had shared with her beloved grandmother, Rose. Maya remembered the countless hours spent learning about the Diwata, the mystical realm, and the balance of nature. She thought of Nykronus and his unwavering dedication to unraveling the secrets of the universe.

With a deep breath, Maya made her decision. She stepped forward, her feet carrying her toward the path of knowledge. As she set foot on the blue-hued path, the bridge beneath her began to transform. The ethereal light solidified, becoming a sturdy, tangible walkway that stretched across the chasm.

Maya's choice revealed her inner strength and commitment to her quest for understanding. She knew that the path ahead would not be easy, filled with obstacles and trials, but she was ready to face them head-on. With each step, she felt a renewed sense of purpose, knowing that the knowledge she sought would aid her in her mission to find Nykronus and help her grow as an individual.

As she traversed the bridge, the soft blue light enveloped her, and Maya couldn't help but smile. She had chosen the path that aligned with her values and the teachings of those she admired most. Whatever lay ahead, she knew she had made the right decision.

As Maya ventured deeper into the mystical realm, she found herself standing at the entrance of a vast cavern. The air thrummed with an eerie stillness, and the faintest whisper seemed to reverberate endlessly through the chamber. This was the Cavern of Echoes, where sound held sway over all else.

Maya took a cautious step forward, her footfall sending a cascade of echoes bouncing off the cavern walls. In the dim light, she could make out the glimmering forms of creatures made entirely of crystal, their facets catching the faint glow and casting prismatic reflections across the stone.

A soft voice emerged from the shadows. Maya turned to see a group of Diwata, their ethereal forms shimmering like starlight. They approached her with gentle smiles, their movements graceful and fluid.

"Welcome, Maya," one of the Diwata spoke soothingly. "This cavern is a sacred place, home to beings of delicate beauty. To navigate these halls, you must embrace the power of silence and tread with the utmost care."

Maya nodded, understanding the gravity of the challenge before her. She took a deep breath, centering herself and focusing on the task at hand. With each step, she moved with deliberate slowness, carefully placing her feet to minimize the echoes that threatened to shatter the fragile creatures around her.

As she progressed deeper into the cavern, Maya encountered more of the crystal beings. Some were small, no larger than her hand, while others towered above her, their forms intricate and mesmerizing. Each step required precision and patience, as even the slightest misstep could send a dangerous reverberation through the chamber.

The Diwata guided Maya, their presence a comforting anchor in the eerie stillness. They communicated through gentle gestures and soft whispers, directing her towards the safest paths and warning her of potential hazards.

Maya's compassion for the delicate creatures grew with each passing moment. She marveled at their beauty and the intricate patterns etched into their crystalline forms. Navigating the Cavern of Echoes became a test not only of her physical prowess but also of her empathy and respect for the beings that called this place home.

As she neared the heart of the cavern, Maya's movements became even more precise, each step a calculated dance of silence and grace. The Diwata watched with approving smiles, their own forms shimmering in the soft light.

As Maya stepped into the clearing, the world around her seemed to shimmer and warp, the edges of reality blurring like a mirage. The Illusionist's Glade, as the Diwata had called it, was a place where nothing was quite as it seemed, governed by an Aswang who reveled in the art of deception.

The air itself felt thick with magic, and Maya's senses tingled with the palpable presence of illusions waiting to ensnare her. She recalled the stories her Lola Rose and her father Elan had told her about the Aswang, tales of their shape-shifting abilities and their liking for trickery. A shiver ran down her spine as she realized she was now face-to-face with one of these legendary creatures—which had been horror stories during her childhood.

Suddenly, the clearing transformed before her eyes. The lush greenery melted away, replaced by a barren, desolate landscape. The ground beneath her feet cracked and crumbled, and the air grew heavy with the stench of decay. In the distance, Maya saw the silhouettes of her loved ones, their faces twisted in agony as they reached out to her, pleading for help.

Fear gripped Maya's heart, and she felt the urge to rush forward, to save them from whatever torment they were enduring. But something held her back, a flicker of doubt that whispered in the back of her mind. She reached for her talisman, the one she had received from the Diwata in the previous trial, and clutched it tightly in her hand.

The talisman pulsed against her palm, its warmth reminiscent of the moment the Diwata had bestowed it upon her. Each beat seemed to whisper truths that cut through the Aswang's illusions, just as Professor Xicato had promised such artifacts would.

As the talisman's energy pulsed through her, Maya's mind cleared, and she saw the illusions for what they truly were. The desolate landscape shimmered and dissolved, revealing the verdant clearing once more. The figures of her loved ones vanished, replaced by the twisted, grinning form of the Aswang illusionist.

"Clever girl," the Aswang hissed, its eyes gleaming with malicious delight. "But can you withstand the depths of your own fears and desires?"

Maya stood tall, her gaze unwavering as she met the Aswang's challenge. "I have faced my fears and conquered them before," she declared, her voice steady and resolute. "Your illusions hold no power over me, for I know the truth of my purpose and the strength of my determination."

The Aswang's grin faltered, and Maya could see a flicker of uncertainty in its eyes. She raised her talisman, its light casting a brilliant glow across the clearing. "I am Maya Durant, daughter of Elan and Kaira, and I will not be swayed by your deceptions. I seek the truth, and I will find it, no matter what obstacles stand in my way."

∼

As Maya ventured deeper into the mystical realm, she stumbled upon a peculiar village. The inhabitants moved about their daily lives with a disconcerting stillness, their faces devoid of any emotion. The air hung heavy with a sense of apathy as if all joy and sorrow had been drained from this place.

A shimmering figure approached Maya, her form radiating a gentle warmth. A majestic golden deer stood by her side, its coat gleaming in the soft light.

"Welcome, Maya, I am Maria Sinukan." Maria Sinukan greeted her, a smile gracing her ethereal features.

Maya recalled the Filipino folklore she had learned, recognizing Maria Sinukan as a Diwata renowned for her benevolence and insight. "Greetings," Maya responded.

Maria Sinukan's smile remained fixed upon Maya, her long black hair flowing in the breeze. "You have entered a village where the inhabitants have lost their ability to feel. Your task is to restore their emotions, to remind them of the beauty and power of the human experience."

Maya looked around, her heart aching for the villagers, who seemed trapped in a state of emotional numbness. She thought of her own journey, her fears, and the hopes that had driven her forward. With a deep breath, she began to share her story.

She spoke of her family, the love and support they had given her, and the lessons they had taught her. She recounted her challenges, the moments of doubt, and the triumphs of perseverance. As she shared her experiences, Maya poured her heart into every word, hoping to ignite a spark of emotion in the villagers.

Slowly, the villagers began to gather around her, drawn by the sincerity and vulnerability in her voice. They listened intently, their eyes gradually losing the dullness that had consumed them. Flickers of recognition and understanding danced across their faces as if Maya's words were awakening something deep within them.

As Maya shared her story with the villagers, she found herself speaking of things she'd never voiced aloud—her fears about Nykronus's disappearance, the weight of her family's legacy, the growing darkness that seemed to be spreading through both this realm and her own.

Maya continued to share her hopes and dreams, vividly painting the world she longed to create—a world where compassion and understanding reigned supreme. She spoke of the power of connection, the importance of empathy, and the strength of embracing one's emotions.

As she finished her story, Maya looked around at the villagers, their faces now alive with a spectrum of emotions. Tears glistened in some eyes, while others wore tentative smiles. The golden deer nuzzled against Maria Sinukan's side as if sensing the change that had taken place.

Maria Sinukan approached Maya, her eyes shining with pride. "You have done well, Maya. Through your words and your heart, you have restored the emotional essence of this village. You have shown them the power of empathy and the importance of connecting with others."

Maya felt a warmth bloom in her chest, a sense of purpose and understanding settling over her. She realized that her journey wasn't just about gaining strength or finding Nykronus; it was also about sharing her humanity, touching the lives of others, and reminding them of the beauty and complexity of emotions.

As Maya approached Mirror Lake, a sense of tranquility washed over her. The water's surface was as smooth as glass, reflecting the ethereal beauty of the surrounding landscape. She knelt at the water's edge, her gaze drawn to her own reflection.

In the mirror-like surface, Maya saw herself as she was—a young woman on the cusp of a great destiny, her eyes filled with determination and a hint of uncertainty. But as she looked deeper, the reflection began to shift and change.

The image in the water transformed, revealing a vision of Maya as she could be. She saw herself standing tall and confident, her powers fully realized and her purpose clear. In this reflection, Maya radiated an aura of strength and wisdom, a true embodiment of the Diwata legacy.

Yet, even in this idealized version of herself, Maya could see the shadows of doubt that lingered beneath the surface. The reflection showed her the fears she still harbored, the insecurities that threatened to hold her back. It was a stark reminder that growth was an ongoing process requiring constant self-reflection and acceptance.

As Maya contemplated the insights revealed by the Mirror Lake, a figure emerged from the treeline. It was Maria Cacao, another revered Diwata known for associating with the cacao tree and the blessings of prosperity.

Maria Cacao approached Maya with a gentle smile, her presence emanating an aura of warmth and understanding. "The Mirror Lake is a powerful tool for self-discovery," she said, her voice soft and melodic. "It shows us not only who we are but also who we have the potential to become."

Maya nodded, her gaze still fixed on the reflections in the water. "I see the strength within me, but also the doubts that linger," she confessed, her voice barely above a whisper.

Maria Cacao placed a comforting hand on Maya's shoulder. "Doubts are a natural part of growth, Maya. They remind us that we are human, that we are constantly evolving. Embrace them, learn from them, and allow them to guide you on your path."

Maya took a deep breath, letting Maria Cacao's words sink in. She understood that her journey was not just about reaching a destination but about the lessons learned and the person she would become along the way.

The reflection showed not just who she could become but how far she'd already come. Each trial in the realm had stripped away another layer of doubt, replaced by an understanding that went beyond her grandmother's stories or Nykronus's teachings.

As the day drew to a close, Maya found herself at the edge of the woods, setting up camp beneath a canopy of twinkling stars. The events of the day played through her mind, each encounter leaving an indelible mark on her soul. She sat cross-legged on her bedroll, her journal on her lap, and began writing.

Maya's pen flowed across the pages, capturing the essence of her experiences. She wrote of the Three Marias—Maria Makiling, Maria Sinukuan, and Maria Cacao—and their profound impact on her journey. These powerful Diwata, once confined to the realm of folklore and fairy tales, had become tangible guides, imparting wisdom and strength through their interactions.

As she reflected on each encounter, Maya realized that the stories she had grown up with were not mere tales but living, breathing entities that held the power to shape her destiny. The challenges she faced, from navigating the Cavern of Echoes to confronting the Aswang illusionist and restoring emotion to the villagers, tested her in ways she had never imagined.

Yet, with each trial, Maya had emerged stronger, her resolve fortified by the lessons she had learned. The Mirror Lake had shown her the depths of her own potential, reminding her that growth was an ongoing process, a journey of self-discovery and acceptance.

Maya closed her journal as the night deepened, feeling a renewed sense of purpose coursing through her veins. The day's challenges had tested her physical and mental prowess and awakened a profound understanding within her. She knew that the path ahead would be fraught with even greater obstacles, but she felt ready to face them head-on.

Maya lay back on her bedroll, gazing up at the stars that seemed to wink at her in encouragement. She closed her eyes, allowing the day's lessons to sink deep into her being, fortifying her for the journey ahead. With each breath, she felt the Diwata's strength, the Three Marias' wisdom, and the power of her determination flowing through her.

CHAPTER

ELEVEN

As Maya ventured deeper into the twilight forest, the boundary between the mundane and the magical blurred, enveloping her in enchantment and mystery. The dense underbrush, alive with the whispers of ancient trees, seemed to call to Maya, and the air was electrified with an energy that sent shivers down her spine. The twilight cast a surreal glow over the forest, painting the world in shades of silver and gold.

Exhaustion weighed heavily on Maya's shoulders, the constant journey taking its toll on her mind and body. She longed for a moment of respite, a chance to catch her breath and gather her thoughts. As she pushed through the foliage, a soft, melodic purring caught her attention, breaking through the eerie silence of the forest. Her heart, heavy with the weight of her quest, was suddenly lifted by the unexpected sound.

Intrigued, Maya followed the sound, her curiosity overpowering her weariness. She parted the branches, stepping into a small clearing bathed in an ethereal glow. Her gaze fell upon a radiant feline nestled in the glade's heart, its coat glistening with an interplay of ebony and amber hues, mirroring the celestial tapestry of a star-strewn firmament.

Maya's breath caught in her throat as she gazed upon the magnificent being. Its eyes, a mesmerizing blend of silver and gold, met hers with an intelligence that seemed to transcend the boundaries of the animal world. The creature's presence radiated an aura of tranquility and wisdom, drawing Maya closer.

Cautiously, Maya approached the feline, her heart pounding with excitement and trepidation. As she drew nearer, the creature remained still, its gaze never wavering from hers. Maya extended her hand, palm up, in a gesture of peace and friendship.

To her surprise, the feline didn't shy away from her touch. Instead, it rose gracefully to its feet and padded towards her, its movements fluid and purposeful. As the creature neared, Maya felt a wave of warmth and comfort wash over her, as if the feline's presence alone could banish the weariness from her bones.

The feline rubbed its head against Maya's outstretched hand, the contact sending a tingle of energy through her skin. At that moment, Maya understood that this was no ordinary creature. It was a being of magic, a guardian of the twilight forest, offering her a silent promise of companionship and guidance.

Maya settled by the small campfire she had lit, the flickering flames casting a warm glow across the clearing. The feline curled up beside her, its presence a comforting balm against the chill of the night. As Maya ran her fingers through the creature's soft fur, she marveled at how its coat seemed to shimmer with an inner light, as if it held the secrets of the stars within its very being.

The feline's purrs filled the air, a soothing melody that wove through the crackle of the fire. Maya was drawn into the creature's gaze, those intelligent eyes holding a depth of understanding that surpassed mere animal instinct. As she looked into those eyes, Maya felt a connection forming, a bond that transcended the boundaries of language and species.

The feline tilted its head, its ears twitching as if listening intently to Maya's thoughts. With gentle nudges and purposeful gestures, the creature communicated its comprehension of Maya's quest. It was as if the feline had been waiting for her, a guardian sent to guide her through the perils of the twilight forest.

Maya's heart swelled with gratitude and wonder. She had never encountered a being like this who could understand her so deeply without needing words. At that moment, she knew that the feline was more than just a companion; it was a kindred spirit, a beacon of hope in the darkness. She felt a warm sense of gratitude towards Asha, knowing that she was not alone in this journey.

"Asha," Maya whispered, the name falling from her lips like a prayer. In an ancient tongue, it meant "hope," and it seemed fitting for the creature that had brought such light into her journey. Asha's eyes sparkled with approval as if the name resonated with her very essence.

As the night wore on, Maya and Asha sat together by the fire, their silence filled with a profound sense of understanding and trust. Maya felt the weight of her loneliness lifting, replaced by a newfound strength and determination. With Asha by her side, she knew she could face whatever challenges lay ahead, secure in knowing she was no longer alone. The bond of understanding and trust between them was a source of strength and security in the face of the unknown.

As the first light of dawn crept through the twilight forest, Maya and Asha set out once more, their bond strengthened by the shared moments of the previous night. The path ahead was uncertain, but Maya drew comfort from Asha's steady presence at her side.

Before long, they reached a crossroads where multiple paths diverged, each shrouded in a veil of mist obscuring their destinations. Maya hesitated, her brow furrowed as she tried to discern which route to take. The air hung heavy with a sense of foreboding, as if the forest held its breath in anticipation.

Asha, however, seemed unperturbed by the eerie atmosphere. The feline stepped forward, her gaze fixed on the paths before them. With a flick of her tail, Asha began to walk towards one of the paths, her steps sure and purposeful.

Maya followed, trusting in Asha's unerring sense of direction. As they navigated the twisting path, Asha's keen senses alerted them to hidden dangers lurking in the shadows. The feline guided Maya around treacherous sinkholes and through dense thickets that seemed to reach out with grasping branches.

At one point, Asha suddenly stopped, her ears pricked forward in alert. Maya tensed, scanning the surroundings for any sign of danger.

Asha's eyes glowed with an otherworldly light, and suddenly, Maya found herself immersed in a vision shared by the feline.

In the vision, Maya saw glimpses of the realm's history, of ancient beings and long-forgotten battles. She witnessed the rise and fall of civilizations, the ebb and flow of magic, and the delicate balance that held the realm together. Asha's memories revealed the complex tapestry of the world Maya had stumbled into, offering her a deeper understanding of the forces at play.

As the vision faded, Maya blinked, her mind reeling from the influx of knowledge. She looked at Asha with newfound awe, realizing that the feline was more than just a guide; it was a repository of wisdom, a guardian of the realm's secrets. The depth of the world she had stumbled into was beyond her wildest imagination, and she was filled with a sense of wonder at the feline's role in it.

Asha met Maya's gaze, her eyes shimmering with understanding. At that moment, Maya knew that Asha would be her anchor in this strange and wondrous land, a constant source of guidance and support as she navigated the challenges ahead.

Maya turned to Asha, her eyes filled with curiosity and wonder. Suddenly, a gentle voice echoed in her mind, startling her with clarity and warmth. "Maya, there is much I wish to share with you," the voice said in a familiar and otherworldly cadence.

Maya's eyes widened as she realized the voice belonged to none other than Asha. The feline's gaze met hers, a flicker of amusement dancing in its luminous eyes. "Yes, Maya, I can communicate with you through the bonds of our minds," Asha confirmed, her telepathic voice tinged with a hint of mirth.

As Maya processed this revelation, Asha began to share glimpses of her past, painting a vivid tapestry of a long-lost civilization that once thrived in harmony with the realm. Through Asha's memories, Maya saw towering spires of crystal reaching toward the heavens, their surfaces shimmering with the reflected light of twin moons. She witnessed the inhabitants of this ancient city, their forms both familiar and alien, as they moved through the streets with grace and purpose.

Asha's voice wove through the visions, narrating the story of a society that had achieved a profound understanding of the realm's intricate balance. They had learned to harness the elements' power, commune with the spirits of the land, and walk the delicate line between the physical and the ethereal.

As the memories unfolded, Maya began understanding the depth of Asha's connection to this lost civilization. The feline had been a guardian tasked with preserving her people's sacred knowledge and wisdom. Through the ages, Asha had watched as the realm shifted and changed, bearing witness to the rise and fall of empires and the ebb and flow of magic.

Asha's voice grew solemn as it shared the burden it had carried for centuries. "I have chosen to share this knowledge with you, Maya," Asha said, her telepathic voice resonating with hope and gravity. "I sense in you the potential to restore balance to the realm, to bridge the gap between the past and the present."

Maya felt the weight of Asha's trust settling upon her shoulders, a mantle of responsibility humbling and empowering her. She understood that Asha had seen something in her, a spark of destiny that had drawn the feline to her side.

As the visions faded, Maya found herself back in the moonlit glade, the air still charged with the echoes of ancient magic. She looked at Asha with newfound reverence, her heart swelling with gratitude for the feline's trust and guidance.

As Maya and Asha journeyed more profoundly into the realm's heart, the path grew increasingly treacherous. The once lush and vibrant landscape gave way to a barren, rocky terrain that seemed to swallow all light and hope. The air grew thick with an oppressive silence, broken only by the occasional whisper of the wind through the jagged crags.

They soon found themselves at the edge of a dark ravine, its depths shrouded in an impenetrable darkness. The path forward seemed to disappear into the abyss, leaving no clear way to proceed. Maya felt a sense of unease grip her heart as she peered into the void, the unknown dangers that lurked within sending a shiver down her spine.

Asha, however, remained undaunted. The feline's eyes gleamed with a resolute determination as if it had faced such challenges countless times before. With a graceful leap, Asha bounded across the ravine, forming a shimmering black and orange blur against the darkness. Maya watched in awe as Asha landed on the other side with effortless precision, her tail swishing confidently.

"Trust in yourself, Maya," Asha's voice echoed in her mind, a gentle encouragement that seemed to chase away the shadows of doubt. "The power to overcome this obstacle lies within you."

Maya hesitated, her heart pounding as she stared at the vast expanse. The idea of leaping into the unknown without guaranteeing safety sent a wave of fear coursing through her veins. Yet, as she looked into Asha's eyes, she saw a flicker of unwavering faith, a belief in her abilities that she had never before possessed.

Drawing a deep breath, Maya closed her eyes and reached within herself, searching for the well of courage that Asha had seen in her. As she focused her thoughts, a warm, tingling sensation spread through her body, emanating from her core and radiating outwards. When she opened her eyes, Maya gasped wonder as she saw her hands aglow with a soft, pulsing light.

Instinctively, Maya raised her hands, directing the light towards the ravine. To her amazement, the darkness parted, revealing a hidden bridge concealed by the shadows. The ancient and weathered bridge stretched across the chasm, offering a path to the other side.

Maya stepped onto the bridge, her footsteps sure and steady as she crossed the ravine. The light from her hands illuminated the way, casting a warm glow that seemed to banish the oppressive darkness. As she reached the other side, Asha greeted her with a proud purr, her eyes shining with approval.

Maya felt a surge of elation and gratitude wash over her. Asha's trust in her had unlocked a power she had never known she possessed. The ability to summon light, banish the darkness, and reveal hidden paths was a gift that filled her with a sense of purpose and responsibility.

As night descended upon the twilight forest, Maya sought refuge in a secluded nook nestled between the gnarled roots of an ancient tree. The day's journey had left her exhausted, both physically and emotionally, yet sleep eluded her. The weight of her mission, the uncertainty of the future, and the fear of failure gnawed at her mind, leaving her restless and troubled.

Maya tossed and turned, her thoughts a whirlwind of doubts and worries. She questioned her abilities, wondering if she could navigate the perils of this strange realm and find Nykronus. Her responsibility seemed to press down upon her, suffocating her with its enormity.

Asha, ever attuned to Maya's emotions, sensed her distress. The feline padded softly towards her, her luminous eyes filled with understanding and compassion. With a gentle purr, Asha curled beside Maya, her warm fur pressing against her skin like a comforting embrace.

As Asha's purrs filled the night air, Maya felt a calm wave over her. The feline's presence was a balm to her troubled soul, a reminder that she was not alone in this journey. Asha's unwavering support and loyalty were a beacon of hope in the darkness. This light guided her through the shadows of her own doubts.

The gentle glow emanating from Asha's fur seemed to chase away the chill of the night, enveloping Maya in a cocoon of warmth and security. As she ran her fingers through Asha's soft fur, Maya felt the tension in her body slowly melt away, replaced by a sense of peace and tranquility.

In that quiet moment, the bond between Maya and Asha deepened, transcending the boundaries of mere companionship. Asha was more than just a guide or a guardian; she was a true friend, a confidant who understood the depths of Maya's fears and the weight of her responsibilities. The feline's presence was a constant reminder that Maya had the strength to overcome any obstacle.

As the gentle rhythm of Asha's purrs lulled Maya into a peaceful slumber, she felt a renewed sense of purpose and determination. With Asha by her side, she knew that she could face the trials and tribulations of this realm and unravel the mysteries that shrouded Nykronus's disappearance.

As the initial rays of daybreak infiltrated the dusky woodland, Maya woke from perhaps the most restful slumber she had experienced since departing her home in California. Her mind was still echoing with the remnants of dreams filled with ancient knowledge and whispered secrets. She blinked away the lingering traces of sleep, her gaze falling upon Asha, who sat nearby, her luminous eyes fixed on the path ahead.

With renewed mental and physical energy, Maya rose to her feet, ready to face the challenges that lay before them. Sensing her confidence, Asha padded softly to her side, her tail swishing with anticipation. The feline's presence was a constant reminder of the bond they shared, a connection that transcended the boundaries of the physical world.

As they set out again, Asha took the lead, guiding Maya through the winding paths of the twilight forest. The feline moved with a grace and surety that spoke of centuries of wisdom, her steps sure and purposeful as it navigated the ever-shifting landscape.

Before long, Asha led Maya to a hidden grove from the main path. The air within the grove was thick with potent magic, a palpable energy that seemed to hum and crackle with each breath. Maya could feel the power coursing through her veins, a tingling sensation that both exhilarated and unnerved her.

Asha's eyes glowed with an otherworldly light, her gaze fixed on the grove's center. "This place is a nexus of ancient magic," Asha's voice echoed in Maya's mind, her tone heavy with significance. "The challenges that await us are drawing near, and we must be prepared to face them."

Maya nodded, her heart pounding with a mixture of anticipation and trepidation. She knew that the path ahead would be fraught with danger, that the forces arrayed against them would stop at nothing to prevent her from finding Nykronus. And yet, armed with Asha's guidance and the knowledge the feline had shared, Maya felt a sense of readiness that she had never before possessed.

As they stood together in the grove, the weight of their shared destiny hung heavy in the air. Maya drew strength from Asha's unwavering support and from the feline's unshakable belief in her abilities. With Asha by her side, Maya knew that she could face whatever lay ahead and that she could rise to meet the challenges that awaited them.

As Maya and Asha emerged from the hidden grove, a vast,

uncharted territory stretched before them. The landscape was a tapestry of rolling hills, dense forests, and shimmering rivers, each promising untold secrets and challenges. The air thrummed with an ancient energy, a palpable presence that seemed to whisper of mysteries.

Side by side, Maya and Asha stepped forward into the unknown, their footsteps falling in perfect synchrony. Asha's sleek form moved with a grace born of centuries, her eyes scanning the horizon with a wisdom that transcended time. Maya, her heart pounding with excitement and trepidation, drew strength from the feline's unwavering presence, knowing they could face whatever lay ahead.

As they journeyed deeper into the realm, the bond between Maya and Asha grew stronger with each passing moment. The feline's ancient knowledge and unwavering support were a constant source of comfort and guidance, a beacon of light in the darkness of uncertainty. Maya, in turn, brought a fresh perspective and a fierce determination, her newfound strength and resolve fueling their shared purpose.

The path ahead was shrouded in mystery, a winding trail that led them through dense forests and across bubbling streams. Each step brought them closer to the realm's heart, to the secrets that had been hidden for so long. Maya's mind raced with the possibilities of what they might discover, the challenges they would face, and the growth they would experience together.

As the sun began to dip below the horizon, painting the sky in a breathtaking array of colors, Maya and Asha paused to take in the moment's beauty. The realm stretched before them, a vast and wondrous landscape promising adventure and discovery. With Asha by her side, Maya felt a sense of hopeful anticipation, united in their quest for truth and understanding.

CHAPTER
TWELVE

ntarctic Plateau, The South Pole

The compass in Elan's hand pulsed with energy as they descended deeper into the underground headquarters. Each step brought them further beneath the ice, where an ancient power seemed to pulse in rhythm with their guide. Their footsteps echoed off the walls, the sound reverberating through the stillness.

Suddenly, the compass began to glow brilliantly, and a hidden mechanism responded to its presence. Gears turned, and stone ground against stone as a section of the wall slid away, revealing the entrance to a locked vault door. Intricate symbols and runes adorned its surface, hinting at the secrets that lay beyond.

Elan and Myst exchanged a glance, their hearts pounding with anticipation. They approached the door cautiously, their breath misting in the cold air. Elan held the compass up to the door, and with a soft click, the lock disengaged. The door swung open, and they stepped into a vast chamber that seemed to stretch on forever.

The chamber stretched before them, its vastness emphasized by towering walls lined with gleaming weapons. Scrolls and relics from long-forgotten civilizations covered ornate shelves, each item a testament to ancient power, their pages holding knowledge lost to the ages.

Elan and Myst moved through the chamber, their footsteps muffled by the thick carpet of dust that covered the floor. They curiously examined the artifacts, their fingers tracing the intricate designs and symbols etched into the metal and stone. Each item held a story, a piece of the puzzle they had been searching for.

As they ventured deeper into the vault, a sense of awe and wonder enveloped them. It was as if they had stepped into a space frozen in time, a place where the secrets of the past were waiting to be unearthed. The compass in Elan's hand continued to pulse with energy, leading them deeper into the heart of the ancient mystery.

As Elan and Myst ventured further into the ancient vault, a central pedestal caught their attention. It stood apart from the other artifacts, bathed in a soft, pulsing light that seemed to beckon them closer. As they approached, they realized that the light emanated from an orb resting atop the pedestal, its rhythm perfectly synchronized with the pulsing of the compass in Elan's hand.

Intricate engravings danced across the orb's surface, shifting in the otherworldly light. Elan's hand moved toward it instinctively, and beside him, Myst leaned forward, both drawn by its inexplicable pull. With reverence and trepidation, Elan reached out and placed his hand on the orb.

Instantly, a surge of energy coursed through his body, and his mind was flooded with a torrent of visions from the past. He saw Nykronus, younger and more vibrant, working alongside a group of figures whose faces were obscured by a shimmering mist. They moved with purpose and urgency, their actions hinting at a momentous task.

As the visions unfolded, Elan and Myst began to understand the true nature of their mission. They saw glimpses of the realm of Aethoria, a realm between heaven and hell, a place of breathtaking beauty and unimaginable danger—purgatory. They witnessed Nykronus and his companions fighting against an undefined threat, their powers combined in a dazzling display of light and magic.

The visions revealed that Nykronus and his allies had formed a coalition to protect the realm. They witnessed them fighting against shadowy figures that would later become known as the Malefic

Assembly, their powers combined in a dazzling display of light and magic.

As the visions faded, Elan and Myst were filled with a deep sense of purpose. They understood that Nykronus's disappearance was not just a personal loss, but a threat to the very fabric of existence. The stakes were higher than they had ever imagined, and the fate of the realm rested on their shoulders. They were determined to uncover the truth and protect the realm at all costs.

Elan and Myst turned their attention back to the artifacts surrounding them. Each item now held a greater significance, a piece of the puzzle that could help them unravel the mystery of Nykronus's disappearance and the looming danger threatening the realm. They knew that they had to press on, follow the compass's guidance, and uncover the truth behind the ancient coalition and the power they sought to protect.

As Elan and Myst pored over the ancient scrolls, the ethereal light cast an otherworldly glow on the parchment, illuminating the intricate scripts and diagrams. The texts were a tapestry of languages, some familiar and others long forgotten, each holding a piece of the puzzle they sought to unravel.

Elan let out a heavy breath as he deciphered a particularly complex passage, his fingers tracing the delicate lines of ink. "This speaks of a mirror hidden in the jungles of Palawan," he said, his voice tinged with excitement. "It's described as a key, a means to access an archway sealed long ago—where Nykronus went."

Myst leaned in closer, his eyes widening as he studied the accompanying illustration. "And where Maya is. The archway seems to be a gateway, a portal to vital locations within the realm," he said, his voice hushed with reverence. "It must have been sealed to protect something of great importance."

As they delved deeper into the texts, the complexity of the languages began to test their knowledge and patience. The scrolls were a labyrinth of ancient dialects and esoteric symbolism, each new passage presenting a fresh challenge. Elan and Myst found themselves working in tandem to unravel the cryptic messages.

Time blurred as they worked. Elan decoded ancient scripts while Myst pieced together fragmented symbols, their complementary skills bringing clarity to the cryptic texts. The ethereal light remained constant, marking their progress through the hours.

As the final pieces fell into place, their shared triumph reflected their growing bond and the weight of their discovery—the location of another mirror in Rub' al Khali, also known as the Empty Quarter, and the ritual needed to activate the portal. This knowledge was a prize won through perseverance, a testament to their shared mission.

With the scrolls' secrets laid bare, Elan and Myst knew their journey was far from over. The mirror in Palawan was only the first step, a key that would unlock the path to the sealed archway and the vital locations within the realm. However, there was no information regarding the second archway, its purpose, or where it led. They gathered the scrolls carefully, their hearts filled with a sense of purpose and a newfound appreciation for the strength of their partnership.

A small panel caught Elan's eye as they carefully rolled the ancient scrolls. It was barely visible, seamlessly integrated into the wall's intricate carvings. The panel clicked and slid open with a gentle push, revealing a hidden compartment. Inside, a single scroll lay untouched, its parchment radiating an ethereal glow.

Elan reached in and carefully retrieved the scroll, his hands trembling slightly as he unrolled it. The parchment crackled softly, its surface adorned with an ancient script that seemed to shimmer in the soft light. Myst moved closer, his eyes widening as he recognized the language.

"It's a prophecy," he whispered, his voice filled with awe and trepidation.

Together, they began deciphering the cryptic text, their minds working in unison to unravel its meaning. The prophecy spoke of a time of great upheaval when an unseen force would threaten the balance between the realms. Amidst the chaos, a Harbinger of Balance figure would emerge, destined to navigate the coming storm and restore equilibrium to the realms.

As they read on, Elan and Myst pondered the implications of the prophecy. Could Nykronus be this Harbinger of Balance? His disappearance and the timing of the prophecy seemed too coincidental to ignore. Or could it be Maya, with her untapped potential and mysterious connection to the realm?

The discovery of the prophecy filled Elan and Myst with hope and dread. They hoped that there was a path forward, a way to restore balance and save the realms from the looming threat. But they also dreaded the realization of the scope of the conflict they faced and the crucial roles they might be called upon to play.

As they stood in the ancient vault, the weight of the prophecy hanging in the air, Elan and Myst knew that their journey had taken on a new significance. They were no longer just searching for a lost friend or exploring a mysterious realm; they were part of something much more significant, a cosmic struggle that would shape the fate of all existence.

As Elan and Myst ventured further into the vault, a sudden rumble shook the ancient walls. Dust fell from the ceiling, and the ground beneath their feet trembled. They exchanged a worried glance, realizing their presence had triggered a long-dormant security measure.

A grinding sound echoed through the chamber. "The entrance!" Myst's warning came as stone scraped against stone, the doorway already half-sealed.

Elan scanned the room, his training taking over. Two pedestals stood on opposite sides, their mechanisms glowing with latent energy. "There!"

They rushed to the pedestals, examining the mechanisms closely. It quickly became apparent that the puzzle required them to work separately but perfectly synchronized. Each pedestal bore a series of symbols that needed to be activated in a specific order, with precise timing.

"Myst, do you see the pattern?" Elan asked, his voice strained with urgency.

Myst nodded, his brow furrowed in concentration. "Yes, but we'll have to trust each other completely. One misstep, and we'll be trapped here forever."

Elan met his gaze, his eyes filled with determination. "I trust you with my life. We can do this together."

They took their positions at the pedestals, their hands hovering over the symbols. Elan counted down, and on his signal, they activated the symbols in perfect unison. The mechanisms responded to their touch, glowing with an ethereal light as each symbol was triggered.

The vault rumbled again, but this time, it was different. The entrance slowly began to reopen, and the tremors subsided. Elan and Myst breathed a sigh of relief, their hearts pounding in their chests.

As they stepped away from the pedestals, Myst's eyes narrowed. "This trap... it's too sophisticated to be a mere security measure. It's almost as if it were designed specifically to test us."

Elan nodded grimly. "You're right. And I have a feeling I know who might be behind it. The Malefic Assembly."

Myst's expression darkened. "They've been trying to undermine our efforts at every turn. But why set a trap here, in this ancient vault?"

"Perhaps they knew we were getting close to something important," Elan mused, his mind racing with possibilities. "Something they desperately want to keep hidden."

As Elan and Myst delved deeper into the vault, their attention was drawn to a peculiar artifact among the ancient relics. It was a fragmented tablet, its surface marred by the passage of time. Yet, the images etched upon it remained discernible. They carefully lifted the tablet, their eyes tracing the intricate lines and symbols that seemed to tell a story across the ages.

The central figure depicted on the tablet was a shadowy entity, its form obscured by an ominous aura. This enigmatic being appeared in various scenes, representing a different historical era. From ancient civilizations to more recent times, the shadowy figure loomed like a specter, its presence a constant thread woven through the tapestry of history.

Elan and Myst exchanged a knowing glance, their minds racing to connect the dots between the fragmented images and the prophecy they had uncovered. The disturbances they had witnessed, the growing unrest in the realm, and Nykronus's disappearance all seemed to converge upon this mysterious entity.

As they studied the tablet more closely, a chilling realization dawned on them. The shadowy figure's appearances coincided with periods of great upheaval and chaos throughout history. It was as if this entity thrived on discord, its presence a harbinger of impending doom.

Myst frowned as he analyzed the implications of their discovery: "If this being is indeed the source of the disturbances, then its return could spell catastrophe for our world, Aethoria, and beyond."

Elan nodded grimly, his grip tightening on the tablet. "And if the prophecy is to be believed, this entity's reemergence is at the heart of the looming conflict."

The revelation brought a sense of urgency to their mission. They understood that the danger facing the realm was far greater than they had initially anticipated. The shadowy figure's return threatened the delicate balance between the realms and the very fabric of existence itself.

They carefully wrapped the tablet and prophecy scroll in protective cloth and secured them with their other crucial finds.

Emerging from the vault, Elan and Myst navigated the labyrinthine passages in contemplative silence, each footstep echoing with the weight of their discoveries. The path back to their airplane stretched before them, but their minds were already focused on the challenges ahead.

Elan's voice broke the silence, his tone filled with determination. "We can't let this prophecy come to pass. Whatever this shadowy figure is, we must find a way to stop it."

Myst nodded, his eyes gleaming with a newfound sense of purpose. "And to do that, we must unravel the rest of Nykronus's mission. We seek answers in Rub' al Khali at the second location."

At the airplane, Elan turned to Myst, his expression softening. "I couldn't have done this without you. Your mom is so proud of the man you've become. We both are."

Myst's hand found his father's shoulder, steady and sure. "We're in this together, Dad. We won't let Nykronus down."

With a final nod, they boarded the airplane, their destination clear and their hearts filled with fierce determination. The ancient Rub' al

Khali archway beckoned, holding the promise of answers and the key to averting the foretold conflict.

Elan and Myst pored over their notes as the airplane took to the skies, piecing together the fragments of knowledge they had gathered. The prophecy, the shadowy figure, and Nykronus's disappearance were all connected, a tapestry of mysteries waiting to be unraveled.

CHAPTER

THIRTEEN

Maya ventured deeper into Aethoria's heart, where the landscape shifted like a living creature, unveiling a labyrinth of ancient trees. The paths twisted and turned, their directions morphing with each gust of wind whispered through the leaves. It was where the very fabric of reality seemed to bend to the whims of an unseen force.

Asha, the intriguing feline companion, walked alongside Maya, her glowing eyes fixed upon the ever-changing paths. With a flick of her tail, she beckoned Maya to follow, leading her into the heart of the forest's mysteries. Asha, a creature of this realm, was not just a guide but a mentor, helping Maya understand the unique nature of Aethoria.

"Listen," Asha purred, her voice weaving through the rustling leaves. "The paths here bend to forces beyond our control, dancing with each whisper of wind."

Maya's face furrowed, trying to make sense of the chaotic web of trails that stretched before her. The shifting paths reminded Maya of the maze-like halls of her old school, but here, at least, she had Asha's guidance. Back home, she'd often felt lost in the crowd, but in Aethoria, each step - however uncertain - felt like part of a greater purpose.

She felt a surge of frustration, a sense of being lost in a world that seemed to defy logic. "How am I supposed to navigate this?" she asked, her voice tinged with uncertainty and a hint of fear.

Asha's eyes coursed with wisdom. "You must learn to sense the subtle shifts in the wind, to anticipate the changes before they happen. Close your eyes and let your instincts guide you."

Trusting in her companion's words, Maya opened her eyelids. She drew in a deep breath, attuning herself to the whispers of the wind. At first, the sensations were overwhelming, a racket of rustling leaves and swirling breezes. Gradually, a pattern emerged: a delicate dance of air currents that held the key to the forest's secrets.

With each step, Maya began to anticipate the rearranging paths, her feet moving in harmony with the wind's gentle guidance. She navigated the labyrinth with growing trust. She had grown from a bewildered traveler to a confident navigator. This newfound trust in her abilities filled her with a quiet strength, a testament to how far she had come.

Maya marveled at her newfound connection with the realm as they emerged from the forest's center. The lesson of the morphing paths had awakened something within her: a deeper understanding of the intricate web of forces that shaped Aethoria. She had grown from a bewildered traveler to a confident navigator, her senses sharpened by Asha's mentorship.

Asha regarded her with a knowing smile. "You've taken your first step in understanding the true nature of this place, Maya. The realm responds to those who can sense its rhythms and flow with its changes."

Maya grinned, a sense of purpose igniting within her. She knew this was just the beginning of her journey, a mere glimpse into the mysteries ahead. Her determination to learn and grow burned bright, each step forward cementing her commitment to this strange new path.

The river defied gravity, its waters streaming skyward into a hovering cloud. Maya's disbelief turned to wonder as Asha demonstrated how to walk the vertical current, their feet finding purchase on what should have been impossible.

With a graceful leap, Asha stepped onto the river's surface and glided upstream, her form moving effortlessly against the water's flow.

Maya's mouth fell open, awe and confusion warring within her. "How are you doing that?"

Asha paused, turning to face Maya with a knowing smile. "It's about aligning your own energy with that of the river. Close your eyes and feel the current, the pulse of the water beneath your feet."

Hesitantly, Maya approached the river's edge, her toes curling against the damp earth. She drew in a deep breath, allowing her eyelids to flutter shut as she attuned herself to the river's peculiar rhythm.

At first, the sensation was strange, the water's upward flow defying every instinct she possessed. But as she focused, Maya began to sense a subtle harmony, a dance of energies that flowed between her own being and the river's ascending current.

With a tentative step, Maya placed her foot upon the water's surface, marveling as it found solid footing. She took another step, then another, her body adjusting to the river's unique flow.

Asha watched with approval, her eyes glinting with pride as Maya navigated the upward current. "You learn quickly, Maya. The realm responds to those who can attune themselves to its energies and find harmony amidst the chaos."

As they left the impossible river behind, Maya's newfound confidence hummed within her, ready for whatever wonder Aethoria might reveal next.

Maya and Asha stumbled upon a valley that seemed to breathe with its own symphony. Stones of varying sizes and shapes littered the landscape, each one emitting a unique musical note as the wind danced through the crevices and hollows.

Maya's eyes widened in wonder, her ears attuned to the ethereal melody that filled the air. It was a song unlike any she had ever heard, a harmonious blend of nature's elements that seemed to hold secrets within its notes.

Asha sat amidst the stones, her tail swaying in rhythm with the wind's steady gusts. "Listen closely, Maya," she purred, her voice a soothing whisper amidst the valley's song. "The stones hold messages, stories of the realm's past and present, encoded within their melodies."

Maya knelt beside her feline companion, her fingers tracing the smooth surface of a nearby stone. As she focused on the music, she began to sense patterns emerging from the seemingly random notes, a hidden language that spoke to her soul.

With each gust of wind, the stones' song shifted, revealing new layers of meaning. Maya closed her eyes, allowing the melodies to wash over her, to fill her mind with images and sensations that transcended mere words.

In the stones' song, she saw visions of Aethoria's creation, of the elemental forces that shaped its landscapes and breathed life into its beings. She witnessed the rise and fall of ancient civilizations, their stories etched into the very fabric of the realm.

As the wind picked up, the melodies intensified, and energy surged through Maya's veins. It was as if the stones' song was awakening something within her, a connection to the elemental aspects of the realm that she had never known existed.

Asha watched with knowing eyes, her voice a gentle guide amidst the swirling melodies. "You have the ability to decipher the messages, Maya. Your connection to the elements allows you to understand the stones' language and unravel the secrets they hold."

With each passing moment, Maya's understanding deepened. The stones' song revealed the delicate balance that existed within Aethoria. She saw glimpses of her own role, of the part she was meant to play in maintaining the realm's harmony.

As the wind died down and the melodies faded, Maya opened her eyes, a newfound sense of purpose etched upon her face. The stones' song had given her a glimpse into the very heart of Aethoria, a window into the mysteries that lay ahead.

Maya and Asha found themselves at the edge of a serene lake, its surface a perfect mirror for the stars that blanketed the sky above. The gentle lapping of the water against the shore created a soothing rhythm, a lullaby that seemed to whisper secrets of the realm's mysteries.

Maya settled onto the soft grass, her eyes drawn to the celestial display above. The foreign constellations seemed to dance across the water's surface, their reflections shimmering with an ethereal light. It was a moment of tranquility, a respite from the trials and wonders she had encountered on her journey thus far.

Asha curled up beside her, the feline's glowing eyes fixed upon the starry canopy. "This lake holds a special place in Aethoria's history," she began, her melodic purr blending with the night's whispered secrets. "It is said that when the realm was first created, the elemental forces that shaped its landscapes gathered here, their energies merging to breathe life into the very fabric of existence."

Maya listened intently, her mind absorbing every word as Asha wove tales of Aethoria's origins. She spoke of the delicate balance between the elements, of the intricate web of connections that bound the realm to the broader universe. As Asha's stories unfolded, Maya began to see her own experiences in a new light, recognizing the threads that tied her own powers to the ancient forces that had shaped Aethoria.

"Your abilities, Maya," Asha continued, her gaze meeting Maya's with a knowing intensity, "are not a mere coincidence. They are a manifestation of the very energies that flow through this realm, a connection to the primal forces that have existed since the dawn of creation."

As Maya absorbed Asha's words, a sense of understanding began to blossom within her. The challenges she had faced, the instinctive way in which she had navigated the realm's shifting landscapes - it all started to make sense. Her powers were not simply a gift but a responsibility, a calling to maintain the delicate balance that held Aethoria together.

Under the starlit sky, Maya felt a profound connection to the realm and the ancient forces that had chosen her for this journey. As she gazed into the lake's mirrored surface, she saw not just her own reflection but the reflection of the entire cosmos, a tapestry of light and energy that stretched beyond the boundaries of Aethoria itself.

In that moment of quiet reflection, Maya knew that her journey was far from over. The secrets of the realm and the true nature of her powers were mysteries that she had only begun to unravel.

The peaceful lake meditation had centered Maya's mind - a clarity she would soon need.

As Maya and Asha ventured further into Aethoria, they found themselves standing at the edge of a vast, open field. At first glance, the field appeared to be a tranquil expanse of gently swaying grasses and vibrant wildflowers. However, as they stepped forward, the landscape began to shift and morph, the ground beneath their feet seeming to ripple like the surface of a disturbed pond.

Maya blinked as trees flickered in and out of existence like ghostly apparitions, her eyes struggling to track the ever-shifting landscape. Paths wound through the field, only to twist and turn in impossible directions, leading nowhere and everywhere at once.

Asha sat calmly amidst the chaos. "This, Maya, is the Field of Illusions. Reality and deception intertwine here, challenging those who seek to navigate its depths."

Maya frowned, her gaze darting from one shifting landmark to another. "How are we supposed to find our way through this?"

Asha's tail swished, and she fixed Maya with a knowing look. "The key, Maya, lies not in what you see with your eyes but what you perceive with your mind. Close your eyes and focus on your inner vision, the truth that resides within you."

Hesitantly, Maya allowed her eyelids to flutter shut, concentrating as she tried to block out the disorienting sensations that assaulted her senses. At first, the darkness behind her closed lids seemed to swirl with the same chaotic energy that permeated the field. But clarity began to emerge as she focused, drawing upon the inner strength that had guided her through the trials of Aethoria.

In her mind's eye, Maya saw the field as it truly was, stripped of its illusions and deceptions. The paths that had once seemed to lead nowhere now converged into a single, clear route, a trail of shimmering light that cut through the darkness like a beacon.

With newfound confidence, Maya opened her eyes, the illusions of the field no longer holding sway over her perceptions. She saw the true path before her, the one that had been obscured by the field's trickery.

Asha purred, a sound of approval and pride. "The Field of Illusions holds no power over those who can see beyond its deceptions."

Maya felt a growing sense of fearlessness and certitude as they navigated the field.

Victory over illusion had barely settled in Maya's heart when the first warning rumble of thunder echoed overhead.

The storm intensified with each of Maya's doubts, lightning fracturing the sky as thunder echoed her internal turmoil. But as the tempest raged, she remembered Asha's teachings - her fears were feeding the chaos.

Sensing Maya's distress, Asha pressed close to her side, the mystical cat's presence a steadying anchor amidst the uproar. "The storm feeds on your fears, Maya," Asha whispered, her voice cutting through the howling wind. "It grows stronger with each doubt that crosses your mind."

Maya's heart raced, her hands clenching into fists as she fought against the rising tide of her own emotions. The storm raged on, the wind tearing at her clothes and the rain pelting her skin like icy needles. It was as if the very fabric of Aethoria was unraveling around her, mirroring the cracks in her own resolve.

But as Maya stood there, buffeted by the storm's fury, something shifted within her. Asha's words echoed in her mind, reminding her that the power to calm the tempest lay within her heart. She closed her eyes, drawing in a deep breath as she focused on the steady rhythm of her own heartbeat.

With each breath, Maya acknowledged the fears and doubts that had fueled the storm, accepting them as a part of herself. She embraced her vulnerabilities, recognizing that they were not weaknesses but rather opportunities for growth and strength.

As Maya's inner turmoil settled, the storm around her dissipated. The wind died down to a gentle breeze, and the rain slowed to a soft patter against the ground. The clouds above parted, revealing a sky filled with stars that seemed to twinkle with renewed brilliance.

Asha purred, her eyes glowing with pride as she watched Maya's transformation. "You have learned to master your emotions, Maya. By facing your fears and accepting your vulnerabilities, you have diminished the storm's power over you."

Maya opened her eyes, a sense of calm washing over her. The storm reflected her inner struggles, a metaphor for the doubts and insecurities that had threatened to overwhelm her. But by confronting those emotions head-on, she had discovered a strength within herself that she had never known existed.

Maya and Asha approached a sacred grove. The trees stood taller, their leaves whispering ancient secrets in the gentle breeze. The ground beneath their feet thrummed with an energy that Maya could feel resonating in her very bones.

At the entrance to the grove, two imposing figures materialized, their forms shimmering with an ethereal light. They were the guardians, the custodians of the realm's knowledge, and their presence exuded an aura of timeless wisdom and power.

The guardians regarded Maya with piercing gazes, their eyes seeming to penetrate the very depths of her soul. "Who seeks to enter this sacred place?" one of them spoke, their voice a deep rumble that echoed through the grove.

Maya stepped forward, her head held high despite the weight of their scrutiny. "I am Maya Durant, daughter of Elan and Kaira, and I come seeking the knowledge and secrets of this realm."

The guardians exchanged glances, their expressions unreadable. "Many have come before you, seeking the same," the second guardian intoned. But the grove's secrets are not freely given. They must be earned through trials of the mind, body, and spirit."

Maya nodded, her resolve unwavering. "I am ready to face whatever challenges you deem necessary."

The guardians circled her like starlight-made flesh, their questions probing the depths of her understanding. Maya's answers drew upon each trial she had faced - the wind paths, the skyward river, the singing stones, the treacherous illusions, the revealing storm. Each word rang with the truth of hard-won experience.

As the guardians continued their relentless examination, a calmness settled over Maya. She understood now that her journey had prepared her for this moment, honing her mind and spirit to face the challenges ahead.

Finally, the guardians stepped back, their expressions softening with a newfound respect. "You have proven yourself worthy, Maya Durant," the first guardian declared. "The secrets of the grove are now open to you, for you have demonstrated the wisdom and understanding necessary to wield them responsibly."

Maya bowed her head in gratitude, a sense of profound humility washing over her. She knew that the knowledge she would gain in the sacred grove was not a prize to be coveted but a responsibility to be shouldered.

The grove awakened before Maya's eyes, sunlight dancing across ancient bark to reveal hidden patterns and symbols. The marks shifted and flowed, weaving Aethoria's creation story in living light. Energy surged through her veins as the realm's essence flowed into her, awakening an awareness of every leaf, blade of grass, and creature that called this place home.

Asha purred, her glowing eyes fixed upon Maya. "You are experiencing the true nature of your connection to this realm, Maya. Your powers are not separate from Aethoria, but an integral part of its very fabric."

As Maya closed her eyes, she saw the threads that bound her to the realm, the invisible ties that connected her to the primal forces that had shaped this magical world. She understood now that her journey had been preparing her for this moment, honing her abilities and her understanding so that she could take her place as a guardian of the realm's balance.

As the light continued to spread across the grove, purpose crystallized within Maya. She was no longer just a wanderer seeking answers but a vital part of Aethoria's tapestry, a guardian entrusted with maintaining the delicate equilibrium that allowed the realm to thrive.

FOURTEEN

As Maya ventured deeper, the cavern air grew heavy with ancient magic, each step stirring echoes of power that had slumbered in the stone for centuries. Crystalline formations jutted from the walls, their facets catching what little light remained and transforming it into dancing shadows that seemed to watch her progress. This was no natural formation – the guardians had carved this labyrinth from living rock, testing those who dared to claim their heritage.

She halted before a barrier that spanned the passageway like a frozen waterfall, its surface rippling with deep crimson light. Veins of darker red pulsed through it in time with her heartbeat as if the magic recognized something in her blood. Maya pressed her palm against the surface, expecting warmth but finding an otherworldly chill that sent shivers racing up her arm.

Her first attempt to breach it – a gentle push of magic – barely caused a ripple. The second, more forceful thrust earned her nothing but a subtle mockery: the barrier's light flickered briefly, almost like laughter. Sweat beaded on her forehead, but frustration crystallized into resolve. She hadn't tracked down her family's ancient grove, hadn't decoded the cryptic messages in her grandmother's journals, hadn't fought through her own self-doubt just to be stopped here.

Maya closed her eyes, awareness turning inward. Past the rapid thunder of her heart, past the tremble in her muscles, down to something deeper – a well of power she'd only glimpsed in dreams. It felt like diving into a bottomless pool, the pressure building in her ears, until...

There.

Something ancient stirred within her chest, unfurling like a flower blooming in fast-forward. Heat rushed through her body, but different from typical warmth – this felt like Starfire in her veins, like the first spark of creation. Her eyes snapped open, blazing with inner light, and when she spoke, her voice carried echoes of her ancestors:

"I claim my birthright."

The barrier exploded outward in a shower of crystalline shards, each catching the light like scattered rubies before dissolving into motes of crimson energy. The release of power left Maya trembling, her fingertips tingling with residual energy she'd never felt. She stared at her hands in wonder, watching tiny arcs of magic dance between her fingers.

But in the aftermath of victory, a deeper understanding settled over her. This barrier hadn't been meant to stop her – it had been waiting for her, testing her strength and determination. Her grandmother's last journal entry suddenly made sense: 'Power without purpose is just force; power with purpose becomes destiny.'

The path ahead beckoned, darker and deeper into the earth. Maya squared her shoulders, the last traces of doubt falling away like the shattered barrier. She could feel more trials awaiting her, each one designed to awaken another facet of her power. For the first time, she was ready to face them all.

As Maya ventured deeper into the cavern, the ancient symbols carved into the walls began to pulse with an otherworldly light. Drawn by an inexplicable force, she reached out, her fingertips grazing the cool stone surface.

In an instant, a vivid and intense flood of memories surged through her mind. She saw a man, tall and broad-shouldered, with features strikingly similar to her grandfather's. He stood in a circle of standing stones, his hands outstretched as he commanded the elements. The wind whipped around him, and the earth trembled beneath his feet.

The scene shifted, and Maya found herself in a grand hall, watching a woman with her Grandma Gianna's piercing eyes. The woman held a glowing orb aloft, its light casting eerie shadows on the walls. She chanted in a language Maya had never heard before yet somehow understood. The orb pulsed in response, its power growing with each uttered word.

The memories cascaded through time - Florence in 1647, Rome during the Republic, and ancient Etruscan temples where her ancestors first learned to speak with stone and flame. Each vision showed her a different facet of her heritage, showcasing an ancestor wielding powers similar to hers. Some commanded fire, others water. Some could heal with a touch, while others could see glimpses of the future.

With each memory, Maya felt a profound connection to her lineage, a sense of belonging she had never experienced before. She now understood that her abilities were not a fluke or a curse but a gift passed down through generations.

Maya found herself in the cavern as the memories faded, her hand still pressed against the ancient symbols. She took a deep breath, feeling the power that had lain dormant within her for so long stirring to life.

She knew now that she was part of something greater, a legacy that stretched back through the ages. And with that knowledge came a clear sense of purpose, a drive to master her abilities and carry on the work of her ancestors.

Maya stepped back from the wall, her eyes alight with determination. She had a long journey ahead of her, but she was ready to face whatever challenges lay in store. With the strength of her lineage behind her, she knew she could overcome anything.

Maya stood at the edge of a gaping chasm, its depths shrouded in an impenetrable darkness. The path in front of her had ended abruptly, and there seemed to be no way to proceed. She peered across the expanse, searching for any means to cross.

As she stood there, a strange sensation began to build within her; a tingling started in her toes, and her spine crept up. It was as if the earth was calling to her, whispering secrets in a language only she could understand. Maya extended her hand, her fingers splayed towards the chasm.

To her amazement, the ground began to tremble, and then, slowly at first but with gathering speed, the rock and soil from both sides of the chasm began to extend outwards, reaching for each other like long-lost friends. They met in the middle, intertwining and solidifying, forming a bridge that spanned the once-impassable gap.

Maya stared at the newly formed path, her eyes filled with shock and awe. With a mere gesture, she had manipulated the earth itself, bending it to her will. The ease with which she had performed this feat was both exhilarating and terrifying. It hinted at a depth of power within her that she had never imagined.

As she stepped onto the bridge, testing its stability with a cautious foot, Maya's thoughts turned to her family. Did Myst possess similar abilities lying dormant within him, waiting to be unleashed? And what of her parents? Had they, too, harbored these powers, keeping them hidden from their children?

The thought was both comforting and unsettling. On one hand, it meant that she was not alone, that her abilities were a birthright, a gift passed down through generations. But on the other, it raised countless questions. Why had these powers manifested so strongly in her, and why now? What was the purpose behind them, and what was the reason for their existence?

Maya shook her head, trying to clear her mind of the swirling thoughts. She had a mission to complete, requiring all her focus and determination. She could not afford to be distracted by the mysteries of her existence, not now.

With a deep breath, she strode forward, her footsteps echoing on the bridge's stone she had created. Whatever lay ahead, whatever challenges she might face, Maya knew she had the power to overcome them. And perhaps, in time, she would unravel the secrets of her abilities and the role they were meant to play in the grand tapestry of her life.

As Maya ventured deeper into the cavern, she was drawn to a peculiar chamber. Upon entering, she was greeted by an astonishing sight. Water flowed against gravity, spiraling around the room in a mesmerizing dance. The liquid ribbons twisted and turned, creating intricate patterns that seemed to defy the very laws of nature.

Intrigued, Maya approached the nearest stream, her hand outstretched. As her fingers neared the water's surface, it suddenly changed course, swirling around her hand in a gentle caress. Emboldened by this response, Maya stepped closer, allowing the water to envelop her completely.

To her amazement, the water formed a protective bubble around her, its surface shimmering with an iridescent sheen. Maya took a tentative breath and found that the bubble gave her ample air. She could breathe and move freely within this aquatic cocoon.

Maya marveled at the sensations surrounding her as she explored this strange new environment. The water was cool against her skin, yet it filled her with warmth and comfort. It was as if the element recognized her, welcomed her, and sought to protect her.

With each passing moment, Maya's understanding of her abilities grew. The water responded to her thoughts and emotions, ebbing and flowing perfectly with her will. She realized that her connection to the elements was not limited to earth alone. Water, too, was a part of her, a force she could command and commune with.

This discovery sent Maya's mind reeling with possibilities. Was this ability unique to her, a gift bestowed upon her alone? Or was it a trait shared by her ancestors, passed down through generations? She recalled the memories she had witnessed of the man who commanded the wind and the woman who wielded the glowing orb. Perhaps they, too, had this profound connection to the elements.

As Maya moved through the chamber, the water continued to dance around her, guiding and protecting her. She felt a sense of profound connection, a unity with the very fabric of the world. And with that connection came a growing sense of purpose, a realization that her journey was not merely about personal discovery but about something far greater.

Maya was greeted by a wall of raging flames that danced with an intensity she had never witnessed before. The heat was tangible, pressing against her skin with a brute force. She could feel the power emanating from the fire, a raw, primal energy that seemed to have a life of its own.

For a moment, Maya hesitated, her instincts screaming at her to turn back and flee from this inferno that threatened to consume her. But something deep within her, a whisper of bravery and will, urged her. She had come too far to be deterred by mere flames, no matter how fierce they might be.

With a deep breath, Maya stepped forward, bracing herself for the searing pain she expected to follow. But to her astonishment, the flames transformed around her, their destructive nature shifting into pure creative energy, each spark a potential waiting to be shaped, as if guided by an invisible hand. She could feel their heat, but it was a comforting warmth, like the embrace of a gentle sun.

Fortified by this discovery, Maya extended her hand, focusing her will on the nearest tongue of flame. To her surprise, the fire responded, coiling around her fingers like a fiery serpent. She could feel its power thrumming through her veins, a pulsing energy that seemed to merge with her own.

Maya's control over the flames grew more refined with each passing moment. She could shape them, command them to dance, and flicker at her whim. It was a heady sensation, a rush of power, unlike anything she had ever experienced.

As she moved through the chamber, the flames continued to bend to her will, parting before her like a fiery sea. Maya marveled at the implications of this new ability. She had already demonstrated a command over earth and water, but now, with fire added to her repertoire, she could sense a pattern emerging.

Each element represented a fundamental aspect of the world, a pillar upon which all creation rested. With her growing mastery over these elements, Maya appeared to be a conduit for their power, capable of maintaining the delicate balance between them.

The realization was both humbling and exhilarating. Maya understood that her journey was not merely one of personal discovery, but of cosmic importance.

As Maya ventured further into the cavern, she stood before a mirror-like surface, its edges jagged and raw as if carved from the rock itself. But instead of her reflection, the surface showed a shadowy figure, its form shifting and flickering like a candle in the wind.

Maya stepped closer, her heart pounding in her chest. Something familiar about the figure tugged at the edges of her memory. As she watched, the figure seemed to solidify, its features becoming clearer and more defined.

And then, with a jolt of recognition, Maya realized who it was. It was her, but not her. This figure was older and wiser, with eyes that had seen the world in ancient life that never *technically* happened. This version of herself carried centuries of wisdom in her eyes - the Maya who had walked the marble-paved streets of Imperial Rome had hidden magic users during the Inquisition and witnessed the rise and fall of a dozen dynasties. Though that timeline had never come to pass, its wisdom remained, seeing the rise and fall of empires and the birth and death of historical figures.

The figure spoke, a whisper that seemed to come from everywhere and nowhere. "Maya," it said, "you have been chosen. Your lineage, your powers, they were given to you for a reason. You are destined to unite the fractured elements of this realm, to bring balance to the forces that have been in discord for so long."

Maya stared at the figure, her mind reeling. Unite the elements?

Bring balance to the realm? The weight of these words settled upon her shoulders like a physical burden, pressing down upon her with an almost unbearable force.

Doubt and fear swirled within her, a maelstrom of emotions that threatened to overwhelm her. Why her? Why now? She was just a girl, a child in the grand scheme of things. How could she possibly be ready for such a responsibility?

The figure seemed to sense her turmoil, its expression softening with an ancient understanding. "I know it's a lot to take in," it said, "but you are stronger than you know. The power within you, the connection you have to the elements, was given to you for a reason. You are ready for this, Maya. You have always been ready."

But even as the figure spoke these words of encouragement, Maya could feel the weight of her destiny pressing down upon her, a burden that seemed too heavy to bear. She had come so far, had discovered so much about herself and her abilities, but this? This was beyond anything she had ever imagined.

At the cavern's heart, the elements converged in symphonic harmony. Earth thrummed beneath her feet, water carved graceful arcs through the air, and flames painted patterns of light across the stone walls, casting a warm glow upon the stone walls. And the air itself seemed to tell secrets, carrying the echoes of ancient wisdom throughout the entire realm of Aethoria.

In this place of convergence, Maya could feel the elements responding to her presence. They swirled around her in a harmonious dance, not in chaos but as if welcoming a long-lost friend. With each breath, she could feel their power flowing through her, a tingling energy that filled her with a sense of purpose and belonging.

As she stood there, bathed in the elemental glow, Maya's remaining fears were buried, replaced by a burgeoning optimism. She realized that her abilities, her connection to the elements, were not a burden but a gift. Yes, it was a responsibility, but also an opportunity to make a difference, to bring balance to a realm that had been in discord for far too long—and to protect her own world.

She thought back to the memories she had witnessed of the ancestors who had wielded these same powers. They had faced their own challenges and fears, and yet they had persevered. They had used their gifts to protect, heal, and bring light to the darkness. And now, it was her turn.

Maya closed her eyes, feeling the elements swirling around her, responding to her silent command. She could sense their eagerness and readiness to follow her lead, and in that moment, she knew that she was ready, too.

When she opened her eyes, a new resolve was etched upon her features. She accepted her role, destiny, and the journey ahead. She knew it would not be easy and that there would be trials and challenges at every turn. But she also knew that she was not alone. She had the strength of her lineage behind her and her ancestors' wisdom guiding her steps.

With a deep breath, Maya stepped forward, ready to embrace her future. She had a realm to save and a balance to restore. With the elements at her command, she knew that anything was possible.

As Maya emerged from the cavern, the daylight seemed to greet her like an old friend. The sun's rays caressed her skin, warming her physically and emotionally. It was as if the world was welcoming her back, acknowledging the profound transformation she had undergone within the depths of the earth.

She took a deep breath, filling her lungs with the crisp, clean air. It tasted different now, richer somehow, as if she could sense the essence of life that permeated every molecule. With each exhale, she could feel the elements stirring within her, eager to be called upon and wielded with the skill and wisdom she had gained.

Maya looked out over the landscape before her, seeing it with new eyes. The trees swayed in the gentle breeze, their leaves rustling with a language she could now understand. The earth beneath her feet thrummed with a steady pulse, a heartbeat that echoed her own. And in the distance, a river wound its way through the terrain, its waters glinting in the sunlight like a ribbon of liquid silver.

Unable to resist the call of her newfound powers, Maya extended her hand, focusing her will on the earth before her. She coaxed a small mound to rise from the ground with a gentle tug, shaping it into a delicate spiral. The soil danced between her fingers, responding to her touch with an eagerness that filled her with wonder.

Next, she turned her attention to the river, reaching out with her senses to feel its flow. With a subtle gesture, she drew a stream of liquid from its course, guiding it through the air in a graceful arc. The water shimmered as it moved, catching the sunlight and refracting it into various colors.

Fire came next, a small flame blooming in her palm with a mere thought. Maya marveled at the warmth and light it cast upon her surroundings. She shaped the fire, molding it into intricate patterns that danced and flickered with a life of their own.

As she played with her abilities, Maya felt a profound sense of joy bubbling up within her. She was meant to do this, what she had been born to achieve. The knowledge of her lineage and the understanding of her destiny all clicked into place like pieces of a cosmic puzzle.

She knew that the path ahead would not be easy and that there would be challenges and obstacles to overcome. But armed with her newfound powers and the wisdom of her ancestors, Maya felt ready to face whatever lay ahead. She would master these abilities, hone them into tools of protection and balance, and fulfill her role, whatever it might entail, with the strength and determination that flowed through her veins.

Maya set forth with a smile and a fire in her heart, ready to embrace the future that awaited her. She had found her purpose, her place in the world, and nothing would stand in her way.

CHAPTER

FIFTEEN

Najran, Saudi Arabia

The scorching sun blazed above the airfield in Najran, Saudi Arabia, the shimmer of heat waves distorting the horizon as jet fuel fumes mingled with the desert air. Elan and Myst stood near a massive CH-53E Super Stallion helicopter, its rotors still as it awaited its passengers. Inside the cavernous belly of the aircraft, a Ford Raptor sat securely fastened, ready for the journey ahead.

A familiar figure approached the duo, her blonde hair whipping in the gentle breeze. Zoe, an old friend with an intimate knowledge of the desert, greeted them with a warm smile as she hugged her companions. "Elan, Myst, it's good to see you both," she said, her voice tinged with joy and solemnity.

Elan absent-mindedly smiled back, memories of his time in the Marine Corps rushing to the forefront as he gazed at the magnificent Super Stallion helicopter. "Zoe." Elan's voice softened. "Been too long. Thanks for dropping everything to come help."

Myst scanned the horizon, his jaw tight. "The Empty Quarter's not forgiving, Aunt Z. We need your expertise on this one."

Zoe's expression grew somber as she shifted her gaze between the two men. "I wish we were meeting under better circumstances," she said, her voice heavy with emotion. "I know you're caught up regarding Professor Xicato's death. I'm sure the Mazza sisters will get to the bottom of his murder."

Elan's jaw tightened, the pain of the professor's murder still fresh in his heart. "It's a tragedy," he said, his voice low. "We can't let his death be in vain. Have you heard from Maya? We discovered the name of the realm she traveled to is Aethoria."

Zoe's head snaps back with a sharp shake, her eyes blazing with determination. "No," she said firmly, her jaw set in determination. "We haven't heard from her since she ventured into… Aethoria." Her voice trembles with worry and anger as she adds, "But I'm sure she will uncover the truth about Nykronus and update us soon."

Myst pulled out the ancient compass, its surface glinting in the early morning light. "We've made some progress," he said, holding the artifact gently. "The compass has led us to hidden vaults and ancient texts that spoke of the gateway in Palawan and the second gateway we're about to uncover."

Zoe studied the compass, her brow furrowed in concentration. "And you believe this gateway can take us to Maya?" she asked, her gaze meeting Elan's.

Elan shrugged, his eyes filled with a mix of hope and concern. "I don't know," he said, his voice tight with emotion. "I hope so. If the legends are true, Aethoria is the key to understanding their fates."

Zoe placed a comforting hand on Elan's shoulder, her eyes shining with determination. "Then we'll find her," she said, her voice firm. "We'll follow the compass and uncover the secrets of the Empty Quarter. Together."

Myst tucked the compass back into his pocket as he watched his father admiring the massive helicopter. "Then let's get moving," he said, gesturing towards the waiting helicopter. "The desert awaits."

The helicopter descended upon a remote, desolate region deep within the Empty Quarter to coordinate the compass, which indicated they were nearing their destination. Elan, Myst, and Zoe disembarked as the rotors slowed, their eyes surveying the barren landscape. They unloaded the Ford Raptor and their belongings and set off towards a series of towering sand dunes that seemed to stretch endlessly into the horizon.

Myst consulted the ancient compass, its needle pointing steadily toward the heart of the dunes. They followed its guidance, the Raptor's powerful engine roaring as it navigated the treacherous terrain. Suddenly, the compass began to glow, and a shimmering mirage appeared in the distance.

As they approached the mirage, it solidified into a hidden structure, its walls adorned with intricate carvings and ancient symbols. They parked the Raptor and cautiously approached the entrance, their hands resting on their weapons.

Inside, the structure was cool and dimly lit, starkly contrasting to the searing heat outside. At the center of the room stood a towering mirror, its surface shimmering with an otherworldly glow. Surrounding the mirror were ancient statues of Roman gods, their stone eyes seeming to follow the trio as they moved through the space.

Elan approached a pedestal laden with ancient tomes, their pages brittle with age. He carefully opened one, his eyes scanning the faded text. "These books speak of a gateway," he said, his voice echoing in the stillness. "A portal to another realm."

Zoe and Myst joined him, their gazes falling upon the mirror. "Could this be it?" Zoe asked, her hand reaching out to touch the cold surface.

As her fingers brushed against the mirror, it began to ripple like water. The ancient statues seemed to come to life, their eyes glowing with an eerie light. Myst consulted the compass once more, its needle spinning wildly.

"The gateway," he breathed, his eyes wide with realization. "It's the mirror. This is it. Hopefully, a path to Maya—and Nykronus."

Side by side, they unraveled the secrets of the ancient text, their voices intoning in a steady rhythm. With each passing phrase, the mirror began to crack and splinter until it shattered into countless pieces, transforming into a solid stone archway. The room was electrified as they were pulled into the archway, replacing the mirror's spot with their bodies. Instantly, they were transported through the archway, leaving behind a swirling vortex of light and color.

As their eyes adjusted, they realized they were now in a parallel room, an exact replica of the previous one but clearly functioning as a library with shelves full of antique books and artifacts lining the walls. Zoe spun around, her eyes searching for an exit, but the only way out seemed to be the stone archway they had just emerged from. "Where are we?" she asked, her voice tinged with wonder and apprehension.

Myst and Elan exchanged a glance, their expressions mirroring the same uncertainty. They had crossed the threshold into a new realm, and the journey ahead was shrouded in mystery.

The walls of the library, filled with ancient books and artifacts, seemed to close in on Elan, Myst, and Zoe. The atmosphere felt stifling, like a prison. The air was heavy with the whispers of ages past, and an eerie silence hung over the room. They searched through the shelves, their fingers tracing the spines of books that seemed to hold the secrets of the universe.

Hours passed as they rummaged through the texts, their eyes straining in the dim light, fingers coated with centuries of dust as ancient leather bindings creaked beneath their touch. Dust motes danced in the air, and the musty smell of old paper filled their nostrils. Just as they were about to give up, Myst's hand brushed against a hidden compartment in one of the shelves. With a soft click, it opened, revealing a cryptic parchment.

Elan and Zoe gathered around as Myst carefully unrolled the fragile document. The parchment was covered in strange symbols and ancient languages, a puzzle waiting to be solved. They worked together, their minds racing as they deciphered the code.

As the meaning of the words became clear, their eyes widened in astonishment. The parchment spoke of a prophecy that linked Nykronus, Aethoria, and a powerful artifact once held by St. Michael himself. The artifact could seal dimensional gates, including the archway Maya passed through in Palawan.

But the prophecy held another revelation. The archway they had entered was different from the actual location of the second gate. The natural entrance to the other realm was shrouded in mystery, its location hidden from all but the most worthy.

Elan leaned back, his mind reeling from the implications of their discovery. "If this artifact seals gates..." Elan's voice dropped to a whisper. "We can't let the Assembly find it first. Maya would be trapped there. Forever."

Zoe nodded, her eyes scanning the parchment once more. "But where do we even begin to look for it?" she asked, her brow furrowed in concentration.

Elan stood up, his gaze fixed on the stone archway that had brought them to this strange library. "We start by finding the true location of the second gate," he said, his voice filled with determination. "And then we find the artifact. We need to look through *all* these books and study the artifacts."

Zoe pored over the ancient maps and astral charts, her eyes scanning the intricate lines and symbols that seemed to dance across the parchment. She traced her fingers along the ley lines, the invisible energy pathways crisscrossing the globe. As she studied the patterns, a realization began to dawn on her.

"Myst, come look at this," she called out, her voice tinged with excitement. "I think I'm onto something."

Myst looked up from the ancient tome he had been studying, his eyes widening as he saw the map Zoe was holding. He hurried over, his gaze following the lines she was pointing to.

"These ley lines," Zoe explained, "they seem to converge at specific points throughout history. And look here," she tapped a finger on a particular intersection, "this is where the artifact was last seen."

Myst's eyes widened as he began to connect the dots. He rushed back to the books he had been reading, flipping through the pages with urgency. "I think I found something, too," he said, his voice trembling with excitement. "These historical events, the ones that changed the course of human history, all seem to coincide with the artifact's appearances."

Elan, who had been quietly strategizing in the corner, looked up at the sound of their voices. He strode over, his eyes scanning the maps and books before them.

"So the artifact has been present during key events throughout history," he mused, his mind racing with the implications. "And these ley lines are like a roadmap to its power."

Zoe nodded, her green eyes shining with the thrill of discovery. "Exactly. If we map out these energy signatures, we can predict where the artifact will appear next."

Elan smiled as he considered the possibilities. "And if we can get to it before the Malefic Assembly, we might be able to use it to seal the gates before they get whatever they're looking for on the other side."

Zoe stressed the urgency, "We have to locate it before they do to ensure Maya's safe return to our world before it is sealed off."

Myst looked up from the books, his expression grave. "If the artifact is as powerful as these texts suggest, it could be dangerous in the wrong hands."

Elan nodded, his jaw clenched. "Then we'll just have to make sure it ends up in the right ones. Take pictures of everything, and carry whatever you think is important. Then let's go."

As Elan, Myst, and Zoe stepped through the archway, a blinding light engulfed them, and they felt the familiar sensation of being pulled apart. Moments later, they found themselves back in the ancient structure in the Empty Quarter, the desert heat hitting them like a wall.

Elan turned to look at the archway, his eyes widening as he watched it crumble before their eyes. The stones fell away, revealing nothing but solid rock behind them. "The path," he whispered, his voice filled with awe and dread. "It's gone. Everything in that library is lost forever."

Zoe and Myst exchanged a glance, the gravity of their situation sinking in, and the weight of their mission seemed to press down on them even more.

Suddenly, a static crackle filled the air, and a garbled voice echoed through the chamber. Myst pulled a small device from his pocket while listening to the intercepted communication.

"It's the Malefic Assembly," he said, his voice urgent. "They're talking about the artifact. They want to use its power to bring someone or something back to Earth."

Elan's jaw clenched, his mind racing with the implications. "And then they'll seal the gateways," he said, his voice tight with anger. "Trapping whatever they bring back here, with no way to banish it back to Aethoria."

Zoe's eyes widened, the realization hitting her like a punch to the gut. "And trapping Maya there too," she whispered, her voice trembling with fear.

The trio stood silently for a moment, the weight of their quest pressing down on them. They knew they were racing against time, and the stakes had never been higher.

Elan squared his shoulders, his eyes blazing with determination. "We can't let that happen," he said, his voice firm. "We have to find the artifact before they do. We have to ensure Maya's safety and stop the Malefic Assembly."

Elan, Myst, and Zoe gathered in a featureless hotel room in Najran, their faces illuminated by the glow of computer screens. They had called an emergency meeting with the Order's leaders, scattered across the globe but connected through secure video links.

Elan stood at the front of the room, his expression grave as he presented their findings. "We've uncovered a plot by the Malefic Assembly," he said, his voice steady despite the urgency of his words. "They seek to use an ancient artifact to bring something back from Aethoria and then seal the gateways, trapping it here on Earth."

The faces on the screens reacted with a mix of shock and concern. Kaira, her eyes fierce, leaned forward. "And what of Maya?" she asked, her voice tight with worry.

Myst stepped forward, his jaw set. "If they succeed, Maya will be trapped in Aethoria, with no way to return."

A heavy silence fell over the room as the weight of their words sank in. Reagan, her expression grim, spoke up. "We cannot allow this to happen," she said, his voice firm. "The Order must act swiftly to prevent this catastrophe. Kaira and I are doing what we can to find Professor Xicato's killer. Maybe they can give us answers."

Zoe nodded, her green eyes blazing with determination. "We need to mobilize all of our resources," she said, her voice ringing with conviction. "We must find the artifact before the Assembly does and ensure the safety of both our world and Maya."

The leaders on the screens murmured in agreement, their faces set with resolve. Stanley, his fingers flying over his keyboard, spoke up. "I'll coordinate our intelligence networks," he said, his voice focused. "We'll track the Assembly's movements and anticipate their next steps."

With a calculated expression, Olivia added, "I'll mobilize our strike teams. We'll be ready to move at a moment's notice."

Austin St. Pierre's weathered face joined Olivia onscreen, the former Special Forces operator's expression grim but determined.

Austin chimed in. "Elan, keep your head up, brother. I'm here for you. Whatever you need."

Elan looked around the room, his heart swelling with pride at the Order's unity and determination. "We face a grave threat," he said, his voice carrying the weight of leadership. But together, we'll prevail. The Order stands united against this darkness."

As the meeting concluded, the leaders signed off individually, their faces disappearing from the screens. Elan, Myst, and Zoe exchanged glances, the gravity of their mission settling upon their shoulders. They knew the coming days would test their resolve and skills, but they were ready to face whatever challenges lay ahead.

Elan, Myst, and Zoe stood in the bustling lobby of the King Khalid International Airport, their demeanors mixed with determination and apprehension. The weight of their mission hung heavy in the air, a palpable presence that seemed to press down on their shoulders.

Elan's gaze flicked through the departure boards, his eyes filled with apprehension. He turned to his companions, trying to calm his nerves by distracting himself from his anxiety. "We need to split up," he said, his voice low but firm. "Cover more ground. Follow the leads we have."

Myst nodded, instinctively reaching for the ancient compass around his neck. "I'll head to Rome," he said, his voice steady. "The Vatican archives might hold clues about the artifact's last known location."

Zoe, her green eyes blazing with resolve, spoke up. "I'll fly with you. When we get there, I'll head straight to the Order's headquarters in Benevento," she said, her tone decisive. I'll work with Olivia and Stanley on the ley lines and historical events. I'll coordinate our efforts from there and keep the lines of communication open."

Elan, his jaw set, looked at his companions. "And I'll go to Greece," he said, his mind already racing with the possibilities. "The ancient texts spoke of a connection between the artifact and the Oracle of Delphi."

They stood silently for a moment, the enormity of their task settling upon them like a shroud. They knew that the path ahead was fraught with danger, that the Malefic Assembly would stop at nothing to achieve their dark goals.

Their hearts raced with adrenaline as they stared at each other, knowing the immense weight of their responsibility. The fate of an entire civilization hung in the balance, and the burden rested solely on their shoulders. Failure was not an option, not when so much was at stake. They shared a determined nod, steeling themselves for the perilous task ahead. The world depended on their success, and they were willing to pay any price to ensure it.

Elan reached out, clasping Myst and Zoe's hands firmly. "We'll find the artifact," he said, his voice filled with a quiet intensity. "We'll stop the Assembly and make sure Maya makes it home."

Myst and Zoe agreed, their expressions emulating Elan's boldness. They knew that they were stronger together, that their bond was unbreakable.

As they parted ways, each heading towards their separate destinations, the weight of their mission pressed heavily on their shoulders. The fate of two worlds hung in the balance.

Three days later, Myst navigated the crowded streets of Rome, his senses on high alert. The ancient city's bustling energy thrummed around him, but he couldn't shake the feeling that he was being watched. As he wove through the marketplace, his hand never strayed far from the concealed weapon.

Suddenly, a flicker of movement caught his eye. A man in a dark suit was pushing through the crowd, his gaze locked on Myst. Myst's heart raced as he realized the Malefic Assembly had found him.

The man reached into his jacket, and Myst reacted instinctively. He dove to the side, knocking over a fruit stand as he rolled to his feet. Civilians screamed and scattered as more Assembly agents emerged from the crowd, their weapons drawn.

Myst's mind raced as he assessed the situation, years of training crystallizing into instant decisions. Tourist families scattered around him, and street vendors dove for cover - too many innocent lives in the crossfire. A full-scale battle would be catastrophic.

He needed to end this quickly and quietly.

He ducked behind a stone column, eyes scanning the marketplace for an escape route. The Assembly agents were closing in, their footsteps echoing on the cobblestones.

Myst's gaze fell on a nearby alleyway, and he knew it was his only chance. With a deep breath, he sprinted from his cover, weaving through the panicked crowd as bullets whizzed past his head.

Breathless and heart-pounding, he dashed into the narrow alleyway, his mind racing as he tried to outrun the ruthless Assembly agents hot on his heels. Suddenly, one of them caught up to him, and they grappled fiercely, the agent drawing a glinting knife with murderous intent. Myst whipped out a dagger from his hilt in a split-second decision and countered the attacks with lethal precision. His baneful blow landed squarely on the assailant's jaw, knocking them back with a sickening crunch. As the dazed attacker stumbled to their feet and made a desperate attempt to flee, Myst lunged forward and grabbed them by their coat collar, only for them to slip out of it like a slippery toad. With gritted teeth, Myst watched as they disappeared into the shadows. But then his eyes landed on a small piece of paper sticking out of the abandoned jacket's inner pocket. He snatched and unfolded it, revealing a detailed map covered in strange symbols and cryptic notes, making his blood run cold. He didn't have time to decipher it now, but he knew it held crucial information that could potentially save his life.

Stuffing the map into his pocket, Myst turned to face his pursuers. They emerged from the alley, their weapons trained on him. Myst raised his hands in surrender, his mind racing as he tried to find a way out.

But before the agents could move, a sudden commotion erupted in the marketplace behind them. Myst seized his chance, lunging forward and disarming the nearest agent with a swift kick. He spun, using the agent as a human shield as he backed towards the opposite end of the alley.

The other agents hesitated, unwilling to risk hitting their comrade. Myst took advantage of their momentary confusion, shoving the agent towards them and sprinting away.

As he ran, Myst's mind reeled with the implications of the map in his pocket. The Assembly was closer to their goal than he had realized, and time was running out. He needed to get this information to Benevento before it was too late.

Elan stood at the base of Mount Parnassus, his heart pounding with anticipation and trepidation. The ancient site of Delphi, once home to the famed Oracle, loomed before him, its crumbling ruins a testament to the passage of time. As he climbed the worn stone steps, Elan couldn't shake the feeling that he was being watched, that some timeless presence was observing his every move.

At the top of the steps, he found himself in a small, circular clearing surrounded by towering columns and ancient statues. In the center of the clearing stood a figure cloaked in shimmering white robes. Elan approached cautiously, his hand instinctively reaching for *Winterstar*.

The figure turned, and Elan looked into eyes that seemed to hold the wisdom of the ages. The guardian's voice was soft, yet it carried an undeniable weight. "You seek the artifact," the guardian said, their tone measured and cryptic. "But do you understand the consequences of your quest?"

Elan grew frustrated, his mind racing with questions. "I know what's at stake," he said, his voice firm despite his uncertainty. "The Malefic Assembly can't be allowed to succeed."

The guardian remained motionless, their expression unreadable. "The artifact holds great power," they said, echoing in the stillness of the clearing. "In the wrong hands, it could bring about a catastrophe beyond imagining. The very fabric of reality could be torn asunder."

Elan's heart raced at the guardian's words, the gravity of his mission pressing down on him like a physical weight. He knew that the consequences of failure were too terrible to contemplate.

The guardian took a step towards him, their robes glistening in the bright sunlight. "You must prove your worth," they declared, their tone growing more intense. "The trials ahead will measure your wisdom, courage, and determination. Only then will you be prepared to confront the obstacles that await you. Therefore, I cannot intervene any further. There are no more solutions to be found here. Leave before it's too late."

Elan knew that the guardian's words were not to be taken lightly, that the world's fate rested on his shoulders. As he turned to leave the clearing, he could feel the weight of the guardian's gaze upon him.

Elan arrived at the entrance of the Order's headquarters in Benevento, greeted by Myst and Zoe, their faces etched with a mix of weariness and determination. The ancient stone walls seemed to hum with an energy, a palpable sense of purpose that permeated the air.

As they entered the central chamber, they found Olivia and Stanley deep in discussion, their voices hushed. Maps and ancient texts littered the large wooden table, a testament to the hours of research and analysis they consumed.

Zoe stepped forward, her green eyes blazing with resolve. "What have you found?" she asked, her voice cutting through the tense silence.

Olivia looked up, her expression grim. "The Assembly is moving faster than we anticipated," she said, tracing a line on one of the maps. "They're closing in on the artifact's location."

Stanley nodded, his fingers flying over his keyboard. "But we've uncovered a pattern," he said, his voice tinged with a hint of triumph. "Their movements, the locations they've targeted... it all points to a specific site."

Elan leaned forward, his gaze intense. "Where?" he asked, his voice low and urgent.

Olivia pointed to a spot on the map, tapping the ancient parchment. "Here," she said, her voice filled with a quiet certainty. "The Temple of the Timeless."

"It's in France, hidden underneath one of the ancient temples of the Knights Templar. And of course, I'm coming with you. I might have even been a Templar Knight in a past life," Stanley Wyatt chuckled.

Myst's eyes widened, recognition dawning on his face. "The map from Rome," he said, his voice barely above a whisper. "It had the same symbol."

Zoe nodded, her mind racing with the implications. "Then that's where we need to go," she said, her voice filled with determination. "We can't let the Assembly get their hands on the artifact."

Elan looked around the room, his gaze meeting each of his companions. "We've come this far," he said, his voice steady and resolute. "We won't fail now. The Order stands united, and we'll stop the Assembly and protect the realms."

CHAPTER

SIXTEEN

San Francisco, California

Kaira and Reagan stood in Professor Xicato's office, where yellow police tape slashed across the doorway like fresh wounds. Papers scattered across the floor told the story of a struggle, each crumpled sheet a silent witness to their friend's final moments. The familiar space, once alive with the professor's enthusiastic theories and warm laughter, now felt hollow with his absence.

Kaira's eyes scanned the room, her mind racing with questions and possibilities. She knew that the professor's work held the key to unraveling the mystery surrounding his death. Reagan, ever the methodical investigator, began sifting through the papers, her industrious eyes searching for any missed clues.

As they searched deeper into the professor's research, Kaira's attention was drawn to a stack of cryptic notes tucked away in a drawer. Kaira traced the ancient symbols etched into Professor Xicato's journal. According to his notes, the artifact wasn't just a religious relic but a key that could bridge the gap between life and death. No wonder Lazarus, a man who had already cheated death once, would kill to possess it. The handwriting was unmistakably Xicato's, but the contents were far more intriguing than his usual academic work.

Reagan leaned over Kaira's shoulder, deep in concentration. "This artifact... it sounds similar to the one Elan and the others have been researching," she remarked, her voice imbued with a mix of curiosity and worry.

Kaira sighed, her mind already connecting the dots. "And this Lazarus... whoever they are, they seem to be connected to it all somehow," she said, her fingers outlining the faded ink on the yellowed pages.

A sense of urgency gripped Kaira and Reagan as they pored over the professor's notes. The murder, the artifact, and the enigmatic figure of Lazarus were all pieces of a colossal puzzle that threatened the very fabric of their world. They were acutely aware of the need to act swiftly to uncover the truth before it was too late. The killer of Professor Xicato was already a step ahead, and time was not on their side.

Kaira and Reagan found themselves in a series of tense, closed-door meetings with members of the Order and close associates of Professor Xicato. The atmosphere was thick with suspicion and unease as they meticulously interviewed each individual, searching for inconsistencies or hidden motives in their relationships with the late professor. The tension in the room was palpable, adding to the weight of their investigation.

In a brightly lit room, they sat across from a quivering young man, one of Xicato's research assistants. Kaira leaned forward, her eyes narrowed. "Tell us about the professor's recent work. Did you notice anything unusual or out of character?"

The assistant shifted uncomfortably in his seat, his gaze darting between the two women. "He... he had been spending a lot of time in the archives, pouring over ancient texts and manuscripts. It was like he was consumed by something, a newfound obsession."

Reagan raised an eyebrow, her pen poised over her notepad. "Obsession? With what exactly?"

The assistant hesitated, his hands clasped tightly in his lap. "He kept mentioning a prophecy, something about a figure named Lazarus. At first, I thought it was just another biblical reference, but the way he spoke about it... it was like he believed Lazarus was a real person, someone dangerous."

Kaira and Reagan shared a look of recognition, the puzzle pieces slowly falling into place. They pressed further, but the assistant's information needed to be improved. His knowledge only scratched the surface of the professor's final days.

As they moved from one interview to the next, a pattern began to emerge. Each person they spoke to had noticed a change in Professor Xicato's demeanor, a growing preoccupation with this ancient prophecy, and the mystifying figure of Lazarus. Yet, no one seemed to have the full picture, only fragments of a larger, more megalomaniacal truth.

In the final interview, a reluctant informant, a close confidant of the professor, finally shed some light on the matter. "He believed it was Lazarus from the Bible. The beggar. Not St. Lazarus of Bethany. He swore that Lazarus was not just a myth or a story, but a very real and dangerous individual," the informant confessed, their voice trembling. "He was convinced that this prophecy held the key to understanding Lazarus's true nature and the threat he posed to our world."

Kaira and Reagan huddled over a disorganized desk in Professor Xicato's private office at Sapienza University, their faces illuminated by the glow of ancient texts and modern screens. The room was a temporary headquarters, away from the nosy eyes of those who had known and worked with the late professor. The air was thick with the musty scent of old books and the hum of computers, a strange juxtaposition of the ancient and the modern.

They delved into the depths of historical records and secret archives, piecing together fragments of information about the biblical figure of Lazarus. As they read, a picture began to emerge—a man who had risen from obscurity, driven by an insatiable hunger for forbidden knowledge. Kaira's brow furrowed as she studied the ancient manuscript, her finger tracing symbols that seemed to pulse with hidden meaning beneath the faded ink. "It says here that Lazarus was not content with the limitations of mortal life. He sought power beyond the grasp of ordinary men."

Reagan leaned in, her eyes scanning the text. "And look at this," she said, pointing to a passage. "It mentions an artifact, one that Lazarus believed could grant him the power he craved. But it also warns that in his hands, the artifact's uses would be unpredictable, even dangerous."

As they continued their research, a disturbing realization began to dawn on them. Lazarus's influence had been spreading silently within their own ranks, a testament to his power and reach. They found references to his name in coded messages and whispers of his teachings in the margins of ancient texts. It was as if he had been watching them, waiting for the right moment to strike.

Kaira sat back in her chair, her mind racing with the implications of their discovery. "If Lazarus has infiltrated the Order, then no one is safe. We have to find a way to stop him before it's too late."

Reagan nodded, her jaw set with determination. "And we have to do it quickly. If he gets his hands on that artifact, there's no telling what he'll do with it."

They looked at each other, a silent understanding passing between them. They had to uncover the truth about Lazarus and stop him before he could ruin their world.

Kaira and Reagan stood at the edge of Lake Bolsena, the moonlight casting a ghostly reflection on the water's surface. The secluded area was the perfect place for an emergency meeting with the Order's inner council, away from snooping eyes and ears. The wind was calm, but the mood was set with tension as they prepared to present their findings, evidence of internal betrayal and manipulation that threatened the very foundation of their organization.

As the council members arrived, their faces etched with concern and curiosity, Kaira and Reagan exchanged a knowing glance. They knew what they would reveal would send shockwaves through the leadership. Still, they also knew it was necessary for the survival of the Order.

Kaira stepped forward, her voice steady and clear. "We have uncovered a web of deceit within our own ranks," she began, her eyes scanning the faces of the council members. "Someone has been working in the shadows, manipulating events and spreading the influence of Lazarus."

The council erupted into a cacophony of voices, some expressing disbelief, others demanding proof. Reagan held up a hand, silencing the room. "We have evidence," she said, her voice unfaltering. "Coded messages, hidden references, and a trail of clues that lead back to one of our own."

The council members' faces grew increasingly somber as they presented their findings. Some shook their heads in disbelief, while others looked at each other with suspicion. Kaira and Reagan knew that they had to navigate the delicate politics of the Order, advocating for unity and vigilance in the face of this new threat.

"We can't allow fear and paranoia to divide us," Kaira said, her voice rising above the hushed voices of the council. "We must stand together, now more than ever, and root out this corruption before it destroys us from within."

But even as she spoke, she could see the skepticism and resistance in the eyes of some of the council members. They feared a witch hunt, a purge that would tear the Order apart. Reagan stepped forward, her voice calm and measured. "We are not suggesting a purge," she said, her eyes meeting those of the skeptics. "But we must be vigilant, be careful who you trust and who you talk to. We need to act swiftly to protect our own."

Kaira and Reagan walked through the serene gardens of the Order's estate, the tranquil surroundings a stark counterpoint to the turmoil in their hearts. The weight of their investigation hung heavy on their shoulders as they contemplated the consequences of their actions.

Reagan sat on a stone bench, her stare fixed on the gentle ripples of the nearby pond. "If we push too hard, we risk fracturing the Order," she said, her voice barely above a whisper. "The council is already divided, and our accusations could tear us apart."

Kaira paced back and forth, her mind racing with the possibilities. "But if we pull back now, Lazarus will only grow stronger," she argued, her hands clenched at her sides. "We can't let him advance his plans unchecked. Professor Xicato's murder cannot go unanswered."

They fell silent, each lost in their own thoughts. The gentle rustling of leaves and the distant chirping of birds seemed to mock the gravity of their situation. Kaira sat down beside Reagan, her eyes searching her sister's face for guidance.

"We have to do what's right," Reagan said finally, her voice resonant with conviction. "Professor Xicato dedicated his life to the Order, to protecting the world from the forces of darkness. We owe it to him to see this through, no matter the cost."

Kaira nodded, her resolve strengthening. "We'll get justice for the professor, even if it means facing opposition from within the Order," she declared, her eyes blazing with determination. "We can't let fear or politics stand in the way of what's right."

They sat there for a moment, their decision made, their commitment to the Order's principles unwavering. They knew that the path ahead would be difficult and that they would face resistance and skepticism at every turn. But they also knew that they had each other and that they would see this through to the end.

As they rose to leave the garden, Kaira placed a hand on Reagan's shoulder. "We'll do this together," Kaira said, gripping her sister's shoulder. "For Xicato." She didn't need to list the others - family, Order, the world. Reagan's eyes said she understood exactly what was at stake.

Reagan struggled to hold back tears as she leaned into her older sister for support, a faint smile spreading across her face. "Together," she agreed, and together, they walked back towards the Order's headquarters, ready to face whatever challenges lay ahead. "I love you so much, Kaira. I don't know how I could keep it together without you."

The Mazza sisters slipped into a forgotten library in Rome, a place lost to time and memory. Dust coated the shelves, and the musty scent of old books filled the air. In the dim light, they spotted a figure waiting in the shadows, his face obscured by a hood.

The figure stepped forward as they approached, revealing himself as Erikson Ghostcloak, a name whispered in the professor's old journals. His eyes, a piercing blue, held a mixture of determination and pain.

"I knew Professor Xicato," Erikson said, his voice low and gravelly. "He was a good man, dedicated to stopping Lazarus."

Kaira and Reagan exchanged a glance, surprised by this unexpected ally. "How did you know him?" Kaira asked, her voice cautious.

Erikson's jaw clenched, a flicker of anger crossing his face. "Lazarus took something from me, something I can never get back. The professor was helping me track him down, to stop him before he could hurt anyone else."

He pulled out a worn, leather-bound journal from his cloak, handing it to Reagan. "This was the professor's personal journal. He left it with me before he died, said it held the key to understanding Lazarus's true motivations."

Reagan flipped through the pages, her eyes widening as she read the cryptic entries. "The artifact," she breathed, looking up at Kaira. "It's not just a source of power. It's a key to something much bigger, something Lazarus has been searching for his entire life."

Erikson nodded, his face etched with dogged persistence. "Lazarus believes the artifact will grant him access to a realm beyond our own, a place where he can reshape reality and bring something…or someone…back. What? I don't know. The professor was close to finding it, but Lazarus got to him first."

Kaira's mind raced with the implications of this revelation. "We have to find the artifact before Lazarus does," she said, her voice urgent. "But we don't even know where to start looking."

Erikson leaned forward, his eyes intense. "I have a lead, a possible location. But it's dangerous, and we'll need to work together if we want to stand a chance against Lazarus and his followers."

Kaira and Reagan looked at each other, a silent conversation passing between them. They knew the risks, but they also knew that they couldn't let Lazarus succeed. With a nod, they turned back to Erikson, ready to forge an alliance that could change the course of their fight against the darkness.

Kaira and Reagan led Erikson through a labyrinth of dimly lit corridors, descending deeper into the bowels of the Order's headquarters. Their surroundings grew tense as they navigated the dark, empty passageways, their footsteps echoing off the stone walls. Finally, they arrived at a heavy wooden door, its surface etched with intricate symbols and runes.

Kaira pushed the door open, revealing a hidden chamber bathed in the soft glow of flickering candles. A large, round table dominated the center of the room, its surface covered in maps, ancient texts, and scribbled notes. Erikson's eyes widened as he took in the sight, a mixture of awe and apprehension on his face.

"This is where we plan our most sensitive operations," Reagan explained, gesturing for Erikson to take a seat at the table. "Only a handful of people know of its existence."

Kaira unfurled a large map, its surface marked with red circles and cryptic annotations. "Based on Professor Xicato's journals," Kaira said carefully, watching Erikson's reaction, "we believe the artifact is hidden in catacombs that ancient texts associate with Jerusalem." She deliberately kept vague the true location she and Reagan had discovered in the professor's private notes.

Knowing the catacombs were not truly in Jerusalem, she also knew they couldn't trust the mysterious Ghostcloak. Reagan leaned forward, her eyes intense. "But we can't just go in and retrieve it. Lazarus and his followers will be watching, waiting for us to make a move."

Erikson nodded, his brow furrowed in thought. "We need to draw them out, force them to reveal themselves."

Kaira's lips curled into a sly smile. "And that's exactly what we're going to do. We'll let it be known that we've recovered the artifact, but we'll make it seem like we're vulnerable, unprepared for an attack."

Reagan picked up the thread, her voice low and conspiratorial. "We'll stage a small, seemingly underprepared team to retrieve the artifact. Lazarus won't be able to resist the opportunity to strike."

Erikson leaned back in his chair, his eyes narrowed. "But we'll be ready for them."

Kaira nodded, her face displaying iron will. "We'll have our best fighters hidden in the shadows, waiting to ambush them when they make their move."

The three of them spent the next several hours poring over the map, discussing strategies and contingencies. They debated the best location for the ambush, the optimal number of fighters to deploy, and the most effective weapons to use against Lazarus's followers.

As the candles burned lower and the night wore on, a sense of relentless drive settled over the room. They knew the risks they were taking, the danger they were inviting. But they also knew that they had no choice. Lazarus had to be stopped, no matter the cost.

Finally, after hours of building a strategy, they sat back, exhausted but satisfied. The plan was set, and the trap was laid. All that remained was to see if Lazarus would take the bait.

As the Order prepared to spring their trap, Kaira and Reagan stalked through the halls like hunters, their faces set with fierce tenacity. They checked and double-checked every detail, ensuring that nothing was left to chance. The fighters were in position, hidden in the shadows, ready to strike at a moment's notice.

But even as they made their final preparations, an unexpected attack shattered the anticipatory silence. Alarms blared through the base of operations as the Order's defenses were breached. Kaira and Reagan raced to the command center, their hearts pounding in their chests.

On the screens, they saw a swarm of Lazarus's followers, their eyes glowing with an unnatural light. They moved with an inhuman speed and coordination, tearing through the Order's outer defenses like they were made of paper.

Kaira barked orders into the comms, deploying the Order's fighters to repel the attack. Reagan's fingers flew across the keyboard, activating the headquarters' emergency protocols. The air crackled with energy as the Order's mystical defenses sprang to life.

The battle consumed every corridor of the headquarters. Order fighters fell back step by step, their enchanted weapons striking sparks against the relentless advance of Lazarus's followers. The air became electrified with spent spells and the metallic tang of blood.

Kaira's sword sang through the air as she dodged a follower's attack, her blade leaving trails of blue fire in its wake. She spun past another attacker, but two more appeared from the shadows for every follower she struck down. Her arms burned with fatigue, and the bitter taste of defeat rose in her throat.

Reagan stood at her side, casting powerful spells to keep the enemy at bay. Her staff glowed with an otherworldly energy as she chanted ancient incantations. But despite her efforts, more and more of

Lazarus's followers seemed to appear out of thin air, overwhelming their defense.

The Knights were beginning to falter, their energy draining with each strike they landed against their formidable foes. Kaira could see the desperation in their eyes as they tried to hold on, but it was becoming clear that they needed reinforcements.

Just when all hope seemed lost, a war horn echoed through the corridors. Kaira's heart soared as Kyran's aerial division appeared on their winged steeds, diving from the heavens like avenging angels.

As the battle raged on, Kaira caught Reagan's eye, sharing a moment of silent concern. The Lazarus followers seemed to have endless soldiers, and the Order's fighters were becoming fatigued. But they continued to fight, refusing to give in to despair.

Erikson, who had joined the Order not long ago, proved himself to be a skilled fighter. His sword flashed in the dim light, cutting down multiple assailants with each strike. Kaira felt a surge of pride for her new ally.

But despite their efforts, the Lazarus followers continued to push forward. Their numbers were too great for the Order to handle alone. Kaira knew they needed a new plan to give them an edge in this seemingly hopeless situation.

She turned to Reagan and whispered urgently in her ear. She nodded with steely resolve and relayed her plan to the other Knights.

Kaira began chanting a powerful incantation, drawing on all of her magical energy as she spoke ancient words of power. The air around her crackled with energy as she finished the incantation and lifted her hands towards their enemy.

A burst of blinding light shot out from Kaira's hands, enveloping the Lazarus followers in its dazzling glow. They cried out in pain and confusion as they stumbled backward, blinded by the sudden burst of light.

Reagan took advantage of this momentary distraction and shouted for their fighters to press forward. They surged through the ranks of their enemies, cutting them down with renewed vigor.

As they fought together with renewed strength and determination, Kaira couldn't help but feel a sense of hope swell within her chest. The

Knights of St. Michael were not just skilled warriors – they were also united by a strong bond forged through years of fighting side by side against evil forces.

And that bond gave them strength when all else seemed lost.

The tide began to turn as more and more Lazarus followers fell under the Order's blades. The remaining attackers, sensing defeat, started to retreat. But even as they gained the upper hand, Kaira and Reagan couldn't shake the feeling that something was wrong.

This attack was too sudden and too well-coordinated. Lazarus had caught them off guard, striking at the very heart of their operations. As they watched the battle unfold on the screens, a chilling realization began to dawn on them.

Lazarus wasn't just a rogue agent, a lone wolf seeking power for himself. He was part of something much more significant, a greater threat that had been lurking in the shadows all along. The artifact, the prophecy, and the whispers of a realm beyond their own pointed to a conflict that was only beginning.

As the last of Lazarus's followers fell and the Order's fighters regrouped, Kaira and Reagan shared a knowing glance, the weight of understanding heavy between them. They had won the battle, but the war was far from over. Lazarus was merely the harbinger of what was to come, and they would need all their strength and cunning to face the challenges that lay ahead.

Kaira and Reagan stood amidst the ruins of the battle exhausted. The once pristine grounds of the Order's headquarters were now littered with debris and the fallen bodies of Lazarus's followers. The smell of the air hung heavy with the acrid scent of smoke and the metallic tang of blood.

Kaira surveyed the damage, her heart heavy with the weight of the lives lost and the destruction wrought. She knew that this was only the beginning, that Lazarus's attack was merely a prelude to the greater conflict that loomed on the horizon. But even in the face of such overwhelming odds, she refused to give in to despair.

Reagan stepped up beside her, her eyes hard with determination. "We can't let this break us," she said. "Lazarus may have caught us off guard, but we won't let him win."

Kaira nodded, her resolve strengthening with each passing moment. "We have to find out what he's really after," she said, her mind racing with possibilities. "The artifact, the prophecy, the realm beyond our own - it's all connected somehow."

They both knew that they couldn't trust Erikson completely. Although he had fought alongside them during the battle, his motives remained unclear. Was he truly an ally, or was he playing some deeper game?

But even with the uncertainty surrounding Erikson, Kaira, and Reagan, they knew they had no choice but to press on. They had to uncover the full extent of Lazarus's plan to protect the Order and prevent the foretold cataclysm.

"We'll need to be careful," Reagan said, her eyes scanning the ruins for any sign of movement. "Lazarus will be watching our every move, waiting for us to make a mistake."

Kaira's jaw clenched with determination. "Then we'll just have to be smarter than him," she said, her voice ringing with conviction. "We'll use every resource at our disposal, follow every lead until we find the truth."

They stood there for a moment, their resolve unshakeable, their dedication to the Order and to each other unwavering. They knew the path ahead would be fraught with danger and uncertainty, but they also knew they had no choice but to see it through.

With a final shared look that spoke volumes between sisters, Kaira and Reagan turned back towards the ruins of their headquarters. The path ahead would be long and arduous, but they would face it as they had faced everything else - together. The battle may have been lost, but the war was far from over, and they would not rest until Lazarus was stopped and the Order was safe once more.

SEVENTEEN

Maya ventured deep into the heart of a mystical forest, her footsteps muffled by the lush, verdant undergrowth. The air hummed with unseen energy as twin moons painted the landscape in layers of silver and pearl. A strange force pulled at her essence as she pushed through the dense foliage, drawing her toward a clearing that pulsed with ancient power.

Ancient ruins rose before her, their weathered stones pulsating with a rhythm that seemed to match the beating of her own heart. The architect in Maya admired the design and intricacies as they displayed something she had never seen before in all her years. Maya's breath caught in her throat as she stepped into the clearing, the air around her shimmering like a mirage. The ground beneath her feet suddenly illuminated, revealing intricate symbols that danced and swirled with a life of their own.

Maya gasped as the symbols resonated deep within her soul. The magic in the air whispered ancient truths, awakening dormant parts of her being that she had never known existed. It was as if the very essence of the realm was reaching out to her, inviting her to tap into its power.

Maya felt a rush of exhilaration and wonder as the energy coursed through her body. She could sense the realm's life force pulsing and flowing around her like an invisible current. The ruins seemed to whisper ancient secrets, tales of lost civilizations, forgotten magics, and the struggles of those who had come before her. The symbols on the ground glowed ever brighter, responding to her presence.

At that moment, Maya realized that this was no ordinary awakening. It was the beginning of a deeper connection with the magic of this mystical realm, a connection that would shape her destiny and the fate of all those around her. This connection wasn't just about power, but about understanding, empathy, and responsibility. As she stood there, bathed in the light of the twin moons, Maya knew that her journey had only just begun and that the true extent of her powers, and the challenges they would bring, was yet to be revealed.

Maya followed Asha through swaying silver grass to the edge of a crystalline lake, where the twin moons' reflection rippled like liquid starlight. The realm's essence wove through the air in melodic threads, humming ancient lullabies that stirred something deep within Maya's soul.

Asha sat by the shore, her glowing fur casting a warm light on the ground around her, her tail wagging and swirling colors into the night sky. "Come, Maya," she said, her voice soft yet filled with wisdom. "Sit with me and let the water speak to you."

Maya settled beside her feline companion, crossing her legs and taking a deep breath. She closed her eyes, allowing her senses to extend outwards, just as Asha had taught her.

At first, there was only the gentle lapping of the water against the shore. But as Maya focused, she began to feel something more. It was as if the lake was alive, its memories and emotions swirling beneath the surface.

Images flashed through her mind, snippets of the realm's history playing out like a movie. Once again, she saw ancient civilizations rising and falling, their stories engrained into the very being of the water. She felt the joy and sorrow of countless beings who had come before her, their experiences woven into the complexity of Aethoria.

As the visions continued, Maya began to understand the true nature of her powers. It wasn't just about manipulating the elements or casting spells. It was about connecting with the essence of magic itself, the life force flowing through every creature and object in the realm.

With each passing moment, Maya felt more attuned to this energy. She could sense the interconnectedness of all things, the way every action and thought rippled into the world around her.

When she finally opened her eyes, Maya was filled with a sense of awe and wonder. The beauty of the realm, the interconnectedness of all things, it was all so overwhelming. She turned to Asha, who was watching her with a knowing smile.

"You see now, don't you?" the feline said, her eyes glinting in the starlight. "Your powers are a gift, a way to understand and connect with the world around you. Use them wisely, Maya, and you will find the path you seek." Her words were filled with wisdom, a guiding light in the darkness.

The twin moons vanished behind gathering storm clouds, sending waves of unease through Maya's body. The wind began to howl, whipping through the trees with a savagery that sent shivers from head to toe. In the distance, she could see a small village nestled in the valley, its inhabitants blissfully unaware of the impending danger.

Maya's heart raced as the storm intensified, its fury building like a tidal wave. Lightning ripped across the sky, bathing the landscape in an otherworldly glow. Lightning crackled across the sky, illuminating the landscape in a harsh, unnatural light. The air crackled with an energy that Maya could feel in her very bones, a raw and primal force that threatened to consume everything in its path.

Asha appeared at Maya's side, her glowing fur standing on end. "The storm is no ordinary tempest," the feline warned, her voice barely audible above the roaring wind. "It is a manifestation of the realm's imbalance, a cry for help from the very essence of magic itself."

Maya nodded, her eyes fixed on the approaching chaos. She knew what she had to do. With a deep breath, she stepped forward, walking toward the heart of the storm. Each step was a battle against the raging winds, but Maya pressed on, her determination unwavering.

At the maelstrom's center, Maya closed her eyes and extended her consciousness into the storm's heart. She could sense the storm's anger, its pain, its desperation. It was a living, breathing entity, lashing out in a primal attempt to communicate its distress.

Words of power flowed from Maya's lips, each syllable resonating with quiet authority. She said to the storm, her words carried on the wind, reaching out to the very essence of the tempest. She acknowledged its pain, its confusion, and its fear. She offered understanding, compassion, and a promise of balance.

As her words flowed, the storm began to calm. The winds died down to a gentle breeze, and the lightning faded into the distance. The clouds parted, revealing a sky filled with stars, their light reflecting off the tranquil surface of the nearby lake.

Maya opened her eyes, a sense of accomplishment and fearlessness washing over her. She had done it. She had not only understood the storm but had also shaped its essence, guiding it back to a state of harmony. In that moment, she realized the true extent of her powers - not just to perceive the realm's magic, but to influence it, to protect and nurture the delicate balance that sustained all life.

The last rays of sunset pierced the forest canopy, illuminating a structure that seemed to materialize from thin air. It seemed utterly out of place in the strange world of Aethoria. She walked around the building, searching for an entrance but finding none. Determined, she closed her eyes and summoned all the knowledge she had gained about the magic in and around her, and just like that, a door materialized on the north wall of the structure.

The door swung open with a whisper of ancient magic, revealing a time-worn library that took her breath away. Its walls were adorned with endless collections of artifacts and books, radiating an ethereal glow from within. The air was heavy with the aroma of ancient parchment and the hum of mystical energy, enveloping Maya in awe as she stepped into this hallowed place.

In the center of the room, her gaze fixated on a pile of shattered stone pieces, as if some crucial structure had been destroyed. The previous library occupants had left their books scattered and open all around. As she looked around, she noticed there were several missing volumes. She couldn't help but let her mind wander, thinking of who may have occupied this room. It had been weeks, maybe even months, since she had seen a familiar face. Questions about her family's well-being plagued her mind. Still, she quickly refocused on her mission at hand - to uncover more about Aethoria, herself, and the fate of Nykronus.

She ran her fingers along the spines of the books, marveling at the intricate symbols and runes etched into their covers. Each one seemed to tell her secrets, inviting her to delve into its mysteries.

One particular tome caught her eye, its cover pulsing with a soft, inviting glow. Maya carefully lifted it from the shelf, its weight heavy in her hands. As she opened the book, the pages seemed to come alive, the words dancing across the parchment in a mesmerizing display.

Maya began to read, her eyes widening with each passing sentence. The tome spoke of a figure known as "The Guardian," a being prophesied to bridge the realms and balance the forces of magic. The Guardian was described as a wielder of immense power, a conduit for the very essence of Aethoria itself.

As she delved deeper into the text, Maya couldn't help but notice the parallels between her own journey and the descriptions of The Guardian. The way her powers had grown and evolved and her connection with the very fabric of the realm aligned perfectly with the prophecy.

Maya's mind raced as she considered the implications. Could it be that her entire life had been leading up to this moment? That her destiny was intertwined with the fate of Aethoria itself?

She thought back to the challenges she had faced and the trials she had overcome. Each one seemed to have prepared her for this role, honing her skills and deepening her understanding of the magical world around her.

As she sat there, bathed in the soft glow of the ancient tomes, Maya felt a sense of purpose settle over her. Whether she was indeed The Guardian or not, she knew that her journey had brought her to this point for a reason. And she was determined to see it through, to unravel the mysteries of Aethoria and fulfill whatever destiny lay before her.

As Maya stood in the library, lost in thought, a sudden movement caught her eye. To her surprise, a door materialized on the south side of the room, its surface shimmering with an inviting light. Curiosity piqued, she stepped through the threshold and found herself in a serene garden, unlike anything she had ever seen.

Crystal flowers chimed like ethereal bells, rainbow-refracting petals dancing harmoniously with luminous vines that twisted in impossible fractals. Each plant pulsed with its own consciousness, whispering ancient secrets into the perfumed air. As Maya walked among them, she could feel their essence reaching her, inviting her to listen and learn.

Asha appeared at Maya's side, her glowing fur casting a soft light on the surrounding foliage. The feline's eyes sparkled with understanding as she observed Maya's awe-struck expression.

"This garden is a sacred place," Asha explained, her voice gentle yet filled with gravity. "It is here that the secrets of the realm are shared with those who have the gift to hear them."

Maya turned to her companion, her brow furrowed in confusion. "What do you mean, Asha? What gift?"

With her regal appearance like a miniature lion, the feline emitted a black and orange aura that radiated around her. She seemed to smile, her tail swishing in an enchanting rhythm. "Your ability to connect with the essence of Aethoria, Maya. It is a rare and precious thing, a power that few possess."

The plants around them began to sway more intently as if on cue, their leaves rustling in a symphony of whispers. Maya closed her eyes, allowing their voices to wash over her, filling her mind with images and sensations she had never experienced.

Through their communication, Maya began to understand the true nature of her powers. She saw how her connection to the realm was not just a tool for her own use but a responsibility, a sacred trust that had been bestowed upon her.

Asha's voice cut through the revelations, her tone filled with wisdom and caution. "Wonderful power brings extraordinary duty, Maya. Your abilities are meant to serve the greater good of Aethoria, to maintain the balance and harmony that sustains all life here."

Maya nodded, humbled by the weight of this realization. She

understood now that her journey was not just about personal growth or discovery but about something much more extensive than herself.

The sacred garden's plants parted like a curtain, revealing a mountain path beckoning Maya upward into the thin air. She ascended a mountain, each step taking her higher into the ethereal landscape of Aethoria. The oxygen grew thinner, and the world around her seemed to blur, the boundaries between sky and land becoming less distinct with every passing moment.

At the mountaintop, Maya settled into a meditative pose, her eyes closing as she focused on the energy flowing through her. The wind whispered around her, carrying with it the realm's secrets. Maya allowed herself to be swept away by its gentle caress.

Her consciousness expanded, unveiling a vision that chilled her to her core. She saw Aethoria engulfed in shadows, a thick and oppressive darkness that seemed to consume all light and hope. The once vibrant landscapes were twisted and distorted, their beauty replaced by an eerie, unnatural gloom. The darkness breached the barriers between realms, consuming her family estate, spreading across California, and engulfing Benevento until all of Earth lay under its shadow.

Amid this chaos, Maya saw a tall figure, a beacon of light amidst the encroaching darkness. As the vision clarified, she realized immediately that the figure was none other than herself.

She watched as her future self stood at a crossroads, the fate of both worlds resting on her shoulders. On one path, the darkness continued to spread, consuming everything in its wake until Aethoria and Earth were nothing more than husks of their former selves. But on the other path, Maya saw herself confronting the shadows, her powers shining bright as she fought to bring balance and harmony back to the land.

The vision shifted, and Maya stood face-to-face with an older version of herself. Their eyes met, and a silent understanding passed between them at that moment. Maya knew this was more than just a glimpse of a possible future—it was a prophecy, a calling she could not ignore.

As the vision faded and Maya returned to her conscious self, she knew now that her journey through Aethoria was not just a personal quest, but a mission that would determine the fate of two realms. She stood as a bridge between two worlds, her destiny woven into the fabric of both Earth and Aethoria.

With a deep breath, Maya opened her eyes, the mountaintop coming back into focus around her. The path before her was evident. She was ready to face whatever came next. For she was Maya, the chosen one, destined to confront the growing darkness and bring hope to a realm on the brink of destruction.

Maya stood at the edge of a cliff, her gaze fixed on the horizon. The gentle breeze tousled her hair, carrying the scent of a new beginning. In her journey through Aethoria, she had experienced so much, facing challenges that had tested her resolve and pushed her to the limits of her abilities.

But now, as she watched the sunset over the ethereal landscape, Maya felt a sense of clarity. The visions she had experienced and the prophecies revealed to her all pointed to a greater purpose, a destiny that she could no longer ignore.

Maya thought back to the moment she first stepped into Aethoria, a world so different from hers. She was uncertain then, unsure of her place in this strange realm. But as she navigated its mysteries and faced its trials, she had grown in ways she never could have imagined.

She had discovered powers within herself that she had never known existed, abilities that allowed her to connect with the very essence of magic itself. Through her encounters with the enigmatic Asha and the whispers of the intelligent flora, she understood the true nature of her role in this world.

Maya embraced her role as The Guardian, recognizing it not as a choice but as a calling woven into the very fabric of her being. The path ahead promised trials that would test her newfound powers, but where fear had once dwelled, the purpose now burned bright. With a deep breath, she turned away from the cliff's edge, drawing strength from Asha's presence beside her - her wise and loyal companion through the trials of Aethoria. Together, they would seek the allies and resources needed to fulfill her role, building upon the knowledge and understanding she had gained on her journey.

EIGHTEEN

Maya and Asha approached the enchanted castle. A deathly silence hung in the air, broken only by their cautious footsteps. The structure loomed before them, its once-grand walls now crumbling and overgrown with twisted vines. The moat surrounding the castle churned with sickly green water that released wisps of acrid vapor, like the breath of a dying dragon. The stench of decay and ancient corruption made Maya's stomach heave, reminding her of the poisoned waters her Lola Rose once warned her about in tales of corrupted elementals.

The castle's architecture seemed to shift between European and pre-colonial Filipino designs - sometimes appearing as towering stone battlements, other times transforming into a vast bahay-na-bato with capiz shell windows that gleamed like trapped souls. Maya recognized the merging of worlds - this was where the old powers of her homeland had followed their people across realms into Aethoria.

She scanned the area, her watchful eyes searching for any signs of life. But there was nothing - no creatures, no movement, not even the rustle of leaves in the wind— or the wind itself. It was as if the castle and its surroundings had been frozen in time, abandoned, and left to decay.

Maya turned to Asha with concern. "I don't like this," she grumbled. "Of all the strange things I've encountered in Aethoria, something about this place feels wrong. Like it's tainted." Her voice dropped lower. "We have to check it out."

Asha resisted, her own eyes constricted as she surveyed the castle. "We must be cautious," she agreed with hesitation. "But we cannot turn back now. We must find a way to cross the moat and enter the castle."

Together, they searched the edges of the moat, looking for a way to cross without falling into the toxic water. After several tense minutes, they found a narrow bridge beneath a tangle of vines. The wood was rotted and unsteady but was the only way across.

Maya took a deep breath and stepped onto the bridge, testing its strength with each cautious step. Asha followed close behind, her lithe form moving with grace and precision. They made their way across the bridge, the toxic water bubbling and hissing beneath them.

As they reached the other side, Maya let out a sigh of relief. But the relief was short-lived as they approached the castle's entrance. The massive wooden doors were ajar as if inviting them inside. Maya hesitated, her hand resting on the hilt of her sword.

"Are you sure about this?" she asked Asha, her voice low.

Asha met her gaze, her eyes glinting with determination. "We have come this far," she said. "We can't turn back now."

Maya pushed open the doors, and together, they stepped into the unknown depths of the enchanted castle.

Maya entered a grand chamber, and the air inside was eerily still, adding to the castle's already lifeless atmosphere. It sent shivers down her arms as she took it all in. The room was vast, its high ceilings adorned with intricate carvings that seemed to dance in the flickering light of the torches lining the walls. A crystal cocoon hovered at the chamber's center, its surface fractaled like frozen lightning. It pulsed with a nightmarish light that painted the stone floor in shifting shadows, each pulse sending out waves of energy that made the air taste like metal and memories. The crystalline structure seemed to whisper in a language Maya almost recognized from her grandmother's oldest chants.

But it was the cocoon guardian who caught Maya's attention.

The Pah, a bakunawa's earthbound cousin, coiled around the base of the cocoon. Like the legendary moon-eater of Filipino lore, its serpentine form rippled with scales that shimmered between deep indigo and obsidian - colors of the ancient underworld. The seven spots along its spine glowed like captured stars, reminiscent of the seven moons its kind once hunted in the age of myths. When it opened its maw, Maya caught the gleam of teeth curved like kris blades, weapons of her ancestors.

The powerful guardian of the crystal cocoon was not to be underestimated. Its eyes, glowing like smoldering coals, fixed on Maya as she approached, a low, ominous hiss escaping from its fanged maw.

Maya's heart thudded in her chest as she grasped the severity of her predicament. It was one of the legendary creatures from Filipino folklore, just like Lola Rose used to tell her about when she was a little girl. Dread consumed her, igniting anxiety within her core. She had come so far and braved so many dangers, all to reach this moment. But now, faced with the Pah, the weight of her quest pressed down upon her like a physical force. The creature's dark vibe filled the chamber, an uneasy presence that seemed to suck the very light from the room.

Ever vigilant, Asha crouched low beside Maya, her fur crackling with protective energy. The spirit cat's eyes glowed with ancient knowing, her form shifting between physical and ethereal as she channeled the protective powers of Maya's ancestral guardians. Like the mystical tigers of Filipino legend, she moved with grace and deadly purpose, ready to defend her chosen warrior.

The Pah, a creature of immense strength and ancient power, uncoiled itself from the base of the cocoon, its sinuous body rippling with barely contained energy. It reared up, towering over Maya, its eyes boring into her soul.

Maya's hand tightened around Moonbow, its form shifting between a traditional Filipino longbow - the busog - and something more ethereal. The arrows in her quiver hummed with the same energy that powered the ancient pangayaw warriors' weapons, each shaft carved with protection sigils her Lola Rose had taught her to draw.

She knew that the Pah would not give up its charge easily and would fight with every ounce to protect the crystal cocoon and its secrets.

The Pah's forked tongue flicked out, tasting the air as it prepared to strike. Maya braced herself, her body tense with anticipation. She knew that the next few moments would determine the fate of her quest and perhaps the fate of Aethoria itself.

The chamber transformed, the flickering torches replaced by an eerie interplay of light and shadow that danced across the stone walls. The air crackled with energy as Maya and the Pah faced off, their wills clashing in a silent battle of determination.

With a deafening roar that shook the very foundations of the castle, the Pah launched itself at Maya, its serpentine body uncoiling with lightning speed. But Maya stood her ground, drawing upon every ounce of the magic and strength she had acquired in Aethoria. The tension in the air was palpable, the outcome of the battle hanging in the balance.

Maya's heart pounded as she watched her arrows miss their mark, the Pah's agility proving a formidable challenge. Without hesitation, she reached for her quiver and drew another arrow, imbuing it with a powerful enchantment.

The Pah's movements reminded Maya of Lola Rose's stories about the bakunawa - how it had once been a guardian of balance before darkness corrupted its purpose. Like the ancient sea serpent that swallowed moons, the Pah seemed to bend light around itself, creating patches of shadow that writhed like living things. But unlike the bakunawa of legend, this creature could be reasoned with, its ancient purpose as a guardian still intact beneath layers of dark magic.

The Pah lunged again, its jaws snapping at Maya's throat. With fierce determination, Maya let the enchanted arrow fly, striking the Pah directly in its gaping maw. A deafening screech filled the chamber as the creature recoiled in pain.

But Maya knew that this was only a temporary setback. The Pah was relentless and would not give up easily. She needed to end this fight quickly before it could regain its strength.

Gathering her energy, Maya channeled it into Moonbow. She let loose a blinding blast of light that engulfed the entire chamber. The Pah roared in agony, its scales sizzling under the intense light. Furious, the Pah hissed and lunged again, but Maya was too quick.

Maya executed a perfect 'sayaw' dodge, her body flowing like water as the Pah's fangs sliced through the space she'd occupied heartbeats before. The martial dance her ancestors had perfected served her now, each movement both defense and preparation for a counterattack.

She sheathed Moonbow and drew the Axiom of the Celestial Divid, humming with divine power. The Pah struck again, but this time, Maya met its attack with Vulcan's shield, the metal ringing with the force of the impact.

In a fluid motion, Maya swung her axe at the Pah's neck, but it was too quick and slithered away. The two circled each other, both waiting for an opening. But Maya could feel her strength beginning to wane. She had been in numerous battles before, but this one felt different - like she was fighting for more than her survival.

Contemplating her next move, Maya remembered the enchanted arrow she had used earlier. She could use it again to weaken the Pah further. She reached for another arrow in her quiver and infused it with magic again.

The Pah sensed her plan and lunged at her again. But this time, Maya was ready. As it opened its mouth to strike, she let loose the enchanted arrow and hit it in the same spot as before - right in its mouth.

The Pah screeched in pain and recoiled once more. Seizing the opportunity, Maya charged forward with her axe raised high above her head. With a mighty swing, she brought it down on the Pah's neck with all her strength, but it wasn't enough.

The Pah prepared to strike again despite being injured and charged at Maya.

The battle raged on, and Maya and the Pah locked in a deadly dance of striking and evading. Maya's movements were fluid and precise, a testament to the depth of her training and her growing connection to the very essence of Aethoria. She countered the Pah's strikes with spells that burst from her fingertips, illuminating the chamber in a dazzling light display.

As the battle between Maya and the Pah reached a crescendo, the crystal cocoon at the chamber's center began to crack. Hairline fractures spread across its surface, the energy within pulsing with increasing intensity. The room shook as if the very fabric of Aethoria was straining at the seams.

Maya sensed the shift in the room's energy and realized that the cocoon was the key to everything. She knew she had to act fast, for if the cocoon were to shatter completely, the consequences could be catastrophic.

In a moment of clarity amidst the chaos, Maya understood that the Pah was not her true enemy. It was a guardian, bound by duty to protect the secrets within the cocoon. She needed to find a way to assert her right to claim what lay within without causing further harm.

Channeling her power, Maya focused her energy into a beam of pure, radiant light. She directed it not at the Pah but at the space around it, weaving an intricate web of magic. The light shimmered and danced, forming a complex pattern that began to encircle the serpentine creature.

The Pah, caught off guard by this unexpected tactic, thrashed and roared as the web of light tightened around it. Its scales shimmered and rippled as the spell's energy seeped into its very being. Gradually, the Pah's form began to shrink, its massive size diminishing as it was compressed by the force of Maya's magic.

Maya drew upon the ancient arts her grandmother had secretly preserved - the same magic that babaylan healers and mystics once wielded in the Philippines. Her fingers traced patterns in the air, forming invisible knots of power similar to the ones woven into traditional tambourine patterns. Each gesture carried the weight of generations who had practiced these arts in secret, waiting for the right time to emerge again.

As the spell reached its climax, the Pah became fully encased in a luminescent cocoon of its own, a prison forged from the very energy it had sought to defend. The creature's roars subsided to a low, rumbling growl, its struggles growing weaker as it was subdued by the power of Maya's light.

Maya remembered the nights spent with Lola Rose, learning the old ways under starlight. Her grandmother had been more than just family - she was a modern babaylan, keeping ancient Filipino traditions alive through stories and secret teachings. Now, facing the Pah, Maya understood why her grandmother had insisted she learn both the warrior arts and healing magics of their ancestors.

"Kapit lang, apo," Lola Rose would say. "Hold fast. Our people's magic flows in your blood." The words echoed in Maya's mind as she faced the Pah, finally understanding that her place in Aethoria was a continuation of her people's ancient role as guardians between worlds.

With the Pah subdued, a ghostly silence fell over the chamber, broken only by the soft crackling of the crystal cocoon as it began to splinter and crack. Maya watched, her breath caught in her throat, as the cocoon shattered, sending shards of glimmering crystal cascading to the floor. Amidst the debris, a figure emerged, weakened but unmistakably alive - Nykronus.

Maya rushed to his side, her heart pounding. Nykronus, the alluring sage she had sought for so long, was finally before her. As she reached him, Nykronus lifted his gaze to meet hers, and in that moment, a profound connection passed between them. His eyes, though tired, shone with pride, gratitude, and understanding, a silent acknowledgment of the trials Maya had endured to reach him.

Nykronus's voice, though strained, carried a warmth that seemed to fill the chamber with life. "Maya," he said softly, "you have done the impossible. You have proven yourself worthy as a guardian of Aethoria and a true protector of its people. You *are* The Guardian."

Maya felt emotion wash over her, the weight of Nykronus's words settling deep within her heart. The tension of the battle, the fear, and the uncertainty that had gripped her for so long began dissipating, replaced by a sense of triumph and relief. She had faced the Pah, one of the most fearsome creatures in Aethoria, and emerged victorious.

As she helped Nykronus to his feet, Maya couldn't help but feel it was all a dream. She had come so far and learned so much, and now, with Nykronus by her side, she knew that anything was possible. The future of Aethoria, and perhaps even the fate of the realms beyond, lay in their hands.

Maya embraced Nykronus, her mentor and dear friend, with tears streaming down her face as she spoke. "Nykronus," she said, struggling to get more words out. Their families had always been close, making Nykronus a second father to her.

Asha, who had watched the scene unfold with wonder and pride, padded over to Maya and Nykronus, her eyes glinting with satisfaction. She rubbed against Maya's leg, a gesture of affection and congratulations, before turning her gaze to Nykronus, a look of profound respect in her feline eyes.

Together, the trio stood amidst the shattered remains of the cocoon, the chamber now filled with new energy - one of hope, determination, and the promise of a brighter future.

As sunlight filtered through the chamber windows, life seemed to be returning to the area surrounding the castle. The once lifeless and toxic moat now shimmered with a newfound vitality, and the barren landscape beyond the castle walls began to show signs of rejuvenation.

Maya and Nykronus stood at the entrance to the chamber, their gazes fixed upon the Pah's restrained form. Once a fearsome adversary, the creature lay subdued, encased in a luminescent cocoon of Maya's creation. Respect and sorrow filled their hearts as they looked upon the Pah.

Nykronus, his strength slowly returning, approached the Pah with a gentle stride. He raised his hand and, with a soft incantation, began to weave his own magic into the spell that bound the creature. The cocoon's intensity softened, its light becoming more soothing, ensuring the Pah was not harmed in its confinement.

"Maya," Nykronus spoke, his voice filled with both pride and understanding. "Your bravery and skill have saved not only me but also the very essence of Aethoria and, as you have probably gathered, our realm. Your actions were necessary, and you have proven yourself to be who I have always known you to be."

He placed a hand on her shoulder, his eyes meeting hers with a profound depth. "But remember, true strength lies not just in the power we wield but in the wisdom to use it judiciously. Mercy, even in the face of adversity, is a sign of the greatest heroes."

Maya nodded, her heart swelling with a newfound understanding. She had indeed saved Nykronus and defeated the Pah, but she had done so in a way that honored the creature's role as a guardian. The Pah, though fearsome, was not an enemy to be destroyed but a being to be respected and understood.

As the chamber filled with the warmth of the Aethorian sun, Maya felt a sense of peace wash over her. The trials she had faced and the challenges she had overcome had not only strengthened her powers but also her spirit. She had learned that true heroism lay in the balance of strength and compassion, power and restraint.

As Maya and Nykronus stepped out of the castle, a gentle breeze caressed their faces, carrying with it the promise of a new beginning. The once desolate landscape had begun to transform, with patches of vibrant green emerging amidst the barren earth. It was as if the land was responding to the triumph of light over darkness, slowly awakening from a long, troubled slumber.

Nykronus, his strength returning with each passing moment, surveyed the horizon with determination and caution. "The road ahead will not be easy, Maya," he said, his voice carrying a weight of experience. "The forces that seek to disrupt the balance of Aethoria are relentless and will stop at nothing to achieve their goals."

Maya nodded, her grip tightening on Moonbow as she stood beside her mentor. "I know," she replied, her voice steady and persistent. "But we'll face them together. We've already proven that when we stand united, there's nothing we can't overcome."

Nykronus smiled, a glimmer of pride in his eyes. "Indeed, we have. And we will continue to do so, no matter what."

As they set off, leaving the castle behind, Maya couldn't help but feel a sense of exhilaration mingled with trepidation. She had passed a crucial test, proving her worth as a guardian of Aethoria, but she knew this was only the beginning. The darkness threatening the realm would not be defeated easily, and she would need to draw upon every ounce of her strength and wisdom to see this fight through to the end.

A sensation Maya couldn't quite define, an amalgam of optimism and awe, suffused her as Nykronus stood alongside her. She was happy she was no longer alone. Despite the uncertainty, one thing was clear: they would not rest until Aethoria was safe and the forces of darkness were banished once and for all.

CHAPTER
NINETEEN

Dense fog cloaked the ancient stone walls of the Chapelle du Temple as Elan Durant and his team converged on the sacred site. Each step echoed against weathered stone, their hearts heavy with the gravity of their mission.

Elan's gaze swept over his companions, measuring their resolve. Myst, his son grown now into a warrior in his own right, stood tall beside him, his eyes burning with the same fierce tenacity that had driven their family for generations.

Olivia's fingers traced the tome's worn spine, its pages crackling with preserved magic. Her scholar's eyes narrowed as she matched the wall's weathered symbols to diagrams in her text, centuries of knowledge flowing through her practiced translation.

Stanley Wyatt's imposing figure cast a long shadow against the temple walls, his red hair blazing like a banner in the dim light. Beneath his gruff exterior lay a heart as steadfast as the ancient knights whose spirits guarded these halls.

Then there was Zoe, her pale hair catching what little light filtered through the fog. Her fingers danced across her electric lute's strings, each note resonating with the temple's ancient harmonies.

Together, they formed a tapestry of skills and experiences, each thread essential to the success of their quest.

Elan's mind raced with the clues they had gathered, piecing together the puzzle that would reveal the Temple of the Timeless entrance. His eyes scanned the chapel's exterior, searching for the tell-tale signs leading them to their destination.

Myst's trained eye caught it first—a subtle indentation in the stone that seemed to shift in the shadows. The team moved as one, their hands finding familiar positions on the ancient mechanism, each touch awakening dormant magic within the walls.

With a low rumble, the stone wall before them shifted, revealing a hidden passageway that descended into the depths of the earth.

Ancient air rushed from the passage, bringing with it the chill of forgotten centuries and the metallic tang of old magic. Dust motes danced in the wan light, swirling like stars in a forgotten cosmos.

Before they crossed the threshold, Elan turned to his team, his voice low and wholehearted. "We've come this far together," he said, his gaze meeting each of theirs. "What lies ahead may test us in ways we can't imagine, but I have faith in each and every one of you. Remember, we're not just here for ourselves. We're here for the world, for the future that hangs in the balance."

With a collective agreement, they steeled their spirits for the journey ahead, each warrior touching the sacred symbols on their weapons as the ancient knights had done before every great quest. United in purpose, bound by a shared destiny, they descended into the Temple of the Timeless, ready to claim the artifact that could change the course of history.

Elan led the way, his footsteps echoing against the stone walls. Olivia followed close behind, eyes scanning the hallowed halls for clues that might aid their quest. The passage narrowed, and the team navigated a series of intricate traps and puzzles, each designed to guard the temple's deepest secrets.

It was here that their individual talents began to shine.

Stanley raised his fist, halting the group with the practiced command of a veteran warrior. His eyes, trained by decades of survival, caught the subtle discoloration in the stone tiles - pressure plates, ancient and deadly. "See how the dust settles differently there?" he growled, pointing to seemingly innocent patterns. "Temple builders always leave a trail if you know where to look."

With each obstacle they overcame, their confidence grew. They moved as one entity, years of shared battles evident in every coordinated step. Zoe's music was already weaving protection where Myst's blade met resistance. When Olivia's translations faltered, Stanley's practical experience filled the gaps. They were more than a team - they were a living legend in the making, each member's strengths covering another's vulnerabilities.

Zoe's nimble fingers quickly worked on the complex lock mechanisms, her skills honed through years of intricate lute playing. The silence was cut short when they heard a low growl from the shadows. All eyes turned to Zoe, whose keen hearing had picked up on the sound.

Her fingers twitched nervously as she reached for her electric lute. Her nimble fingers flicked through chords and melodies like second nature. With a sharp strum, she unleashed a sound that echoed through the chamber.

The shadows coalesced into a nightmarish form - a beast born of ancient curses. Its body rippled with muscles beneath scales dark as forgotten depths, crowned with spiraling horns that seemed to absorb light. Crystalline claws scraped against stone, leaving trails of phosphorescent marks, while its eyes blazed with eldritch intelligence.

But Zoe's music seemed to affect it, causing it to falter and hesitate. Her voice rose above the lute's ethereal tones, weaving an ancient ballad of binding:

> "By starlight's grace and shadow's reign,
> Ancient powers I dare constrain,
> Through strings of fate and melody's might,
> Yield thy fury to songs of light!"

The beast's movements grew sluggish as each word seemed to wrap around it like chains of silver sound. Taking advantage of the distraction, Elan stepped forward with his sword drawn. Olivia followed suit, her bow primed and ready.

Together, they charged at the beast, their weapons clashing against its thick hide.

With one final blow from *Winterstar*, the beast roared in defeat before crumbling to dust.

Breathing heavily but exhilarated from their victory, the team shared smiles and high-fives before continuing their exploration of the chamber.

Myst's knowledge of ancient languages proved invaluable as they continued into the temple. He deciphered cryptic inscriptions carved into the walls with a focused intensity. His brow furrowed in concentration.

Olivia marveled at Myst's abilities, having known him primarily as a skilled Marine. But here, in this ancient and mysterious place, he seemed like a different person altogether – more confident and knowledgeable than ever.

Myst's translations allowed them to navigate hidden passageways and avoid potentially deadly traps. Each new room held its own challenges and puzzles, but they could overcome them all with Myst's guidance.

They entered a vast circular chamber that took their breath away. The domed ceiling stretched into darkness above them, while the curved walls bore intricate patterns of inlaid silver and crystal. As their torchlight played across the surface, the patterns shifted like living things, revealing themselves as star maps of impossible constellations. The chamber held no apparent exit, but the air thrummed with ancient purpose.

Myst studied the markings with intense scrutiny before speaking up. "These are constellations," he said, pointing to a particularly intricate image on the wall. "If we can align them correctly, I believe it will reveal an exit."

The team quickly got to work, moving heavy stone slabs around the room to align the symbols correctly. It was no easy task—each movement had to be precise, or they risked triggering some kind of trap.

But after several tense minutes of careful maneuvering, the last piece clicked into place, and a section of the wall slid open.

They entered a small chamber beyond and found themselves face-to-face with what appeared to be an ancient guardian – a towering figure adorned with armor and a massive sword.

Elan stepped forward confidently, drawing *Winterstar*. But before he could move, Zoe stepped forward and began playing her lute softly.

The guardian seemed mesmerized by her music, frozen in place as she continued to play. Taking advantage of the distraction, Elan lunged forward. It struck the guardian with his sword, causing it to shatter into pieces.

The hallowed halls revealed their stories as they delved deeper into the temple. Intricate murals adorned the walls, depicting the history of the artifact they sought and the guardians who had sworn to protect it. The images were vivid and striking, portraying epic battles and moments of great sacrifice.

Olivia paused before one remarkably detailed mural, her fingers tracing the ancient lines. "This is it," she breathed, her voice filled with reverence. "The artifact we seek... it's more than just an object of power. It's a symbol of hope, of the eternal struggle between light and darkness."

Elan nodded, his eyes fixed on the mural. The weight of their mission settled heavily on his shoulders, but he drew strength from the determination he saw in his companions' eyes. They were here to ensure that the artifact didn't fall into the wrong hands and to protect the delicate balance that hung in the balance.

As they pressed on, the temple's magic seemed to guide their steps, leading them closer to their goal. The air hummed with anticipation, and Elan could feel the ancient power that lay just beyond their reach.

They were close now, so close to uncovering the secrets that had been hidden for centuries.

As they entered the heart of the temple, a sense of darkness consumed the ancient chamber. In the center stood a towering figure, its form a fusion of stone and ethereal energy. The protector, a creation of ancient magic, is bound to protect the artifact at all costs.

Elan and Myst exchanged glances, a silent understanding passing between father and son. They stepped forward, their weapons ready, as the creature's eyes flared to life with a dark glow.

Magic and steel sang in deadly harmony as they engaged the protector. *Winterstar* blazed in Elan's grip, its ancient enchantments awakening at the presence of its ancient kin. Each strike left trails of silver light in the air while the protector's counters rippled with waves of primordial power.

Myst joined the fray, his blade weaving a deadly dance as he sought to find a weakness in the protector's defenses.

Olivia, her bow in hand, provided crucial support from a distance. Her arrows, imbued with ancient incantations, found their mark, chipping away at the protector's stony exterior. Stanley, his sword wrapped in mystical energy, delivered powerful blows that shook the very foundations of the chamber.

And then there was Zoe, her music a symphony of power. Her melodies wove through the air, bolstering her companions and seeking to unravel the protector's magical defenses.

The battle raged on, a testament to the team's cohesive strength. They worked as one, their movements synchronized, their powers intertwined. Each blow, each spell, each note of Zoe's music brought them closer to victory.

But the protector was relentless, its power ancient and unyielding. It lashed out with waves of magical energy, seeking to overwhelm the intruders who dared to challenge its sacred duty.

Elan, however, saw beyond the protector's aggression. He recognized the same resolve that burned within his own heart—the desire to protect, to safeguard that which was most precious. At that moment, he understood they were not here to conquer but to prove their worthiness.

With a shout of determination, Elan lowered his sword. "We're not your enemy," he declared, his voice ringing through the chamber. "We seek the artifact not for power but to ensure its power is used for the greater good."

The protector hesitated, its glowing eyes fixed upon Elan. The others followed suit, lowering their weapons and fading their magic.

In that moment of stillness, the protector and the intruders reached a profound understanding. They had proven their resolve and commitment to a higher cause.

The protector stepped aside slowly, and the path to the artifact was now clear. Elan and his companions had passed the final test not through conquest but through the strength of their hearts.

As the protector stepped aside, Elan and his companions entered the Temple of the Timeless sanctum. Ancient wards flickered to life as they entered, bathing the chamber in light that seemed to flow like water down the walls. Constellations unknown to mortal astronomers danced across the ceiling, their patterns shifting in response to their presence. The air hummed with the weight of accumulated power, centuries of magical resonance making their enchanted weapons vibrate in sympathy. The artifact they had sought for so long was in the center of the room, resting on an ornate altar.

Elan approached the altar, his heart pounding in his chest. The others followed close behind, their eyes wide with wonder. As they drew closer, the artifact hung suspended in a column of light that seemed to bend around itself. Its surface shifted like liquid metal, ancient runes swimming beneath its skin in patterns that hurt the eyes to follow. With each pulse of its inner light, the air grew thick with power, and whispers of long-dead languages echoed in their minds.

With trembling hands, Elan reached out and touched the artifact. The moment his fingers made contact, a surge of energy coursed through his body, and his mind was flooded with visions.

The visions crashed over each of them like waves of liquid time, uniquely personal yet universally devastating. Elan witnessed armies clash beneath skies torn by magical warfare, the weight of leadership crushing countless souls. Myst saw the fall of ancient bloodlines, the price of failure written in the bones of his ancestors. Olivia's mind burned with the destruction of sacred knowledge, and libraries of power turned to ash. Stanley relived the last stand of legendary warriors, their sacrifices echoing through time. And Zoe heard the final songs of dying worlds, their melodies twisted into screams by Verendana's corruption.

Their weapons blazed with forgotten power. The air seemed to bleed as reality buckled under the weight of forces never meant for mortal hands. He witnessed the sacrifices made by ancient heroes, their lives given freely to seal the realm and protect the world from darkness. Their final moments showed them what was at stake - Verendana's army, poised to strike at the heart of all they held dear.

The visions faded, and Elan returned to the sanctum with his companions. They, too, had experienced the same revelations, their faces etched with awe and determination.

"This is it," Olivia whispered, her voice trembling with emotion. "The key to stopping Verendana and protecting the world."

Myst nodded, his eyes fixed on the artifact. "But it won't be that easy, will it? We've seen the battles that await us, the sacrifices that may be required."

Elan looked at each of his companions in turn, seeing the resolve in their eyes. "We knew this wouldn't be easy when we started," he said. "But we also knew that it was necessary. The world needs us, now more than ever."

The Knights of the Order of St. Michael had come this far, and they would not falter now, not when the fate of the world hung in the balance.

As Elan and his companions prepared to leave the Temple of the Timeless, an unsettling realization dawned upon them. Their actions had not gone unnoticed, and the forces they sought to thwart were now closing in.

Olivia was the first to sense it, a prickling unease that crept up her spine. "We're not alone," she whispered, her eyes darting to the shadowed corners of the sanctum. "The Malefic Assembly—Verendana's forces... they're coming."

The urgency in her voice spurred the others into action. They knew they couldn't risk letting the artifact fall into the wrong hands. They hastily gathered their gear and began their retreat, navigating back through the temple's winding corridors.

The once serene halls now felt oppressive, filled with an ominous presence that seemed to lurk just out of sight. Every shadow held the potential for danger, and every echoing footstep reminded me of the pursuit that followed.

Elan led the way, his senses heightened and his grip tight on *Winterstar*. Myst and Stanley flanked him, their own weapons at the ready, while Olivia and Zoe brought up the rear, their keen eyes watching for any signs of their pursuers.

The chase was on, a desperate race against time and the forces that sought to undo all they had accomplished. They moved swiftly and silently, their training and instincts guiding them through the labyrinthine passages.

The sounds of pursuit echoed through the ancient halls - the screech of metal on stone, the chittering of shadow-spawn, and worst of all, the measured tread of the Malefic Assembly's elite guard. Their whispered incantations seemed to seep through the very walls, turning friendly shadows into reaching claws. The air grew thick with the copper taste of hostile magic, and each breath became a struggle against the encroaching darkness. The clatter of armor and the snarls of dark creatures echoed through the stone halls. Verendana's minions were closing in, driven by a relentless determination to reclaim the artifact.

With a final burst of speed, Elan and his companions burst into daylight, the temple's entrance sealing shut behind them with a resounding thud. They paused momentarily, catching their breath, their hearts pounding with the exertion and weight of their narrow escape.

But even as they stood there, the artifact pulsing with power in Elan's grasp, they knew this was only the beginning. With Verendana's forces on their heels and the fate of the realm hanging in the balance, they were no longer mere seekers of history.

They were the key players in a battle that would determine the future, and they were more determined than ever to win.

CHAPTER

TWENTY

B enevento, Italy
Modern technology had found its place even in the Order of St. Michael's ancient headquarters in Benevento, where the most sensitive archives were kept. Kaira and Reagan hunched over the ancient texts, the bright glow of massive computer screens illuminating their faces. The musty smell of old parchment mingled with the hum of modern technology, a testament to the Order's long history and ongoing mission to maintain the balance between realms.

Reagan, with her piercing blue eyes and auburn hair tied back in a practical bun, squinted at the faded script. Though they ran the Order's San Francisco chapter, some research could only be done here, in the heart of their organization. "Kai, here's something about a prophecy," she whispered so only Kaira could hear, tracing the lines with her finger. "A 'Harbinger of Shadows' who will challenge the balance between realms."

Kaira leaned in closer, her eyes scanning the cryptic messages. "It's not a straightforward prophecy," she said, her voice tinged with excitement and concern. "There are hidden codes within the text, almost like a puzzle."

The Mazza women worked tirelessly, cross-referencing the ancient tomes with the digital archives on their tablets. Hours passed as they deciphered the complex layers of meaning, piecing together the fragments of the prophecy.

As the final piece fell into place, Kaira and Reagan exchanged a look of dawning realization. The description of the Harbinger of Shadows, destined to disrupt the equilibrium of power, bore an uncanny resemblance to the biblical figure Lazarus and his recent actions.

"It's as if he believes he's fulfilling this prophecy," Kaira hushed, a chill running down her spine. "As if he sees himself as the catalyst for some great upheaval."

Her expression grew somber, her grip on the device intensifying. "And if he truly believes that, there's no telling what he might do to make it a reality."

The weight of their discovery and the implications of Lazarus's potential role in the prophecy were inking in. They knew they had to act fast and find a way to counter whatever plans he might have set in motion.

But even as they began to formulate their next steps, Kaira and Reagan couldn't shake the feeling that they were just scratching the surface of something much larger and more dangerous than they had ever faced.

San Francisco, California

After their discovery in Benevento, the sisters returned to San Francisco, where their responsibilities as leaders of the West Coast headquarters awaited. The bustling American city couldn't have been more different from the ancient Italian town they'd left behind. While Benevento held the Order's history in its stones, their modernized base of operations hidden beneath a tech startup's façade represented its future.

Kaira and Reagan navigated the crowded streets, their footsteps echoing on the littered sidewalks as they wound through narrow alleys. The city's beautiful architecture towered over them, a lone witness to the clandestine meeting about to unfold.

They arrived at a small, unnoticeable café, its craggy wooden sign creaking in the gentle breeze. Entering the equally worn interior, they spotted Erikson Ghostcloak seated at a corner table, his broad shoulders hunched over a steaming cup of espresso.

As they approached, Erikson looked up, his stormy eyes meeting theirs with a look of recognition. Kaira and Reagan slid into the torn seats opposite him, their expressions mixing hope and apprehension.

"Thank you for meeting us, Erikson," Kaira said, keeping her voice low. "What did you find out?"

Erikson leaned forward, his voice a deep rumble. "Lazarus is on the move. He's been gathering ancient artifacts, relics of immense power. But that's not all."

He paused, his gaze intense. "He's been making alliances with dark entities, beings from realms beyond our understanding. It's as if he's building an army that spans across dimensions."

Reagan's eyes widened, her grip tightening on the table's edge. "An army? For what purpose?"

"From what I've gathered," Erikson continued, "Lazarus isn't content with just power in our world. He wants to control the very forces that maintain the balance between good and evil. He believes that by harnessing these artifacts and aligning with these entities, he can reshape the fabric of reality itself."

Kaira and Reagan looked at each other in growing alarm. Lazarus's ambition was staggering, far beyond anything they had anticipated.

"Do you have any leads on where he might be heading next?" Kaira asked, her mind already racing with potential counter-measures.

Erikson reached into his pocket and pulled out a small, worn leather journal. "This contains the locations of several ancient sites and hidden vaults that Lazarus has been researching. I believe these are his next targets."

He slid the journal across the table to Kaira, who took it with gratitude. "Thank you, Erikson. This information is invaluable."

As they rose to leave, Erikson's hand shot out, grasping Kaira's wrist. "Be careful," he warned, his eyes boring into hers. "Lazarus is not to be underestimated. He's grown powerful, and he has allies in dark places. To make matters worse, he has the full army of the Malefic Assembly at his disposal."

Kaira met his gaze steadily. "We'll be careful. But we can't let him succeed. Too much is at stake."

With a final nod, Erikson released her, and the Mazza women slipped out of the café.

The Order's West Coast headquarters, hidden beneath the façade of a tech startup in downtown San Francisco, housed a council chamber that buzzed with tension as Kaira and Reagan stood before assembled members of the Order of St. Michael. The walls seemed to press in, amplifying the gravity of their revelations. Kaira's steady and clear voice cut through the murmurs of the gathered council.

"Lazarus is not just a rogue agent or a minor threat," she declared, her eyes sweeping over the faces of her colleagues. "He's become a force that threatens the very balance of our world."

Reagan stepped forward, her tablet in hand, and with a few swift taps, holographic images sprang to life above the council table. Ancient texts, decoded prophecies, and surveillance footage merged into a complexity of impending doom.

"He's been gathering artifacts of immense power," Reagan explained, highlighting critical points in the glowing display. "Each one a piece of a larger puzzle, a plan to directly assault the pillars that sustain the equilibrium between good and evil."

The council members leaned forward, their expressions shifting from skepticism to growing alarm as the evidence mounted. Kaira and Reagan laid out the intricacies of Lazarus's network, the alliances he had forged with dark entities, and the whispers of his growing army.

"This is not a matter of containment or counterintelligence," Kaira said, her voice heavy with the weight of their findings. "Lazarus is on the verge of something catastrophic, something that could reshape the very fabric of our reality. He needs one last artifact, one of immense and mysterious power, to achieve his goal." Her hand unconsciously moved to the silver chain at her throat, where her wedding band rested beside her Order medallion. "As we speak, Elan and his team are on their way to retrieve it before Lazarus can. If anyone can succeed in this mission, it's him."

The council members shifted uneasily, aware that their West Coast leaders were sending their best operative - and Kaira's husband - into extreme danger.

As the presentation drew to a close, a heavy silence settled over the chamber. The council members exchanged uneasy glances, the realization of their own unpreparedness sinking in like a cold weight in their guts.

Kaira and Reagan stood resolute, their eyes conveying the situation's urgency. They had laid bare the uncomfortable truth: Lazarus's reach and power had grown beyond their worst fears, and the Order faced a threat unlike any they had encountered before.

The hushed conversations of alarm and resolve drifted to Kaira and Reagan's ears as the council members filed out of the chamber. The pair lingered, burdened by the gravity of what had been disclosed, the implications bearing down on them as if they were tangible entities. The holographic images still hovered above the table, a silent testament to the enormity of the threat they faced.

Kaira sank into a chair, her shoulders slumping as if the burden of leadership had suddenly become too heavy to bear. "Reagan," she said, her voice lacking energy, "do you think we're ready for this? Lazarus, his army, the artifacts... and now Elan..." She trailed off, the weight of sending her husband into danger adding to her concerns.

Reagan moved to her side, placing a comforting hand on her shoulder. "I don't know, Kai," she admitted, her doubts surfacing in the quiet of the empty room. "But I do know that between your leadership here, the main headquarters' support, and Elan's skills in the field, we've never been better positioned to face a threat like this. Even if it feels different. Even if we're on the brink of something we can't fully comprehend."

They sat silently for a moment, the weight of their responsibility pressing down on them. The Order had faced countless threats over the centuries, but never one that seemed to strike at the very heart of the balance they had sworn to protect.

"What if we're not strong enough?" Kaira asked, her eyes fixed on the glowing images before them. "What if, despite all our efforts, Lazarus succeeds in his plans?"

Reagan squeezed her shoulder, a gesture of solidarity and shared concern. "We can't think like that, Kai. We have to believe in the strength of the Order, in the power of the alliances we've forged."

Kaira nodded, drawing strength from her sister's words. "You're right. We can't let doubt paralyze us. We have to act and act decisively."

They rose to their feet, a boldness perching over them. They understood the necessity of unity in the face of such a profound threat, and they knew that their next steps would be crucial in rallying their allies and strengthening their defenses.

"We start by reaching out to every contact, every friend of the Order," Kaira said, her voice steady and resolute. "We pool our resources, our knowledge, and our strength. And we don't stop until we've done everything possible to stop Lazarus."

Reagan smiled. "Together," she said, clasping Kaira's hand. "We face this together, no matter what comes."

Kaira and Reagan dove back into the archives with fiery fervor, their eyes scanning tomes and digital records aggressively. The musty smell of old parchment mingled with the hum of the computers, creating a strange harmony of the old and the new.

They worked diligently, poring over records of battles and agreements, never losing their concentration. The stakes had never been higher, and they knew that every piece of information could be the key to stopping Lazarus.

Days blended together as they tirelessly searched for answers. And then, amidst the countless pages of forgotten lore, Reagan found something promising.

"Kai, look at this," she called, her finger tracing ancient symbols. "It references a ritual, something about severing bonds between mortals and dark entities. Most of it is encrypted, but..."

Kaira leaned in, her expertise in ancient languages complementing her sister's skill with patterns and codes. "If we can decrypt this fully, if this ritual is what we think it is..."

"It could give us a way to cut off Lazarus from his dark allies," Reagan finished, their eyes meeting with cautious optimism. "But we'll need help from the scholars in Benevento to decode it completely."

"Then we work with both headquarters," Kaira said firmly. "We use every resource the Order has. Between this potential ritual, Elan's mission, and our combined strength..." She straightened, new determination filling her. "We might just have a chance."

They knew it wouldn't be easy. The ritual was complex, requiring rare ingredients and precise timing. But it was a chance, a way to strike at the heart of Lazarus's strength before he could bring his plans to fruition.

Kaira and Reagan gathered the necessary components and studied the intricate details of the ceremony. They knew they had to act fast, for every moment they delayed was another moment for Lazarus to grow stronger.

Hope began to spread throughout the Order's senior council members. This forgotten ritual, this ancient knowledge, could be the turning point they desperately needed. It was a chance to defend against Lazarus's onslaught and take the fight to him, to weaken his grip on the dark powers he sought to wield.

Kaira and Reagan stood before the assembled Order. The great hall was filled to capacity, every member hanging on their every word as they outlined the plan of action.

"We face a threat unlike any we've encountered before," Kaira began, her voice clear and strong. "And the Order has seen and experienced so much! Lazarus's power grows by the day, and his alliances with dark forces threaten the very balance of our world."

Reagan stepped forward, her eyes sweeping over the gathered faces. "But we aren't powerless. We have knowledge, we have strength, magical artifacts, celestial weapons, skills the average person would never dream to know, and most importantly, we have each other."

They spoke of the ritual they had discovered, the glimmer of hope in the face of the gathering darkness. They outlined the steps needed to prepare, from gathering the necessary components to studying the intricate details of the ceremony.

"But this ritual is only one part of the fight," Kaira continued. "We must fortify our sanctuaries, strengthen our defenses, and be ready for battle on all fronts."

Reagan smiled, her expression profound. "We must also seek out allies, both in this realm and beyond. We can't face this threat alone."

They called for unity, for every member of the Order to stand together in the face of this adversity. They spoke of the stakes, of the potential consequences if Lazarus succeeded in his plans.

"This is not just a fight for the Order of St. Michael," Kaira said, her emotion-filled voice. "This is a fight for the very soul of our world. For the balance that we have sworn to protect."

As they finished speaking, a hush fell over the hall. Then, slowly at first but growing in strength, a cheer began to rise from the assembled Order. It was a cheer of unity, determination, and an undaunted commitment to stand together against the darkness.

Kaira and Reagan looked out over the sea of faces, their hearts swelling with pride and hope. At that moment, standing before the assembled Order, they knew they were not alone. Together, they would face the coming storm. Together, they would fight for the light.

CHAPTER
TWENTY-ONE

Maya's eyes snapped open, her pulse thundering as ancient warnings reverberated through her mind. She bolted upright, sweat-soaked bedroll clinging to her skin, and drew a ragged breath. The celestial expanse of Aethoria stretched before her, its ethereal beauty now tainted by writhing shadows.

She turned to find Nykronus and Asha awake, their eyes filled with concern as they watched her. Maya pushed herself to her feet, her legs unsteady beneath her. She walked over to them, the dream still vivid in her thoughts.

"I had a vision," she whispered, her breath ragged. "A dream. A warning from an ancient spirit. It spoke of a trial that will demand more from me than before."

Nykronus's face depicted curiosity, his eyes scanning Maya's face. "Tell us everything you remember," he said, his voice gentle but firm.

Maya recounted the spirit's appearance and the overwhelming intuition that had flooded her senses. As she spoke, Asha moved closer, her otherworldly glow emitting a comforting warmth against Maya's leg.

When she finished, Nykronus was silent for a long moment, his thoughts reserved. "This is a sign," he said at last. "A challenge that could alter the fate of Aethoria itself."

Maya felt her skin prickle. She knew this was no ordinary dream from the moment she'd awoken. But to hear Nykronus confirm it made it all the more real.

"What do I do?" she asked, her voice steady despite the fear that gnawed at her insides.

"You must rest, Maya. This trial will test you in ways you've never been tested before. It will require all of your strength, all of your courage, and all of your wisdom."

Asha rubbed her head against Maya's hand, her purr a soothing rumble. "We will be with you every step of the way," she said, her voice a soft mew in Maya's mind. "You are not alone in this."

Maya nodded, drawing strength from their support.

Together, they began to plan, discussing the skills Maya would need to hone and the knowledge she would need to acquire.

This was her destiny, the reason she had been drawn to Aethoria in the first place. She knew she was ready.

Maya, Nykronus, and Asha ventured deeper into the mystical forest. An unnatural fog crept around them, its tendrils curling and twisting like ghostly fingers.

The fog parted like a silver curtain, revealing a circular clearing where ancient magic pulsed beneath their feet. Violet energy arced through the air like lightning, raising goosebumps along Maya's arms as the raw power pressed against her skin.

From the swirling mists, a figure emerged—a Babaylan, her eyes ancient and knowing. "She spoke her name—Liwaya—each syllable resonating with centuries of ancient power." Maya instinctively knew this was the manifestation of her trial, a test of her resolve and character.

Liwaya's gaze pierced through Maya, seeming to see into the depths of her soul. "Maya Durant," she spoke, echoing through the clearing, "you stand at a crossroads. A darkness threatens to engulf this realm, and the choice to stop it falls upon you."

Maya's heart raced as Liwaya continued, "But this choice comes with a price. To halt the spread of this darkness, you must sacrifice something of immense personal value. Something that defines you that holds a piece of your heart."

A chill ran down Maya's spine as the weight of Liwaya's words sank in. Her mind raced with the possibilities of what she might have to give up—her powers, her memories, her connection to her family.

Asha pressed against Maya's leg, offering silent support, while Nykronus watched somberly, understanding the gravity of the choice before her.

Maya grappled with the decision, her heart torn between the desire to protect what she held dear and the duty to safeguard the greater good. She knew the consequences of allowing the darkness to spread unchecked—the suffering it would cause and the lives it would destroy.

But the thought of losing something so integral to her being, something that made her who she was, filled her with an aching sense of dread.

Maya closed her eyes, the weight of Liwaya's words bearing down upon her. She retreated into the depths of her mind, the outside world fading away as she confronted the turmoil within.

Memories flooded through her—the rigorous training sessions with her family, the love and support they had always shown her, and the desire to stand out that had driven her to Aethoria. She thought of the people she'd met in both lifetimes, the lives she had touched, and those who had touched hers in return.

As she delved deeper into her psyche, Maya confronted her fears— the fear of failure, of not being strong enough to protect those she cared about, of losing herself in the process. She grappled with the desires that pulled at her heart—the yearning for a simple life, the freedom to choose her own path, and the chance to explore the depths of her own power.

But amidst these conflicting emotions, a realization began to dawn on Maya. Her journey had never been about her own desires or fears. It had always been about something more significant—a duty to protect, serve, and safeguard the innocent from the encroaching darkness.

She thought of the lessons she had learned, the wisdom imparted by Nykronus, and the insights gained from her own experiences. She understood power was not an end but a means to fulfill a higher purpose. And sometimes, that purpose demanded sacrifice.

As the guardian, the mantle of leadership had been placed upon her shoulders. She had accepted it willingly, knowing full well the responsibilities that came with it. Now, faced with the choice to protect Aethoria, Maya understood that her desires paled in comparison to the needs of those she had sworn to defend.

Maya opened her eyes, and her decision was made. She stood tall before Liwaya, her voice steady as she spoke. "I understand the weight of this choice, and I'm ready to bear it."

She plunged into the depths of her being, past layers of memory and magic until she touched the molten core of her power—that sacred fusion of ancestral magic and hard-won knowledge that defined her existence. She drew it forth with trembling hands: a crystalline sphere shimmered with opalescent light, its surface rippling with fragments of her most precious memories. Each pulse matched her heartbeat, sending cascades of color through the clearing.

Nykronus and Asha watched in solemn silence, their eyes filled with sorrow and admiration as Maya held out the orb to Liwaya. The Babaylan reached out, her ancient hands cupping the offering with reverence.

As the sphere left Maya's grasp, ice spread through her veins. The warmth of her magic—a presence so constant she'd never truly noticed it until now—drained away, leaving behind an echoing void. Each heartbeat resonated through this newfound emptiness, a hollow drum beating to the rhythm of all she had lost. Memories that had once blazed bright flickered like dying stars just beyond her reach.

Liwaya held the orb aloft, its light casting an ethereal glow across the clearing. "Your sacrifice is accepted, Maya Durant," she intoned, her voice resonating with the realm's power. "The balance shall be restored."

With those words, Liwaya began to fade, her form dissipating into the swirling mists. As she vanished, the orb of light sank into the ground, suffusing the earth with its radiance.

Maya sensed the ground beneath her feet shift, a subtle but unmistakable change in the fabric of Aethoria. The corrupting darkness that had threaded through Aethoria's fabric like black veins receded, driven back by the force of her sacrifice.

But even as the realm stabilized, Maya acknowledged the weight of her loss settled upon her shoulders. She had given up a part of herself, a piece of her identity, to protect this world. It was a price she had been willing to pay, but the pain of it was no less acute.

Nykronus approached Maya, his ancient eyes filled with sadness and amazement. He placed a hand on her shoulder, his touch a comforting weight. "What you did today, Maya," he began, his voice low and solemn, "was an act of true bravery. You've shown wisdom beyond your years and a willingness to sacrifice for the greater good."

Maya looked up at him, tears glossing her eyes, and nodded—words inadequate to express the storm of emotions within her.

Asha padded over, her glowing form pressing against Maya's leg. "Your choice has altered the course of our battle," she purred, her voice a soothing balm to Maya's troubled heart. "The darkness has been pushed back, and it's because of you."

Maya reached down, running her fingers through Asha's soft fur. She drew strength from their presence, from the knowledge that she wasn't alone in this fight.

As they stood there in the clearing that had witnessed her sacrifice, Maya knew the weight of her decision settle upon her. The void left by her sacrifice ached, a constant reminder of what she had given up.

But amidst the pain, there was also a sense of clarity. Maya understood now, more than ever that her journey was not just about wielding power. It was about the wisdom to use that power for the greater good, even when it demanded the ultimate price.

She recalled her training and the lessons her family had instilled in her. They had taught her to be strong, to fight with skill and courage. But they had also taught her the importance of compassion, of putting others before herself.

At that moment, Maya realized that her sacrifice had been the ultimate embodiment of those lessons. She had chosen to put the needs of

Aethoria before her own, to give up a part of herself to protect the realm she had grown to love.

It was a bittersweet realization that filled her with pride and sorrow. But as she stood there, surrounded by the support of Nykronus and Asha, Maya knew that she had made the right choice.

She took a deep breath, squaring her shoulders as she looked over the now-peaceful forest. The battle was far from over, she knew. The darkness would return, and she would need to be ready to face it.

But for now, in the aftermath of her trial, Maya allowed herself a moment of respite. She had proven her worth, not just as a warrior, but as a leader willing to make the hard choices for the sake of others.

Maya, Nykronus, and Asha continued their journey through the dreamlike forest of Aethoria, the path ahead seeming to open up before them. The mists that had once obscured their way parted, revealing a more straightforward trail that wound through the ancient trees.

But it wasn't just the physical path that seemed more defined. For Maya, the way forward had never been more apparent. The trial she had faced and her sacrifice had left an indelible mark on her soul. Though a part of her had been diminished, given up for the greater good, she found that her resolve had only grown stronger.

The emptiness left by her sacrifice had been filled with a profound understanding of what it truly meant to be a leader, to put the needs of others before her own. She thought back to the pain of giving up a piece of herself. But now, as she walked through the tranquil forest, she understood that it had been a necessary pain.

Nykronus and Asha walked beside her, their presence a constant reminder of the support she had. They had witnessed her trial and the depth of her courage and selflessness. And in their eyes, Maya saw a newfound respect, a recognition of the leader she had become.

Maya embraced a sense of calm that settled over her as they journeyed on. The fears and doubts that had once plagued her seemed to fade away, replaced by a quiet confidence. She had faced one of her life's most significant challenges and emerged stronger for it.

She had proven to herself and those who relied on her that she was willing to make hard choices and sacrifice for the greater good.

With each step along the ancient path, Maya forged ahead—no longer just a wielder of magic, but a guardian who understood the true price of power. The trial had stripped away her innocence, but in that void bloomed something far more precious: wisdom earned through sacrifice and strength tempered by loss. She emerged not just transformed but transcendent.

CHAPTER
TWENTY-TWO

The ancient trees of Aethoria whispered secrets in their melodic tongue as Maya and Nykronus made their way through the shifting shadows of the forest. Luminescent moss carpeted the ground beneath their feet, each step releasing tiny sparks of ethereal light. Maya noticed a change in Nykronus's demeanor - his usually alluring expression had grown distant, his steps becoming more measured as if the air around him carried a newfound weight.

Asha padded silently beside them, her fur rippling with shadows and starlight, occasionally pausing to taste the air with a flick of her whiskers. The mystical feline's ears swiveled forward as they entered a clearing, where shafts of golden light filtered through the ancient canopy, creating a natural sanctuary.

In this hallowed space, Nykronus paused. The filtered light caught the angles of his face, deepening the ancient wisdom etched there. His eyes, when he turned to Maya, held a gravity that made the air itself seem to be still.

Maya became uneasy, but she nodded, encouraging him to speak.

"I came to Aethoria not just to explore its mysteries but to find a way to stop Lazarus." Nykronus's words hung heavy in the air, the ponderosity of his mission palpable. "His ambitions, if left unchecked, threaten the very balance of our worlds."

Maya's eyes widened, a chill running down her spine. Beside her, Asha's fur suddenly stood on end, her golden eyes narrowing to slits. "Lazarus? From the Bible?"

"Yes. My journey was meant to lead me to purgatory," Nykronus continued, "through a gateway hidden within the depths of Aethoria. There, I hoped to find knowledge or power that could help me counter Lazarus effectively."

Maya understood the pressure of this revelation settle upon her. The scope of their struggle had suddenly expanded, encompassing not just their immediate battles but the fate of entire realms.

"Why didn't you tell me this before?" Maya asked, her voice barely above a whisper.

Nykronus sighed a sound that carried the responsibility of centuries. "I wanted to protect you, to not burden you with the full extent of our plight. I could tell you were going through a transformation from being brought to this realm."

Nykronus traced a symbol in the air, leaving a trail of silvery light that formed into the shape of a three-pointed star. "The prophecy speaks of three forces united - Wisdom, drawn from the ancient powers," the first point blazed blue, "Compassion, born of mortal understanding," the second point glowed golden, "and Nature's own wild magic," the third point shimmered green.

"When you first arrived in Aethoria, Maya, your aura was purely golden - the mark of human empathy. But as you've grown, I've watched threads of blue wisdom and green wildness weave themselves into your spirit. The prophecy foretold of one who would bridge all three realms of power, someone who could understand both the light and shadow of existence."

Maya watched as the glowing symbol reflected in Asha's knowing eyes, the three colors swirling in their depths like ancient memories awakening. The mystical feline's tail traced patterns in the air that mimicked the three-pointed star, her whole body resonating with power. She had been drawn to Maya from the first moment - not by chance, but by destiny's own design. "Is that why Asha chose to guide me?" she asked softly.

Nykronus smiled. "The guardians of nature's magic have always known where to position themselves for destiny's turning points. Asha recognized in you what I hoped to find - a heart capable of healing the wounds that traverse all realms."

Maya nodded, a newfound determination rising within her. She now understood their mission's genuine stakes and pivotal role in the cosmic balance.

"I'm with you," she said, her voice steady despite the moment's gravity. "We'll find a way to stop Lazarus together."

Nykronus placed a hand on Maya's shoulder, a gesture of comfort and solidarity. In that moment, amidst the tranquil beauty of Aethoria's forest, a new chapter of their journey began - one where the fate of worlds hung in the balance.

Their path wound through the heart of Aethoria until they came upon a stream that sang with voices older than time. Crystal-clear waters danced over rocks that gleamed with internal light, creating patterns that seemed to mirror the very thoughts weighing on Maya's mind.

Asha approached the water's edge with deliberate grace, each paw step leaving circles of green energy that spread like ripples through time itself. Her whiskers quivered as she tasted the ancient magic in the air, and when she settled beside Maya, her purr carried harmonies that seemed to echo the stream's ageless song. The mystical feline settled gracefully beside Maya as they rested, her presence a steady anchor amid the swirling uncertainties.

The stream's gentle song encouraged confession, its waters reflecting the shifting expressions that crossed Nykronus's face as he turned to Maya, his features both sad and compassionate.

"To truly understand our mission," he began, his voice low and measured, "You must first understand Lazarus. His story is not one of simple villainy, but of a tragic figure overtaken by his own quest for power."

Maya leaned in, her eyes wide with curiosity and a hint of trepidation.

"There is much more than what is told in the Book of Luke and the parable pertaining to Lazarus. Lazarus, like many of us, was drawn to Aethoria by its mystical allure, its promise of knowledge and power beyond the mortal realm. He believed that by harnessing the darkness within this realm, he could protect the innocent, right the wrongs of the world."

Nykronus paused, his gaze distant as if reliving a painful memory.

"But the darkness of Aethoria is seductive, all-consuming. It whispers promises of greatness, of invincibility. And Lazarus, in his desperation to make a difference, fell prey to its siren song."

Maya noticed a chill run through her, a sense of unease settling in the pit of her stomach. Asha's ears flattened against her head, her tail lashing in agitation. She pressed closer to Maya as if trying to shield her companion from the mere mention of such darkness. Maya had never seen the usually composed feline so disturbed.

"He lost himself," Nykronus continued, his voice heavy with sorrow, "consumed by the power he sought to wield for good. The Lazarus we face now is a shadow of the man he once was, a being twisted by the darkness he once hoped to control."

As Nykronus's words sank in, Maya's perspective began to shift. She had always seen Lazarus as an enemy, a force to be defeated at all costs. But now, through Nykronus's tale, she began to see him in a more nuanced light - a tragic figure, a cautionary tale of the perils of unchecked ambition.

"Our mission," Nykronus said, his eyes meeting Maya's with a newfound intensity, "is not just about defeating an enemy. It's about addressing the underlying tragedy that led him astray, about finding a way to bring balance back to Aethoria and to all the realms it touches."

Maya nodded, a sense of understanding dawning upon her. Their journey, she realized, was not just a battle against darkness but a quest for redemption, for healing the wounds that had led to Lazarus's fall.

As they traversed the lush, ethereal landscapes of Aethoria, Maya couldn't shake the profound magnitude of Nykronus's revelations. The story of Lazarus, once a figure of pure villainy in her mind, now took on a more complex hue. She grappled with conflicting emotions - the steadfast determination to protect her world and the budding empathy for the tragic figure they faced.

Asha, ever-attuned to Maya's moods, sensed her companion's inner turmoil. The mystical feline nuzzled against Maya's leg, offering a comforting presence amidst the swirling thoughts. Her purring was a soothing balm to Maya's troubled mind.

"I can see it in your eyes," Asha purred, her voice a soothing balm. "The struggle between duty and compassion."

Maya sighed, her hand absently stroking Asha's glossy fur. "I always thought our mission was clear-cut. Defeat the villain and save the world. But now... now I see the shades of gray, the humanity behind the monster."

Nykronus, overhearing the exchange, approached with a gentle smile. "It's a heavy burden, isn't it? To see the complexity of our foes."

Maya inclined her head, locking eyes with Nykronus's timeworn stare. "What can we do to end this? We have to stop Lazarus, but at the same time, I want to rescue him from his own inner demons."

Nykronus placed a comforting hand on Maya's shoulder. "That, my dear, is the true test of a hero. To find the path that leads to healing, even in the face of great darkness."

As they walked, Maya mulled over Nykronus's words. The idea of redemption, of reaching out to Lazarus with understanding rather than condemnation, began to take root in her heart.

"What if..." she began, her voice tentative yet hopeful, "what if we could find a way to reach him? To offer a chance at redemption?"

Nykronus's eyes sparkled with pride. "It's a noble thought, Maya. One that speaks to the strength of your character."

At that moment, amidst the beauty of Aethoria and the warmth of her companions, she recognized a glimmer of hope. Through understanding and compassion, they could find a resolution that healed rather than harmed—a way to bring balance back to Aethoria and the soul of a fallen man.

The mountain loomed before them, its jagged peaks piercing the lavender sky of Aethoria like ancient spears. Maya's breath caught in her throat as they drew closer, her steps crunching on crystalline gravel that seemed to whisper ancient secrets. The air grew thick with an electric tension, making her skin prickle and her hair stand on end.

Beside her, Asha's fur bristled, the orange patches seeming to glow against her black coat like embers in the strange, shadowy light. The mystical feline's tail twitched in a complex pattern that Maya had learned meant danger and power intertwined.

Nykronus halted at the mountain's base, where smooth obsidian rock met rough granite. His weathered hand traced ancient runes carved into the stone, symbols that pulsed with a faint blue light at his touch. "Here," he whispered, his voice carrying despite its softness. "The ancients sealed this gateway to purgatory centuries ago, hoping to prevent exactly what Lazarus now attempts."

The wind shifted, bringing with it the scent of ozone and something older that reminded Maya of church incense and autumn leaves. She shivered, remembering the significance of Nykronus's earlier revelations about Lazarus. "Those who sealed it," she ventured, "did they know he would come?"

"They knew someone would try." Nykronus turned to face her, shadows dancing across the deep lines of his face. In the strange light, his eyes held both starlight and sorrow. "The power beyond this gate has always drawn those who seek to change their fate. But you, Maya —" He extended his hand, palm up, revealing a mark that glowed with the same blue light as the runes. "You're the first to come with the intention of healing rather than conquest."

Asha pressed against Maya's legs, her purr deepening to a resonance that seemed to vibrate through the very foundations of the mountain. Her fur shimmered with an inner light that pulsed in harmony with the ancient runes, green energy flowing from her like rivers of starlight. As guardian of nature's magic, she was no mere companion but a vital key to the power they now sought to unleash. The vibration seemed to awaken something in the mountain itself, causing tiny crystals embedded in the rock face to flicker like distant stars.

Maya placed her hand in Nykronus's, gasping as warmth rushed up her arm. It felt like sunlight and shadow intertwined, an ancient and new power. Asha stretched up, placing one paw atop their joined hands. Where her paw touched, Maya felt a wild magic join the mix, like wind through summer leaves.

"The gateway requires three kinds of power," Nykronus explained, his voice taking on the rhythmic quality of ritual. "The wisdom of ages." His hand pulsed with blue light. "The courage to face darkness with compassion." Maya's hand began to glow with a soft golden radiance. "And the balance of nature itself." Asha's paw emanated a green shimmer that twined with the other colors.

"Together," they spoke in unison, their voices harmonizing with an otherworldly resonance that echoed off the mountainside.

The ground beneath them shuddered. A line of light traced its way up the mountain face, following the path of ancient runes that had been invisible moments before. The crack that appeared wasn't just in the physical rock but seemed to split the very fabric of reality. Through it, Maya glimpsed swirling shadows and dancing lights, and the boundary between worlds was made manifest.

The portal widened, edges crystallizing into an archway of obsidian and light. The air that drifted through carried the impact of centuries and the whispers of countless souls. Maya inhaled deeply, tasting metal and mysteries on her tongue.

"The path is open," Nykronus murmured, "but remember—in purgatory, intentions matter more than power. Your compassion, Maya, may prove to be our greatest strength."

Maya squared her shoulders, drawing strength from Asha's steady presence and Nykronus's quiet confidence. The portal beckoned, its swirling depths holding both answers and dangers. But now, understanding the true nature of their quest—not just to stop Lazarus, but to heal the wounds that had created him—she felt ready to face whatever waited on the other side.

Maya, Nykronus, and Asha stood before the entrance, their resolve unwavering. They understood that the path to stopping Lazarus lay in confronting the place he sought to escape, facing the darkness that had consumed him.

"Are we ready?" Maya asked, her voice a mix of determination and uncertainty.

Nykronus placed a reassuring hand on her shoulder. "We are."

With those words, the trio stepped forward as one. Asha took the lead, her tail held high like a beacon of nature's power, her paws leaving traces of green energy that seemed to light their way into the unknown depths of purgatory. Whatever lay beyond, they would face it together, armed with a deeper understanding of their mission and a resolve to find a solution that could bring healing to both the realms and the soul of a fallen man.

CHAPTER

TWENTY-THREE

S omewhere near the France Border approximately 118 kilometers from San Sebastián, Spain

Elan's grip tightened on *Winterstar* as shadows materialized from the morning mist, taking the form of the Malefic Assembly's elite guard. Their discovery of the group's sanctuary in Azur's farmlands sent a chill through his bones that had nothing to do with his blade's ancient magic. The first attacker approached him with impossible speed—a blur of crimson robes and gleaming steel.

Winterstar answered before Elan could think, the sword's consciousness merging with his own in that familiar dance of battle. Ice-blue energy crackled along the blade's length as he dodged, the impact sending shockwaves through his arms. Time seemed to slow. Each movement flowed into the next: a slash that split the air with sapphire light, a thrust that left frost crystallizing on his opponent's robes, and a sweeping strike that scattered three attackers like leaves in a storm.

The ancient sword's song filled his mind—a melody of ice and starlight that had guided warriors for centuries before him. Its power coursed through his veins, transforming his muscles into living steel, his reflexes into lightning. A defender leaped at him from the left, shadow-magic writhing around their blade. Elan pivoted on his back foot, *Winterstar*'s edge catching the morning sun as it described a perfect arc through the air. The collision of ancient steel against shadow-forged weapons rang out across the battlefield like a temple bell.

Yet for every foe he felled, two more emerged from the mist. Sweat froze on his brow as he held the line, each breath burning in his lungs. The weight of their mission—the artifact, his friends, the fate of it all— pressed down on him like a physical force. But as *Winterstar* hummed in his hands, a sound like distant avalanches, Elan felt his will crystallize into something unbreakable. He had sworn an oath, not just to the blade or the cause, but to everyone who fought beside him. As long as he drew breath, that line would hold.

Beside him, Stanley fought with fierce determination, his fists connecting with the enemy in a flurry of powerful blows. The former MMA fighter's skills were tested as he dodged and weaved, his red hair whipping wildly in the wind as he moved with a speed that belied his muscular frame. Each punch was delivered with precision and force, fueled by the adrenaline coursing through his veins and the unwavering resolve to protect those he held dear. Stanley's cowboy hat threatened to fly off with every rapid movement. Still, he paid it no mind, focusing solely on the battle and the relentless onslaught of foes before him.

Zoe's fingers danced across the strings of her electric lute, the instrument's haunting melody intertwining with the sounds of battle. Her music immediately affected the battlefield, bolstering her allies and disorienting their foes. The enchanting notes swirled through the air, a symphony of power and emotion that wove into the conflict's very fabric. With each skillful pluck of the strings, Zoe's music became a force to be reckoned with, a weapon as potent as any blade or spell. Her allies felt their spirits lift and their resolve strengthen. At the same time, their enemies faltered, their minds clouded by the beguiling tones. At that moment, Zoe was not merely a musician but a conduit for ancient and primal magic, and her song was a catalyst for victory. Her long blond hair was slick with sweat as she poured her heart into the performance.

Myst, ever the protector, stood guard over the artifact safely tucked in his jacket pocket, his hands weaving intricate patterns in the air as he cast defensive spells alongside Olivia. His brow furrowed in concentration, the ancient words of power flowing from his lips like a magic river. The air around them shimmered and crackled with energy, a testament to the strength of their combined efforts. Myst's eyes darted across the battlefield, constantly vigilant, always ready to defend against the next attack. He could feel the weight of the artifact against his chest, a constant reminder of the importance of their mission and the trust placed in him to keep it safe. The young man's focus was unwavering, his connection to the ancient magic of his lineage evident in the shimmering aura surrounding him.

The battle raged on, the farmhouse's once peaceful grounds now a chaotic whirlwind of clashing weapons and crackling energy. Elan and Stanley fought back-to-back, their movements synchronized as they pushed back against the relentless onslaught of the Malefic Assembly.

The sound came first—not a scream, but something worse: a soft, surprised exhale that cut through the chaos of battle like a blade through silk. Elan knew that sound. He'd heard it before, in other battles, in other losses, but never from—

"Olivia!"

Time fractured. *Winterstar*'s colors faltered mid-swing as Elan turned, each heartbeat stretching into eternity. Olivia stood twenty paces away, her spell-tome still clutched in one hand, the other pressed against her midsection. Their eyes met across the battlefield. Hers held no fear, only a terrible understanding.

Then, her knees buckled.

The spell-tome hit the ground first, ancient pages fluttering like broken wings. Olivia followed, her descent somehow both graceful and devastating. The impact drove the breath from her lungs in a wet gasp that misted red in the morning air. Where her hand fell from her stomach, darkness spread across her gray sweater—not the familiar shadow-magic they'd fought so many times before, but something far more mundane and infinitely more terrible.

Her pixie-cut hair, still perfect despite the battle's chaos, formed a dark halo around her head. The silver pendant she always wore—a gift from her grandmother, from her first life, she'd told them one night around the fire—glinted once in the sunlight before becoming slick with blood. Each breath whistled through her lips, shallow and racing as if her body tried to fit a lifetime of air into these final moments.

"Strange," she whispered, her voice steady despite everything, "I always thought it would hurt more."

The scent of ozone and copper filled the air—Zoe's healing magic tangling with the metallic smell of blood. But even as the bard's power washed over Olivia in waves of golden light, Elan saw the truth written in the growing shadows under her eyes, in the way her fingers had already begun to cool when they brushed against his hand.

Some wounds, he realized with growing horror, magic couldn't touch.

Elan and Stanley exchanged a look, a silent understanding passing between them. With a roar of fury, they redoubled their efforts, their attacks becoming more aggressive as they sought to end the fight quickly. Elan's blade flashed in the sunlight, cutting down foes with a newfound urgency, while Stanley's fists struck with a force that sent enemies flying.

But it was too late.

Amidst the chaos, the group huddled around Olivia's still form. Elan, his face etched with worry, cradled her head gently while Myst and Stanley worked frantically to stem the flow of blood from her wounds. Zoe, her hands glowing with healing energy, poured every ounce of her power into Olivia's battered body.

Despite their combined efforts, Olivia's life force continued to ebb away. Her breaths grew shallow, and her skin took on a deathly pallor. The realization that they could not save her settled over the group like a suffocating blanket.

Olivia's eyes fluttered open, her gaze hazy with pain. "My friends," she whispered, her voice barely audible above the crackling of the dying embers in the fireplace. "You must... continue the fight."

Elan leaned closer, his eyes brimming with unshed tears. "We will, Olivia. We won't let your sacrifice be in vain."

A faint smile graced Olivia's lips. "The darkness... it must be stopped. Promise me... you won't give up."

Stanley, his usually boisterous demeanor subdued, placed a comforting hand on Olivia's shoulder. "We promise, Olivia. We'll see this through to the end."

Her voice choked with emotion, Zoe added, "Your strength will guide us, always."

As Olivia's eyes drifted closed for the final time, a sense of profound loss settled over the group. They had lost not just a comrade but a dear friend, a sister in arms. The weight of their mission, the fight against the encroaching darkness, had never felt more real or urgent.

In the silence that followed, broken only by the soft sobs of those gathered, a solemn determination took root.

As the group prepared to leave the refuge, the weight of their loss and the pressure of their mission began to take their toll. Tensions simmered beneath the surface, threatening to boil over at any moment. Elan and Myst, their mission already tainted by the recent events, found themselves at the center of a growing storm.

Stanley was the first to voice his discontent, grief and fear manifesting as anger. "We can't keep going on like this," he growled, his fists clenched at his sides. "We're flying blind, and it's costing us lives. Olivia's blood is on our hands."

Zoe, her eyes red-rimmed from crying, nodded in agreement. "We need a plan, a real plan. We can't just keep reacting to whatever the Malefic Assembly throws. We need to be proactive."

His grief and frustration bubbling to the surface, Elan snapped back. "You think we don't know that? We left headquarters for the Artifact and got what we came for. This sucks, I know. But I don't see why you're taking it out on us, Stanley. We're doing the best we can with what we have. This isn't easy for any of us."

Myst, caught between his loyalty to his father and his own doubts, tried to intervene. "We're all hurting right now, but turning on each other isn't helping. We need to stick together, now more than ever."

But Stanley wasn't having it. "Sticking together is what got Olivia killed. We need to change our approach, or we're all going to end up like her."

The words hung heavy in the air, a painful truth none wanted to acknowledge. For a moment, it seemed the group might fracture under their grief and fear.

But then, something shifted. Elan, his voice heavy with emotion, spoke up. "Olivia believed in this cause, in us. She wanted to be here. Just like you did. Just like Zoe did. She gave her life fighting for what she knew was right. We can't let her sacrifice be in vain."

Trembling but determined, Zoe added, "Olivia would want us to keep going to finish what we started. We owe it to her to see this through. You're right, Elan. I wanted to be here, and I am still here."

As the group looked around at each other, they saw the same pain and determination reflected in each other's eyes. They had lost one of their own, but they were still together, still united in their cause.

Stanley, his anger fading into a grim resolve, nodded. "For Olivia, then. We keep fighting, no matter what."

Dawn painted the hilltop in watercolor hues - the kind Olivia used to photograph on their early morning watches. Dew sparkled on the wild sage that had already begun growing around her marker—not the traditional wooden cross they'd first erected, but a standing stone carved with ancient runes that Myst insisted would help guide her spirit home. The morning light caught the crystalline formations in the rock face, making them shimmer like tears.

Elan knelt before the stone, his knees sinking into earth still soft from yesterday's rain. *Winterstar* hummed softly at his hip, its usual icy song subdued, as if the blade too mourned their loss. His fingers traced the runes Myst had carved: Scholar. Warrior. Friend. Guardian. Aunt. Below them, in Olivia's precise handwriting—copied from her last field journal—were the words she'd lived by: "Knowledge guards the light."

"I brought something from the library," Elan said, his voice barely above a whisper. He withdrew a smooth river stone from his jacket, its surface worn by centuries of patient water. "Remember that day in Benevento? You spent hours explaining how these stones in the library's foundation had witnessed centuries of scholars coming and going, preserving knowledge through wars and plagues and darkness."

He placed the stone at the marker's base, where it joined other tokens of remembrance: Zoe's silver lute pick that Olivia had once used to mark her place in ancient texts; Stanley's worn MMA hand wraps from the day she'd asked him to teach her self-defense; a pressed flower from Myst's grimoire—wolfsbane, her favorite for its dual nature as both poison and cure.

"You were right about the stones," Elan continued, watching the sunrise paint shadows across the marker. "They endure. They remember." His fingers brushed the cool surface of the river stone. "This one was beneath your favorite reading spot. The librarian said... she said you sat there so often, she started calling it 'Olivia's Corner.'"

The wind picked up, carrying the scent of sage and morning dew. For a moment, Elan could almost imagine it was her voice in the whisper of leaves—could almost see her there, cross-legged on the library floor, surrounded by ancient texts and modern tablets, looking up with that slight smile that meant she'd found something extraordinary.

"We found something in your notes," he said, his voice growing stronger. "About the artifact. About what the Malefic Assembly is really planning." His hand tightened on *Winterstar*'s hilt. "You knew, didn't you? That's why you pushed us to check the Benevento archives. You were always three steps ahead of us."

The standing stone stood silent in the growing light, but the runes seemed to pulse gently, matching the rhythm of his words. Myst had said the stone would remember their vigils, words, and promises. Would hold them like the library stones held centuries of whispered knowledge.

"We'll finish what you started," Elan promised, rising slowly. "We'll protect what you died defending." He touched the stone one last time, feeling the warmth of the morning sun on its surface. "And we'll make sure they remember. Not just what you died for—but what you lived for."

As the morning stretched on, none of them wanted to be the first to say it, but they all felt the compass's steady pulse growing more insistent with each passing hour. The artifact that had guided them to Azur— and to their loss—now thrummed with an almost anxious energy.

"The compass's song... it's changed," Elan said, his hand resting on *Winterstar*'s hilt, the sword's own icy melody clashing with the compass's increasingly erratic rhythm. "It hasn't felt like this since the night Nykronus entrusted it to us."

Myst retrieved the compass from his jacket pocket, its bronze face catching the late morning light. The intricate runes etched along its edge—symbols Olivia had spent countless hours trying to decipher— seemed to shimmer with an inner fire. "She was translating these, you know. The night before..." He swallowed hard. "She said they weren't just decorative. That they were some kind of warning."

"Or instructions," Zoe added softly, her musician's ears picking up the subtle changes in the compass's resonance. "Remember how she used to say magical artifacts don't just point the way—they teach us how to walk it?"

The small town of Azur stretched out below them, its medieval streets and terracotta roofs a stark contrast to the modern Ford Explorer waiting at the bottom of the hill. They'd chosen this place for its obscurity, its distance from the Malefic Assembly's usual haunts. Now it would forever be marked in their memories as something else —a tomb, a testimony, a turning point.

"We don't have her expertise anymore," Elan said, his eyes sweeping over the town one last time, memorizing the place where they'd lost so much. "But we have her notes. Her research. And we have each other."

The compass's pulse quickened as if responding to his words. The needle, which had been swinging erratically, suddenly snapped to attention with such force that Myst nearly dropped it. It pointed unerringly southeast—toward San Sebastián.

They made their way down the hill in silence, each lost in their thoughts but bound together by shared purpose. The Explorer's dark bulk waited for them, its modern lines incongruous against the ancient cobblestones. As they loaded their gear, the compass's song grew stronger, more urgent—a crescendo building toward something none of them could yet comprehend.

What had begun as a subtle hum now felt like a physical presence, the artifact's energy filling the vehicle with an almost electric tension. As Elan guided them through Azur's narrow streets, each turn seemed to amplify the compass's power. They were leaving more than a fallen companion behind—they were driving toward whatever truth Olivia had died protecting, whatever secret had made the Assembly desperate enough to strike so boldly.

The medieval town receded in their rearview mirror, its bell towers and ancient walls growing smaller until they merged with the Spanish countryside. But the compass's song only grew stronger, its needle unwavering. Sitting in the passenger seat, Myst traced the intricate engravings on its surface, his eyes growing wide as the runes began to pulse with an inner light.

"Wait," he exclaimed, his voice filled with sudden understanding and trepidation. "Something's happening. I can sense it—it's not just guiding us, it's—"

The air around them crackled with unseen energy, reality itself seeming to bend and warp. Stanley let out a startled grunt from the backseat. "What the hell?"

"Myst, what do you mean it's—" Zoe's words were cut short as a blinding light engulfed them, accompanied by a deafening roar that seemed to shake the very foundations of the earth.

In an instant, the group found themselves whisked away, their senses overwhelmed by the sudden shift in their surroundings. Elan swerved and brought the vehicle to an abrupt stop. The familiar Spanish countryside had vanished, replaced by an alien landscape that defied description. As they struggled to regain their bearings, they knew their journey had taken an unexpected and potentially perilous turn, leading them into uncharted territories where the rules of reality no longer applied.

CHAPTER
TWENTY-FOUR

San Francisco, California

The command center of the Order of St. Michael thrummed with tension, magic, and technology seamlessly intertwined in the air like static before a storm. Before a wall-sized display, Kaira and Reagan studied a haunting map - its crystalline surface pulsed with veins of amber light, each marking another breach where Lazarus's darkness had taken hold. With every new flicker, another piece of his sinister puzzle fell into place. The ghostly illumination carved shadows beneath Reagan's sharp cheekbones and glinted off the silver streaks in Kaira's dark hair as they tracked the spreading corruption.

Reports and intelligence lay scattered across the table, painting a grim picture of the scale of Lazarus's plans. Deep in concentration, the leaders pored over the documents to assess the growing threat. Each piece of information added another layer of urgency to their already weighty task, the fate of countless lives resting on their shoulders.

The room was heavy with anticipation of their decision, and every member of the Order waited for guidance from their leaders. They looked to Kaira and Reagan, their eyes filled with hope and apprehension, seeking reassurance in the face of an uncertain future.

Kaira's voice cut through the silence, her tone sad and heavy with the strain of their recent loss. "As some of you know," Kaira said, her finger hovering over a dark spot on the map that pulsed like an open wound, "we've lost Olivia." The name hung heavy in the air, drawing sharp breaths from those who hadn't heard. "Our friend, our guiding light, fell defending the Spanish sanctuary. Her death..." Kaira's voice hardened, "serves as a stark reminder of the lengths Lazarus will go to achieve his goals and the price we may all have to pay to stop him."

Reagan nodded, her eyes brimming with tears that she fought to hold back. She reached out, placing a comforting hand on Kaira's shoulder, a silent gesture of support and shared grief. "We can't let her loss be in vain," she said, her voice steady despite the emotion that threatened to overwhelm her. "We have to honor her memory by standing united against this threat, no matter the cost."

The air was charged with a palpable sense of urgency, the imposition of impending doom casting shadows over their faces as they contemplated the road ahead. They knew that the choices they made at that moment would shape the course of the battle and that every decision would carry the potential for great triumph or devastating loss.

Later, seeking privacy to process their grief, the sisters retreated to Reagan's study. Unlike the sterile command center, this room breathed with personal history - medals of valor hung beside candid photos of Order members in happier times, and Olivia's smiling face featured in many of them. Reagan's fingers traced the edge of one such photo as she and Kaira settled into the worn leather chairs where they'd spent countless hours strategizing with their now-fallen friend. They were not just leaders but also individuals with their fears and doubts, struggling to find the strength to lead their people in the face of such a daunting task.

The leaders paused their deliberations after the heavy silence surrounding the knowledge of Olivia's death. Reagan turned to her sister; her usually steady and resolute voice trembled as she spoke. "I remember the first time I met Olivia," she began, her eyes distant with memory. "Her strength, her wisdom..." Reagan's voice softened with memory. "Her faith was extraordinary. Picture Times Square on New Year's Eve - thousands of people, chaos everywhere, every exit blocked. But with Olivia, it was like having an invisible path laid out just for you. No matter how dark things got, she always knew the way forward, and somehow made you believe you'd make it through anything."

Kaira smiled, soft words playing on her lips. "She had a way of bringing light into even the darkest of moments," she said, her voice thick with emotion. "Her guidance, her unwavering faith in our cause... it was a beacon for us all. I remember first meeting her...in my *other* life..."

As they shared memories of Olivia, each story painting a vivid picture of the remarkable woman she had been, the conversation took on a profoundly emotional tone. They mourned not only a fallen leader but a dear friend, a sister in arms whose absence left a gaping void in the fabric of their lives and in the heart of the Order. Her death had shaken them to their core, and the pain of her loss was a constant reminder of the stakes they were fighting for.

The realization of Olivia's sacrifice, the ultimate embodiment of their struggle against the darkness, brought a painful clarity to their situation. Her loss was a stark reminder of the stakes they faced, the lives that hung in the balance with every decision they made.

"Our plan," Reagan said, her voice steadying with resolve, "must honor Olivia's memory. We cannot let her sacrifice be in vain."

Kaira reached out, clasping Reagan's hand in solidarity and shared grief. "She would want us to carry on," she said, her eyes shining with unshed tears. "To fight, to protect, to stand united against the darkness that threatens to consume us all."

The room had transformed when Kaira and Reagan returned to the command center. Gone were the scattered reports and whispered conversations. Their most trusted advisors and lieutenants stood at attention, their ceremonial robes catching the amber light from the map display. Magic crackled in the air like lightning before a storm as the sisters took their positions at the head of the room, the weight of centuries of Order tradition settling on their shoulders.

Kaira's voice rang out, clear and resolute. "We have made our decision," she announced, her gaze sweeping over the assembled faces. "We will confront Lazarus directly, meeting his forces head-on in a battle that will determine the fate of our world." She outlined their plan, detailing the strategies they would employ and the risks they would face, building tension and anticipation for the impending battle.

Reagan stepped forward, her posture mirroring her sister's determination. "We know the risks, the dangers that lie ahead," she said, measured and deliberate. "But we also know that the alternative is unthinkable. We cannot allow Lazarus to continue unchecked, to spread his darkness and corruption across the land."

The room seemed to hold its collective breath as Kaira unveiled the details of their plan. "We will invoke the ancient rite of the Celestial Convergence," Kaira declared, her voice resonating with power that made the very air crackle. The gathered advisors drew sharp breaths - some making warding gestures, others gripping their chairs white-knuckled. The last time the Convergence had been attempted, according to Order records, it had torn a hole in the fabric of reality itself.

"The alignment of the seven celestial anchors," Reagan continued, pulling up an intricate diagram of interconnected constellations on display, "will create a weapon of pure light - one capable of cleaving through Lazarus's darkness. But the power required..." She met her sister's eyes, both knowing the unspoken cost. The last Convergence had claimed the lives of three of the seven mages who attempted it. A veteran mage near the front went pale, his hands trembling as he made the Order's ancient sign against death. He had been there for the last attempt - had watched those mages burn from the inside out as they channeled powers beyond mortal comprehension.

Whispers of disbelief and excitement filled the air, the audacity of the plan leaving many stunned. The Celestial Convergence was a legend, a mythical feat that had never been attempted in living memory.

Reagan's voice cut through the chatter, her tone unwavering. "We know the risks, the potential consequences of wielding such immense power," she acknowledged. "But we also know that we have no choice. This is our last, best hope to save our world from the darkness that threatens to engulf it."

As the reality of their decision settled over the room, a palpable sense of unity and determination began to take hold. The Order, galvanized by their leaders' resolve, stood tall in the face of the looming battle.

"We stand together," Kaira declared, her voice ringing with conviction. "As one Order, one force against the darkness. We will not falter. We will not fail. For the sake of all we hold dear, we will prevail."

The room erupted in a rallying cry, a chorus of voices pledging their allegiance and lives to the cause. Kaira and Reagan stood at the helm, their resolute expressions a beacon of strength for the assembled Order members.

Suddenly, a commotion erupted from the back of the room. Flushed with urgency, an intern pushed her way through the crowd, shouting to get Kaira's attention. "Kaira! Kaira, please listen!"

The room fell silent, all eyes turning to the young woman as she reached the front, her breath coming in short gasps. Kaira's brow furrowed with concern as she met the intern's panicked gaze.

"Kaira!" Sarah - the intern who had earned her position through perfect test scores and an unmatched talent for tracking spells - burst through the crowd, her usual composure shattered. At nineteen, she was the youngest member of the Order's intelligence division, and never, in her meteoric rise through the ranks, had she looked this terrified. Her tablet clattered to the floor, its screen still displaying the last known coordinates of Elan's team, the tracking runes she had personally crafted now dark and lifeless.

"It's - they're -" She sucked in a breath, forcing herself to deliver the report with the precision her training demanded. "Elan's team was crossing the Spanish border when our tracking spells detected a massive surge of dark energy. Then nothing. All seven tracking signatures, the satellite feed, even their magical anchors - everything went dark simultaneously." She pulled up a holographic replay, showing seven bright points of light snuffed out in an instant, leaving behind a void that seemed to swallow even the background magical noise of the area.

Kaira's hand found Reagan's arm, squeezing tight enough to bruise. They'd seen this pattern before - the night Olivia died.

A wave of shocked murmurs rippled through the room, the news hitting like a physical blow. Kaira and Reagan exchanged a look of alarm, the implications of this development sinking in.

The advisors stepped forward, their faces etched with worry. "We can't proceed with the plan without the other leaders of the Order," one declared grave. "We don't even have Maya or Nykronus. How can we hope to confront Lazarus without their strength and guidance?"

Kaira held up a hand, silencing the rising tide of concerns. Her eyes met Reagan's, a silent communication passing between them. With a nod, Kaira turned back to the assembled group, her voice steady despite the gravity of the situation.

"We understand your concerns," she said, her gaze sweeping over the room. "This news is deeply troubling, and we cannot ignore its impact on our plans. Let's not jump to conclusions."

Reagan stepped forward, her expression mirroring her sister's determination. "Kaira and I will convene in our private quarters to determine our next actions," she announced, her words measured and deliberate. "For now, we'll table our current plan until we gather more information and assess the situation fully."

The room fell into a tense silence, the moment's gravity settling over them all. Even in the face of this unexpected setback, Kaira and Reagan's leadership provided a glimmer of hope amidst the uncertainty.

The sanctuary's ancient garden had weathered centuries of Order leaders seeking its wisdom. As Kaira and Reagan walked the worn stone path between beds of herbs used in healing spells, the enchanted roses - bred by the first Order mages - turned their blooms to track their movement. Here, where the veil between worlds ran thin, and the air hummed with accumulated power, they could finally let their guards down. No wards or surveillance spells penetrated this sacred space - only the whispers of past leaders, their wisdom soaked into the very soil, bore witness to the sisters' vulnerability.

Amidst the gentle rustling of leaves and the soft chirping of birds, the Mazza's finally let their carefully maintained facades crumble. Here, away from the watchful eyes of their followers, they could be more than leaders - they could simply be sisters, sharing their fears and doubts in the sacred quiet.

Kaira's voice trembled as she spoke, her words a confession of the fears that haunted her. "I can't help but wonder if we're making the right choice," she admitted, her gaze fixed on the delicate petals of a blooming rose. "The lives we're risking, the sacrifices we're asking others to make... it weighs heavily on my heart."

Reagan reached out, her hand finding Kaira's in a gesture of comfort and understanding. "I feel it too," she whispered, her own doubts rising to the surface. "The responsibility, the uncertainty... it's a burden we bear together."

In the garden's stillness, the sisters allowed themselves to express the depths of their fears, the doubts that gnawed at their resolve. They spoke of the personal toll their leadership had taken, the sleepless nights spent grappling with impossible decisions, and the constant fear of failing those who looked to them for guidance.

Yet even amidst the vulnerability, a thread of determination wove through their words. Their commitment to their cause, to the fight against the darkness that threatened to engulf their world, burned brightly within them.

"We can't let our fears consume us," Kaira said, her voice gaining strength as she spoke. "We have to trust in each other, in the strength of our bond and the righteousness of our cause."

Reagan nodded, her own resolve mirroring her sister's. "Together, we'll face whatever lies ahead," she affirmed, her grip on Kaira's hand tightening. "We'll bear this burden as one, drawing strength from our shared purpose."

As their thoughts turned to Elan and his team, a flicker of hope ignited within them. A constellation of stars peeked through the gathering dusk through the garden's enchanted roses - the same formation they would need for the Celestial Convergence. Perhaps it wasn't a coincidence that Elan had disappeared just as they discovered this ancient solution. If anyone could survive Lazarus's darkness and find their way back, it would be him. And maybe, his return would bring the missing piece they needed to make the impossible ritual possible.

ACT THREE

"Life's most persistent and urgent question is, 'What are you doing for others?'"
— *Martin Luther King Jr.*

TWENTY-FIVE

Maya and Nykronus emerged from the sealed gateway, their senses overwhelmed by the transit from Aethoria. Purgatory, a realm of half-light and shadows, enveloped them in its solemn embrace. The air hung heavy with the whispers of past lives, a symphony of penance and redemption that echoed through the shifting mists. The mystery of this place, sealed for a reason, stirred a deep curiosity in Maya and Nykronus.

As they navigated this liminal space, Maya was struck by the striking beauty that surrounded them. The muted colors and soothing undulations of the terrain created a dreamlike atmosphere, a stark contrast to the vibrant chaos of Aethoria and the dark machinations of their world. Nykronus seemed to find solace in the quietude that permeated the realm, a beauty that filled Maya with a sense of wonder.

Asha, however, remained wary. The feline companion, her glowing orange and black fur standing up on her back, padded close to Maya's side. "This place was sealed for a reason," she groaned, her voice a soft growl amidst the stillness. "The secrets it holds, the power that lingers here... it's not meant for mortal eyes." Her caution filled the air with a sense of impending danger.

Maya, her initial awe giving way to a somber reflection, couldn't help but ponder the nature of this place. The souls that lingered here, trapped between worlds, sought closure or redemption. This concept resonated deeply with her understanding of the world's growing complexities. The weight of their journey, the sacrifices they had made, and the challenges that lay ahead seemed to find a mirror in the souls that wandered purgatory's misty paths.

As they ventured deeper into the realm, the echoes of past lives grew louder, whispering secrets and sorrows that tugged at Maya's heart. She couldn't help but wonder about the stories behind each soul and the choices that had led them to this place of penance. The realization that even in death, the struggle for meaning and purpose continued struck a chord within her.

Nykronus, sensing Maya's introspection, placed a comforting hand on her shoulder. "This place is a reminder," he said, his voice a tender rumble amidst the stillness, "that the path to redemption is never easy, but it is always worth pursuing. Just as these souls seek to atone for their past, we must confront the darkness within ourselves and the world around us."

As Maya and Nykronus traversed the eerie terrain, a once-grand estate loomed before them, its crumbling facade a testament to the ravages of time and neglect. The sprawling ruins seemed to mirror the rich man's life, symbolizing his earthly wealth and subsequent downfall.

Amidst the decaying grandeur, a figure emerged from the shadows, his movements cautious yet purposeful. As he approached the travelers, his composure flickered with caution and relief, the weight of countless years of isolation etched upon his face.

"Travelers from another realm." The words rasped from his throat, hoarse from disuse. "It has been an age since I've seen another soul."

Maya and Nykronus exchanged glances, their curiosity piqued by the man's unexpected presence. They stepped forward, their postures guarded yet open to the encounter.

The rich man, sensing their willingness to listen, began to pour out his story, the words tumbling from his lips in a torrent of raw emotion. He spoke of his life, vast wealth, and the choices that had led him to this desolate place, his voice trembling with regret and resentment. As he delved deeper into his tale, his gaze looked haunted, as if reliving each painful moment.

With each revelation, a twisted truth began to emerge, one that challenged the very foundations of the parable Maya and Nykronus had known. The rich man's words painted a picture of betrayal, where he had been unjustly condemned, his actions misinterpreted, and his character maligned. In contrast, Lazarus, through deceit and manipulation, had managed to ascend to a position of power, exploiting the very system that had once oppressed him. The rich man's story served as a powerful catalyst, shattering the characters' preconceived notions of good and evil, and forcing them to confront the complexity of morality in their world.

"The judgment that befell me was flawed." His demeanor burned with conviction. "Lazarus, the one deemed virtuous, was not as he seemed. His actions were cloaked in a veil of righteousness, masking the darkness that lurked within."

Maya and Nykronus listened intently, their minds grappling with the implications of the rich man's revelations. Once evident in the parable, the thin line between virtue and vice blurred before their eyes.

As the rich man's story unfolded, the travelers questioned the nature of cosmic judgment, the scales of justice that had seemingly condemned one and elevated the other.

The rich man led Maya and Nykronus through the crumbling halls of his once-grand estate, the echoes of their footsteps mingling with the whispers of the past. As they entered what remained of a grand salon, the rich man gestured for them to sit among the faded remnants of his earthly attachments—tattered tapestries, broken furniture, and the ghostly traces of a life long gone.

Settling into a weathered armchair, the rich man fixed his gaze upon Maya, holding wisdom born of centuries of reflection. "In this place—" He paused, words barely a whisper against the pressing silence, "I have come to understand the intricate web that binds our worlds together—a tapestry woven from the threads of revenge and mercy, action and consequence."

Maya leaned forward, her attention rapt as she absorbed the rich man's words. He spoke of the cycles that perpetuated the dance between darkness and light, how each act of vengeance or mercy rippled through the realms, shaping the destinies of countless souls.

"To break these chains," the rich man continued, "one must learn to see beyond the surface, to understand the motivations and pain that drive others. Only through understanding and forgiveness can we hope to transcend the patterns that bind us."

Asha's tail twitched uneasily as she circled the weathered furniture, her luminous eyes fixed on their mysterious host. Her presence comforted Maya silently as the rich man's tale unfolded.

As the rich man's words washed over her, Maya felt her worldview expanding, the rigid lines between good and evil blurring into shades of gray. She began to see her fight against darkness in a new light—not just as a battle against external forces, but as a struggle for the souls caught in these cycles, including Lazarus's. The rich man's story deeply impacted Maya, shaping her understanding of redemption and the complexity of morality and influencing her future actions in the narrative.

The realization that even her greatest enemy was, in some sense, a victim of the same forces that she sought to overcome filled Maya with a profound sense of empathy. She understood that true victory would not come from vanquishing Lazarus but from understanding the pain that drove him and offering the mercy that could break the cycle of vengeance.

As the rich man fell silent, the weight of his wisdom hung in the air, a substantial presence amidst the salon's decaying grandeur.

As they walked through the twisted paths of purgatory, Maya and Nykronus found themselves surrounded by the echoes of countless souls, each trapped within their own tales of regret and hope for redemption. The rich man, his tone filled with a deep understanding, pointed out the various figures that dotted the landscape, their forms shimmering in and out of existence as they grappled with the weight of their past actions.

"Each soul here," he explained, his voice a soft whisper amidst the affectionate moans of the lost, "is caught in a web of their own making, a tapestry woven from the choices they made in life. Yet, even in this place of penance, there is hope for change, for growth, and for the balance of the cosmos to be restored."

Maya, her mind still reeling from the rich man's earlier revelations, found herself drawn to the stories that unfolded around her. She saw in each soul a reflection of her struggles, the temptations she had resisted, and the sacrifices she had made. In their eyes, she recognized the same longing for redemption that had driven her journey.

Sensing Maya's growing understanding, the rich man placed a hand on her shoulder, his touch a subtle reminder of the wisdom he sought to impart. "The true balance of the universe," he said, "lies not in victory through force, but in the transformation of hearts and minds. Where condemnation fails, compassion may yet succeed."

Maya felt a profound shift within herself as the words sank into her soul. She began to see her role as a warrior, a champion of light against the forces of darkness, and a beacon of hope and forgiveness.

This realization solidified her resolve, transforming her approach to the impending confrontation with Lazarus.

No longer would she seek to vanquish him through force alone. Instead, she would strive to understand the pain that had driven him to this path, to offer the mercy and redemption that could shatter the chains of vengeance that bound them both. In this newfound clarity, Maya found a strength she had never known before, a power born not of violence but of empathy and grace.

As the shimmering gateway back to their world materialized, Maya and Nykronus prepared to depart from the solemn realm of purgatory. The rich man, his gaze filled with newfound peace, approached them, his steps measured and purposeful.

"Travelers," he said, his voice a patient whisper amidst the swirling mists, "your presence here has been a reminder of the world beyond these walls, a world still caught in the endless dance of light and shadow."

He reached into the folds of his tattered robes, his fingers closing around a small, unassuming object. With a reverent gesture, he pressed the item into Maya's palm, his gaze holding hers with an intensity that spoke of the weight of his words.

"Take this coin," he urged, his voice filled with a quiet solemnity, "as a reminder of the lessons learned in this place. May it serve as a symbol of the wisdom and mercy that you must carry with you on your journey."

Maya looked down at the object in her hand, a simple yet elegant coin, its surface etched with intricate patterns that seemed to dance in the half-light of purgatory. Her eyes traced the delicate engravings adorning each side of the coin—one face portraying the celestial realm of paradise. At the same time, its counterpart illustrated the fiery depths of the infernal abyss. She could feel the weight of its significance, a tangible representation of the rich man's story and the fundamental truths it had revealed.

As they stood at the threshold between realms, the gateway's shimmering light casting an ethereal glow upon their faces, Maya lost herself in deep reflection. The encounter with the rich man had left an indelible mark upon her soul, a transformative experience that had reshaped her understanding of the world and her place within it.

She thought of Lazarus, the adversary who had once seemed a figure of pure malevolence, now revealed to be a complex tapestry of pain, ambition, and the consequences of a cosmic imbalance. The insights gained in purgatory had granted her a new perspective, a deeper understanding of the forces that had shaped his path, and the role she must play in restoring the delicate balance between light and shadow.

Maya pressed the coin to her heart, its cool metal a reminder of all she had learned in this realm of shadows and redemption. Lazarus would test the very limits of her strength and resolve, but now she possessed something greater than mere power – understanding. Within her burned not the fierce confidence of a warrior, but the steady resolve of one who had glimpsed the truth behind justice itself.

CHAPTER

TWENTY-SIX

As Maya, Nykronus, and Asha prepared to leave the muted, barren terrains of purgatory, the rich man beckoned them for one final conversation. They gathered under the perpetual gray light of the realm between Heaven and Hell, their faces cast in an otherworldly glow.

"Before you depart," the rich man began, his voice low and solemn, "there is one more truth I must impart to you."

Maya leaned in closer, her curiosity piqued. "What is it?"

The rich man's eyes flickered as he spoke. "There is a figure, a being of immense power and knowledge, who has played a crucial role in the lives of Lazarus. Her name is Verendana."

Nykronus's face flooded with concern. "Verendana…"

The rich man nodded. "Verendana is a very powerful woman dating back to the days of Jesus Christ. It was Verendana who resurrected Lazarus and Dante and raised them as her sons, shaping their destinies from the shadows." The rich man's expression darkened. "Some whisper she seeks to restore an ancient balance, others say she aims to overturn it entirely."

Asha's ears twitched, her feline eyes narrowing. "But why? What purpose did she have in molding their lives? How do you know this?"

"That, I cannot say for certain," the rich man admitted. "But know this: their fates and the crisis you now face are intricately woven together by Verendana's hand. From the souls trapped around us, I have learned much. After all, I have nothing but time."

The revelation sent a shiver through Maya's body as she grappled with the understanding that an invisible puppet master had been orchestrating their fates all along. She thought of her family, of all they had endured—were their trials part of Verendana's grand design as well? It tied back to her history and her struggles back on Earth. Verendana's name resurfaced, a haunting echo of Maya's trials and tribulations. They had overcome Dante, but the specter of Lazarus loomed even more ominously than the vengeance of St. Valentine.

"So, our conflict with the Malefic Assembly," she said slowly, "it's not as cut and dry as I've thought but about a much larger tapestry of destiny?"

The rich man inclined his head. "Indeed. The actions of the past, the choices made by Verendana and those she influenced, have set in motion a chain of events that have led to this moment."

Nykronus stroked his beard thoughtfully. "This knowledge changes everything. We must tread carefully, for we are dealing with the machinations of a being far more powerful than we realized."

The revelation that Lazarus, the duplicitous character who lay at the heart of their trials, was once an inhabitant of purgatory caused a seismic change in Maya's perception of reality and her role in it, introducing an additional layer of complexity to their strife.

"Lazarus was here in purgatory?" Maya asked, her voice barely masking her shock.

The rich man nodded solemnly. "He was a familiar presence, a soul seeking redemption like so many others. But then, decades ago, he vanished without a trace."

Nykronus's brow furrowed. "Vanished? How is that possible?"

"It was a mystery that confounded us all," the rich man explained. "But as time passed, whispers began to circulate among the souls here. Whispers that Lazarus had been reincarnated granted a new life in the mortal realm."

Maya's mind raced with the implications of the reincarnation she and her family had experienced, wondering if they were connected. "Reincarnated?"

The rich man's gaze drifted to the distant horizon. "The forces at work here are beyond our comprehension. But many believe that Lazarus's reincarnation was part of Verendana's grand design, a piece of a larger puzzle we cannot yet see."

Asha's tail twitched, and her feline eyes narrowed in contemplation. "So, Lazarus's actions in the mortal realm might be influenced by his experiences here, by his past life in purgatory."

"It's a possibility we cannot ignore," Nykronus said gravely. "This knowledge adds a new layer of complexity to our struggle against him."

Maya nodded, her resolve hardening. "But it also gives us a new perspective, a new way to understand our enemy. If Lazarus was once a soul seeking redemption, perhaps there is still a glimmer of hope, a chance for us to reach him."

The revelation hung heavy in the air as Nykronus strode back and forth, his mind racing. "Lazarus vanished years ago, as he was reborn through the power of the Dagger of Love. That blade was stained with his very essence," he mused aloud. "Is it possible the Lazarus mentioned in Luke's Gospel and Lazarus of Bethany are one and the same? His blood was the key to forging that dagger. This implies that when Verendana and Dante were given new life, Lazarus too was resurrected." The weight of this revelation was palpable, casting a solemn shadow over their understanding of the past.

Maya's words carried a solemn weight. "This signifies we bore witness to the darkness that was set loose upon the earth."

As the trio stood at the boundary separating purgatory from their path back, the rich man's revelations weighed heavily on their minds. The eternal twilight of purgatory carved deep shadows across their faces, each line a testament to their growing understanding of the truth, mirroring the moral ambiguity that now clouded their mission. The impact of the revelation was like a thunderclap in the silence of their thoughts.

Maya turned to Nykronus, her brow furrowed. "If Verendana has been orchestrating Lazarus and Dante's lives, raising them as her sons, shaping their choices and fates, how can we hold them fully accountable for their actions?" The complexity of their moral dilemma was like a heavy fog, obscuring the path of righteousness.

Nykronus sighed, his eyes distant. "It's a complex question, Maya. While Verendana's influence cannot be ignored, Lazarus and Dante still make their own choices. They are not absolved of responsibility."

Asha's tail flicked as she chimed in, "But how much of their path was truly their own? If Verendana raised them and molded them from the start, where does her culpability end and theirs begin?"

Maya nodded, her gaze drifting to the ethereal landscape. "It feels like we're facing an adversary who is as much a victim as a villain. How do we confront someone whose very existence is so entangled with the machinations of a higher power?"

Nykronus placed a comforting hand on Maya's shoulder. "We must remember that understanding their circumstances does not excuse their actions. Lazarus and Dante have caused immense harm, regardless of Verendana's influence."

"But does that mean they are beyond redemption?" Maya asked, her voice barely above a whisper. "If we defeat them, are we truly serving justice, or are we just perpetuating a cycle set in motion by forces beyond our comprehension?"

Asha's ears twitched. "Our role is not to judge but to restore balance. To break the cycle, rather than blindly continue it."

Maya turned to Nykronus, her eyes searching his face. "What do you think is the right path forward? How do we navigate this ethical minefield?"

Nykronus took a deep breath, his gaze meeting Maya's. "We must strive to act with wisdom and compassion. We must understand the complexities of our adversaries' lives, but not let that understanding paralyze us. We have a duty to protect the innocent and prevent further harm. But we must also seek ways to break the cycle of violence and manipulation, to find a path towards healing and redemption."

Maya nodded slowly, absorbing Nykronus's words. As they stood there, the weight of their mission settled upon their shoulders—a burden and a calling that had grown more complex with each revelation.

As Maya, Nykronus, and Asha turned towards the gateway, the weight of the rich man's revelations hung heavy in the air. The flickering light of the portal cast an ethereal glow on their faces, illuminating the mix of emotions that played across their features – determination, apprehension, and a newfound sense of purpose.

Maya took a deep breath, her gaze fixed on the gateway. The path ahead was no longer simple but fraught with moral complexities and difficult choices. The knowledge of Verendana's influence, of the intricate web of destiny that had shaped Lazarus and Dante's lives, added a new layer of responsibility to their mission.

She glanced at Nykronus and Asha, her companions on this journey. Their presence comforted her, a reminder that she was not alone in facing the challenges that lay ahead. Nykronus's wisdom and Asha's intuitive guidance would be more valuable than ever as they navigated the murky waters of their adversaries' motivations.

Maya stepped forward with a nod of resolve, leading towards the gateway. Each step felt heavier than the last, as if their newfound knowledge was a physical weight upon their shoulders. Yet, amidst the heaviness, there was also a sense of clarity, a renewed sense of purpose.

The rich man's words echoed in Maya's mind as they approached the shimmering portal. The complexities of Lazarus and Dante's lives and the influence of Verendana's machinations would not deter them from their mission. If anything, it strengthened their resolve to find a path toward healing and redemption, to break the cycle of violence and manipulation that had ensnared their adversaries.

As they stood on the threshold of the gateway, Maya paused, turning to face Nykronus and Asha. In her eyes, they saw a flicker of the determination that had carried her through countless trials. "We go forward," she said, her voice steady, "not just to confront our enemies, but to understand them. To find a way to restore balance, to end the suffering that has plagued us all."

The rich man watched them with ancient eyes. "Remember," he said softly, "even the most carefully laid plans can be undone by the simplest acts of free will. That is both our greatest weakness and our greatest strength."

Their realm's vibrant hues and humming energy washed over them as they stepped through, life itself palpable in each breath—a stark contrast to purgatory's muted essence.

Maya paused, her gaze sweeping over the familiar landscape. The revelations in purgatory weighed heavily on her mind, the complexities of their mission now laid bare. She turned to Nykronus and Asha, her companions on this journey. She saw the same mix of determination and contemplation etched on their faces.

"Our task has taken on a new depth," Maya said, her voice carrying a note of solemnity. "The knowledge of Verendana's influence, of the intricate web of destiny that has shaped Lazarus and Dante's lives, has changed everything. We have to go home—now, while we still have time to act on what we've learned. The Malefic Assembly's next move could already be in motion."

Nykronus nodded, his eyes reflecting the wisdom gained from their experiences. "We must approach this not merely as a confrontation but as an opportunity to untangle the threads of fate and free will. To bring peace, we must understand the forces that have set these events in motion."

Asha's tail swished, her feline eyes gleaming with determination. "Our battle is not just against Lazarus and Verendana but against the very machinations that have ensnared them. We must find a way to break the cycle, to restore balance to the realms." Asha's tail moved in a perfect circle. "Perhaps that's why we were chosen—not to continue the pattern, but to transform it."

Maya reached out, placing a hand on her companions' shoulders. "Together, we'll unravel this tangle of destinies. We won't break down in our commitment to our cause. Still, we'll approach it with the nuance and understanding that our experiences in purgatory have granted us."

CHAPTER
TWENTY-SEVEN

Unknown Coordinates

The black Ford Expedition kicked up a cloud of sand as it came to a stop. The vehicle, stark against the verdant backdrop of the oasis, seemed out of place in this lush haven amidst the desert's expanse.

Elan stepped out of the driver's seat, his eyes squinting against the bright sunlight. Myst, Zoe, and Stanley followed suit, their faces a mix of awe and relief at the sight of the unexpected oasis.

"Well, would you look at that," Stanley remarked, his weathered face softening. "A little slice of paradise in the middle of nowhere. You know we're not in France anymore, right?"

Zoe stepped forward, blonde hair catching the sunlight as she traced her fingers along a palm frond. "It feels different here. Like we've crossed some invisible boundary."

Myst stepped forward, his gaze sweeping over the lush vegetation. "It's like a mirage, but real. The perfect place to catch our breath and regroup."

Elan remained silent, his eyes scanning the surroundings with a trained intensity. The tranquility of the oasis, with its sounds of trickling water and rustling leaves, offered a stark contrast to the recent tensions they had endured.

"We should set up camp," Elan finally said, calm but authoritatively. "We should take advantage of the shade and water while we can."

The others nodded in agreement, already moving to unload their gear from the Expedition. As they worked, the gentle sway of the palm trees seemed to welcome them, a silent invitation to find solace in this unexpected refuge.

Zoe paused, her hand resting on the rough bark of a palm tree. "It's strange, isn't it? Finding something so alive in the middle of all this emptiness."

Stanley chuckled. "Life has a way of surprising you, darling. It's what makes the journey worthwhile."

Myst glanced at his father, a flicker of understanding passing between them. They had both seen their fair share of good and bad surprises in their quest to unravel the mysteries of the compass.

As the team settled into the oasis, the severity of their mission seemed to lift, if only for a moment.

Elan reached into his pocket, his fingers instinctively seeking the reassuring presence of his cell phone. As he pulled it out, the others mirrored his action, their faces illuminated by the blue glow of their screens.

"No service," Myst murmured, his brow furrowing as he tapped at his phone. "Not even a single bar."

Zoe held her phone up, turning in a slow circle. "Same here. It's like we've been cut off from the world."

Stanley frowned, his fingers dancing across his screen with practiced efficiency. "This isn't right. We should have coverage out here. There's no reason for a total blackout. The Starlink satellites aren't connecting either."

Elan glanced at his son, a flicker of concern in his eyes. "What do you think it could be?"

Stanley shook his head and stroked his mustache as he pondered the question. "Could be some sort of signal interference. Something blocking the towers from reaching us. But out here? It doesn't make sense. The satellites should be able to reach us anywhere. Which could mean…we're not anywhere on Earth."

Zoe chuckled, but there was an edge of nervousness in her voice. "Maybe we've crossed over into another realm. You know, like in those old stories. Stepped through a portal without realizing it."

Myst raised an eyebrow, a hint of a smile playing at the corners of his mouth. "You think we're in Aethoria or something? Is this the paradise Maya has been living in?"

Zoe shrugged, her green eyes sparkling with mischief. "Hey, stranger things have happened. Especially with this group."

Elan tucked his phone back into his pocket, his gaze sweeping over the oasis again. The loss of communication with the outside world added an edge of uncertainty to their situation. Out here, in the middle of nowhere, they were vulnerable in a way they hadn't been before.

"Whatever the reason," Elan said, his voice steady and calm, "we need to stay alert. We don't know what we're dealing with here."

The others nodded, the gravity of their situation settling over them like a brick. Once a haven, the oasis now felt like a trap, its beauty a deceptive mask hiding unknown dangers.

As the group settled into the oasis, the compass in Elan's hand suddenly came alive. It emitted a pulsing glow, casting intricate light patterns on the sand at their feet. The rhythmic hum emanating from the ancient device filled the air, drawing the attention of everyone present.

Elan's brow furrowed as he studied the compass, its needle spinning erratically before settling in a direction deeper into the heart of the oasis. "We need to go," he commanded.

Myst stepped closer to his father, his eyes fixed on the glowing compass. "It's like it's calling us, guiding us somewhere. The artifact wasn't its final destination."

"Zoe's voice carried an almost musical quality as she said, 'The adventure continues.'"

Zoe and Stanley exchanged glances, their expressions mirroring the intrigue and unease in the air. "I guess we follow it then," Stanley said, adjusting his hat. "Not like we have much choice out here."

Elan stared at the terrain around them. "We can't take the SUV; we have to walk. Grab your stuff; we leave in 30 minutes."

Drawn by the compass's insistent beacon, the group navigated through the oasis's heart, where the vegetation grew denser, and the air felt charged with anticipation. The towering palm trees seemed to lean in closer, their fronds whispering secrets as the group passed beneath them.

As they pushed deeper into the oasis, the compass's glow intensified, pulsing in time with their heartbeats. The ground beneath their feet shifted from soft sand to a more solid, almost metallic surface hidden beneath the lush greenery.

Elan held up a hand, signaling the others to stop. A large sphere stood before them, nestled by the water's edge. Its surface reflected the oasis around it. Yet, it remained untouchable by the natural world as if existing in its own realm.

Myst approached the sphere cautiously, his hand outstretched. As his fingers neared the surface, a ripple of energy pulsed outward, causing the air to shimmer and distort. He pulled back, his eyes wide with wonder. "What is this thing?"

Elan shook his head, the compass pointing directly at the sphere. "I don't know, but the compass led us here for a reason."

Zoe stepped forward. "It's like a doorway," she whispered, her voice filled with awe and trepidation. "A gateway to somewhere else."

Stanley frowned and braided one side of his mustache as he studied the sphere. "Or a trap," he grumbled, his hand instinctively reaching for the knife at his belt. "We need to be careful."

As they walked around the perimeter of the sphere, a previously unseen entrance materialized, inviting them into an entirely white, luminous room that blinded them with its brilliance upon entry.

Elan shielded his eyes, squinting against the overwhelming brightness. "What is this place?"

Myst blinked rapidly, his vision adjusting to the stark white surroundings. "It's like stepping into a blank canvas. Everything is just... white."

Inside, the starkness of the white room was a canvas of pure potential. In the center of the room stood a table with a precise cutout, unmistakably meant for the compass.

Zoe approached the table, her fingers trailing along its smooth surface. "It's like it was made for the compass. Like it was waiting for us."

Stanley frowned, his eyes scanning the room for any signs of danger. "I don't like this. It feels too easy. Too perfect. Aliens, is this an alien spaceship?"

Elan stepped forward, the compass heavy in his hand. He glanced at his companions, a silent question in his eyes. They nodded, their expressions a mix of anticipation and apprehension.

With a sense of ceremony, Elan placed the compass into the cutout. The moment it settled into place, the room's overwhelming brightness dimmed to reveal a single scroll on the table.

Myst reached for the scroll, his hands trembling slightly. "What do you think it is?"

Zoe leaned in closer, her eyes wide with curiosity. "Maybe it's a map. Or a message from whoever built this place."

Stanley crossed his arms, his mustache quivered with skepticism. "Or it could be a trap. We need to be careful."

Elan held up a hand, his gaze fixed on the scroll. "We've come this far. We can't turn back now."

With a deep breath, he unrolled the scroll, the ancient parchment crackling beneath his fingers. The others gathered around him, eyes scanning the cryptic symbols and diagrams covering the page.

As they studied the scroll, the room around them seemed to pulse with energy as if the walls were alive with anticipation. Now firmly embedded in the table, the compass glowed with a pulsing light.

As the group huddled around the ancient scroll, their eyes widened with each revelation. The cryptic symbols and diagrams gave way to a narrative that unfolded like a tapestry of myth and history intertwined.

Elan's fingers traced the intricate lines, his voice hushed as he read aloud. "It speaks of St. Michael, trapped in an eternal battle against the forces of darkness, led by Satan himself."

Myst leaned in closer, his excitement conveyed through his wide smile. "His location—it's been hidden until now. The scroll—it's like a map leading us to him."

Zoe's hand rested on the compass, glowing and illuminating in the table's cutout. "It's as if everything has been leading us to this moment. The compass, the oasis, this room. It's all connected."

Stanley's mustache bristled as he studied the scroll, his eyes narrowed. "This isn't just a mission anymore. It's a calling. A destiny. *Satan*. This is huge. And let's not forget, we *are* the Order of St. Michael. "

The significance of their discovery settled over the group like a mantle of purpose. They stood in silence, each lost in their own thoughts as the gravity of their task sank in.

Elan's voice broke the stillness, his tone solemn. "We're not just fighting for ourselves anymore. We're fighting for something greater. For the very balance of good and evil."

Myst nodded, his eyes shining with determination. "And we'll face it together. As a team. As a family."

Zoe's fingers tightened around the compass, her voice tender but resolute. "For Maya. For St. Michael. For the world."

Stanley adjusted his hat, his stance resolute. "Well then, what are we waiting for? Let's go save the world."

As the gravity of their discovery settled upon them, the group gathered around the table, exchanging glances that conveyed a newfound sense of purpose. The lore surrounding St. Michael, the celestial protector against the forces of darkness, now intertwined directly with their quest, elevating their role in this cosmic struggle.

Elan's eyes met each of his companions, his voice steady as he spoke. "This isn't just about us anymore. We're part of something bigger, a battle that has been waged for centuries."

Myst nodded, his fingers tracing the intricate symbols on the scroll. "And now we know our place in it. We're not just searching for answers; we're fighting for the very balance of good and evil."

Zoe's gaze fell upon the compass, its beautiful glow a constant reminder of its significance. "I wonder if Nykronus knew what this compass could do. It's like the compass chose the Order, for this quest, and guided us to this moment. We can't turn back now."

Stanley adjusted his hat, with pride. "We won't. We've come too far to let fear hold us back. St. Michael needs us, and we'll be there to answer the call."

The revelation that the compass served as both a key and a beacon set their course with renewed urgency. Freeing St. Michael from his eternal battle was not merely a step towards thwarting Satan's plans but a crucial act in restoring the delicate balance that hung in the balance.

Elan tucked the scroll away with careful precision, each movement deliberate. The impact of centuries of warfare settled onto their shoulders yet somehow made them stand straighter.

"Nykronus's disappearance," Zoe said suddenly, her green eyes wide with realization. "It wasn't random. He knew something about this."

"No," Elan agreed, his voice heavy with certainty. "Nothing about this has been random. We're part of something ancient, something bigger than ourselves." He looked at each of them in turn - his son, his trusted friends, his team. "And we're going to see it through."

The compass continued its steady pulse, a heartbeat of light in the otherworldly chamber, marking the rhythm of their newfound purpose.

CHAPTER
TWENTY-EIGHT

San Francisco, California

The grand hall of the Order's San Francisco headquarters cast long shadows across the ancient wooden floors, its towering windows offering glimpses of the Golden Gate Bridge shrouded in evening fog. Banners bearing the marks of centuries-old victories hung heavy with history, seeming to droop under the weight of recent losses. Olivia's empty seat at the council table was a stark reminder of why they had gathered.

The room hummed with tension as members from various factions filed in, their faces etched with grief and determination. Some materialized through shimmering portals, while others appeared on floating magical displays, their images casting ethereal blue light across the weathered stone walls. Leaders from every branch of the Order had been summoned—a gathering unprecedented in the last decade.

Kaira strode to the podium, her ceremonial robes crackling with barely contained magical energy. Behind her, Reagan's more practical combat gear spoke to their complementary leadership styles—one the diplomatic face of the Order, the other its tactical backbone. Both women carried the shadows of sleepless nights beneath their eyes, having spent the week since Olivia's fall planning this moment.

"Three days ago," Kaira began, her voice carrying to every corner of the hall without magical amplification, "we lost one of our finest. The Malefic Assembly's attack on Olivia wasn't just a tragedy—it was a declaration of war. They've moved beyond shadows and whispers, and we must respond in kind."

Reagan stepped forward, her battle-scarred hands bringing up a shimmering tactical display. "Our enemy has grown bold, thinking Olivia's death has weakened us. They don't realize it's given us clarity of purpose. That's why we're implementing Plan B—the contingency Olivia helped design."

The display shifted, showing a complex web of magical ley lines crisscrossing the city. "First phase: we embed deep-cover operatives within their ranks. Not just spies—we're placing our combat specialists, our ward-breakers, our best and brightest. The Assembly thinks they know our playbook. They're wrong."

Murmurs rippled through the crowd, a mix of surprise and grim satisfaction. Kaira raised her hand, and the room fell silent. "This goes beyond our usual methods. Each operative will be equipped with Olivia's latest innovation—untraceable communication crystals. No more lost agents. No more ambushed teams."

The war room briefing that followed was intense and focused. Magical projections danced across reinforced walls as team leaders received their assignments. Kaira's diplomatic expertise helped smooth ruffled feathers as traditional rivals were forced to collaborate, while Reagan's tactical mind caught and solved potential field problems before they could develop.

Hours later, as twilight painted the bay in purple and gold, the Order gathered in their warded courtyard. The Golden Gate Bridge stood sentinel in the distance as hundreds of candles flickered to life— one for each year of service Olivia had given to their cause.

"We don't just mourn tonight," Kaira addressed the assembly, her voice thick with emotion. "We remember. We learn. We grow stronger." She held up a crystal that pulsed with soft blue light. "These communicators were Olivia's last gift to us. She knew the escalation was coming. She prepared us for this moment."

Reagan stood at her side, unusually subdued. "Olivia taught me everything I know about combat magic," she shared, earning surprised looks from younger members who knew her only as the Order's fearsome battle commander. "But more importantly, she taught me that strength means nothing without compassion. That's what the Assembly will never understand—and that's why they'll fail."

As the memorial continued, stories of Olivia flowed freely. Tales of her legendary magical innovations mixed with quieter moments: her patient mentoring of new recruits, her dry humor during crises, and her absolute dedication to protecting innocent lives. With each story, the shared resolve in the courtyard grew stronger.

The gathering ended with a ritual of remembrance, each member adding their magical essence to a central flame until it burned with all the colors of the aurora. As the light danced across tear-stained faces, Kaira and Reagan exchanged a look of fierce determination. The Order wasn't just honoring Olivia's memory—they were becoming something new, more substantial, forged in the crucible of loss and united by an unshakeable purpose.

The Malefic Assembly had meant to break them. Instead, they had given the Order precisely what it needed: a reason to evolve.

CHAPTER
TWENTY-NINE

Jungle outside the Province of Palawan, Philippines

The vortex's energy crackled and swirled as Maya, Nykronus, and Asha emerged into Palawan's embrace. Behind them, the ancient stone archway shuddered, its weathered surface spider-webbing with cracks before dissolving into dust. Chunks of masonry crashed through the glass-like remnants of the portal's threshold, the sound startling a group of macaques into raucous protest. Above them, hornbills took flight, their massive wings casting fleeting shadows through gaps in the emerald canopy.

Maya inhaled deeply, the thick Palawan humidity filling her lungs with the rich perfume of orchids and damp earth. After the crystalline air of Aethoria, with its sharp tang of raw magic, each breath felt like coming home. The glass beneath her feet, iridescent with lingering otherworldly energy, crunched as she shifted her weight—a final whisper of the realm they'd left behind.

Nykronus, his antique eyes reflecting the dappled sunlight filtering through the dense canopy, surveyed their surroundings with quiet recognition. Centuries of traversing between worlds had taught him to read the subtle signs of a successful crossing. "The archway may be gone," he mused, his voice a gentle rumble that seemed to harmonize with the forest's pulse, "but our connection to Aethoria remains unbroken. The threshold between worlds has simply... shifted."

Maya smiled, unconsciously reaching out to stroke Asha's glowing fur. The feline's presence was a comforting constant, a living embodiment of their bond with the mystical realm.

As they stood there, letting the sounds and sensations of the jungle wash over them, Maya could feel the pulse of that mystical realm beathing in sync through her veins. It was thrumming energy, a reminder that her experiences in that otherworldly domain had left an unforgettable mark on her existence.

She closed her eyes, focusing on the sensation. It was as if a part of Aethoria had taken root within her, intertwining with her essence. The power she had discovered, the wisdom she had gained, and the connections she had forged now resided within her, waiting to be called upon.

Asha purred softly, her glistering eyes meeting Maya's gaze with an understanding that rose above words. The cat's presence was a testament to the enduring influence of Aethoria, a living bridge between the realms.

Nykronus placed a reassuring hand on Maya's shoulder, his touch a grounding force amidst the swirl of emotions. "The journey may have ended," he said, his voice filled with a quiet conviction, "but the impact of Aethoria will continue to guide us, to shape our path forward."

Maya nodded, a small smile tugging at the corners of her lips. "Let's go home."

With the pulse of that mystical realm beating in sync with her own heart, she felt stronger than ever. The journey home beckoned, and with it, the challenge of carrying Aethoria's gifts across the divide between worlds.

~

San Francisco, California

Their journey from Palawan's verdant depths to San Francisco's urban canyons unfolded like the turning pages of a spell book. Each stage of travel pulled them further from the raw magic of their return point: first a bumping jeepney ride through mountain roads where the jungle slowly gave way to villages, then a small propeller plane that lifted them above the archipelago's scattered emeralds, and finally a commercial flight that carried them across the vast Pacific.

Maya spent those hours of transition with her hand resting on Asha's fur, watching through various windows as one world gradually transformed into another. The feline's coat still sparkled with Aethorian energy, though the glow had dimmed to match their reentry into the mundane world—now visible only to those who knew to look for it.

"It's different this time," Maya murmured to Nykronus as their final flight descended toward San Francisco, the city's fog-shrouded towers piercing the clouds like modern megaliths. The last rays of sunset painted the sky in colors that reminded her of Aethoria's ever-changing atmosphere. "Coming back. I can feel both worlds now, like overlapping melodies."

Nykronus nodded, understanding flickering in his ancient gaze. "That's the true gift of your journey," he said, his words nearly lost in the aircraft's descent. "Not just visiting another realm, but learning to carry its essence within you, even here."

They emerged from the airport into a San Francisco evening, where streetlights buzzed with ordinary electricity instead of magical energy, and the crowds moved with the hurried purposefulness of those anchored firmly in a single realm. The city's famous fog wrapped around them like a ghostly embrace, carrying the salt-tang of the bay and the distant echo of foghorns.

As their Lyft wove through the city's steep streets, Maya pressed her hand against the window, feeling the thrum of the mundane world against her palm. Yet beneath that ordinary pulse, she sensed something else—ley lines, ancient and powerful, crisscrossing beneath San Francisco's streets like spiritual subway tracks. The Order hadn't chosen this location by chance.

The Victorian mansion that housed their headquarters emerged from the fog like a ship coming to port. Its weathered facade, painted in heritage blues and grays, presented a perfect mundane disguise to passersby. But Maya's enhanced senses detected the complex lattice of wards and protective spells that wrapped the building like invisible ivy. Years ago, she would have barely noticed them. Now, after Aethoria, they sang to her, a familiar melody drawing her home to waiting hearts.

Asha, ever attuned to Maya's moods, padded softly beside her, the feline's glowing presence a constant reminder of their shared connection to Aethoria. The cat's eyes, glistening with a pearl of otherworldly wisdom, seemed to offer silent support, a wordless assurance that the lessons learned in that mystical realm would not be lost amidst the clamor of the city.

As they navigated the crowded sidewalks, Maya turned to Nykronus, her voice low but filled with determination. "The things I learned in Aethoria," she began, her gaze distant yet focused, "the power I felt, the understanding I gained... I know it's not just for that realm. It's meant to be used here, to help the Order, to face whatever challenges lie ahead."

Nykronus grinned. "The wisdom of Aethoria is not bound by the borders of that world," he agreed, his voice a gentle rumble amidst the city's din. "It is a part of you now, Maya, a well of strength and insight that you can draw upon whenever you need it."

Maya smiled, the weight of her experiences settling into a sense of purpose. She knew that the journey back to headquarters was more than just a physical one; it was a transition, a chance to integrate the lessons of Aethoria into her life on Earth. She was ready to face the challenges that awaited her, armed with the wisdom and power she had gained.

Asha brushed against Maya's leg, the cat's soft fur a tactile reminder of their connection. Maya reached down, running her fingers through Asha's glowing coat, drawing comfort from the contact. The feline's presence was a constant reassurance, a living embodiment of the bridge between worlds.

Anticipation swelled within Maya as the Order's headquarters came into view. The prospect of reuniting with her mother, father, and brother filled her with eager joy. She yearned to regale them with tales of her exploits and take her place in thwarting the Malefic Assembly's schemes.

The Order's spelled doorway recognized them instantly, ancient magic rippling across their skin like warm water as they crossed the threshold. With its soaring ceilings and carved wooden panels, the grand entrance hall hummed with activity. Maps and tactical displays hovered in the air, their ghostly light casting moving shadows across the antique wallpaper. A dozen conversations in multiple languages filled the space, but all fell silent as Maya's family registered their arrival.

Lola Rose reached her first, moving with the grace that belied her years. Her small hands cupped Maya's face, and Maya felt the subtle probe of her grandmother's gift—the ability to read the energetic imprints of other realms. "Ah, anak," she whispered, her accent thickening with emotion, "you've carried back more than memories, haven't you?"

Grandma Gianna approached more slowly, her researcher's eye taking in every detail of their return. The copper pendants and crystals adorning her neck clinked softly as she moved. "The theoretic implications alone..." she began, then caught herself, emotion overtaking academic interest as she pulled Maya into a fierce embrace. "We felt the moment you crossed back," she murmured. "The ley lines beneath the city practically sang."

The familiar scent of her grandmothers—Lola's sampaguita flower perfume and Grandma Gianna's mix of old books and dried herbs—grounded Maya in the moment, a bridge between her old life and new understanding. They held her together, their own magical talents recognizing and celebrating the growth in hers.

Movement caught Maya's eye—her father Reagan slipping a crystal-studded headset off his ear, abandoning what looked like an essential tactical discussion with several international Order members on the floating displays. His face lit up with that particular smile he reserved just for her, which had welcomed her home from every adventure since childhood. But this time, she saw something new in his expression: recognition of an equal rather than protective pride for a child.

Maya barely had time to breathe before Jhan, Austin, and Kristinn converged on her, their excited energy starkly contrasting to the grandmothers' reverent welcome. Already tapping notes into his ever-present smart tablet, Jhan fired off questions about Aethoria's magical frequency patterns. "Did you notice any correlation between the realm's ambient energy and the effectiveness of different spell types? My research suggests—"

"Forget the technical stuff," Austin interrupted, his martial artist's eye studying her stance, noting how she carried herself differently now. "Did you learn any new combat applications? That thing you did with the light before you left—can you teach us?"

Kristinn, always the most empathetic of the three, noticed how Maya's hands still trembled slightly from the crossing. She pressed a steaming cup of ginger tea into Maya's hands—a family comfort drink their mother had always made after challenging training sessions. "What was it like?" she asked softly. "Not the magic or the missions, but just... being there?"

Maya sipped the tea gratefully, its warmth spreading through her chest as she considered how to explain. "It's like..." she began, then smiled as Asha jumped onto a nearby desk, scattering Jhan's carefully arranged crystals. The cat's fur still sparkled with lingering Aethorian energy, casting tiny rainbow refractions across their faces. "Remember when we were kids, how we'd shine flashlights through Mom's crystals to make light patterns on the walls? Aethoria is like being inside one of those light patterns, but the light is alive, and it teaches you its dance."

Reagan and Kaira exchanged glances at this description, their tactical minds already spinning with possibilities. Maya recognized their expressions—the same ones they wore when plotting complex operations. But there was something else there, too: a parent's pride tempered with the bittersweet recognition that their daughter had grown beyond their protection. In that moment of understanding, the air in the room seemed to shift, as if the very walls of the headquarters sensed a coming revelation.

As the excitement of reunion settled into a warmer rhythm, Grandma Gianna drew Maya toward the library alcove—their special place since Maya was small enough to sit on her grandmother's lap during story time.

From a hidden compartment behind a worn copy of "Dimensional Theory and Practice," she retrieved a box Maya had never seen before. It was carved from Filipino holy wood, its surface inlaid with mother-of-pearl symbols that matched the oldest protection wards in the head-quarters' foundations.

"Your Lola Rose and I have been waiting for the right moment," Grandma Gianna began, her fingers tracing patterns on the box that made the inlays shimmer like living things. "This pendant belonged to your great-great-grandmother Isabella Durant. She was the first in our family to recognize what we now know as cross-dimensional reso-nance patterns—though back then, and they called her touched by the spirits."

Maya's hands trembled as she accepted the box, feeling the weight of history in more than just its physical form. The wood felt warm against her palms, responding to her touch like a sleeping cat rousing itself.

When she lifted the lid, her breath caught. The pendant wasn't beautiful in any conventional sense—its metal was dark and almost organic-looking, like a midnight drop caught in silver. But as she watched, iridescent symbols shifted across its surface: the sharp angles of protection wards melting into the flowing scripts of healing runes, then reforming into configurations she recognized from Aethoria's geometries. At its center, a stone that wasn't quite a stone pulsed with a light that seemed to reach toward her.

"Isabella created this during her final expedition," Grandma Gianna explained, her voice taking on the tone Maya recognized from essential lessons. "She called it the Nexus Heart. It's said she forged it at a confluence of ley lines during a celestial alignment, incorporating materials from seven different dimensional planes. But its true power isn't in its construction—it's in its ability to adapt, to grow with its bearer's understanding of the spaces between worlds."

Maya lifted the pendant from its nest of aged velvet. When it touched her skin, she felt a resonance with her newly enhanced connection to Aethoria—like two tuning forks finding the same note. The symbols on its surface flickered rapidly before settling into a new configuration she somehow knew had never existed before.

"It's been waiting," Grandma Gianna said softly, watching the pendant's response to Maya. "Just as we all have, in our own way, for you to find your path between worlds."

Grandma Gianna's eyes sparkled with wisdom as she watched Maya's reaction. "This pendant symbolizes your role within our family, Maya. You are a bridge between worlds, a conduit for the mystical energies that flow between Earth and Aethoria. It is a reminder of the strength you carry within you and the unique path you have chosen to walk."

Maya felt the weight of her legacy settling upon her shoulders, a mantle of responsibility and power that she embraced with a newfound sense of purpose. She clasped the pendant around her neck, feeling its energy harmonize with hers, a perfect symbiosis of the earthly and the ethereal.

As she turned back to face her family and allies, Maya could see the awe and admiration in their eyes. Her connection to Aethoria, once a distant marvel, now felt like a vibrant, living force that enriched her very being. It was a testament to her growth, the trials she had overcome, and the wisdom she had gained.

The family sat in respectful silence, absorbing the profound truths that Maya's journey had unearthed. They recognized that her words were not mere recollections but living lessons imbued with the power to shape their paths and guide their actions in the battles to come. As if responding to an unspoken signal, Lola Rose stood, her eyes bright with ceremonial purpose. "It is time," she said simply, gesturing toward the stairs that led to their most sacred space.

～

The Durant-Mazza family gathered in the headquarters' rooftop garden, where generations of their lineage had conducted their most sacred ceremonies. Ancient roses, their stems wrapped around spelled trellises, bloomed out of season, their petals shimmering with stored magical energy. Herbs from both mundane and otherworldly sources filled the air with an intoxicating blend of scents: sage and rosemary mingling with the sharp sweetness of star-blessed nightshade and dawn-caught dew moss from the hidden valleys of Aethoria.

Maya stood at the garden's heart, where the building's strongest ley line emerged from the earth like a fountain of invisible light. The Nexus Heart at her throat pulsed in rhythm with this ancient power, sending ripples through the carefully tended plants. Around her, floating witch lights cast their warm glow over the assembled faces of her family, their light mixing with the stars above San Francisco's fog-wrapped streets.

The pendant's resonance with the garden's magical energies created subtle auroras in the air—threads of light that wove between the mundane and magical plants, between the earthly and otherworldly elements that her family had so carefully balanced here for genera-tions. As Maya gazed at her gathered family, she sensed how this place had always prepared her for this moment, this confluence of powers and possibilities.

Maya's steady voice, imbued with the charisma of Aethoria, broke the silence. "My family," she began, her gaze sweeping over the assem-bled faces. The journey I have undertaken has not only granted me power and understanding but has also shown me the true potential of our legacy."

She paused, letting her words sink in, the weight of her revelation palpable in the night air. "The connection I now share with Aethoria is not merely a tool for the battles ahead but a means to forge deeper understandings and new paths for us all."

As Maya spoke, the pendant around her neck seemed to pulse with an otherworldly light, a tangible manifestation of her bond with the mystical realm. "I pledge to use this connection, this gift, to not only protect our world but to bridge the gap between the earthly and the ethereal, to bring forth a new era of unity and purpose for the Durant-Mazza legacy."

The family listened, their eyes fixed upon Maya, their hearts swelling with a renewed sense of purpose. They could see her transformation and how her journey had shaped her into a beacon of hope and strength. Her words, filled with conviction and wisdom, resonated deep within their souls, igniting a fire of determination and unity.

As the ceremonial energy began to settle, the family members rose one by one, each pausing briefly before Maya. Some offered quiet words of support, others simply touched her shoulder or smiled with understanding. The already strong bonds between them had been fortified by the truths she had brought forth from Aethoria.

Kaira approached last, her eyes shimmering with pride and emotion. She placed a gentle hand on her daughter's shoulder, her touch conveying the depth of her love and support. "Your father and I are so proud of you, Maya," she said, her voice soft yet filled with conviction. "You have grown in ways we could never have imagined, and your strength gives us all hope for the battles to come."

Maya leaned into her mother's embrace, drawing comfort and strength from the warmth of her presence. In that moment, the weight of her destiny felt not like a burden but like a mantle of purpose and responsibility, made lighter by the support of her family.

After Kaira departed, Maya, Nykronus, and Asha lingered in the garden, sharing a moment of quiet confidence. The trials they had endured together, the battles they had fought side by side, had forged an unbreakable connection between them. They stood as a united front, their shadows merging in the witch-lights' glow.

"The path ahead won't be easy," Nykronus murmured, his ancient eyes reflecting the starlight.

Maya nodded, feeling Asha's reassuring presence against her legs. "But we won't walk it alone."

Eventually, even they departed, leaving Maya alone with her thoughts. She stood at the garden's heart, where the ley line's power thrummed strongest, a contemplative figure bathed in starlight and magical radiance. Her connection to Aethoria, once a hidden thread in the tapestry of her life, now shone as a guiding light, illuminating the path ahead for her family and the broader struggle against the encroaching shadows.

The garden's peace belied the tumultuous times ahead. Still, Maya stood ready, a warrior tempered by experience and empowered by the confluence of her worlds. She gazed into the night sky, her eyes reflecting the infinite possibilities that stretched before her. The Nexus Heart pulsed gently against her skin, its rhythm matching the beat of her heart and the flow of magic through the garden's sacred space. At that moment, she knew that no matter what challenges the future might bring, she would face them with the strength and wisdom born of her extraordinary journey—and with the unshakeable foundation of her family's love and trust.

CHAPTER
THIRTY

The Order's great bronze doors groaned open at sunset, splitting shadows that had waited centuries for this moment. Elan led his team through them—Myst, no longer a boy but a warrior gripping *Winterstar*'s ancient hilt; Zoe and Stanley, their armor bearing fresh scars from battles yet untold. In Elan's hands, the artifact blazed with blue fire, its power awakening echoes in the very stones of their fortress.

Inside the grand hall, hundreds of candles cast dancing light across the vaulted ceiling, where mosaic scenes of the Order's history glinted like captured stars. The assembled members parted in reverent silence, their whispers rising like autumn leaves: "They've returned... They found it..."

At the hall's heart stood Kaira, her ceremonial silver robes a stark contrast to the weeks-old traveling clothes of the returning party. Her emerald eyes met Elan's across the distance, with years of shared battles and quiet moments passing between them in that glance. Beside her, Reagan's usual stoic demeanor cracked into a rare smile, her hand tightening on the hilt of her sword—a warrior's gesture of respect.

For a heartbeat, silence held the hall in its grip. Then, a single cry of triumph shattered it, and the Order celebrated. The sound echoed off ancient stone, setting the enchanted crystals in the ceiling humming with sympathetic magic. Kaira crossed the space between them in measured steps that belied her racing heart. When she reached Elan, her embrace carried the strength of mountains and the gentleness of morning light.

Kaira's fingers traced the new scar along Elan's jawline. "Welcome home," she whispered, the words carrying the weight of a thousand prayers spoken during sleepless nights.

"We found it." Elan pressed his forehead to hers, their shared gesture since their first days as young warriors. In his peripheral vision, the artifact's blue glow pulsed in time with their heartbeats. "But the cost..."

She silenced him with a gentle touch. There would be time for burdens later. Her attention turned to Myst, who stood taller than when he'd left, his father's sword now fitting naturally at his hip. The boy she'd sent off had returned a man, his eyes holding shadows she recognized from her battles.

"Mom." Myst's voice had deepened during his absence. He accepted her embrace but kept his gaze fixed on the artifact. "Olivia should be here to see this."

The name fell like a stone into still water. Zoe's sharp intake of breath and Stanley's tightened jaw spoke volumes. Even the artifact's glow seemed to dim as if acknowledging their loss.

The artifact was laid before the assembly, its ancient power drawing them closer like moths to flame. In its crystalline depths, secrets waited to be unraveled, prophecies yet to be spoken.

Out of nowhere, a lone member of the Order began applauding, their palms slapping together in a frenzied rhythm. The rest of the Order quickly joined in, their voices rising in triumphant cheers. "With the Durant-Mazza family and our leaders restored, it's time to return to the offensive!" Someone bellowed above the jubilant noise, their eyes burning with determination.

The celebration fell silent as the great hall's doors swung wide again. Where candlelight touched the threshold, shadows deepened instead of retreating. Maya stood in that darkness, midnight blue robes of a Shadowmender rippling like liquid twilight. Her staff's crystal peak sang to the artifact, their resonance making the air tremble.

Beside her walked legend made flesh: a Shadowcat, its obsidian and flame-colored fur rippling like liquid night. Ancient runes shimmered beneath its pelt with each movement, its eyes holding the wisdom of centuries. Each pawstep left briefly glowing sigils on the stone floor, marks of power not seen since the Age of Twilight.

"Dad. Mysty." Maya's voice carried the strength of her new station. She placed a hand on the Shadowcat's shoulder, her fingers disappearing into the ethereal fur. "This is Asha, Daughter of the Twilight Court. She chose to bind her fate with mine when I needed her most."

Her voice resonated directly in their minds when she spoke, rich with power and warmth. "The children of Elan Durant carry the old blood strongly. It is an honor to stand with your family in these dark times."

Even Nykronus, ever unshakeable, raised an eyebrow at this. The implications of a Shadowcat's allegiance hung heavy in the air—such beings hadn't walked beside humans since the Age of Twilight.

As they drew closer, a figure emerged from the shadows, his presence eliciting gasps and whispers of astonishment from the assembly. Nykronus, his ancient eyes filled with wisdom and knowledge, stepped into the light, his robes swirling around him like a living entity.

Myst and Elan, momentarily stunned by this unexpected appearance, rushed forward to embrace Nykronus. The emotion of the reunion was palpable, a tangible force that seemed to fill the courtyard. Tears of joy and relief mingled with laughter as they held each other close, the weight of their shared journey evident in every gesture.

Maya watched as her family welcomed Asha and Nykronus, their bonds stronger than any ancient magic. The moment of reunion passed swiftly as all eyes turned to the artifact, its presence drawing them back to their purpose.

Elan stepped forward, his voice steady and commanding. "Our

journey has been long and filled with danger," he began, his gaze sweeping over the assembled crowd.

Myst stood beside him, his eyes shining with the knowledge they had gained. "The artifact before you is more than just a relic of the past," he said, gesturing towards the gleaming object. "It's a key, a beacon that will guide us to St. Michael's location."

A murmur rippled through the crowd, a mix of awe and anticipation. Zoe and Stanley exchanged glances, their discoveries burning on their tongues.

As Elan and Myst continued their narration, detailing the twists and turns of their quest, the members of the Order listened with rapt attention. Each revelation was met with a collective intake of breath, a shared understanding of the magnitude of their mission.

The hall's grandeur amplified the significance of their words, the ancient stones bearing witness to the unfolding of destiny. As the tale ended, silence fell over the room, filled with resolve, determination, and the weight of what was to come.

Kaira stepped forward, her eyes shining with fierce determination. "We have been given a great gift," she declared, her voice ringing through the hall. "A chance to rescue one of our own, to confront the forces that seek to destroy us. Let us not waste this opportunity."

Kaira found Elan in their garden sanctuary, where moonflowers turned their faces toward the artifact's glow like ancient sentinels awakening. The flowers' silver light caught the new scars on his face, marks of a victory that felt too much like a warning.

The artifact's glow, visible through the cloth wrapping at Elan's belt, cast shifting patterns across the midnight roses—flowers bred by the first Orders to detect dark magic. Their petals remained silver tonight, untainted. Safe, at least for now.

Kaira traced her fingers along the garden wall's runes, feeling the familiar pulse of protection spells laid down by generations of their predecessors. "Do you remember teaching Maya to read these?" Her voice carried pride and pain. "She could barely reach the lowest ones."

"Now she's writing new ones." Elan's hand covered hers, his sword calluses familiar against her skin. "Did you see how the runes responded to her? A full Shadowmender at her age... and Myst." He shook his head, wonder and worry warring in his expression. "Leading the artifact recovery team like he was born to it."

The moonflowers turned their faces toward them, sensing the surge of parental emotion. One blossom unfurled, releasing a soft chime that echoed their daughter's laughter from years past.

"We wanted to protect them from this life," Kaira said, resting her head against Elan's shoulder. The ceremonial robes of the Order's leadership felt heavier tonight. "Instead, they've surpassed us both."

Elan's arm tightened around her. Above them, the stars wheeled in their ancient patterns, the same stars they'd named for their children in quieter times. "They protect each other now. Maya with her Shadowcat bond—something not seen in three ages—and Myst..." He touched *Winterstar*'s hilt reflexively. "The blade answered him today. Called to him over me."

The admission hung in the perfumed air. Another threshold was crossed, another change they hadn't prepared for. But Kaira heard the pride beneath his words, the fierce joy of seeing their children come into their power, even as it meant watching them step into danger.

The midnight roses swayed in a breeze too subtle for the human senses. Tomorrow would bring councils and plans, strategies, and sacrifices. But here, in their sanctuary, Kaira allowed herself to remember the weight of tiny hands in hers, the echo of small feet on ancient stones.

"They'll need us differently now," she said finally, facing her husband. The moonlight caught the silver threading through his dark hair, badges of their years together. "Not to lead them, but to stand beside them."

Elan's answer was to draw her closer, their shadows merging on the rune-carved stones. Around them, the garden kept its ancient vigil, witness to another generation rising to meet its destiny.

~

Professor Xiacto's study remained unchanged since his sacrifice at the Battle of Twilight Gate. His last cup of tea still sat petrified on the desk, the leaves long since read by seers for any final messages. Elan avoided looking at it as he entered—some wounds never fully healed.

The room hummed with contained power. Artifacts from a thousand victories lined the walls: the Sword of Dawn's First Light, still gleaming though its wielder fell three centuries past; the Codex of Shadowed Truth, its pages turning by themselves in response to the artifact's presence; the Mirror of Lost Ages, which showed only darkness since the professor's passing.

Nykronus stood at the window, his form shifting between elderly scholar and ageless being with each flicker of the enchanted candlelight. The flames burned blue in his presence—they always had, though few now remembered why.

"Watch," Nykronus commanded, his voice ancient as the stones around them. He gestured to where Myst stood in the courtyard below, the artifact's light pulsing in time with his heartbeat. "The old powers remember what we have forgotten."

Elan's hand tightened on *Winterstar*'s hilt. "You chose him for this. Before he was born."

"The powers chose." Nykronus turned, his form shifting like smoke. "I merely read the signs in time to prepare him."

"Just as Xiacto knew when he chose to hold the Twilight Gate," Nykronus said, his eyes holding galaxies of memory. "Some choices echo through generations, Elan. Your children now stand where we once stood, but the wheel turns differently for them."

The artifact pulsed, sending ripples through the study's collection. The Codex's pages rustled faster, and the Mirror of Lost Ages flickered briefly with light.

"The Shadowcat's arrival changes everything," Nykronus continued, moving to examine the artifact. His fingers traced symbols in the air above it, leaving trails of blue fire. "Such beings don't choose lightly. Maya's power, Myst's leadership, the artifact's awakening... the patterns align too perfectly for chance."

"And St. Michael?" Elan asked, watching the symbols fade.

Nykronus smiled, an expression that held both infinite wisdom and profound sadness. "Ask yourself why a Saint—an Angel. No, a Paladin of his experience would allow himself to be taken. Why now, when Maya has bonded with a Shadowcat and Myst has proven himself ready to bear *Winterstar*'s burden."

The implication settled like frost across Elan's consciousness. "A gambit."

"The opening moves were made long before any of us drew breath, old friend." Nykronus placed a hand on Elan's shoulder, his touch carrying memories of countless battles fought together. "Our task now is to prepare them for what comes next. The game changes, but the stakes remain eternal."

Dawn came to the Order's fortress as it had for a thousand years: first touching the highest spire where the Eye of Morning kept its eternal watch, then cascading down the ancient walls like liquid gold. But this morning, the light revealed an unprecedented gathering.

They assembled in the Chamber of First Light, where every major campaign in the Order's history had been planned. The circular chamber's walls bore moving frescos of past battles, their enchanted pigments shifting in response to the gathering power. As sunlight streamed through the crystal dome above, it scattered across the assembled leaders in fragments of prophecy and purpose.

The artifact sat at the chamber's heart, no longer wrapped, its crystalline surface now alive with swirling patterns. Around it stood the Order's present and future: Elan and Kaira at the northern point, their ceremonial armor catching the dawn's first rays; Maya and Asha to the east, the Shadowcat's presence causing the chamber's ancient wards to shimmer with recognition; Myst at the south, *Winterstar* humming softly at his hip, its blade reflecting light that hadn't existed for centuries; Zoe and Stanley flanking the western approach, their battle-worn gear a stark contrast to the chamber's grandeur.

Nykronus completed the circle, his form seeming to blur at the edges as the sun's power filled the room. The moving frescos slowed their eternal dance as if the past itself waited to hear what would come next.

"The pieces align," Nykronus began, his voice resonating with the chamber's acoustics. Above them, even in daylight, the crystal dome began to map the stars' positions. "St. Michael's capture was no defeat, but the gambit we've waited three ages to see played."

Maya stepped forward, Asha moving like her shadow. "The Twilight Court stirs," she said, her new authority evident in every word. "Asha's kin speak of movements in the deeper realms. The barriers thin."

"Which is why they took him." Myst's hand rested on *Winterstar*'s pommel, and the sword's crystalline core pulsed in time with the artifact. "St. Michael guards more than just our realm. His presence in their territory changes the rules of engagement."

The artifact flared suddenly, projecting a map onto the chamber floor: a sprawling visualization of layered realms, showing paths and passages that hadn't been walked in millennia. Asha's eyes gleamed as she studied it.

The old ways open again, the Shadowcat's voice echoed in their minds. *What was sundered seeks to reunite.*

Kaira moved to the map's center, her shadow falling across ancient territories. "Then we use their own gambit against them. Maya, your Shadowcat bond gives us access to paths they thought were lost. Myst, *Winterstar*'s awakening to you isn't just succession—it's preparation."

"The blade knows what comes," Elan added, exchanging a knowing look with Nykronus. "Just as the artifact's timing was no coincidence. We're not just mounting a rescue; we're fulfilling a convergence centuries in the making."

Stanley stepped forward, his practical nature grounding the discussion. "We'll need to move in phases. Maya and Asha scout the shadow paths while Myst's team creates a diversion at the known gates. Meanwhile, the artifact—"

"Will show us the way," Zoe interrupted, pointing to where the projected map was shifting, revealing new paths as the artifact pulsed. "Look—it's not just showing us routes, it's showing us timing. The realms don't just overlap in space."

"They overlap in time," Nykronus confirmed. "St. Michael knew this. His capture ensures he'll be exactly where we need him, when the barriers are thinnest." He turned to Maya and Myst. "But the price of walking these paths... you must be certain."

The siblings shared a look about battles already fought and bonds forged in fire. Maya's hand found Myst's, and the artifact's glow intensified.

"We've been preparing for this our whole lives," Maya said, while Asha's tail curved protectively around them both. "Whether we knew it or not."

Myst nodded, and Winterstar sang softly in its scabbard. "The old powers are waking. It's time we did the same."

The artifact's light suddenly died, plunging the Chamber of First Light into shadow. In that darkness, Asha's eyes blazed like twin stars.

They come, the Shadowcat's voice rang in their minds. *The Twilight Court stirs. They know we've found it.*

Myst drew *Winterstar* in a single fluid motion, its crystal core igniting with blue fire. Shadows deeper than night crept across the floor, leaving only three lights in the darkness: the sword's azure flame, Asha's star-bright eyes, and the artifact's final, answering pulse before it went dark.

$\sim$

The hunt had begun.

CHAPTER

THIRTY-ONE

The Durant Estate within Prairie Creek Redwoods State Park, Orick, California

The Durant-Mazza estate rose from its foundations like a bridge between worlds. Ancient battle artifacts hung beside smart displays, spell-worn shields reflected the glow of fiber optic cables, and centuries-old tapestries shared walls with holographic art. Each room told the story of a family who had mastered the delicate dance between magical heritage and modern innovation.

The family gathered in the spacious living room one by one, creating a sense of togetherness and belonging. The fireplace crackled, its comforting heat spreading throughout the room. The furniture had been thoughtfully arranged to promote closeness, with soft couches and chairs placed near each other, encouraging conversation and bonding.

Maya paused at the threshold, drinking in the sight of her parents. Elan and Kaira sat entwined on the leather sofa, their fingers laced together with the easy familiarity of decades. Myst's presence at her shoulder steadied her, as constant as a heartbeat. From his carved oak throne, Nykronus surveyed them all, centuries of wisdom etched into the lines of his face, his eyes bright with an emotion that straddled the line between pride and concern.

As they settled into their seats, an air of anticipation filled the room. Each member carried the importance of their recent experiences, the trials and triumphs etched into their faces and woven into their very beings. The silence that fell was not one of emptiness but of a shared understanding, a recognition of their profound journeys.

Elan leaned forward, his eyes meeting each family member's in turn. "We've all walked difficult paths," he began, his voice low and laden with emotion. "Paths that have tested us, our faith, and our love for one another."

Kaira nodded, her hand tightening around Elan's. "But we've come out of it stronger," she added, her voice resonating with certainty. "Each trial has taught us something; each victory has brought us closer to understanding our purpose."

Maya felt the encumbrance of her own journey settle upon her shoulders, the memories of the realm between heaven and hell still vivid in her mind. She glanced at Nykronus, seeing in his eyes a reflection of the wisdom and pain she had witnessed her entire life.

The stage was set for sharing stories and for putting together the tapestry of their shared destiny.

Elan and Myst sat side by side, their posture mirroring the unity of their quest. As the family's attention turned to them, Elan reached for the artifact on the mantel, its surface gleaming in the firelight. He held it reverently as if it were the key to unlocking the very secrets of the universe.

"Our journey wasn't without its trials," Elan began, his voice steady and robust. "We faced adversaries seeking the power of this artifact for their own ends."

Myst nodded, his eyes distant as he recalled the challenges they had overcome.

As Myst spoke of their journey, his voice caught on Olivia's name. The empty chair in the corner—always her favorite spot—seemed to draw every eye in the room. Some losses cut too deep for time to heal.

As they delved into the details of their quest, the room seemed to come alive with the echoes of their adventure. They spoke of ancient ruins, hidden temples, cryptic riddles, and treacherous traps. Each obstacle they described was met with a collective intake of breath, a testament to the danger they had faced.

Yet, amidst the danger, there were moments of triumph and discovery. Elan recounted the moment they had finally uncovered the location of St. Michael, the knowledge an imposition upon their shoulders. Myst spoke of the bonds they had forged, the trust and loyalty that had seen them through the darkest times despite losing their beloved Olivia.

As their tale drew to a close, the family felt assured. They had accomplished what many would have deemed impossible, securing the artifact and the knowledge to turn the tide against Lazarus.

But there was also a heaviness in the air, a recognition of the responsibility that now rested upon their shoulders. The quest had changed Elan and Myst, not just in skill and knowledge, but in the very fabric of their being. They had seen the depths of evil and the heights of courage and knew that the battle ahead would demand everything they had to give.

Maya sat amid her family, and Asha curled contentedly on her lap. As the attention shifted to her, a hush fell over the room, the magnitude of her experiences in Aethoria materializing in their surroundings. She took a deep breath, her eyes reflecting the profound changes she had undergone.

"Aethoria," Maya breathed the word like a prayer, or perhaps a warning. "It was a realm where wonder and terror danced as partners." Her fingers absently traced the new scars on her wrist—silvery marks that seemed to shimmer with otherworldly light. "Every story Lola told us, every creature from our Filipino legends—they were all real. The Three Marias, Liwayas, Babaylans, Diwatas. Just knowing they exist and facing them—those are different kinds of truth." Each challenge, she explained, had forced her to dig deeper within herself to unlock potential she had never known existed.

"But it wasn't just about power," Maya continued, her hand absently stroking Asha's fur. "It was about what to do with that power. It was about knowledge, about understanding the very fabric of the realms that surround us."

She delved into the revelations she had uncovered, the truths about Purgatory, the rich man, and Lazarus's role in the cosmic balance. Her words painted a picture of a far more complex and interconnected universe than any of them had ever imagined.

As Maya spoke, her family listened in rapt attention. They could see the change in her, not just in how she carried herself but in the depth of her gaze and the wisdom in her words. She had walked paths they could scarcely comprehend, and it had transformed her in profound and humbling ways.

"I've come to understand that our battle is not just about good and evil," Maya said, her voice vibrating with resolve. "It's about balance, about the delicate equilibrium that holds our worlds together. And each of us, in our own way, has a part to play in maintaining that balance."

Her words hung in the air, a testament to the growth she had undergone and the gravity of the responsibility they all shared. At that moment, the Durant-Mazza family saw Maya not just as a daughter or a sister but also as a leader and a beacon of hope in the fight that lay ahead.

The heft of Maya's revelations settled over the room like a heavy cloak. Kaira and Reagan exchanged knowing looks—the kind that passed between sisters who had spent decades fighting the same shadows. Without a word, they moved to the war room, where the maps waited. The time for stories was over; now they needed plans.

Kaira and Reagan sat at the large oak table, a map of the Malefic Assembly's stronghold spread out before them. The room was dimly lit, the only illumination source being the soft glow of the lamp hanging above the table. The two women, sisters by blood and leaders by choice, were deep in discussion, their voices low and intense.

Kaira's finger traced the winding path across the weathered map, her nail catching on the parchment's raised wards. "Every route into the Malefic Assembly's stronghold is trapped, warded, or both." She met Reagan's eyes across the table. "But they've left one vulnerability—their own arrogance."

Reagan leaned forward, candlelight catching the battle-scars on her knuckles. "A slow infiltration." She said the words like she was tasting them. "We position our pieces carefully, build our network inside their ranks. They're so convinced of their superiority, they'll never suspect their own could turn against them."

They had spent countless hours poring over intelligence reports, analyzing their foes' movements and patterns. It had been a painstaking process but yielded a plan as daring as it was calculated.

"Targeting Verendana and Lazarus first is key," Kaira continued, tapping the locations on the map that marked their targets. "If we can eliminate their leadership, we can throw the entire organization into disarray."

"And that's where Erikson Ghostcloak comes in," Reagan added, leaning back in her chair. "His position within the Malefic Assembly's higher circle gives us a crucial advantage."

When Erikson's name was mentioned, the room fell silent. Elan, Zoe, and Stanley exchanged uneasy glances, their expressions clouded with doubt.

"Can we trust him?" Elan asked, his voice heavy with concern. "We knew an Ivar Ghoastcloak once, and he betrayed us in the past. How can we be sure Erikson won't do the same?"

"Let's not forget his brother Leif turned on the Order, too," Stanley grumbled.

Kaira and Reagan looked at each other, and silent communication passed between them. They had considered this question themselves, weighing the potential risks against the invaluable intelligence Erikson had provided.

"He nearly died for us in the battle at the headquarters," Reagan said, her voice firm with conviction. "That kind of loyalty cannot be faked."

"And we cannot let the sins of the brother taint our judgment of Erikson," Kaira added, her gaze sweeping over the assembled family members. "He has proven himself time and again."

Nykronus, who had been listening silently, spoke up, carrying the force of centuries of wisdom. "We must give trust a chance," he said, his eyes meeting each of theirs in turn. "For without trust, we have no hope of prevailing against the darkness that threatens to engulf us all."

As the tales of their journeys wound down, a profound sense of unity settled over the Durant-Mazza family. The living room, once just a space for gathering, had transformed into a sanctuary of shared purpose and determination. The echoes of their stories hung in the air, a testament to the trials they had faced and the transformations they had undergone.

Elan stood, his gaze sweeping over his family. "We have each walked our own paths," he said, his voice filled with emotion, "but those paths have led us here, to this moment, to this shared mission."

Kaira nodded, her hand finding Elan's. "And we have emerged stronger for it," she added, her words ringing with conviction. "Each challenge has taught us something about ourselves, about the depths of our resilience and the power of our love."

Maya felt the substance of her transformation settle upon her shoulders. She had walked the realms between heaven and hell and had faced trials that would have broken lesser spirits. Yet here she stood, among her family, ready to face whatever lay ahead.

"The road before us will not be easy," Nykronus said, his ancient eyes filled with pride and solemnity. "But we have something that our enemies can never understand: the strength of our unity, the power of our bonds."

As they looked around at each other, the Durant-Mazza family saw not just individuals but a tapestry of shared history, love, and sacrifice. They had been forged in the crucible of adversity, their bonds tempered by the fires of their trials.

The firelight caught the determination in their eyes, the set of their shoulders, the way they unconsciously moved to protect each other's flanks—a family forged into something stronger than blood alone could create. Now, as darkness gathered beyond their walls like a rising tide, they faced it not just as family, but as warriors who had already survived the impossible. Their weapons were ready, and their magic hummed in the air, but their greatest strength lay in the unspoken promise between them: no one fights alone.

CHAPTER

THIRTY-TWO

Maya stepped into the tranquil gardens of the Durant-Mazza estate, where morning mist clung to the roses. A time-worn stone bench beckoned her from its sanctuary among wisteria vines and swaying cypress branches. As she settled onto its cool surface, nature embraced her with its melody—wrens trilling their morning songs, leaves whispering ancient secrets in the breeze.

In this moment of solitude, Maya allowed her thoughts to wander, sifting through the tapestry of her journey. The victories won, the losses mourned, and each experience had left an indelible mark on her soul.

She reflected on the person she had become, a warrior tempered by trials, forged in the crucible of adversity. The challenges she faced and her decisions each played a part in shaping her into the woman she is today.

Yet, amidst the weight of her experiences, Maya found a flicker of hope. The love and support of her family, the unbreakable bonds that had carried her through the darkest times, reminded her that she was not alone in this fight.

In this sanctuary of green and gold, Maya found more than mere solitude—she discovered a peace born of acceptance, an understanding that every step of her arduous journey had led her precisely where she needed to be.

She rose from the bench, her steps measured and determined. The warrior within her, tempered by the trials of the past, was ready to face future challenges. And with the love and support of her family, she knew that no obstacle was insurmountable.

Maya's fingers traced the ancient token, its metal warm against her skin. As she turned the coin, its engravings caught the morning light— one side depicting the soaring spires of Heaven, the other the shadowed depths of Hell. Her mind wandered to Aethoria, that mystical realm so inexplicably intertwined with Earth, and she wondered if it also served as a bridge between undiscovered worlds. Was Aethoria between two realms? What other places were there to explore? As she traced the depictions on the coin with her finger, memories of her adventures flooded her mind, each step a reminder of the knowledge she had gained.

With each step in her journey, Maya had uncovered secrets that few could comprehend, powers that defied the very laws of nature.

The revelations of realms beyond, the whispers of untold powers, and the looming threat of Lazarus all converged in her mind, painting a picture of the responsibility she now bore.

She understood, with a clarity that thrilled and terrified her, that her role in the balance between light and darkness was pivotal. The fate of worlds, seen and unseen, rested upon her actions and the choices she would make in the face of the challenges.

The garden around her seemed to pulse with new energy as if the very earth beneath her feet recognized the significance of her realization. The rustling leaves and gentle birdsong became a symphony of encouragement, a reminder that she was not alone in this fight. She shut her eyes and honed the magic taught to her in Aethoria, communicating with the natural world surrounding her and relishing the strong connection she shared with it.

Maya put the coin in her pocket, tucking it away as a cherished relic of her past and a guide for her future. In this moment, surrounded by the beauty of the garden and the weight of her knowledge, Maya found a strength within herself that she desired to show the world around her.

The garden's spell broke softly as familiar footsteps approached. One by one, her family emerged from the estate's shadow into the morning light, transforming the solitary sanctuary into something far more precious. Elan, his presence as solid as the earth beneath their feet, walked alongside Kaira, her grace and wisdom evident in every step. Myst moved with a quiet purpose, his eyes holding a depth of knowledge beyond his years. Meanwhile, Reagan's fierce loyalty and determination radiated from her very being.

They gathered around Maya, forming a circle of love and support. At that moment, no words were needed. The silence that enveloped them was one of understanding, shared experiences, and unbreakable bonds. They stood together, a family forged in the crucible of adversity, each member a testament to the strength of their unity.

Maya felt a surge of gratitude and determination as the silence stretched on. She looked at each face, seeing the reflections of their shared journey. Elan's steadfast courage, Kaira's unwavering faith, Myst's insightful wisdom, and Reagan's fierce protection – each of them had shaped her into the woman she had become.

Slowly, the silence gave way to soft-spoken discussions. They spoke of the challenges ahead, the strategies they would need to employ, and the roles each of them would play. Their voices, though hushed, carried a weight of resolve. They were a family united, ready to face whatever lay ahead.

Maya absorbed each word and gesture, watching Elan's strategic mind complement Kaira's intuitive wisdom, and Myst's mystical knowledge balanced Reagan's earthbound strength. Together, they weren't just family—they were an unbreakable chain, each link essential and irreplaceable.

As their voices wove together in the morning air, Maya felt the strength of their bond pulse like a living thing. The love and support of her family, the knowledge that they stood with her, ready to face the trials ahead, filled her with a determination that burned brighter than ever before. She was proud of her family, bound by love, strengthened by adversity, and united in their resolve to protect the balance of the worlds they held dear.

As the sun crested the horizon, its golden rays painted the garden in a warm, ethereal glow. The Durant-Mazza family stood together, their faces turned towards the light, each lost in their own thoughts yet united in their shared purpose.

Maya stepped forward, her voice steady and strong as it carried across the tranquil space: "We stand here, on another beautiful day, facing challenges that would shake the very foundations of our world. But we don't stand alone. We stand together, a family bound by love and strengthened by the trials we have faced."

She paused, her gaze sweeping over the faces of her loved ones. "The path ahead twists through shadow and light, through realms known and unknown. Powerful enemies await us at every turn. But I know, with a certainty that burns brighter than the sun itself, that we'll win. The knowledge I have gained and the powers I have unlocked are not mine alone. They're ours, a gift to be wielded to defend the balance we hold dear."

Maya's eyes shone with fierce determination. "I stand before you and make this vow," her voice carrying the weight of destiny itself. "Every power within me, every lesson learned, every battle fought—it all leads to this moment. Lazarus must fall. St. Michael must be saved. And the realms we cherish must be protected." Her eyes met each of theirs in turn. "But this isn't my battle alone. I need your strength, your wisdom, your unwavering hearts beside mine."

Elan stepped forward, placing a gentle hand on Maya's shoulder. "We stand with you, Maya. Always. Your fight is our fight, your purpose our own."

Kaira, Myst, and Reagan nodded in agreement, their faces etched with love.

At that moment, standing in the golden light of dawn, they were more than family—they were guardians of balance, warriors of light, bound by bonds stronger than blood and tempered in fires hotter than fate itself. Whatever darkness lay ahead would find them unshaken, unbroken, and utterly unafraid.

EPILOGUE

Mexico City, Mexico

Ancient Aztec ruins slumbered beneath the sprawling streets of Mexico City, their stone foundations intertwined with a more recent sanctuary - the fortress of the Order of St. Michael. As twilight painted the sky in shades of amber and violet, steam rose from street vendor carts and the scent of roasting elotes drifted through narrow alleyways. But in the shadows, darker forces gathered.

Verandana traced her fingers along the obsidian pendant at her throat, its surface drinking in what little light remained. Her silver-streaked hair caught the dying sun as she surveyed the stronghold from their vantage point in an abandoned bell tower. Beside her, Lazarus stood motionless, his angular features carved from the same cold stone as the church walls around them.

"The spy's intelligence was precise," he murmured, dark energy crackling subtly around his clenched fists. "Their wards are weakest at the southern wall, where the old Aztec ley lines interfere with their sanctified barriers."

Verandana's lips curved into a razor-thin smile. "The Order believes ancient magic beneath their notice. Such arrogance." Her voice hardened. "The same arrogance that led them to take your brother from us."

Lazarus's usual mask of indifference cracked slightly at the mention of Dante. "They claim to protect humanity while they hold him prisoner. Tonight, we discover where they've hidden him."

Below them, robed figures moved through the stronghold's courtyard, lighting blessed lanterns against the encroaching darkness. None looked up to notice the gathering shadows that moved against the wind or the subtle distortion of air that marked Verandana and Lazarus's forces taking position.

Their strike force was an elite cadre, hand-picked and bound by dark oaths. Necromancers whose power drew from the death-soaked grounds of ancient sacrificial sites. Shadow-weavers who had trained in the lightless caverns beneath the city. Each chosen for this moment, this strike at the Order's heart.

Verandana raised her hand, dark energy coalescing around her fingers. "Begin," she commanded.

The attack unfolded like a lethal dance. Shadow-weavers struck first, their magic snuffing out the blessed lanterns and plunging the courtyard into darkness. The Order's defenders scrambled to respond, but their formations were split by waves of necromantic energy that rose from the very ground beneath their feet.

Lazarus vaulted from the bell tower, his descent cushioned by writhing shadows. Where he landed, the stone cracked and darkened. His magic pulsed outward in waves of absolute darkness, extinguishing light and hope. Order members caught in its path stumbled, their blessed weapons dimming.

"Your walls will fall," Verandana's voice echoed across the battlefield as she descended, carried by wings of shadow. "Your secrets will be torn from your minds. Tell us where you keep Dante; perhaps some of you will survive this night."

The Order rallied behind their senior members, circles of holy light pushing back against the darkness. A priestess in white and gold raised her staff, sending a beam of purifying energy skyward. "We do not yield to darkness!" she declared. "The Order stands!"

The battle transformed the stronghold into chaos. Ancient stones, witnesses to centuries of history, crumbled under the assault. Magical energies clashed in spectacular displays - shadow against light, death magic against blessed barriers. The air itself seemed to shake with the power being unleashed.

Lazarus carved through their defenses with cold precision, each strike calculated and lethal. But beneath his efficient violence lay a personal fury that surfaced in brief, devastating bursts. "Where is my brother?" he demanded, power wrapping around a fallen defender's throat. "Where does the Order hide its prisoners?"

Verandana's attacks were different - fluid, almost artistic in their destruction. She turned the Order's defenses against them, corrupting their holy symbols and transforming their protective circles into traps. Her laughter rang out across the battlefield, a sound of genuine pleasure mixed with vengeance long-awaited.

As the battle reached its peak, the Order's defenses finally shattered. The great doors of the stronghold burst inward, and darkness flooded the sacred halls. But in their moment of victory, Verandana and Lazarus found their primary goal unfulfilled - no sign of Dante, no clue to his prison's location.

"This is only the beginning," Verandana declared, watching Order members retreat through hidden passages with their wounded. "We will hunt you through every sanctuary, every sacred ground, until we find him. The Order of St. Michael's time is ending."

Lazarus stood amid the rubble, his cold facade cracking as he picked up a fallen Order medallion. "We will find you, brother," he whispered. "Whatever they've done to you, wherever they hide you, we're coming."

Dawn approached as Verandana and Lazarus melted back into the shadows with their forces. The first rays of sun illuminated the devastation - ancient stones scarred by dark magic, blessed grounds defiled, the proud stronghold broken but not destroyed.

The surviving Order members emerged from their shelters, led by the priestess in white and gold. Her voice rang out with unwavering resolve despite her wounds: "We endure. We rebuild. And we keep our sacred trust, no matter the cost." Her followers began clearing rubble, tending to the injured, and reinforcing what barriers remained.

But in the shadows of Mexico City, as street vendors began setting up their morning stalls and early workers hurried past the damaged church without noticing anything amiss, Verandana and Lazarus were already planning their next strike. This battle was lost, but the war for Dante - and for the soul of the world itself - was only beginning.

In the distance, church bells began to toll, their sound carrying both morning's promise and a requiem for the night's dead. Neither light nor darkness had claimed total victory, but the balance had shifted. The Order of St. Michael's age of unchallenged power was over, and a new, darker era was dawning.

ACKNOWLEDGMENTS

I wrote *Between Realms* immediately after *Echi Eterni*. Before even editing the first book, I was already immersed in this one, brainstorming ideas for the third, fourth, and fifth. Looking back at the dedication page, I realize it took grief—no, tragedy—to find this creative outlet and begin my journey toward healing. Writing became a way to mend my heart while I was living in Hawaii, and through that process, I also found my true love. It allowed me to heal and to grow into a better version of myself, though I'm still striving every day to be my best self.

I chose *1 John 4:19* for the dedication because it holds a truth I've come to embrace: to truly love others—and myself—I must first love God. I know I wouldn't be where I am today without Him.

Thank you to my entire family.

Thank you to my readers for giving me a chance.

ABOUT THE AUTHOR

Erhrole Navarro is a first-generation Filipino American author, active-duty Master Chief in the U.S. Navy, a proud husband to Violet, and stepfather of two daughters. Originally from San Jose, California, he now resides in San Diego, California, living each day to honor his late son, Ethan.

His debut novel, *Echi Eterni*, began as a story he penned in seventh grade, and he continues his journey with *Between Realms*, Book 2 of the Mystic Chronicles series. Erhrole enjoys DJing, comic books, and motorcycle rides along the California coast when not writing or serving his country. Through his work and life, he embraces resilience, compassion, and the enduring strength of the human spirit.

Also by Erhrole Navarro

The Mystic Chronicles Series

Echi Eterni (2024)

Between Realms (2024)

Book 3 (TBD)